Fresh as a Daisy
is the third novel by the author of
The Wrong Sort of Girl and
The Wrong Mr Right

'Feel-good fiction at its best' *Jill Mansell*

'Heartwarming' *Katie Fforde*

'Very much an author to watch' *Bookseller*

'A fun read' *Company*

'A must for old-fashioned romantics' *Best*

Also by Valerie-Anne Baglietto

The Wrong Sort of Girl
The Wrong Mr Right

About the author

Valerie-Anne Baglietto was born in Gibraltar in 1971. Her grandfather and great-grandfather were both writers, so Valerie-Anne keeps the tradition in the family and writes under her maiden name. Although she always wanted to be a novelist, she worked in London as a graphic designer for a couple of years while scribbling fiction in her spare time. In 2000 she won the Romantic Novelists' Association New Writers' Award for her first novel *The Wrong Sort of Girl*. She lives in North Wales with her husband and young family.

VALERIE-ANNE BAGLIETTO

Fresh as a Daisy

CORONET BOOKS

Hodder & Stoughton

Copyright © 2003 by Valerie-Anne Baglietto

First published in Great Britain in 2003 by Hodder and Stoughton
Published simultaneously as a Coronet paperback in Great Britain
in 2003 by Hodder and Stoughton
A Division of Hodder Headline

3 5 7 9 10 8 6 4

A CIP catalogue record for this title is
available from the British Library

ISBN 0 340 82417 4

Typeset in Plantin Light by Palimpsest Book Production Limited,
Polmont, Stirlingshire
Printed and bound by Mackays of Chatham Ltd, Chatham, Kent

Hodder and Stoughton
A division of Hodder Headline
338 Euston Road
London NW1 3BH

For my children . . . the noisy one and the fidget.

And for Gaylord – a special little boy . . .
Because he existed.

ACKNOWLEDGEMENTS

Thank you as always to Dinah Wiener, and to Carolyn Caughey and the team at Hodder. To my family and friends, and anyone else who may have helped in any way during the writing of this book – even if it was unwittingly! And to the RNA, simply for being there, especially to my comrades in THE WELSH DRAGON CHAPTER/ SEFYDLIAD Y DDRAIG GYMRAEG.

'There are only two or three human stories, and they go on repeating themselves as fiercely as if they had never happened before.'

O, Pioneers, Willa Cather

I

Daisy Kavanagh couldn't remember when she'd last been this tongue-tied and clammy-palmed. Then again, she'd never had in-laws to meet for the first time before.

All the greetings she'd rehearsed on the journey here had been forgotten, swallowed up by sheer awe of her surroundings. Ben had said that Greenacres was a fairly large old house, but he'd been so blasé about it, so laid-back, that Daisy had never – in the twelve long weeks that she'd known him – imagined it to be a third of the size of Buckingham Palace.

Trembling, she stuck out her hand towards the man who looked nothing like her husband but was clearly her father-in-law. Ben had given it away by calling him Dad.

'Hello,' croaked Daisy, her mouth dry. She forced her lips into a smile. 'I'm very pleased to meet you.'

Howard Kavanagh stared at her without forcing his lips to do anything. At last, his hand came out and shook hers weakly. 'Likewise.'

Ben slung a protective arm round her shoulders, and turned her to face his stepmother. 'Vivienne, I'd like you to meet the latest Mrs Kavanagh. Not that there've been any others. Not on my side, at least . . .'

Daisy sensed him bite his tongue.

The older woman – who seemed over forty, even

though Daisy had inside knowledge that she wasn't – looked her up and down with sharp aquamarine eyes that gave nothing away. Daisy gulped, but couldn't rid herself of the lump in her throat. Suddenly she felt painfully conspicuous. She had taken such care to look her best today. In fact, she was wearing the same outfit she'd worn for the wedding ten days ago. Dating from the sixties, it comprised a short, red, sleeveless dress and matching coat. Daisy had found knee-length, leather boots to go with it, with only a modest heel, so they didn't look too tarty.

She'd bought the whole ensemble the morning they'd applied for the marriage licence. After their appointment with the registrar, Ben had whisked her to the nearest ATM and taken out the maximum amount possible in one go. Daisy had demurred, telling him he couldn't afford to spare that much, but he'd handed her the wad of cash anyway and told her not to come back to his flat until she'd bought herself something special.

'And I don't want any change,' he'd grinned. 'Get shoes and jewellery and whatever else you need. In fact, if that isn't enough—' But she'd hurried off before he could work out how to give her more.

On her own in London's West End, though, she'd walked straight past the intimidating designer bridal shops with their Scarlett O'Hara skirts and sculptured, embroidered bodices. It wasn't as if the wedding was taking place in a historic little church, with a chauffeur-driven Daimler and half a dozen frilly bridesmaids in attendance.

In fact, they hadn't even had a best man. Just two witnesses, plucked from obscurity and then waved off with ecstatic thanks following the brief, simple ceremony. Daisy and Ben had had a quick drink to celebrate at the nearest pub before dashing back to the flat, changing into more casual clothes, throwing their luggage in the boot of the car and going off on honeymoon.

Looking at her stepmother-in-law now, who was wearing a crisp white shirt and grey trousers, Daisy felt ridiculously overdressed, in spite of her surroundings. Ben had assured her she looked fine this afternoon when they'd set out, but why couldn't he have been honest and warned her she'd gone over the top? Or maybe it was her own fault for not realising that while Ben was looking smart himself, he hadn't gone as far as wearing the dark taupe suit he'd worn for the wedding.

'You'll have to excuse our behaviour,' said Vivienne Kavanagh suddenly. She leaned over and kissed the air by Daisy's left cheek. 'It's just . . . Ben's never done anything like this before . . . It's not every day he returns home after such a long time away. Especially not with a new wife.' She seemed to realise that sounded odd, and hastily added, 'Or any wife, for that matter.'

'At least I didn't just turn up with her,' Ben defended himself. 'I did write and warn you first.'

'A postcard from Cornwall,' frowned Vivienne. 'Is that what you refer to as writing?'

Chewing her lip, Daisy stared at the parquet floor. Her nerves were so thinly stretched she felt as if they might snap.

'We were on honeymoon,' explained Ben. 'There wasn't much time to write pages and pages, if you get my drift.'

'Facetious as always,' snorted his father. 'Even marriage won't make you grow up, will it?'

Daisy peered through her lashes to find Howard Kavanagh staring at her rather than his son. His expression seemed to imply that she wasn't the sort of girl who would smooth Ben's path to maturity. Luckily, there was an abrupt yelp to her right which prevented her from dwelling on this. A boy came careering into the entrance hall on a unicycle. He seemed to fly off – on purpose or by accident, Daisy couldn't tell – landing in a bony heap at her feet. Scrambling up, he frowned at her, his eyes the same pale shade of blue as his mother's. This was obviously Ben's half-brother.

'How many times do I have to tell you?' Vivienne hissed at him. 'You mustn't ride that thing inside the house.'

The boy mumbled something that sounded like, 'Sorry,' but Daisy couldn't be certain.

'Hello, Robert,' said Ben cagily. 'You've grown a bit, haven't you? How are you keeping?'

'I'm ten. And I've grown a lot.' The boy frowned, his gaze still riveted on Daisy. Then he turned to his mother. 'I wasn't upstairs,' he contested. 'I know that last time—'

'That's not the point,' interrupted his father, with evident disapproval. 'Someone could get hurt, and not just you. Think about it, you wouldn't ride a normal bicycle round the house like that.'

Fascinated, Daisy reached out to pick up the unicycle, wondering why Ben had spoken about his half-brother so coolly. Robert seemed cheeky, but not a brat.

'Oi,' snapped the boy, swiping at her hand. 'Gedorff!'

She took a step back, as if she'd narrowly missed walking into a snake pit.

'It's mine!' scowled Robert. 'You're a girl. If you tried riding it, you'd fall off.'

'Robert,' admonished his mother, 'don't be so rude!'

Daisy realised that Ben probably hadn't been exaggerating about his half-brother, after all. 'Wouldn't most people fall off at the first attempt, even boys?' she challenged, ready and able to fight the majority of her own battles, although she'd had no intention of leaping on to the unicycle and turning herself into a laughing stock. She felt uncomfortable enough as it was. 'It's a unicycle – they're not easy to get the hang of. How did you learn to ride something like that? I would have thought you'd prefer a skateboard, or rollerblades.'

'It's just a fad,' frowned Vivienne, by way of explanation, her voice rigid as she closed this line of conversation. She straightened her son's shirt, then glanced at her watch. 'Ben, it's almost time for dinner, so I suggest you take Daisy upstairs to your room rather than give her the grand tour. She might want to freshen up or change.'

'Upstairs?' Daisy looked at her husband in confusion. 'I thought—'

'It's just for a couple of nights.' Ben took her arm, and before she could protest, started leading her towards the broad sweeping staircase. 'Until we review our situation.'

'Situation?' She glanced over her shoulder as a middle-aged man in a grey suit clattered through the front door carrying their luggage. 'What's going on?' she muttered. 'Who's that?'

Ben glanced back, too. 'Henries. He's a sort of butler and valet and . . . What? What are you looking at me like that for?'

Daisy was breathless as he ushered her along an endless corridor. On either side were dark polished doors and gilt-framed landscapes. Oh, God, help! Could one or more of the paintings be a Constable or a Turner?

'Why didn't you tell me the truth?' Daisy gasped at last, as they came to a halt in front of a door which looked no different from all the others they'd just passed. 'Ben, why didn't you tell me your family's out of bloody *Harpers & Queen?*'

With a disconcerting abruptness, the honeymoon seemed well and truly over, but Ben Kavanagh couldn't pinpoint why. It was a feeling rather than a concrete fact, because after all, they'd only spent five days in Cornwall and he'd still felt as if he was on honeymoon when they'd returned to London. Now, however often he reminded himself that what lay ahead was a fresh start for both of them, he lacked the necessary enthusiasm to buoy him up.

Smoothing a hand across his freshly shaven face, he gazed down at his wife from the door to the en suite bathroom. She was barely visible beneath the heavy embroidered bedspread and monogrammed sheet, but a long tendril of hair lay curled over the pillow, almost forming a perfect spiral. Sunlight slanted in through a gap in the curtains, highlighting a swarm of dust particles which looked as if they were taking part in a slow, sedate Elizabethan court dance.

Last time he'd stood on this spot had been two and a half years ago. Back then he hadn't been a married man, though, and he hadn't yet turned into the prodigal son and started driving up and down the M1 trying to sell vacuum cleaners for a living. Neither had he taken to stopping off at a particular service station in the hope that a certain girl would be working a shift behind the counter at Burger King . . .

He dressed quietly so as not to wake his wife, then let himself out of the bedroom and headed down the airless gloom of the corridor towards the galleried landing and main staircase. It was only just gone eight, he might as well let Daisy have a lie-in; she often had trouble getting off to sleep. Although he couldn't blame her yesterday after that disaster of a dinner.

He'd had difficulty coaxing a single word out of her during the meal, let alone a coherent sentence. Sitting in the large formal dining room with his family stationed round her, she'd retreated into a shell he hadn't realised existed. She'd always been so open with him, so refreshingly honest. But mulling it over last night in bed, he'd realised that, in essence, most people were like tortoises with invisible shells. Some of them, to give them fair dues, also had larger brains and an ounce of compassion, but in his twenty-nine years he hadn't met as many as he would have liked.

In fact, his faith in human nature had definitely been on the wane.

Until Daisy.

Until she'd asked him if he'd prefer a coffee to Diet Coke because the fizzy drinks machine wasn't working properly and everything was coming out slightly flat. And she'd smiled – that now familiar sunrise of a smile, her eyes crinkling beneath the cap of her casual uniform. It felt as if something inside him had slammed into something else. He'd stared at her, daft sod that he was, struggling to form the words, 'Yes, thank you.'

And that had been it – a cynic converted. Love at first sight, they called it. A heady, potent, obsessive combination of desire and curiosity and a longing to see her, again and again, dishing out burgers and fries and grinning as if there was no place on earth she would rather be while her gaze returned with helpless frequency to the clock on the wall.

'Ben! Watch where you're going. You're miles away . . .'

He blinked at his stepmother. 'Sorry . . . Er – do you

still have breakfast served in here?' He gestured to a door leading to a small, informal dining room, feeling like a young tearaway up to no good. He didn't know how Vivienne managed to reduce him to this when she was only eight years his senior. She'd just always had that knack from the first day she'd come to live at Greenacres, even though she had only been brought in as a replacement wife, not a new mother.

'It's self-service these days,' she said lightly, as she opened the door, then tittered in a hollow fashion at her feeble attempt at humour. 'There's scrambled egg and bacon, if you've got the stomach for it.'

As if he wouldn't be able to fathom this out for himself from the dishes lined up on the sideboard.

'I still can't get your father out of the habit,' she went on. 'But at least he doesn't mind things grilled any more. If, like me, you prefer cereals and croissants however . . .'

Ben's usual fare was cornflakes. Today, as a treat, he aimed for the egg and bacon and discovered some mushrooms also keeping warm on the hotplate. His favourite! He helped himself to generous portions, then joined his stepmother at the small oak table.

'Dad not up yet?' he asked, when the silence seemed interminable.

Vivienne looked up from the *Daily Mail*. 'Your father's been and gone. He always has breakfast at seven thirty and then takes the dogs for a walk.'

'I, um, didn't think he'd be quite so regimented now that he's retired. Not that he was ever in the army, but—'

'*Semi*-retired. And you know he's not the type to laze around in bed all morning. Where's, er . . . Daisy, by the way?'

'In bed,' muttered Ben, through a mouthful of egg. He

swallowed. 'It was a long day yesterday. I thought I'd let her rest.'

'Of course, that's very considerate of you. Coffee?'

'Please.'

She poured him a cup from the grotesque silver pot that had always stood on the breakfast table for as long as he could remember. It had probably stood there when his great-grandparents were alive, waiting for the day when it could finally be considered a family heirloom.

'So,' said Ben, offering his stepmother a brisk smile, 'it feels just like old times.' He groaned inwardly at the cliché, but it was too late, he'd said it.

'Mmm . . .' She stared down at the newspaper.

Ben tried to relax. It seemed that no one was going to jump on his case, figuratively speaking. Unless they were waiting to catch him off guard.

'. . . Except that it won't ever be like "old times", will it?' continued Vivienne, folding up the *Daily Mail* and pushing it to one side. 'It can't be. Too much has happened.'

'Well, I know there's Daisy to consider now.'

'Actually, I was referring to your father.'

Ben raised an eyebrow. 'Dad? What's up with him?'

'He's just turned sixty-one, as you're aware, and I think he's starting to feel the years take their toll. Before you left . . . when you were being trained to head the firm and leading everyone to believe you were going to marry Geraldine, including the poor girl herself—'

Ben almost choked on a mushroom. 'I didn't leave without telling Geraldine how I felt. I was always straight with her. And I did care about her, whatever anyone thinks.'

'But you *love* Daisy? Even though you've only known her for – what? Two minutes – compared to how long you'd known Geraldine. Yet, suddenly, kaboom!' Vivienne waved her hand about expressively, as if she was still performing Shakespeare for that small touring theatre company. 'I'm going to be frank with you, Ben, this is about as puerile as you've got. "Running away" was bad enough, but coming back home with a child bride in tow . . .'

Ben put down his cup so vehemently that coffee sloshed across his hand, trickling under the cuff of his shirt before he could grab a napkin. 'She's twenty-four. That hardly makes her a child.'

'She looks about seventeen. And tell me, is that her real hair colour?'

'No,' bristled Ben. 'Is that yours?'

'More or less. I only use highlights to disguise the grey. I wouldn't pretend to be a natural blonde if I wasn't one.'

Ben tried to wrap his head around that before replying. 'Daisy likes to experiment with colour, but then so do lots of women. It's not permanent.' Although, from what he'd seen, she would probably colour it again before it washed out completely.

'So, it's a sort of maroon shade this week. Very . . . studenty.'

Ben scowled. His stepmother always seemed to know how to ruin his appetite. 'You're just jealous,' he said accusingly. 'You can't stand the fact that you're not the only Mrs Kavanagh round here any more. You're afraid Daisy will usurp your position. After all, you still think of my mother as a threat even though she's been dead thirteen years.'

Vivienne's eyes flashed, but to his perverse annoyance she didn't continue the argument. She just said, rather calmly, 'So, you're planning to stay on at Greenacres then?'

'You can't throw me out.'

'Your father and I have no intention of attempting to. Please don't be so dramatic. I just noticed last night that your . . . "wife" wasn't under the impression that you were staying.'

Ben glared out of the French windows into the conservatory. Time seemed to have stood still out there. The same wicker chairs and coffee tables were placed in their usual positions between grandiose potted palms, and ornate lamps with neatly pleated shades stood in perfect alignment on the wide windowsills. Did anyone ever use that room, or was it still his mother's haunting ground? It used to smell of lavender. The way Daisy smelled when she dabbled with aromatherapy to help her sleep.

'No,' said Ben, after an awkward silence, 'we're not going to cramp your style, Vivienne. I've already told Daisy about the Gatehouse.'

His stepmother shrugged. 'Well, legally it *is* yours – now that you're a married man. You know that better than I do. It's up to you if you want to live there or not. It could have been your home two years ago.'

'Well, that just goes to show, doesn't it? If I was in this for what I could get, I'd have married Geraldine and gone along with everything else Dad expected of me.'

Vivienne unfolded the newspaper and spread it out in front of her again. She began to pour herself another coffee. It seemed to signal the end of the conversation, but then she added in a low voice, 'You're back *now*, though. And you're married. That's very convenient, Benjamin, wouldn't you say?'

2

'I'm starving,' yawned Daisy, stretching out her hand to the other side of the bed. Instead of the warm body she was expecting to find, there was a cold emptiness. She opened her gummy eyes and sat up slowly, blinking round her. A shaft of light sliced the gloom through a gap in the thick, heavy curtains. As far as she could make out, there wasn't a clock in the room, and Ben's high-tech, digital radio alarm was still packed in one of the boxes in the boot of his car.

Daisy fumbled about on the expanse of bedside table and found her watch. It was almost ten. No wonder she was hungry. Why hadn't Ben woken her up? And where was he anyway . . . ? Swinging her legs over the edge of the mattress, she lowered herself carefully to the floor. She was five-foot-five, not small, not tall, but this four-poster bed was far from average. When she'd first set eyes on it last night, she'd felt as if she'd stumbled across a display in a stately home; except that there wasn't a thick burgundy rope barring her way, or a little plaque requesting her not to touch the furniture or ornaments and going on to state that Lord Such-and-Such or Lady Blah-de-Blah Once Slept In This Bed.

Ben had practically dragged her into the room, smiling at her reluctance. 'Don't you think it's romantic?' He'd pulled her close and kissed her. 'I used to hate this bedroom. I longed for a futon and halogen spotlamps and self-assembly pine shelves like the kind I'd seen in Argos.'

'Which is exactly what you had in your flat,' she'd reminded him, still confused and out of her depth. 'It was about as different from this as you could get, bar an igloo.'

'Don't I know it.' Ben had groaned and collapsed backwards on to the bed, Daisy stifling a gasp of horror as he'd crumpled the immaculate bedspread.

Now, she padded over to the window and dragged back the curtains. They seemed to contain lead and reached all the way to the floor, but eventually she managed to scoop them back and secure them in silken braids with tassels as large as her fist. The window wasn't double-glazed. As a chill assaulted her through her nightie, her nipples stood to attention and she realised why the curtains were so thick. They provided welcome insulation. Right now, it felt more like January than April.

Daisy shivered with dismay as well as cold as she realised that she had next to nothing on. Outside in the garden, surrounded by a pack of dalmatians – she couldn't tell how many there were at a glance, but it was definitely less than one hundred and one – was her father-in-law Howard Kavanagh. He was staring straight up at her, his face puckered in consternation.

Waving at him wouldn't be a good idea, thought Daisy, mortified. She retreated into the centre of the room. Glancing round, she remembered that there was an en suite. Maybe Ben was in there?

But he wasn't. Daisy looked down at the arctic-white tiles and matching roll-top bath and wondered what to do. Ben probably wouldn't be long. He wouldn't desert her in a strange house, even if it was his family's.

Although she was hungry, she decided to get washed and decently dressed before confronting her in-laws again. Slipping on a dressing-gown and padding in her furry slippers to the kitchen didn't seem appropriate. It was what she would usually do, though, aiming straight for a kettle and some tea bags before she could face a bath or shower. Mainly because most of the bathrooms she'd ever known had been like fridges. She'd needed the luxury of a hot drink inside her before daring to undress.

One of the main problems here was the fact that she didn't know where the kitchen *was*. Maybe she would ask Ben to draw her a map so she could find her way round the house when he wasn't with her.

A thought struck her, and she peeked into the bedroom, scanning it for a kettle and some cups and saucers. But this wasn't a hotel or B&B. Resigned to her fate, Daisy used the toilet and ran a bath – praying for hot water and thanking God when it came sputtering out – then slipped out of her nightie and knickers. With a sigh, she twisted her hair into a knot and sank into the bath. Bliss. Nirvana. Damn. She'd forgotten to put her towel within reach. It was miles away by the basin.

With a grumble of frustration, she glared at the wheezing radiator. It was barely emitting any heat. There'd been something similar at her junior school, she recalled dimly. In the girls' toilets. The memory struggled to get out, even as she resisted it, making her shudder in spite of the warm water. If she'd survived her childhood, thought Daisy, squeezing her eyes shut, she could probably survive anything.

'What are you doing?' said a boy's voice, petulant and disdainful. 'That's the kitchen. You can't go in there.'

'Er . . .' Daisy stopped in her tracks. Half an hour after her bath, it seemed that she'd instinctively navigated herself to the door she'd been after (although she'd cautiously opened a few others along the way). But now Ben's half-brother was about to put the kibosh on her plans. 'Why can't I?' she asked warily.

'Because it's not allowed.'

'But I want to have breakfast.'

'It's nearly eleven.'

'Well . . . brunch then.'

'You can't do that.'

'Why not? I'm not a bad cook really. I only want to make something simple now, though.'

'That's not the point. You can't just walk into the kitchen and start cooking.'

'I'm sure I could figure out where everything's kept. I wouldn't like to bother your mother, after all . . .'

'No.' Robert Kavanagh rolled his eyes. 'If you want something to eat, you've got to ask Mrs White. She hasn't got a husband any more, but she still calls herself Mrs.'

'Who is she?'

'The cook, of course. She doesn't let anyone near her utensils.'

'Oh.' Daisy chewed on a fingernail. She was faint with hunger. Ben hadn't returned to their room, so she'd had no choice but to venture out into Greenacres without a guide. 'If I can't go into the kitchen, how can I tell Mrs White that I want something to eat?'

Robert looked pensive for a moment. 'You'll have to proceed through the proper channels.'

'And that would be . . . ?'

'You'll have to go through the housekeeper's office.'

This was utterly surreal. 'The housekeeper's office?'

'Mrs Peacock,' Robert nodded sagely. 'She's in her study. The room with the blue door. You can't miss it.'

Daisy frowned in suspicion. 'I suppose she's busy talking to Reverend Green at the moment, though?'

Robert appeared unfazed that she'd caught him out.

Just then, the kitchen door opened and a woman stepped out. Her smile seemed pleasant enough, but her tone was businesslike and brisk. 'I thought I heard voices. You must be the new Mrs Kavanagh.'

Daisy was beginning to feel sick. Her sugar levels were plummeting rapidly, even as her annoyance rocketed. 'And you're Mrs White,' she replied testily, 'according to this young gentleman here.' She jabbed a thumb in Robert's direction.

The sight of Ben coming round a corner and striding eagerly towards them did nothing to placate her, although Robert took this as his cue to scarper.

'Oh look!' Daisy huffed at her husband. 'It's Colonel Mustard.'

'Sorry?' About to wrap an arm round her, Ben recoiled. He looked from Daisy to the older woman. 'I see you've met Mrs White.'

'Mrs . . .' Daisy's jaw dropped.

The cook didn't look impressed. 'It's that old Cluedo thing, I suppose. People don't always believe it first time. Nice to have you home again, Mr Kavanagh.'

She was about to retreat into the kitchen when Daisy put out a hand to stop her. 'Wait! Don't go.'

Mrs White blinked at her. 'Sorry, was there something you wanted?

'Are you all right?' asked Ben, concerned.

'No,' said Daisy. 'No, I'm not.' She'd been abandoned

by her husband – albeit temporarily – spotted semi-naked by her father-in-law and publicly humiliated by a ten-year-old. 'I'm hungry,' she complained. 'I'm having a lousy morning and all I want is a cup of tea and some toast. With jam if there is any. Some jam would be great. Preferably strawberry, but—'

Ben cut her short, steering her past the cook into the kitchen. 'Sorry, Mrs W., this is an emergency. Never mess with Daisy Kavanagh when her stomach's empty. Not unless you fancy being on the menu yourself. Believe me,' he looked rueful, 'I know.'

Once she was fed and watered, Daisy reverted to normal. The characteristic peachy bloom returned to her cheeks, and the lustre to her light brown eyes. Ben watched her drain the last of her tea. She regarded him sheepishly, all trace of gruffness gone, then turned her attention to the vast kitchen. They were alone. Mrs White had been summoned to see Vivienne.

'This room isn't how I would have imagined,' Daisy admitted in hushed tones, as if she were in a church confessional.

'Oh?'

She shrugged. 'If you'd only told me you grew up in a Jacobean manor house, I suppose I would have expected something baronial. And I wouldn't have thought you were boasting. I would have imagined lots of dark wood everywhere, and a high ceiling with beams all across it. On the other hand, what I would have *liked* to see was one of those huge farmhouse kitchens in antique pine, with an Aga and a massive battered table in the middle.' She tapped the pristine glass surface of the small octagonal table they were seated at, which was just to the right of the door. In the centre of the room was a multi-functional 'island' with a dark granite worktop.

Ben's voice was husky as he reminisced, 'It used to be more welcoming – before Vivienne came on the scene. She packed off our old cook to a retirement home and headhunted Mrs White. Between them, they had the kitchen redesigned and modernised. A bit too Starship Enterprise, even for me. But Vivienne does a lot of entertaining.'

'I never would have guessed,' said Daisy, in the pert way that always made Ben chuckle. She picked up her mug and plate. 'I'm assuming there's a dishwasher round here somewhere?'

'Two actually, but they're totally integrated.'

'You mean, invisible.'

He snorted. 'Just leave that stuff in the sink, don't worry about it.'

The circular, stainless steel sink looked buffed within an inch of its life. It was empty, and Daisy seemed to be wondering if it had ever seen a dirty dish in its life. 'Are you sure?'

'Trust me.' He held out his hand to her, smiling. Slowly, she smiled back. He wanted to kiss her, but resisted, in case Mrs White came back and caught them in an embarrassing clinch. 'Besides . . .' Ben went on, aware that Daisy was oblivious to his compulsion, and contemplating how she would respond if she was telepathic '. . . it's about time I took you on a little mystery tour.'

3

Ben opened the rickety little gate and stood akimbo, one foot on paving stones, the other on the grass verge.

Daisy shook her head at him, bemused. 'What are you doing?'

'D'you see my left foot? Well, technically it's now in Wales. As is' – he scanned his body – 'most of my leg and the tip of my elbow. If I shift along a bit' – which he did – 'exactly half my body's now in Flintshire. The other half is still in Cheshire.'

Daisy was impressed. 'So we're right on the border here?' A moment later she frowned dubiously. 'How can you be so exact?'

'Because, young lady, as a qualified solicitor I know the law like the back of my hand.'

'Aren't you rusty? And what's the law got to do with map-reading?'

'Conveyancing has a lot to do with map-reading. I'm sure it'll all come flooding back to me. Anyway, it's common knowledge in the family that this fence is right on the border and that the Gatehouse' – he gestured to the building in front of them – 'is in a different county – a different country even – from the bulk of the Greenacres estate.'

Daisy gazed up at the house. 'So this is the Gatehouse . . .'

Ben came to stand beside her. He put an arm round her

shoulders and asked, with a hint of nervousness, 'What do you think?'

Daisy tried to nod encouragingly, but the house was so plain and square and . . . depressing. Built of grey stone, with a forbidding black front door, its peeling sash windows stared at her blankly, all the curtains drawn as if it was the middle of the night. As for the garden, which seemed to border the front and left-hand side of the house, the kindest way to describe it would be to say it was well stocked.

'Why didn't we come past here yesterday?' she asked, trying to conceal her disappointment and persuade herself that first impressions weren't as important as people made out.

'This is the old driveway.' Ben stepped on to the smooth, winding track they'd followed all the way from the main house. 'When the bypass was built for the village, Dad had another approach – tarmacked and everything – laid directly to the new road. That's the one we used when we arrived.'

Daisy pointed to an imposing, weathered iron gate and the overgrown lane beyond. 'So I'm guessing that leads to civilisation then?'

'Very astute. Nettlesford's less than a quarter of a mile to the left.'

'You're already talking like a solicitor.'

'Do you think so?' Ben shrugged. 'I must be getting into character already.'

'I hadn't realised you weren't going to be yourself once you came back here,' muttered Daisy.

A gust of wind made the trees and shrubs swoop sideways. She rubbed her eye where a speck of something had blown into it. The eye began to water. She turned her head away, in case Ben thought she was crying, and walked up the path towards the house. 'I take it we can go inside?'

Ben hurried to join her, brandishing a key. He forced it into the lock, and turned it one way and then the other. 'Bugger, it's rusted up.'

'Maybe you're trying too hard.' Daisy took the key from him and carefully, gently, turned it in the lock. The door creaked open as she pushed it. 'See?' She blinked in the dark as they stepped inside, a strong musty smell assaulting her nostrils.

'Shit,' hissed Ben. 'What did I just tread on? It felt alive.'

'When I was a kid, our front door was always playing up,' said Daisy, drawing back the nearest set of curtains and opening the window to let in some air. 'If you forced it, you didn't get anywhere. You had to – eek! A spider!' She moved on quickly to the next set of curtains.

The room that was now filling with watery spring light was, in actual fact, three rooms in one. It seemed as if she and Ben had been mysteriously whisked back into the past, although history never having been her strong point, Daisy wasn't sure which past exactly. The space, as she decided to refer to it, also reminded her vaguely of a loft apartment. But only because it was open plan; the similarity more or less ended there. It was smaller than a rounders pitch, and was dominated by one wall made entirely of grey stone, identical to the outside. The other three walls had been plastered, in what seemed a rustic, slap-dash fashion. Inset in the stone wall was a large fireplace, about four feet high and five feet across, with something resembling a cauldron hanging empty and limp in the dank alcove. Built round the fireplace, a few wooden cupboards – in dire need of waxing – were arranged higgeldy-piggeldy to pass for a kitchen.

Daisy bit her lip, a dozen emotions charging through her. Like the rest of Greenacres, this place wasn't quite how her husband had described it. But perhaps, she mused, it was her imagination that was at fault on this occasion for being far too idealistic.

A pale-faced Ben was still looking round the quarry-tiled floor for the 'something alive' that he thought he'd trodden on. But the only suspect was the edge of a rolled-up rug.

At last, he spoke, sounding like an estate agent this time. 'If I can just point out the light switches and the kitchen taps, you'll realise that Aunt Eleanor wasn't batty enough to get by without water or electricity . . .'

Daisy's heart lifted a little with relief.

'And there's a bathroom upstairs – just about,' Ben went on. 'It's small, but at least they managed to squeeze in the necessary facilities. You haven't got to go outside, or wherever the original occupants would have had to go. The thing is, this is a listed building, so there's all sorts of red tape when it comes to renovations.'

'Who were the original occupants?' asked Daisy, surprised that her interest was genuine.

'The gamekeeper and his family, I think. Dad doesn't talk about Greenacres' history because, basically, he doesn't know a lot. He only married into the family, after all. And when my grandparents and my mother were alive . . . I suppose I never got round to asking them about it much. I wasn't that kind of boy, interested in stories about dead people, even if they were my ancestors. Aunt Eleanor was the only one I could sit and listen to for hours, but she wasn't living in the past, she was just . . . nuts. Anyway, the Greenwood family have owned the estate since the middle of the eighteenth century, although, as I told you last night, it's been around since the reign of James I. The Gatehouse was built later, though. Circa 1800, I think. There's a plaque above the front door, but the little canopy or porch or whatever you want to call it – built on even later – hides it, unless you stand on a ladder.' Ben sighed. 'I wish I did know more about them now, to be honest. My family,' he added, to avoid any ambiguity.

'Was Greenwood your mother's maiden name?'

Ben nodded. 'I had told you, hadn't I? Or maybe it just didn't come up. The Greenwoods of Greenacres,' he said grandly and a little tongue-in-cheek. 'Except now it's the Kavanaghs of Greenacres, which doesn't have quite the same ring.'

Daisy peered tentatively under some armchair-shaped dust sheets in the lounge area. 'Very . . . floral.' She let the sheet drop back. 'And that must be the "dining room".' She looked at the small round table and fiddle-back chairs. A narrow Welsh dresser stood against the wall, which was painted a dingy mustard colour.

Ben was scratching his head. 'It's not exactly how I remember it. I don't think anything's been changed since Aunt Eleanor died, it's just . . . the memory plays tricks on you.'

Daisy didn't reply. She had turned her attention to the staircase tucked away in a corner. The stairs were bare wood, narrow and steep, and led to a small landing carpeted in a mossy green which ran into each of the three rooms. A bathroom, which mercifully had a fairly decent white suite with brass fittings; a poky bedroom with a single bed and a rocking chair; and then a larger bedroom overlooking the front garden. Daisy pulled back

the curtains in this last room, then turned round to survey
the low double bed. She lifted the edge of a dust sheet
and discovered a patchwork quilt and brass bedstead. A
wardrobe – mahogany, perhaps – stood in one corner;
beside it was a matching dressing-table with legs that
were so spindly they looked as if they might give way at
any second.

Ben had followed her upstairs. It was fortunate that he
was under six feet, just about, or his untidy blond hair
would have skimmed the low beams. He stared glumly
across the bed at Daisy.

'When my aunt lived here, it seemed such a getaway
from the main house. My mum always had to have
everything in its place, but my aunt was a bit more relaxed.
Don't get me wrong, Mum was great, but sometimes living
with her was like treading on eggshells. You know I'm not
the neatest of people, even though I try to be. I guess
that's why I used to spend so much time here. Aunt
Eleanor didn't mind me slobbing out. She was a bit of
a slob herself, when she wasn't skipping round catching
butterflies or picking bluebells in the wood.'

Daisy raised her eyebrows.

'It's OK,' Ben assured her, smiling for the first time
since they'd set foot in the Gatehouse. 'I used to tease
her, but she wasn't really mad. Just eccentric. She never
married, and she didn't have a career. My grandfather
was old-guard and couldn't stomach the thought of either
of his daughters working for a living. My aunt must
have been bored and kept herself occupied in her own
way.'

'So,' broached Daisy, recalling what he'd already told
her, 'if she left the Gatehouse entirely to you, does that
mean there's no mortgage or rent to pay?'

Ben shook his head. 'Just the other bills, of course. Council tax, water, electricity . . .'

'Is there a phone?'

'Not at the moment. We were going to get a line put in when . . .' he tailed off and frowned out of the window.

'When you and Geraldine moved in?' Daisy completed the sentence for him. 'I don't need shielding, Ben. We've all got baggage.'

'Some more excess than others, though.' He was referring to himself, unaware of the chord it struck in her too. 'Anyway,' he continued, 'Geraldine planned to revamp the place, as far as she was able to.'

'Is that what your aunt would have wanted?'

'It was what Geraldine wanted. And you haven't met her yet. She can be demanding at the best of times. I don't think she really wanted to live here. Looking round now, I can't blame her.'

He seemed so dejected, Daisy went over to him and wrapped her arms round his waist. 'Listen, there's nothing wrong with this place that a lick of paint can't fix.'

'But I bet you've never cooked on a range before? I don't mean an Aga-type thing, I mean that fireplace you saw downstairs. And there's no central heating.' He seemed to have been saving that detail for last.

Daisy gulped. 'I'm sure I could learn to cook on it, or *in* it, or whatever,' she said, as gamely as possible. 'If your aunt managed it, so can I. It must be a bit like a barbecue. And I've always liked the idea of real fires. They're much more . . . atmospheric.'

'Well, on a plus point, there's the boiler contraption in the kitchen which heats the hot water – that makes the downstairs quite warm. And upstairs, portable electric heaters would be OK, provided we remember to switch them off when we're supposed to.'

'Don't worry,' Daisy reassured him, 'it's going to be fine. Summer will be here soon anyway.'

'We ought to get a proper cooker, though,' sighed Ben. 'I don't know about you, but thinking about it, I couldn't cope without a hob. And if you *really* want – be honest now – we can go the whole hog and do the place up properly . . .'

She put a finger to his lips, snuggling closer. 'Shut up. I like it. We'll go to the nearest B&Q tomorrow and buy some paint.'

Ben was finally beginning to relax. She could feel the tension easing away as she rubbed the curve of his back. His body arched closer to hers, their mouths meeting in a kiss that was both sweet and sensual, and went on for far too long to just end there. With the presumptuousness of newlyweds, they negotiated themselves on to the bed. Ben kicked off his loafers, Daisy her mules. The mattress was lumpy and sagged in the middle, the entire bedstead creaking loudly at their combined weight.

'Aunt Eleanor was a feather,' murmured Ben. 'There was nothing to her.'

Daisy wrenched at the top button of his jeans. 'What the hell made you sell your futon? Did you fancy a change?'

'The only thing I fancy right now is *you*.' He kissed her roughly on the lips. 'You're so gorgeous . . .' His mouth trailed downwards, following his hands as they tugged at her buttons.

They made love urgently, still half-clothed, the sunlight glistening down on them through the yellowy voile nets. Afterwards, tangled in a dust sheet, Daisy lay dozily against Ben's chest. For her, so far, this was the best part of being married. The security of the post-coital moment. The luxury of enjoying the afterglow without wondering if the man she had just slept with would still be there in the morning, let alone the following week. Not that there'd been many men, but enough for her to know that this was infinitely better.

Ben ran his fingers slowly through her hair. 'You aren't going to colour it again in a hurry, are you?' he asked suddenly, out of nowhere. 'I'd like to see it the way nature intended. It struck me this morning that I married you and I don't even know what your real hair colour is, apart from a "dull brown".'

'It *is* dull,' sighed Daisy, tweaking at one of his chest hairs.

'Ouch,' winced Ben.

'Sorry. What I mean is, it's boring. It reminds me of . . .'

'What?'

Daisy had been about to say it reminded her of her mother's hair, but she didn't want to go into that now.

'It's ours,' she said simply, after a pause.

'What is?'

'This place. It's ours, isn't it?' She propped herself up on one elbow and looked at him, excitement flickering in her stomach at the realisation that this was their home. 'I've never had anything that was "ours" before.'

'Even if it's decrepit?'

'It's not!' smiled Daisy. 'Just neglected. That's easier to fix. It needs a clean, but it's not too cobwebby. OK, so it hasn't been loved very much lately, but no one's let it fall into disrepair either.'

He stared at her, caressing her face with the back of his hand. 'My aunt would have adored you . . .' a slow grin slid on to his lips '. . . you're almost as barmy as she was.'

Daisy giggled and rolled on to her back. She stared up at the ceiling. There was mildew in one corner, grey and ominous, but it couldn't dampen her enthusiasm.

'Why don't we go shopping and buy some food and wine, maybe some champagne?' she suggested. 'Nothing too expensive, of course. We could bring it back here tonight and—' She was about to say, 'Watch a video,' but then remembered she hadn't even seen a television downstairs. Still, there was always Scrabble.

'Er, we can't.' Ben was fastening his jeans. 'Not this evening.'

Daisy's heart began its inevitable downward descent. She couldn't bear the thought of sitting with his family again round that huge, French-polished dining table at the main house. Not two nights in a row.

'We're going to the Headless Horseman,' said Ben. 'Our local. There's karaoke on a Saturday.'

'Oh . . .' Daisy was a little taken aback. It wasn't what she would have expected from a sleepy village pub. She sat up and scanned the room for her knickers.

Ben went on quickly, 'I called some old friends while you were still in bed this morning. They're going to be at the Headless Horseman tonight, too. They're dying to meet you.'

'Tonight?'

Daisy suddenly remembered the spot on her chin; the fact that she'd overplucked her right eyebrow the other day, although Ben had said he couldn't tell the difference; and finally – worst of all – she remembered what a torture it had been meeting Ben's family. What if it was the same with his friends?

'I can't,' she spluttered. 'I'm not ready.'

'Of course you are!' Ben sounded so confident, Daisy cringed. 'You'll be fine. They'll love you.' He fished her knickers from underneath the dressing-table and deposited them on the bed. 'Now come on, Mrs All-It-Needs-Is-A-Lick-Of-Paint, let's go find a phone book, or ask someone where the nearest DIY store is. We might even have time to go today.'

4

'What do you think I should wear?' asked Daisy.

Ben strolled out of the en suite with a towel round his waist. His mouth fell open. Daisy had emptied the entire contents of her suitcase over the four-poster bed.

'This?' she said, holding up black pants and a mauve shirt. 'Or this?' She held a skimpy, silky dress up to her chest, then shook her head. 'No, it's just a pub, isn't it? And these pants, I'd forgotten they're a bit tight. After those fish and chips earlier, I won't fit into *anything*.'

'Of course you will, you're not fat.'

'But I'm not thin, am I?' Daisy flung clothes left, right and centre.

'Darling' – Ben dared to step closer – 'you're perfect.'

'You always say that!' She pulled up the bra strap which seemed determined to slide off her shoulder. 'I'm just average. I've got an average sort of face, an average sort of figure—'

'Well, wouldn't you rather be average than ugly?' Ben was aware he had to defuse the situation fast.

Daisy's nostrils flared. 'That's not the point!'

'What is, then?' If he tried to calm her down by remaining calm himself, it would only antagonise her more. And if he attempted to make her laugh, it would probably have the same effect. The only way to handle her when she was in this sort of mood was to act moody and mulish himself.

'I . . . I don't know what the point is,' stammered Daisy. 'Except that I've got nothing to wear.' She tried perching on the bed, but it was too high, her bottom kept slipping off. 'Maybe you should go on your own tonight,' she frowned, rubbing her forehead.

'Why?' he asked, frowning himself. He'd been afraid of this. 'Have you got a headache?'

'A headache? No . . .'

She seemed to regret answering so quickly. If she'd thought about it, Ben speculated, she probably would have had one, after all.

'Well,' he shrugged, rummaging through his own suitcase and pulling out stonewashed jeans, 'you don't have to come if you don't want to. Nobody's twisting your arm.'

'But . . .'

He turned and looked at her. She was holding her bra strap in mid air, her mouth open.

'But what?' he prompted.

'Don't you want me to come? Wouldn't you be disappointed if I didn't?'

Of course he'd be disappointed. In fact, he wasn't going to the Headless Horseman without her. But his plan wouldn't work if he came across as desperate.

'I'd get over it,' he bluffed.

'It's just . . .' Daisy seemed to have a lump in her throat '. . . I've never met your friends before.'

Ben let his towel drop to the floor, and reached for some underpants. 'I'm aware of that.'

'They might hate me,' she muttered.

He should have known. He should have realised she

was still agonising over that. 'No one's going to hate you,' he said soothingly. Scrutinising the jumble of clothes on the bed, he picked out a white T-shirt, pink cardigan and denim skirt. 'What about these?' he suggested, injecting his voice with the assurance she currently lacked. 'They're all my favourites. You look great when you wear them together. This is cashmere, isn't it?' He held up the cardigan.

'Acrylic, actually.' She sniffed and rubbed her nose.

'Well, it looks as if you paid a fortune for it.'

She hesitated, then gazed up at him, misty-eyed.

Ben held his breath. To his continual surprise, he had yet to see Daisy cry properly. Her eyes would get watery, but nothing seemed to actually spill on to her cheeks. There were never any tears of distress or rage, let alone joy. She claimed she hadn't cried like that since she was a little girl, and the trend had persisted even on their wedding day. Now, as had happened so often before, her eyes glistened . . . but nothing came of it.

With a resigned sigh, Ben pretended to punch her on the chin. 'Come on, where's your spirit? My friends aren't going to eat you. I vetted them thoroughly while we were at school together. If they weren't going to be nice to my future wife, I wasn't going to have anything to do with them.'

Her lips broke into a tiny smile.

'See,' he brushed his mouth against the top of her head, 'I was thinking of you even then.'

'But you didn't know me.' Daisy leaned her head against his chest. His heart thumped faster as she nuzzled against him.

'I knew that there'd *be* a you, if that makes sense,' Ben continued. He gasped involuntarily as her hands roamed his body. 'What are you doing? Is this some new scheme to get out of going tonight?'

Daisy's strap had slipped completely off her shoulder. She stared up at him in mock innocence. 'Would I do that? Well – maybe I'm just trying to make us a little bit late.'

'You cow,' Ben moaned and kissed her, knowing full well, for the second time that day, that it wouldn't stop there.

'So come on, you two, let's see the rings then.'

Ben instantly stretched out his hand, but Daisy held back. It wasn't that she was ashamed of her wedding ring, she just knew that nobody else would find it half as beautiful as she did.

'I didn't want anything fancy,' Ben was saying, as Alice and Stella studied his hand.

'It's got an unusual patterned edge,' Alice observed, as if she knew about these things.

She looked at Stella, who added, 'Understated but elegant.'

'Oh, for shit's sake,' sighed Kieran, 'it's a bloody ring. I'm not wearing one when I get married, I can tell you that now. A watch – that's all the jewellery a bloke needs to wear. You'll never see me poncing about in chains and rings—'

'Oh, shut it,' said Ben good-naturedly. 'Who'd want to marry you anyway?'

'Let's see yours then.' Alice turned to Daisy, who reluctantly held out her hand. Her ring was eighteen carat gold, plain and narrow, with no unusual patterned edge. And her nails could have done with a good filing.

'Very . . . understated,' said Stella. 'Where's your engagement ring?'

'I don't have one.'

Alice's pale red eyebrows shot heavenwards. 'Why not? How could you let the bastard get away with it?' She thumped Ben on the arm.

Daisy shrugged. 'It seemed silly for such a short time. We had to buy the wedding rings in a rush. I suppose I felt I didn't need anything else.'

'That's not the point,' said Stella. 'He's supposed to fork out a month's salary. It's a tradition, isn't it? Although even a tiny diamond would be better than none.'

'Well,' Daisy retorted quickly, without thinking first, 'I preferred having a honeymoon, and we couldn't have afforded both.'

Ben coloured slightly, and squeezed her knee under the table. She probably shouldn't be discussing their finances in public, but she'd felt compelled to stick up for him.

'So where did you go then?' asked Kieran. 'Somewhere hot? Although you don't look very tanned.'

'Cornwall,' said Ben offhandedly.

'Mevagissey,' Daisy elaborated. 'We stayed in a B&B, and we found this great little fish restaurant in the harbour. We went to St Ives and Bodmin Moor and Land's End, and we even made it to a beach a couple of times, just for a paddle, it was too cold for anything else.'

'Do you remember when we all went to that villa in Florida?' Alice interrupted, just as Daisy had been about to describe how the sand went on for miles. 'We had our own pool, and Geri kept trying to get us to go skinny-dipping in the middle of the night.'

Ben snorted at the recollection. 'But what's with all this "Geri" stuff? She used to hate us shortening her name.'

'Well, if Geri Halliwell can reinvent herself, so can our very own Geri Parr.' Adam, as freckled and ginger as his twin sister Alice, had just returned to the table with the second round of drinks. 'Just you wait till you see her again, mate. You won't recognise her. She changed completely after you left. You did her the world of good dumping her.'

'I didn't dump her,' said Ben tetchily. 'It was a mature, mutual agreement.'

'That wasn't what she went round telling everyone.' Stella sipped her Bacardi Breezer and gave Kieran a sideways glance, as if to say, 'Poor Ben has no idea.'

Daisy shifted along the banquette, closer to her husband, pressing herself gratefully against his warm, muscular thigh. Grateful for alcohol, too, she lifted her drink to her lips. Eeuch! She almost spat it out again.

'This is vodka and tonic!' She glared accusingly at Adam.

He looked at her blankly. 'Isn't that what you wanted?'

'I asked for vodka and lemonade.' She frowned, realising that he probably hadn't done it on purpose, but still vexed. The evening seemed to be going from bad to worse. She was convinced Ben's friends didn't like her, and she wasn't exactly warming to them either.

'Sorry,' shrugged Adam. 'Look, I'll go get you another.'

'It doesn't matter, I'll do it myself.'

Daisy sprang to her feet, glad of the excuse to escape, if only for a couple of minutes. Before Ben could protest, she was gone. A few people – locals probably – turned to stare at her curiously as she made her way across the smoky, low-ceilinged room. The bar was crowded, so she headed for the far end where it was quietest. Another advantage from here was that she couldn't see the table by the fruit machine where Ben and his friends were sitting. Trying not to meet anyone's eye except for the nearest barmaid's, she focused her attention on getting served sometime before Christmas. Not that she was in a hurry, but she would feel even more self-conscious if she was ignored.

'I'd offer to buy you a drink, but you already seem to have one.'

The voice, coming from somewhere to her left and faintly Liverpudlian, sounded as if it was directed at her. She looked sideways and saw a man in a faded denim jacket. Her first sweeping impressions of his face were that his eyes were dark and deep set, his jaw shadowy with stubble and his lips in urgent need of a smile.

He inclined his head towards her glass. 'That *is* your drink, I'm assuming?'

She nodded, hastily wondering whether to be friendly or remain aloof. It was a reflex response. She'd worked behind a bar when she was nineteen, learning how to handle herself as capably as any of the other girls in the club. It had depended on the customer; Daisy had usually been able to suss straight away if he was going to be a nuisance. This one seemed lonely, which unfortunately could swing either way. He was propped against the bar with a pint of Guinness by his elbow, three-quarters full. By the slight glaze in his eyes, Daisy guessed it wasn't his first drink of the night.

'Right spirit, wrong mixer,' said Daisy matter-of-factly, catching the attention of a barmaid as she said it. 'Vodka and lemonade – at least, it ought to be.' Daisy rolled her eyes at the young woman, pleading for female solidarity.

'Was it Adam who ordered it? He definitely asked for tonic water.'

'Er – yes, I know. But he got it wrong.'

'That isn't my fault . . .' The archetypal busty barmaid had probably known Adam for years and wasn't about to

be disloyal. 'If you want another drink, I'm afraid you'll
have to pay for it.'

A blush filtered into Daisy's cheeks. She'd left her
bag at the table; it would be humiliating to have to go
back for it.

'Oh, come on.' The swarthy stranger in the denim
jacket frowned at the barmaid. 'Give the girl a break.
She's obviously new round here. What sort of a welcome
is that? Not very good for customer relations. If you're
really that bothered, I'll pay for the drink.'

'Thank you, really, but that isn't necessary . . .' Daisy
tried to work out if there was another way out of her
dilemma.

'I know it isn't,' said the stranger, 'but I'd like to
anyway.'

'OK, OK, no need for the knight-in-shining-armour
routine,' said the barmaid at last, oozing sarcasm from
every pore. 'I'll let you off this time.' After mixing a
vodka and lemonade, she bustled off to serve another
customer.

Daisy looked down at her new drink, cupping her hand
round the glass. Her wedding ring twinkled up at her, shiny
and unscratched. Like her marriage.

'Thank you,' she said, grudgingly confronting the would-
be hero beside her. 'It was very kind of you.'

'Kind,' he echoed, as if he was feeling the shape and
texture of the word on his tongue. He frowned pensively
into his Guinness. 'Now "kind" always suggests to me that
there's no ulterior motive, which, in this particular case,
wouldn't be true.' He turned and fixed his gaze on her.

Daisy squirmed inwardly. 'What about a heavenly
reward? Couldn't that be classed as an ulterior motive?'

The stranger blinked, nonplussed.

'Some people are kind because they don't want to go to hell,' Daisy explained.

'Uh-huh, I see. Too late for me then, I'm sorry to say. I'm currently having impure thoughts about a married woman.' His gaze swept down to her ring and then back to her face, which felt warm and flushed. He held out his hand. 'Jerome Wallace,' he said, still without smiling.

'Daisy Miller.' She shook his hand. 'I mean, Kavanagh.'

'Can't you decide?'

'Kavanagh. Daisy Kavanagh. It's just—'

'You haven't been married long.'

She paused and frowned. 'How did you know?'

He took a sip of his drink, and licked away the froth from his lips with the tip of his tongue. 'Because you were almost forgetting you've got a new surname. That happens quite often with newlywed women. And divorcées, if they've chosen to revert to their maiden name.'

'Right.' Daisy clutched her own drink tightly. 'I suppose it does, although I only know about the former.'

'And I know practically everything about the latter. Makes us a good team, don't you think?' He seemed amused at last, although in an edgy, brittle sort of way. 'Kavanagh, you said? Any connection with the Kavanaghs up at Greenacres?'

'Howard Kavanagh's my father-in-law.' Daisy didn't savour admitting it. She wished her father-in-law was someone normal who lived in a thirties semi and drove a beige M-reg Volvo. Someone with a patched cardigan and a hearty laugh who'd hug her as if he meant it. Not that Howard had hugged her at all; she would probably get frostbite if he tried it, he seemed such a cold man. Oh, why couldn't Ben have stayed an ordinary bloke instead of turning into Somebody's son?

'So you're Benjamin Kavanagh's wife?' Jerome Wallace seemed almost challenging. Or was it defensive? Daisy couldn't tell. 'I didn't know he was back in Nettlesford already. I'd heard he was coming home, but . . .'

'He's back all right. Are you a friend of his?'

'Your husband's never met me; he'd already left when I moved here. I know his family, but not him personally.'

'I see.' Daisy took a sip of her drink. 'Maybe I should introduce you.'

Jerome shifted his elbow on the bar and leaned closer. His unexpected smile lacked conviction. 'Now, wouldn't that be a novel idea?' he uttered softly.

'I don't see why,' she said, with a primness that didn't suit her. 'It's a perfectly innocent acquaintance.' Now she sounded like a character from a Jane Austen novel. Obviously she was out of practice at this; or could becoming a wife do that to you? 'You and me, that is, not him and—'

'Christ,' grunted Jerome Wallace. Daisy wasn't fond of people saying this out of context. 'Where on earth did he find you?' He sounded as if he was smothering a laugh.

She bristled with indignation. Just as a voice over a loudspeaker announced that the karaoke was about to start, Jerome reached out and grabbed her arm, preventing her from stalking off.

'I'm sorry,' he said. 'I didn't intend for it to come out like that. I meant it in a nice way.'

'Of course you did.' Daisy shook off his grip. 'Thanks for the offer of a drink, anyway. As I said, it was very kind of you.'

Without looking back, she picked her way across the pub towards her husband and the sanctuary of his warm, sinewy thigh. Except that, as the table came into view, she noticed that Adam had taken Stella's seat and that Stella was now on the banquette next to Ben. He didn't appear to have missed Daisy; he was regaling his friends with a 'D'you Remember When?' story. With a brief smile in her direction, he gestured to a vacant stool and continued with the tale. Deflated, Daisy sat down, while the landlord, presumably, of the Headless Horseman clambered on to a small platform and switched on the karaoke machine.

'Stella means star in Latin, you know,' proclaimed Alice, staring spellbound at her friend, who was performing 'Like a Virgin'.

A beanpole version of Madonna, Stella gyrated stiffly round the tiny stage. Her blonde hair flapped, her beaded top shimmered and her voice grated. At least, it did to Daisy. Stella's friends seemed in awe of her, including Ben. OK, so she'd been better than any of the previous acts, but that wasn't saying much.

'Isn't it spelt S,T,E,L,L,A,*R*?' asked Daisy.

'What?' Alice wrinkled her brow, her freckles merging into an orange blur.

'*Stellar*. The Latin for star.'

'Ssshhh,' said Kieran.

'You don't know Latin,' Ben whispered to Daisy.

'I know a bit,' she said, neglecting to keep her voice low. 'I know *tempus fugit*.'

'*Tempus* what?' frowned Adam.

'Time flies.' Ben put a finger to his lips and looked pointedly at Daisy. This only riled her more.

'I never was any good at Latin,' muttered Adam, 'but things don't usually end in R, do they? *Luna*, for instance. Isn't it us who added the Rs, rather than the Romans?'

'Who gives a toss?' Kieran folded his arms over his

chest. 'I'd like to hear Stella sing, if that's OK with everyone.'

But the song soon came to an end. Stella gave a bow as the pub erupted into rapturous applause. Daisy wondered if the applause grew louder because Stella's top gaped slightly as she leaned over. The tall blonde tottered off the stage and rejoined the group. Kieran kissed her on the cheek, and instantly she giggled and broke out in a blush.

'You were great,' he enthused.

She rubbed at her black suedette trousers, as if she had an itch above both knees. 'Thanks.' Her head ducked low. She seemed coy for the first time that night.

Just then, Daisy's attention was diverted by the sound of her name. It rang out from the loudspeakers, crackily yet unmistakable. 'Daisy Kavanagh.' Everyone must have heard it. And according to the landlord of the Headless Horseman, she was due to sing the next song.

Ben frowned across at her. 'I didn't know you'd put your name down.'

'I – I didn't.' Daisy glanced round the table. 'Is this some sort of joke?'

But everyone was looking as baffled as she was. Either they were very good actors, or . . .

'Daisy Kavanagh?' came the voice again, more enquiringly. The landlord was on the stage, peering into the audience. 'You're down to sing "My Heart Will Go On".'

Ben's frown deepened. 'From *Titanic*. That's your favourite film!'

Daisy felt accused of a crime. 'I know. But I honestly didn't put my name down.'

'Have you ever done karaoke before?' asked Adam.

'No . . .'

'Well, you can't be expected to do it now then,' said Stella. 'There's obviously something dodgy going on.' She looked suspiciously round the group, and then back at Daisy. 'I mean, you're no Celine Dion.'

At this, Daisy rose defiantly to her feet. 'I suppose I've heard Celine belt it out enough times, though.'

Ben looked flustered. 'Darling, come on, sit down. I don't know what's going on, but if you like I'll go up myself and say it's all been a stupid misunderstanding.'

'Afraid I'll make a fool of myself?' said Daisy. 'Or afraid I'll make one of you?'

Ben's mouth opened and closed, and his eyes regarded her helplessly, but he didn't reply. Not verbally, at least.

Daisy turned on her heel and started making her way towards the small stage, her heart thumping violently as if it most definitely would *not* go on once the ordeal was over.

5

'If I'd known you could actually sing . . .'

Ben squinted after Daisy along the deserted country road. The moon was having trouble bouncing light through the patchy clouds. It didn't help that his wife's coat was dark, and that she would stride along in front of him for a few yards before her pace and temper would slacken and she would appear abruptly at his side again, like a ghost out of thin air.

'What difference would it have made?' her voice called back to him, and then, suddenly, there she was, eyes glinting at him out of a pale, silvery face.

'All the difference. "My Heart Will Go On" isn't the kind of song you can cock up without it being painfully obvious. I know karaoke's only supposed to be a laugh—'

'Someone ought to tell Stella that. She looks as if she's auditioning for *Pop Idol*, except that she's too old.'

'Oh, come on, Daisy, give her a break. That's always been her dream. To sing professionally.'

'She should have had lessons then.'

'She did when she was younger. What about you – did you have lessons? Have you ever sung professionally?'

She was walking ahead of him again. 'Just because I can sing, doesn't mean I have to do it for a living.'

'It seems such a waste . . .'

'You've heard me in the shower before now, why didn't you say anything then?'

'That's not the same.'

It wasn't as if she belted out showstoppers while shampooing her hair. Sometimes she just hummed. What had happened back there in the Headless Horseman had commanded Ben's attention in the same way as when he'd first seen her smile. Inside him, something indefinable had slammed into something else. Love at first sight, all over again. Except that it was love at first song.

How many men back there had felt the same? Coveting her for her voice, her face, her body . . . Ben's chest tightened in a possessive, primeval fashion, even as something akin to an electrical charge passed through him. She was his. All his. Daisy Kavanagh – the sublime girl in the pink cardigan who had silenced a heaving pub with a voice that ought to be immortalised on CD, selling at HMV like hot cakes.

'It's not simply that you can sing.' Ben scoured his brain for the right words. 'It's just . . . you poured out your soul while you did it. I've got to be honest, that song's not one of my favourites. In fact – No, forget it. What I'm trying to say is that you made me listen to it in a completely different way.'

'That's only because you know me. You don't know Celine Dion from Adam. Well, actually you do know an Adam, but—'

'Daisy, you made me listen to the words. You made me want to reach out and hug you, because you seemed so . . . so sad and alone up there.'

Her pace slowed again. She appeared against the backdrop of the hedgerow. 'I've made you talk like a girl.' There was a hint of a smile in her voice.

He latched on to that. 'Yes, fine, I admit it. I'm talking through my arse. Not that I'm saying girls talk through their arses, it's just . . .'

'Quit while you're behind, Ben.'

He wanted to reach out and hug her now, but her arms were folded over her chest, barring him from trying. Tonight hadn't gone well, and his brain was in knots attempting to analyse why. There had to be more than one reason, because things seemed to have got progressively worse as the evening wore on. He knew Daisy had been nervous about meeting everyone, but they were OK really. He'd known most of them since primary school, and even when he'd been living in London he had still kept in touch via regular phone calls or e-mails. It was his family he had been trying to get away from when he'd left Nettlesford.

He couldn't understand why Daisy would dislike his friends. They'd done their best to include her in the conversation, even though most of it had been about old times. Unfortunately, being a reunion of sorts, this reminiscing had been unavoidable. But as people, they were all perfectly approachable; and thoroughly, irrefutably human. They had their faults, idiosyncrasies, Achilles' heels . . . and the sense that they were young and invincible – like kids. In fact, Ben realised, that was largely what they were. 'Teenage' twenty-somethings in the process of growing up, like a second adolescence without the gawkiness and spots. Still convinced that they were going to leave Nettlesford behind one day and head out into the big wide world for good.

Most of them had left when they were eighteen, to go to university. Kieran had even travelled as far afield as Southampton. But they'd all trickled back, as if irresistibly drawn by a magnet they had no control over. As far as Ben could see, the big wide world and its numerous adventures now lay in Chester. Kieran had even gone as far as to buy a flat there, near the canal; although, by the sound of it, he visited Nettlesford regularly for his mum to do his washing and replenish the supply of home-cooked meals for his freezer.

And Stella . . . the golden girl. Apple of her parents' eye. By now she had to know she wasn't good enough to be a professional singer. Why else would she nurture the dream without trying particularly hard to achieve it? So she worked in the family stables and pretended she didn't enjoy it because in truth she was into glitz and glamour, not horse shit. But Ben knew her as well as any of the others could claim to, apart from Kieran perhaps (in spite of her denials, there was definitely something going on there). She was the first girl Ben had ever kissed. The first he'd dated. And vice versa. They'd fallen into that 'relationship', and out of it again, while managing to stay friends because, after all, they had only been fifteen at the time.

As for Adam and Alice, they were both still sharing that same terraced house that their grandfather had left them. Both still teaching at the primary school where they'd been pupils themselves. Both still single and searching. If it hadn't been for the difference in their gender, you could have been fooled into thinking they were identical twins.

Ben had been the first to take the leap into the next dimension – *marriage*. He acknowledged now that he would probably be the first to navigate the dimension after that. But, fingers firmly crossed, children wouldn't be coming along for a while yet. Marriage alone seemed draining enough at times like this.

'I love you,' he said abruptly, but it was almost as if he was talking to himself. His wife had vanished into the darkness again.

She reappeared, standing by the old entrance to the Greenacres estate. The Gatehouse loomed behind her, edged in silver.

'I love you, too,' she said quietly. 'I'm sorry I'm such a bitch.'

'You're not.'

'I am. And I have sung in public before. Once or twice at school . . . and then as a sort of cabaret act.'

'Cabaret?' Ben's eyebrows shot up. 'So you got paid for it?'

'Peanuts. It was this tiny basement comedy café that played live jazz on a Thursday night.'

'You sang jazz?'

'The job only lasted a few weeks. I couldn't hack the pace.' Her voice was barbed with sarcasm.

'You told Adam that you'd never sung in front of an audience.'

'I said I hadn't done karaoke. That's the truth. I hadn't – before tonight.'

'But why . . . ?'

'I don't sing in public any more because I get too nervous,' explained Daisy impatiently. 'Actually *sick* with nerves. I felt like throwing up tonight, but I was so angry . . . Besides, I didn't have a long build-up. There wasn't time to get myself in a tizzy about it.' She paused, her brow ridged with a frown. 'It's not as if I live to sing. It's no great passion of mine, so why put myself through it if I don't have to?'

'That's the problem with talent and ambition,' Ben sighed concedingly. 'You've got the former, but it's Stella who wants it. People think they come as a package.'

'They don't. Not always. I suppose that makes it one of life's ironies.'

Ben stretched out and took her hand. 'I understand. And I'm sorry, too.'

They walked side by side past the Gatehouse.

'I wish we were living here already,' Daisy commented softly.

'We can start bringing our stuff over tomorrow, if you like.'

'What stuff would we need for one night? Nothing essential . . .'

He was silent for a moment as he let this sink in. He couldn't resist teasing her. 'What about our toothbrushes? And Colgate? I can't say I'm keen on going to bed without my breath smelling of its usual minty freshness.'

Their pace was slowing. Side by side, they came to a halt and turned to face each other. Daisy smiled.

'I've got some Polos in my bag.'

Ben laughed, stroking her cheek. 'Where on earth did I get you from?' He felt her recoil. 'What? What's wrong?'

'Nothing. It's just, what you said . . .' She shrugged. 'Don't worry, it doesn't matter. Just me being silly. Are they expecting us up at the house?'

'Dad and Vivienne? They've probably retired to their separate bedrooms by now.' He smiled darkly at the thought. 'I said we'd let ourselves in and that we'd probably be late. I don't think they'd be worried, if that's what you're getting at. The house is so big, they wouldn't hear us coming in anyway.'

'Do you have the key with you? To the Gatehouse?'

He dug a hand into his pocket. The few keys he owned were all attached to an old, scuffed leather keyring. 'Lucky me, eh?'

She leaned over, and brushed his lips with her own. 'Lucky us.'

The card came a couple of days later, addressed to '*Mrs Daisy Kavanagh*' at Greenacres. It was forwarded to the Gatehouse by Vivienne herself.

'Which gives me a pretext to visit.' She smiled stiffly as Ben fished out an extra tea bag.

'We've just put on a brew,' he said. 'Do you fancy one?'

'Earl Grey?' His stepmother didn't sound hopeful.

'PG Tips.' Daisy dusted down her jeans, which were faded and baggy and had cost her a fiver in a charity shop. Help the Aged, possibly, she couldn't remember. She'd been twenty-three and between jobs, and it had seemed an extravagance at the time. Daisy frowned at the mop in her hand and the rustic tiled floor of the Gatehouse, which she'd been about to wash down. But the sense of panic generated by the memory only lasted a few seconds. Ben's hand came to rest on her shoulder, his fingers gently kneading her neck, and she knew beyond doubt that this was the safest she had ever felt.

'Doing a spot of cleaning, I see.' Vivienne glanced round, her nose screwed up as if the faint whiff of bleach in the air was distasteful. 'Although, I hope you realise that this place would have been in a far worse state if I hadn't made sure it was cleaned thoroughly at least a couple of times a year and any minor jobs that needed doing were taken care of.'

'I appreciate that,' said Ben.

'Just protecting your investment.'

'It was very good of you . . .' Daisy peered curiously out of the corner of her eye at the envelope lying on the worktop. '. . . especially when looking after the rest of Greenacres must take up so much of your time.'

Vivienne settled on a kitchen stool. It wobbled precariously, but this failed to ruffle her. Daisy wished she had that sort of innate composure herself. When she'd first sat on the stool, she had sworn at it as she'd almost toppled off. Ben had been meaning to take a look at it to see if it could be fixed, but Daisy was rapidly becoming aware that DIY wasn't his strong point.

'I employ the best staff – whether permanent or temporary – in order to get the best work done,' Vivienne expounded. 'I rarely have to ask them to do anything twice.'

She was acting as if she was in a business meeting, rather than chatting casually over a cup of tea.

Daisy continued to peer at the envelope. Who would be writing to her at Greenacres? It was a personal letter, not a circular, addressed in block letters in a nondescript handwriting she didn't recognise.

'Aren't you going to open it?' Vivienne asked.

Ben jerked his head towards it. 'Who's it from? Do you know?'

As she picked it up, Daisy noticed that the postmark was local; dated yesterday afternoon. It also felt like a card rather than a letter. She wished she could make her husband and stepmother-in-law vanish, just for a couple of minutes, while she read it.

'I'll open it later,' she said decisively, jamming it into a back pocket.

Ben pouted in disappointment. 'But I wanted to know who it was from!'

'It isn't anything important. Don't be so nosy.' She pretended to rap his knuckles.

Vivienne sipped her tea and gazed round, eyes as hauntingly blue and vigilant as ever. She could probably spot a speck of dust a mile off, frowned Daisy, who had already come to the conclusion that the Gatehouse was one of those places notoriously and inexplicably difficult to keep clean.

As Ben and Vivienne chatted, mostly about Geri and her imminent return from holidaying in Cuba with her fiancé Declan, the mysterious missive seemed to burn a hole in Daisy's pocket. She was actuely aware of her posterior as the card moved stiffly against it. It was no good, she couldn't hold out any longer. She was going to have to open it.

'Back in a mo,' she said distantly, hitting on an excuse. 'I'm desperate for the toilet. It must have been the tea . . .' She hurried upstairs and bolted the bathroom door behind her.

Perched on the lid of the loo seat, she stared breathlessly at the envelope, a dart of trepidation shooting through her. She didn't have any friends locally. Not that she had any real friends anywhere else. It was sometimes harder to know if you had an enemy.

A mixture of defiance and curiosity finally compelled her to rip open the envelope. The picture on the front of the card showed a Forever Friends bear cradling a bunch of flowers and looking sheepish. Below the bear was a squiggly 'Sorry . . .'

Daisy opened it, utterly intrigued.

'My dear Mrs Kavanagh.'

Well, if that wasn't taking the mickey just a little bit . . .
Daisy frowned as she read on.

> *'Re: the karaoke.*
> *I was the one who put your name down.*
> *You'll never know how pleased I am that you turned*
> *the joke back round on me, so until I can apologise in*
> *person – will this do?*
> *Your faithful servant,*
> *J. W.'*

Jerome Wallace?

Daisy read it three times from start to finish, her mind
racing. Until now, she'd been privately blaming Kieran.
For some reason – his shifty eyes, maybe? – she trusted
him the least out of Ben's friends. He looked capable of
playing a prank like that and bluffing his way out of it.
But the confession in this card made more sense, even
though it seemed a cross between a laconic e-mail and an
old-fashioned business letter.

Yet – did it make sense? She frowned at it again.

Men had long since lost their mystique for Daisy. They
were simple creatures really. Even the more sensitive,
intelligent ones like Ben functioned primarily on a few
basic levels. Her own sex were the enigmas. Women like
Vivienne, for instance: beautiful and sophisticated enough
to have any man, but settling for a cantankerous bully more
than twenty years her senior.

What was so simple about Jerome Wallace, though?
Who the hell was he? Daisy couldn't define what lay
behind the 'joke' he'd played, or this card. Fair enough,
maybe he fancied her; but why do something like this
when he knew she wasn't for the taking? She couldn't help
thinking that there was more to it, her heart fluttering with

fear, perverse excitement, panic, because in a childish way she felt stalked.

A knock on the door made her leap off the loo. Suddenly she realised that she did need to use the toilet after all, but it was too late.

'Are you all right?' asked Ben.

'Er, yes – fine.'

'Vivienne's gone.'

'Right.' She put the card back in the envelope and slid it into her pocket again, then flushed the loo and washed her hands. 'So soon?'

'You know what she's like.'

Actually, thought Daisy, I don't. She unbolted the door and stepped out on to the narrow landing.

'Our first visitor.' Ben smiled, rubbing a hand over his glittering stubble. 'I would have shaved if I'd known she was coming.'

Daisy hoped her cheeks weren't too rosy. 'We'll have to ask Vivienne and your dad over for dinner.'

'Yeah, right.' He tugged at a lock of hair curling over his brow and yawned dramatically. 'I need a bath. I feel like someone's dragged me through some manure.'

'It's only half past three.' Daisy brushed past him down the stairs. 'Come on, there's work to do. We can't let one little interruption throw us off course.'

'You're a slave-driver.' Following her down the stairs, he remarked nonchalantly, 'It was good of Vivienne to bring the letter over herself, though.'

'Mmm.' Daisy was non-committal.

'I assume it was a letter?'

'I haven't opened it yet. I recognise the writing, though. It's . . .' Should she keep lying, or should she confide in him? The fact of the matter was, she didn't know how he would react. Would he start wondering if she'd actually encouraged this Jerome Wallace? She didn't want him to think that, or doubt her, even for a second. The safety she'd felt earlier seemed tenuous now, like a balloon with a needle hovering over it.

'From . . . ?' Ben prompted.

'An old friend.' Her back to him, Daisy closed her eyes briefly, praying that he hadn't spotted the postmark. 'Ellie . . . Findus. Haven't I mentioned her before?'

'Er—'

'I must have. You've just forgotten.' Daisy picked up the mop and resumed cleaning. 'She was my best mate back in Norwich. I wrote to her after the wedding.'

'When did you last see her?'

'Oh . . . a couple of years ago. She's married, too. With three kids. Another on the way.'

'Blimey.'

'Exactly. She rarely leaves Norfolk now. Too busy.'

'You should give her a call sometime. Catch up on old times.'

Daisy hated lying, yet she'd been doing it from the first occasion she'd sat down to have a coffee with him, in the service station. He was wearing that same earnest, boyish expression now. There was something about Ben that reminded her of Luke Skywalker from *Star Wars*, even though he didn't look anything like the actor who'd played him.

It had fascinated her in the early days, how a stranger could fall for her when she wasn't dressed in a skimpy outfit, her face glossy with make-up. So she had put him to the test, and he had passed. She had let him see her at her hormonally challenged, temperamental worst, and he had still wanted to put his arms round her. To hold her. To let her know she was everything he had ever wanted, and then, out of nowhere on that blustery February afternoon as they'd walked through Hyde Park, ask her to be his wife.

'You'll have to get a phone connected here first,' said Daisy chirpily, swishing the mop round the floor. 'I'm not calling Ellie from your mobile, she'd cost you a fortune.'

'I get free talktime.'

'That still wouldn't be enough.' She wrung out the mop into a bucket. 'Trust me, you've never met Ellie.'

Even if she existed, Daisy doubted he ever would have.

6

'Any other preferences, in case they don't have *Monsters, Inc.*?'

'I don't know . . .' Daisy shrugged distractedly, leaning back to survey her handiwork. '*Shrek*, maybe?'

Ben paused by the front door. 'All these kids' films you're into doesn't mean you're pregnant, does it? This isn't some weird modern craving? Fifty years ago, foetuses wanted tuna and banana sandwiches. Now they want Gameboys and DVDs.'

Daisy pulled a face. 'No craving, no baby. I just don't fancy anything heavy. I'm sick of all that violence and swearing.'

'Fine, fine. No gangster movies. I think I can cope.' He ducked to avoid the cushion Daisy aimed at his head, and dodged out of the front door, laughing.

Daisy glanced at the DVD player, sleek and silver beneath a matching thirty-two-inch widescreen TV. Ben had already got round to fixing small speakers in various strategic positions for the 'full cinematic experience', even though he hadn't attempted to mend the dodgy kitchen stool yet. The whole high-tech system had arrived yesterday, much to their astonishment. They'd thought it was a mistake when the delivery man had knocked on their door, until he'd mentioned Howard and Vivienne Kavanagh. As it turned out, they'd wanted to give Ben and Daisy a belated wedding present. 'We couldn't think of anything else,' Vivienne had told Ben when, still in shock, he'd called to thank her. 'A toaster or vacuum cleaner seemed inadequate.'

'A new three-piece suite would have been nice,' Daisy had frowned, when Ben had finished talking to his step-mother.

'You're kidding, right?' Ben had looked as if all his Christmases had come at once. 'I never expected anything from them, let alone this.'

'I don't know . . . Yes,' she'd gone on hastily at the look on his face, 'you're right. This is great. I'm being ungrateful.' Yet she couldn't quite shake off the feeling that it somehow smacked of bribery.

Daisy turned back to the wall in front of her. It was no longer a dingy mustard colour. The base coat was a dark green, and the top coat, dabbed on with a sponge, was paler and called – rather dramatically – Sage Skies. Wandering round B&Q last Saturday, staring up at the shelves stacked with hundreds of tins, Daisy had decided against pastels and had talked Ben into trying their hand at a paint effect. Except that she'd done most of it while Ben had listened to football on the radio ('You do realise it's nearly the end of the season?'). It wasn't that he was lazy, he'd simply been too gung-ho about the whole thing. Daisy had wanted to do it properly, preparing the wall first, sugar soaping, sanding, that sort of thing. Ben hailed from the slap-it-all-on-and-hope-for-the-best school of thought. It wasn't something he enjoyed, therefore he wanted to get it over with as quickly as possible.

The last time Daisy had wielded a paint brush with any notable effect had been during art class at school. Since then, she'd wanted to redecorate her various digs over the years, but each time the landlord had mulishly refused permission. So she'd learned to live with peeling wallpaper, or plain magnolia, or psychedelic orange (her last bedsit had been owned by an ex-hippy). Now that she had her own home, she was going to spend as long as she wanted and be as meticulous as she liked to get it looking just right.

'*Love* the colours!' exclaimed a voice from behind. 'Did you choose them yourself, or was it Ben?'

Daisy swung round to confront a tiny female with chocolate-brown eyes and streaky dark hair cut into a sharp, shoulder-length bob. She looked almost anorexic, apart from her breasts, which were like two firm peaches threatening to spill out of her plunging black top. Daisy would have bet against them being real.

'Please don't shatter my illusions and tell me it was Ben,' the woman went on pleafully, in a voice that was neither common nor posh. 'I'd hate to think he'd developed some taste.'

'I'm sorry,' Daisy finally managed to utter, 'but who are you?'

'Listen, *I'm* the one who should be sorry, barging in like this. But the door was open . . .' The woman breezed forwards, holding out her hand. 'Geri Parr, Ben's cousin. Well, third cousin – by marriage, I think. Genealogy's so complicated.'

Daisy's first impulse, based on vanity, was to sweep back the ancient polka-dot scarf keeping her hair off her face. Her second was to straighten the shirt she was wearing, covered in flecks of green paint. Finally, she held out her own hand to shake Geri's.

'I'm Daisy,' she muttered.

'Well, of course, who else would you be? You're not my

idea of a professional painter and decorator. Besides, you fit Vivienne's description virtually to a tee. Where's Ben, anyway? Skiving probably.'

'You've just missed him. He's gone to get a takeaway and a video. I mean, a DVD,' Daisy blathered. 'For tonight. We were going to stay in.'

'Very romantic.' Geri sighed. 'That's the kind of thing I wish Declan was into. He always prefers to go out to a restaurant or a club, you know how it is. Now and again I wish he'd take me to the cinema, or ten-pin bowling. Something that doesn't involve me dressing up.'

Daisy didn't know how to react, or what to say next, so she tried putting herself in the other woman's shoes.

'I know what you're thinking,' said Geri, flopping into an armchair. 'But I'm not here to be nosy . . . Well, all right, I'm human – of course I'm curious. You're Ben's *wife*, for crying out loud! His WIFE! I've known Ben too long to be mad at him for – for nothing. And I still love him in my own platonic way. I can't wait to see him again, and I couldn't wait to meet you. But I'm not harbouring any grudges. It wouldn't have worked out between Ben and me, and now I've got Declan, which is kismet, really. It's not perfect, but then whose relationship is? Except yours, probably.' Geri waggled an endless, metallic-blue finger-nail. 'You must still be in that rose-tinted honeymoon phase, especially considering that you haven't known each other long. You've managed to get past the awkward early stage while still enjoying all the good parts.' She paused. 'I'm sorry, I go on a bit, don't I?'

'Would you like a glass of wine?' asked Daisy, deciding it wouldn't be tactful to agree out loud. She didn't know Geri well enough, and the question might have been rhetorical. 'Ben put a bottle in the fridge to chill.'

'Sounds great.'

'It's only a Liebfraumilch,' Daisy added quickly. 'Nothing fancy. I'm not into dry.'

'Neither am I, the sweeter the better. Sometimes – don't tell Declan – I'll crack open a bottle of Asti and drink it in the bath. Well, only a glass. I'm not an alkie.'

'Right.' Daisy hunted for the corkscrew. Ben had only used it a couple of days ago. 'Damn,' she mumbled, 'where is it?'

'We ought to go out sometime.' Geri had sprung to her feet and then promptly dropped down again, this time into a kneeling position on the rug in front of the TV. She proceeded to press a few buttons on the DVD player. Daisy winced. Ben half-jokingly wouldn't let her near it in case she messed something up. 'I know it can't be easy coming halfway across the country,' Geri was rabbiting on. 'Leaving your job and your friends and . . . Was Vivienne serious when she said you'd worked at Burger King?'

'Deadly,' frowned Daisy.

'I had a waitressing job when I was sixteen. Just for the holidays. It was in this olde-worlde coffee shop. Hardly fast food, but I still couldn't cope.' Geri grinned at the memory, then jumped as the television crackled into life. 'Oh, I must have pressed "on". Anyway, I've heard that in places like Burger King and McDonald's you can climb the career ladder really quickly. Is that true?'

'Well—' Daisy had never attempted scaling it herself.

'Because ideally that's what you need nowadays, a job with prospects. I'm not a career woman myself, not at the moment, but I wouldn't be averse . . . Great, *Blind Date*'s on! Or one of those "Best Of" shows, at least.'

Daisy found the corkscrew at last. For some unfathomable reason, it was in the cupboard under the sink. Typical.

She opened the wine and poured out two glasses, carrying them through to the lounge.

'So,' she said, because for the first time Geri seemed to have lost her tongue, 'where's your fiancé tonight then?'

'Pick number three,' Geri growled at the TV. 'Three, you nob-end, *three*!' She groaned as the contestant picked number two. 'Have you seen how much glitter she's got in her hair? Half a can, at least. Complete tart. Still, I think he can still "ditch" her, can't he?'

'Your fiancé?' prompted Daisy. 'Declan?'

'Declan? "Ditch" her?' Geri frowned. Then she twigged, and smothered a giggle. 'Oh, Declan's in Boston. The one in Massachusetts. Is that what you were asking? He flew out practically the moment we touched down from Cuba. But that's him – always on the go. Cuba was a holiday, before you ask. Boston is business. He doesn't know for sure when he'll be back, so I'm at a loose end. *I know*' – she seemed even more animated, if that were possible – 'you can help me out with some of the wedding stuff. There's still loads to do. Vivienne has been a godsend, but sometimes a girl needs someone her own age.'

'Vivienne isn't that old.'

'Not in theory, no. But that's what you get when you marry someone as prehistoric as Uncle Howie. Well, he's not technically my uncle, but I've always thought of him as one, do you know what I mean?'

Daisy was dying to ask the burning question, the one Ben shied away from. *Why* had Vivienne married him? For his money or social standing? Surely someone like Vivienne could have had someone even wealthier or more influential? Unfortunately, Cilla Black had just announced that 'Clerr' and James were off on a blind date to Bognor

Regis. Geri seemed to find this hysterical. To Daisy, Bognor was better than nothing.

'Er, Geri, would you mind if I went upstairs to change? I feel a bit of a scruff.'

'What? Oh, of course not. But you look fine, don't change on my account. Or even for Ben. You're married now, let him see you how you really are. By the way, though, you've got paint on your chin . . .'

Daisy hurried upstairs. At first, she could hardly bring herself to look in a mirror, aware that she had to be a state compared to Geri. When she finally took the plunge, she discovered a smudge of Sage Skies below her bottom lip, as she'd feared. She could hear Geri downstairs, ordering the commercial break to 'Hurry up and get on with it!'

Another enigma, she decided dolefully. Another complication. For the umpteenth time since arriving in Nettlesford, Daisy found herself speculating: friend or foe?

Ben pushed the door open with his foot, and shuffled into the Gatehouse bearing a Chinese takeaway and *Monsters, Inc.*

'Hi, honey, I'm home!' It was his best American drawl.

'Well, hi honey yourself! You look amazing! Marriage obviously agrees with you.'

He turned and gawped at the young woman sitting cross-legged on the lounge rug. She looked the same . . . yet completely different. He couldn't work it out at first. It was so unmistakably Geraldine – no one had eyes like hers, and that smile was a dead give-away – but the girl he'd grown up with had been flat-chested and short-haired. Elfin, really. He'd always found her skinny frame a little unhealthy, and it hadn't helped that she'd had a tomboyish dress sense which consisted mainly of jodhpurs, jeans, baggy sweaters and shirts. She would never have worn boots like these with such a high, narrow heel, in spite of her diminutive height. And she would never have contemplated cosmetic surgery. Surely a bra alone, however expensive or 'miraculous', couldn't defy nature to such a drastic extent?

'Do you think being engaged suits *me*?' she asked, clambering to her feet and bounding towards him. 'Second time round, that is.'

'Geraldine—'

'*Geri*. And, here, let me help you with that.' She relieved him of the takeaway and DVD, plonked them both on top of the small shoe cabinet where the phone was going to go once he got one, and then wrapped her arms round him, squeezing him tight. She had to be on some sort of fitness regime. She'd never been this strong a few years ago.

'You do look great, really,' she went on. 'Growing older agrees with you. And I like your hair like that – all curly, like a spaniel. It never suited you when you had it too short.'

'I thought it was getting a bit long now,' said Ben vacuously. 'I'll be able to tie it in a ponytail soon.'

'Don't exaggerate.' Geri leaned back and surveyed him at length. He felt as if he were an exhibit in her fiancé's art gallery, although not a *pièce de résistance*. From what Vivienne had said, Declan Swannell could spot a modern masterpiece at ten paces. He must have seen potential in Geri.

'Vivienne said you were flying back from Cuba yesterday,' Ben went on. 'I assumed you'd still be in Liverpool, recovering from jet lag or something. Declan's got a flat there, hasn't he?'

'A small one. And I do stay there some of the time. Declan had to head off to the States, though, so I wasn't

going to hang around on my own. Besides, I couldn't wait
to come and see you. And meet the lucky woman who
nabbed you, of course.'

'Speaking of which . . . ?'

'Daisy's upstairs. She said she was going to get changed,
but then I heard her running a bath. She's been up there
ages now. A little quiet, isn't she? I suppose she's shy.'

Ben snorted. 'Daisy? Quiet?' Then he remembered that
first dinner with his father and Vivienne.

'Well,' grinned Geri, 'compared to me. But I like
her. She's sweet. And I'm not saying that to sound patronising.'

'She is sweet,' said Ben, 'but she's also—' He stopped
and mumbled, 'Shit.'

Daisy was coming down the stairs wearing an outfit he'd never seen before. At least, he'd never seen
her wearing the skirt, which was long and clingy with
a deep split. The top was another matter. He'd only
ever seen it within the confines of the bedroom. One
of those bra tops which went down to the waist, in
black satin, with a row of hook and eye fastenings just
crying out to be undone. And she was wearing too much
make-up. There was dark stuff smudged round her eyes,
and her lips weren't their plump, natural pink but a
vampish red.

'That's better,' she was saying, flicking at her hair,
which she'd scraped over one shoulder. 'I feel a little
more presentable now.'

Ben glanced at Geri, who seemed as flummoxed as he
did.

'Did you get the takeaway?' Daisy asked, reaching for
her glass of wine on the coffee table. She took a sip, and
smiled at him provocatively.

'Er . . . yes. And I got you those sesame things on toast you like so much.'

'Great. I'm starving.'

'I got *Monsters, Inc.,* too.'

'I'll get the trays out then. We can eat in front of the TV.'

'Um, are you planning on going out later? Only, I thought we were staying in tonight.'

'Sorry?'

'It's just – you've got yourself all . . . dressed up.'

'Oh, this.' She looked down insouciantly. 'I was fed up with all the tatty old gear I've been throwing on this past week.' She turned to Geri. 'You know how it is, a girl can't wear Kookai or Monsoon when she's cleaning and decorating, can she?'

What about Ann Summers? thought Ben. He didn't know what was going on, but he knew he didn't like it.

Geri stared down at the floor. 'I'd, um, better be off . . .'

'Why don't you stay and have something to eat with us?' Ben asked, keen to catch up with her, and apprehensive at being left alone with his wife if she was in one of her strange moods. He was too hungry to get into an argument right now.

Daisy looked peeved. 'There won't be enough food. If we'd known beforehand . . .'

'There's plenty of food. I always order too much. Come on,' he cajoled, smiling at Geri, 'don't rush off. You'll have to take us as you find us, though.' When she didn't instantly demur, Ben hurried on, 'I'll lay the table.'

'No need,' said Geri, 'I'm happy eating off my lap, too. It'll be cosy.'

'Isn't Vivienne expecting you home?' asked Daisy, clattering plates in a dangerous manner.

'I can ring and let her know. She won't mind.'

'Mrs White might.'

Ben turned to Daisy, muttering through partly gritted teeth, 'Leave it, darling, I'm sure no one's going to mind.' He turned back to Geri. 'Do you want to borrow my mobile to call them? We haven't got a landline set up yet.'

'Can I? I've left mine in my bag up at the house. To be honest, I'd prefer to eat here. You know what Vivienne and your dad's dinner parties are like.'

'Oh, have they got company tonight?'

'Just someone form the council and his la-de-da wife. No one important. I'm upsetting their numbers anyway. An extra girl, and all that. You know what a stickler your dad is.'

Geri winked at Ben, and smiled conspiratorially. The way he remembered her best.

'I don't know how you can just pick up where you left off like that . . .'

'What?' Ben didn't bother glancing up from the TV. It was a few hours later, and Geri had left a while ago.

'As if nothing had happened. As if you hadn't decided you weren't right for each other.'

'I assume you're talking about Geri and me. In which case, you can stop worrying.'

'I'm not worried.' Daisy sank down on the sofa beside him, rearranging the split in her skirt so that it wasn't indecent.

'Yes, you are. You're jealous. You went and got changed and made yourself look completely over the top.'

Daisy wrestled the remote control out of his hand. 'Will you at least look me in the eye when you're insulting me.'

He sighed. 'I'm not insulting you. I just think you're over-reacting. I wish Geri hadn't caught you on your own at a bad moment. But she did, and it's over with. You've met her and she's met you, and both of you lived to tell the tale.'

'Can I switch this off now?'

'I'm watching it.'

'I don't like football.'

'Well, I do.' Ben reclaimed the remote control. 'Listen to us, we sound just like that couple who tore each other to shreds on *Blind Date*.'

Fear fluttered in the pit of her stomach. What had happened to them since they'd come to this place? They'd only been here a week, but already their relationship had entered new territory.

'It's just . . . Geri wasn't what I'd expected. She wasn't how you'd described her.'

Ben sighed again. 'She's changed. She could always talk for England, but she's more . . . confident now, I suppose. The thing I like about *you* is that usually you know when to shut up.'

'Why did you break it off between you, Ben?'

'Why? Bloody hell, did you see that goal!' He rocked with elation. 'I love it when United get thrashed!'

'You're being evasive.'

'Huh?'

Daisy nibbled on a blunt nail. They still needed filing. Some were a couple of millimetres longer than others, which looked odd at the best of times, but compared to Geri's talons . . . 'Or maybe you're just being a man,' she murmured.

'OK.' He turned to face her, giving her his full attention now that the routine match analysis had replaced the actual football highlights. 'You want to know about Geri and me? Besides what I've already told you, which was everything.'

'I don't think you told me exactly why you broke up.'

'You're my wife, not my psychiatrist. Anyway, I don't know "exactly" why. I suppose I realised I didn't love her enough. We'd drifted into the engagement, egged on by my dad, and I started waking up in the mornings wondering if I was making a big mistake. I think Geri realised it, too, it's just that I was the first to actually say anything.'

'But you still ran away.'

Ben shook his head, exasperated. 'I wasn't running from *her*. I was trying to get away from becoming someone I didn't want to be. I felt as if my father was trying to turn me into a clone of himself, like Dolly the sheep, and Vivienne was his accomplice. They were doing it to Robert, too, except that with him they were going to succeed. He was already like them, even at eight.'

'So why are you back now?'

'You know why. I'm a crap salesman. I hated it. The only other thing I'm trained for is being a solicitor.'

'You could do something else, learn new skills—'

'My dad will have me counting paper clips as it is.' His brow wrinkled, and he hit the 'off' button on the remote. 'Where's all this coming from? You didn't have any problem with our plans before we came to Nettlesford. What's changed now that we're actually here?'

She wished she hadn't started this.

'I'm going to be thirty in a couple of months,' Ben went on. 'I could keep running from my past and all its problems, I suppose, but what kind of a man would I be?'

Wriggling in her bra top, the wires of which were digging into her ribcage, Daisy shrugged and ventured, 'A happy one?'

7

The village of Nettlesford was erupting into blossom. Daisy couldn't get over how abruptly it had happened, or how many trees were paraded down the High Street. She hadn't seemed to notice them before. Armed with an old wicker shopping basket she'd discovered in the cupboard under the stairs, she'd strolled up the lane from the Greenacres estate, her mood lifting by the minute. It was one of those early spring days which had to be equivalent to a hefty dose of anti-depressants, without any side-effects.

It was a Monday, and Ben's first day at work, and Daisy was slowly beginning to shake off the loneliness she'd felt earlier that morning when she'd waved him off. He hadn't taken a packed lunch, so she was going to surprise him with a 'picnic' in the office. It was lucky that he didn't work a long distance away. Theoretically, he could come home at lunchtimes if he wanted. She could rustle up a salad, or his favourite club sandwich. It would break the monotony for her.

She frowned slightly. If she was already thinking of her new housewife state as monotonous, this was rather worrying considering it was only her first day. Since the wedding, she'd effectively walked round with her head in the clouds, veiled in the novelty of being a brand new wife. This morning, without Ben, she had taken on a new role, one that she hadn't really given much thought to before. The Daisy of the last seven years had been more or less self-sufficient. In her experience, relying on other people only culminated in being let down.

A small Co-op appeared ahead on the other side of the road. Daisy crossed over, aware that this was the only supermarket she would have easy access to. She'd never had the opportunity to learn to drive. Before Ben had come along, no one had ever offered to teach her, and she couldn't have afforded proper lessons. In London, this hadn't posed a problem, not with buses and the Underground. When she'd worked at the service station, she'd relied on lifts from co-workers, which hadn't been as bad as it sounded. Around here, she would have more difficulty. From Nettlesford, there was only one bus an hour which would take her to Chester, and the nearest train station was five miles away.

The supermarket wasn't as busy as she'd expected, and as she wandered down the aisles filling her basket, she conjured up an image of Ben in his new grey suit, adjusting his tie in front of their bedroom mirror and anxiously asking if he looked the part. 'My hair really does need a cut,' he'd grumbled, patting down the sticky-out curls above his ears. 'Dad will probably say I look like a vagrant and won't let me near clients till I have it all chopped off.'

'You're rejoining a firm of solicitors,' Daisy had reminded him, smiling indulgently in spite of her downcast mood, 'not the Royal Marines.'

What was it about Ben that had made her trust him from so early on? The question niggled at her as she stood in the bakery section debating between pitta bread and bagels. It was the same question that had haunted her when she'd initially found herself opening up to him; exposing herself to hurt and betrayal for a second time in her life. She had made herself vulnerable because she'd felt so secure, even while she'd put his devotion to the test, but she still couldn't work out why she'd felt so safe in the first place.

Finally, she chose the bagels. Smoked salmon was on special offer, which was lucky, and Daisy added cream cheese, plastic knives and lavender-coloured napkins to her basket before heading for the check-out.

Outside again in the exhilarating spring air – no one could ever reproduce that in a fabric conditioner, whatever they claimed – Daisy spotted a charity shop over the road, nestling beside a coffee shop. It was still too early to surprise Ben, but now she had two ideal ways to pass the time.

She went to the charity shop first, and eventually narrowed her selection to a couple of dog-eared paperbacks, a long, simple dress in the gypsy style she loved, a little cardigan the same shade of purple as the napkins, and a pair of brass and mother-of-pearl candlesticks, which would come in handy for the romantic candlelit dinner she planned to cook later in the week. Her purchases in total came to just under twelve pounds. Harvey Nicks could never compete! Then she went to the coffee shop next door and succumbed to a different sort of temptation – hot, frothy cappuccino and a huge, moist slab of carrot cake with not just one but two layers of butter icing.

From a strategic spot in one corner, she watched the other customers. A couple of young mums were chatting over caffe lattes and flapjacks while their toddlers slept in awkward positions in buggies. A vicar or priest – could you tell the difference by their dog collars? Daisy wasn't sure – dropped in to buy a cake for the 'Bishop's visit' that afternoon. Over a second cappuccino, Daisy immersed herself in one of the paperbacks she'd bought, until she got to the end of chapter one and decided it was time to head for Ben's office.

'Messrs Kavanagh & Co.' was written in gold and black lettering on the small window beside the main door. Daisy pressed a buzzer, heard the door latch click and found herself at the foot of a steep, narrow staircase carpeted in a heavy-duty brown twist. This led to a small, stuffy waiting room, with a corridor leading off to the left flanked by Georgian-style white doors. The only person visible was a receptionist seated in front of a window, the backdrop of light transforming her smooth blonde hair into a halo.

'Hello,' she smiled. 'Can I help you?'

'Yes.' Daisy smiled back. 'I've come to see Ben.'

'Mr Benjamin Kavanagh, certainly. Is he expecting you?'

'Er, no. But I'm his wife . . . It doesn't matter that he isn't expecting me, does it?'

Comprehension flitted across the girl's face. 'I see. Of course, Mrs Kavanagh, I'm sorry. Please take a seat and I'll let him know you're here.' She proceeded to press a couple of buttons on her phone and mumble into the mouthpiece. A moment later, Ben appeared, beaming.

'What are you doing here?' Abruptly, a shadow crossed his face. 'Is everything all right?'

Daisy threw herself into his arms. She'd missed him more than she had realised. His own embrace was warm and strong. Aftershave still clung to his neck. If it hadn't been for the receptionist trying not to stare, Daisy would have nibbled his ear. Instead she began to babble excitedly.

'I thought I'd surprise you – so here I am! I've been out shopping, after I did the washing-up, of course, like a proper housewife. I bought a few bits and bobs, and went into that coffee shop, you know, opposite the Co-op. And look' – she pointed to her basket – 'I brought a picnic for us.'

'A picnic?' He seemed bemused. 'For now?'

'To eat in the office, or if you know somewhere else we can go . . . You haven't had lunch yet, have you?'

'No, but—'

'Were you waiting for me, Ben?' It was Howard Kavanagh, approaching from the far end of the corridor, pulling on his jacket. 'Oh.' He noticed Daisy. 'What are you doing here?'

'Dad said he'd shout me lunch,' Ben explained to her sheepishly.

'We'll mainly be talking business,' Howard went on, 'it really wouldn't interest you.'

'I wish you'd phoned,' Ben murmured. 'It would have saved you a trip.'

'How could I surprise you if I warned you first?' Daisy's spirits were no longer bubbling but sinking rapidly. 'Besides, you forgot to leave me your mobile, so I didn't have a phone.'

'We could have the picnic tomorrow,' he suggested hopefully.

The bagels would probably be rock hard by then, and the smoked salmon's 'best before' date was today. Daisy felt too choked up to reply. She didn't want to look like a wimp in front of her father-in-law. Looking stupid was bad enough.

'Here.' Ben handed her his mobile. 'We'll have to see about getting you your own one, I suppose.'

Some cheap and chunky pay-as-you-go model, no doubt. She knew they had to be careful with money. Ben was still repaying his car loan and an ever-increasing Visa bill.

'I'll be home around half five, maybe earlier.' He winked and kissed her briefly on the lips. 'Have a nice afternoon.' And leaving her with a faint whiff of his aftershave, he followed his father, who was already thudding heavily down the stairs.

Daisy stood in the middle of the waiting room, trying not to meet the receptionist's eye. She picked up the shopping basket as nonchalantly as possible, but compared to before it seemed to weigh a ton. Along the corridor, a door opened and closed and Daisy sensed the receptionist spring to attention.

'Hello, Mr Wallace,' she simpered. 'Are you joining the two Mr Kavanaghs for lunch?'

'No alas, Michelle, the invitation didn't extend to the "& Co." part of the firm. But that's nepotism for you.'

Daisy froze. The male voice was as familiar for its slight accent as it was for its sardonic, who-gives-a-damn tone. It couldn't be, it couldn't . . . And yet it could. It was like the missing piece of a jigsaw.

Oh, God, please make her invisible.

'Daisy . . . ?'

She lifted her head and turned slowly in his direction.

'It *is* you,' said Jerome Wallace. 'Mrs Kavanagh, in the flesh.'

It was the way he said 'in the flesh' that made her shiver. She forced out a stiff smile of recognition, but she didn't know what to say. 'Oh, it's you, too,' seemed so weak.

'What brings you here?' he asked cheerily.

'I should have thought you could have worked that out

for yourself,' she said at last. 'Why didn't you tell me who you really were?'

'I did. I told you I was Jerome Wallace.'

'You know what I mean!'

'Oh, the fact that I work for your father-in-law?'

There was another pause. 'You look . . . different.' The words left her mouth before she could stop them. His hair was as neat as it had been at their first meeting, but the rest of him seemed to have caught up, too. His suit, shirt and tie were faultless. He was even wearing a matching waistcoat.

'Well,' his manner was arch, 'I find these trousers don't really go with my denim jacket, so I only tend to wear them for work.'

'I see.' As the shock of seeing him again – here of all places – wore off, Daisy became aware of the receptionist staring. When the girl realised she'd been rumbled, she pushed back her chair and stood up.

'Think I'll make myself a coffee,' she muttered. 'Would anyone else like one?' When Daisy and Jerome shook their heads, she excused herself and headed down the corridor.

'Can I help you carry your shopping somewhere?' Jerome asked, pointing to the basket. 'Is your car parked nearby?'

'I don't drive.'

'You walked all the way from Greenacres?'

'It's not that far. Besides, Ben and I are living at the Gatehouse, which is nearer.'

Jerome nodded. 'Are those bagels real, by the way?'

'What?' Daisy looked down and saw the packet of bagels poking out from the Co-op bag in her basket. 'Of course they're real.'

'Then we could eat them, I suppose. That would help lighten your load. I was just going to the coffee shop to buy a sandwich, but I much prefer bagels. I went to New York once, and I used to have them for breakfast. Do you have cream cheese in there, too?'

Daisy found herself slapping his hand as he prodded about in the bag. The familiarity of the gesture took her aback; it was the kind of thing she might do to Ben. Jerome chuckled.

'Plastic knives, I see. Were you planning a picnic, or do you just hate washing-up? I'd bet good money on the first.'

'What planet are you from?' she huffed. 'You nose around in other people's shopping. You put down names other than your own to sing karaoke, when I bet you wouldn't have the nerve to sing yourself. And why did you pick "My Heart Will Go On"? Of all the songs—'

'It was at the top of the ballad list. Don't blame me. If the landlord had had them in alphabetical order you would have been singing "Abide With Me".'

'That's a hymn,' she pointed out scathingly.

Jerome shrugged. 'Whatever. Now, seeing as your husband is off having lunch with your father-in-law, whom I'm sure you're very fond of already, why don't I help you with his share of the bagels? I assume you were intending them for him, and it would be a shame to waste them, especially when I know an ideal spot in the park—'

'There's a park?'

'A couple of minutes away, by the war memorial. Perfect for a picnic, especially on a day like today. Your husband won't see us, if that's what's worrying you. The Headless Horseman's in the other direction.'

In spite of feeling to the contrary, bravado urged her to respond, 'I'm not worried about anyone seeing us!'

'Well then, there's nothing to stop us, is there?' And he took the basket out of her hand and steered her towards the stairs.

The ideal spot turned out to be a bench scattered with bird droppings in the shade of a large gnarled tree. They managed to find a couple of clean patches to sit on. Apart from some more mums with toddlers, who were playing on the swings and roundabout, the park wasn't what Daisy had expected, not compared to the sprawling London ones. It seemed more of a modest village green, except that there wasn't a duck pond.

'The coffee shop will be packed now,' remarked Jerome. 'No one seems to appreciate the great outdoors any more.' Rummaging in the basket, he pulled out the smoked salmon, cream cheese and bagels, and set about assembling the ingredients as if he was an old hand at it.

'There.' He offered it to her when he'd finished. 'Not quite Manhattan deli, but it'll have to do. Go on,' he urged, 'take it.'

Reluctantly, she did. To be truthful, she wasn't hungry. The carrot cake was still too recent a memory, and sitting here with a man who made her feel that it might be preferable to be single, while all the time making her conscious that she wasn't, was enough to put her off any delicacy, even smoked salmon.

'Pluto, by the way,' he said abruptly, as he tucked into his own bagel.

'Sorry?'

'The planet I'm from. You asked me before.'

'Right.' Daisy wiped cream cheese from her wrist. If the

man was mad, then was she afraid of him only because his gaze made her feel as if she'd forgotten to put on her underwear that morning? 'So you're an alien then?'

'Only between the hours of midnight and six a.m. As you can see, I'm quite human during the day.'

In spite of the alarm bells going off inside her, Daisy giggled, scattering crumbs and hastily wiping her mouth with one of the lavender napkins.

'Now I can die happy,' he declared triumphantly. 'I've finally raised a laugh. You've been a difficult project, Daisy Kavanagh. Although not quite as hard as your husband's going to be. I'm sorry to say that he doesn't seem to like me.'

Daisy frowned. 'Why shouldn't he?'

With the unreachable look in his eyes that she recognised from their first meeting, Jerome sighed. 'He probably feels that I've taken his place in the family firm. And to an extent, I have. But then he buggered off and left his dad in the lurch, so who's actually to blame?'

Out of loyalty to her husband, even if she knew he was guilty as charged, Daisy didn't answer.

'The thing is, in a way I'm glad he's back,' Jerome admitted. 'The workload's crazy now that your father-in-law's semi-retired. We take on too much, but Howard Kavanagh can never say no, even if he won't be dealing with it directly. The pound signs light up in his eyes every time a potential client rings up. I've been saying for ages that we needed more manpower, but I didn't actually mean Ben. That spoils my plans, you see. I was being groomed to take over when Howard retired completely, but with the return of the prodigal son . . .'

Daisy's discomfort grew.

'You're probably wondering why I'm confiding in you, of all people?' said Jerome.

She watched as he assembled another bagel, slapping on the cream cheese and being over-generous with the salmon. He held it out to her, but she hadn't made it through her first yet.

She shook her head. 'No, thanks.'

'Oh, well. The things a man has to do . . .' And he dug his teeth in.

'So, why exactly *are* you telling me all this?' she asked. 'I'm hardly unbiased.'

He looked as if he was about to speak with a full mouth but then thought better of it. Daisy waited, if not patiently, then in no hurry to end the conversation. Jerome Wallace might be a Whopper short of a Burger King, but at least he was company. Oddly enough, in spite of any ulterior motives he might harbour, he felt more of a friend than anyone Daisy had met in the last fortnight.

'I'm not sure why I'm telling you,' said Jerome. 'Just that I don't want Ben to think of me as some sort of rival. I was only joking about the prodigal son part. The low-down,' he continued, 'is that your husband's speciality is conveyancing and mine's always been family law. Take divorce, for instance. A nasty business, but someone's got to do it. Ironic, really. Your husband will be helping out all those happy bright young things who are so much in love, buying their first "nest" together, eager to share a new life. Then a couple of years down the line, I'll be helping them carve it all up. *C'est la vie.*'

'That's a terrible attitude. It's so—'

'Cynical?'

'You're saying that love doesn't last. That all marriages are doomed.'

'Love can last – of course it can. I'm sorry if I implied otherwise. The thing is, it's dynamic, which is what people seem to forget. It changes as the relationship changes. Everyone expects too much from marriage nowadays, but that's partly the power of advertising for you. All those ideals. Couples want the buzz to last, that initial "high". They feel they deserve it. Society doesn't always learn from past mistakes. Usually we forget the most important ones, which is why the human race will never be perfect. Most of us still haven't realised that the first flush of romance fades, and that anything and everything that follows has to be worked at. Nowadays' – Jerome grunted derisively – 'we're so lazy and complacent, we want it all handed to us on a plate.'

During this tirade, Daisy had finally deduced that he was talking from his own personal experience. This put a different aspect on things. He seemed a man on a mission.

'You're divorced, aren't you?' she asked gently.

He didn't look at her. 'It's been two years now . . . I came to Nettlesford because I was trying to get away from it all. From *her*. But the truth is, we failed because we were lazy. We expected it to stay as wonderful as it was on our wedding day. We wanted kids, that seemed part of the package, except that . . . Well, let's just say that nothing happened in that department. The years went by and the gloss faded and . . .'

'You had an affair?' prompted Daisy, trying to second-guess.

'No.' He shook his head, but he still didn't look at her. 'My wife did. And she instantly got pregnant and decided that was the end of "us" and a new beginning for her. So in the course of time there was another wedding, although

this time I wasn't there. And, as far as I know, she already
has a boy and a girl and a labrador.'

Daisy wet her lips. 'Is she still with the man she –
um . . .'

'The last I heard, they were separated, which was quick
work. But he's still supporting the kids – something I mercifully never had to do. Believe me, people in the wedding
trade are making a killing out of gullible sods like us.'

Daisy chewed on a nail. 'Ben and I had a very simple
wedding. More of an elopement, really. At least, that's the
way I like to see it.'

Jerome glanced at his watch, then turned to look at her.
The smile on his face was the same one that never quite
reached his eyes. 'I'm glad,' he said. 'Marriage isn't just
for a day. What's the point of starting wedded bliss in debt
because you wanted four tiers on the cake rather than just
two, or expecting someone else to fork out for it all, even
if he is your father?' Jerome looked at his watch again
and sighed heavily. 'Listen, I'm supposed to be meeting
a client in five minutes.'

'Oh . . . You'd better hurry then.' Daisy dusted down
her skirt, sending crumbs flying on to the asphalt path.
She was more conscious than ever of Jerome's physical
presence as he stood over her. His shadow on the grass
seemed to stretch for miles.

'Thanks for lunch.' The sudden sincerity and warmth
in his voice caused her stomach to flip over. 'I hope Ben
appreciates you. He's a lucky man.'

Unable to trust herself to speak without a quaver in her
voice, she inclined her head.

'I'll see you around, Mrs Kavanagh.' He made an
old-fashioned, cocky motion, as if tipping back an invisible
hat. Or was it more of a salute?

Daisy stared after him as he walked away. He had engaged her sympathies, there was no disputing that. And now that she knew the reason for the distant look in his eyes and the loneliness behind the smile – which sounded so like the lyrics of a love song it was untrue – she wondered if there was anything she could do about it that wouldn't be termed drastic.

Ben had female friends, so why couldn't she have a male one? Strictly platonic and above board. After all, she had just shared a public lunch with Jerome. That was hardly the kind of thing you did if you had something to hide. Yet, as she packed the leftovers of the lunch back into the basket, Daisy wondered how and when she would broach the subject with Ben. It ought to be easy – she'd made a friend, which was a good start, surely? – but somehow it was going to be the hardest conversation she'd had with him so far.

8

Ben frowned down at the contents of the remaining bucket outside the shop. The roses would have been perfect, if they weren't already looking a little tired. They were overpriced, too, considering they weren't going to last long once he took them home.

A teenage shop assistant shuffled out and scooped up the bucket. 'We're about to shut up for the day . . .' Indolently chewing gum, she left the sentence hanging in the air. When Ben dithered, she shrugged and turned to go back inside.

He followed her in. There was nothing else for it. It was going to have to be the extortionate roses. This was the only florist's in Nettlesford. Ben was walking home, and it didn't make sense to go back to the Gatehouse, pick up his car and drive to the retail park. He wanted to give Daisy the flowers as soon as he saw her, not make up some excuse about nipping to Tesco's.

Selecting the perkiest of the bouquets, Ben consoled himself with the knowledge that Daisy was worth every penny. Buying her flowers would ease his conscience at letting her down over the surprise picnic, but his main intention was to reassure her that she was the top priority in his life.

Ben set off home quickly, only pausing outside the Co-op when – sod's law – he spotted a flower stand

just inside the door. He'd forgotten about this place. It
had been a traditional village general store linked to the
adjacent off-licence when he'd left Nettlesford two and a
half years ago. But now the two shops had been knocked
through into one large one. Ben gave a cursory glance at
the flowers on offer, which were only tulips and carnations.
They might be cheap and cheerful, but they didn't cry out
romance. Satisfied that he'd made the right decision, he
continued on his way home.

Daisy opened the front door before he could even push
his key in the lock. This had to be a good sign – unless it
was because she couldn't wait to give him an earful. But her
smile looked genuine. There was a towel wrapped round
her head, which meant that she'd washed her hair again.
Gradually, the brown was emerging, and it didn't look dull
or boring to Ben.

'Flowers!' She lifted her eyebrows. 'Are they for me?'

'Who else?' He kissed her, holding the bouquet to one
side so that it wouldn't be crushed in their embrace.
'Something smells good.'

'My perfume? I just sprayed some on . . .'

'I meant, in the kitchen.'

'Oh, that.' She smiled again. 'Just a French-style casserole. Loads of garlic and red wine. My own recipe, so
keep your fingers crossed.'

Ben noticed the dinner table, elegantly laid with a
tablecloth, gleaming cutlery, sparkling wine glasses, and
a couple of tall white candles waiting to be lit. He couldn't
remember having seen the candleholders before. Maybe
Daisy had unearthed them from the cupboard under
the stairs. There seemed no end to the bric-à-brac his
aunt had stored away in there, and which nobody, until
now, had bothered to sort out. Daisy kept discovering

'hidden treasures'. Ben knew better than to refer to it all as junk.

'Are you spoiling me,' he grinned, 'or is it going to be like this every day?'

'I just thought it would be nice, considering we didn't have lunch together. I was planning to do this on Friday night, but . . .'

'I'm sorry about today.' Ben sighed and reached out to rub her shoulder, which felt tense. 'You don't know what my dad's like. He would have been impossible with me if I'd asked for a raincheck. I'd much rather have joined you for a picnic. In fact, before Dad cornered me this morning, I'd thought about coming home for lunch to surprise *you*.'

She was blushing and staring at the floor.

'So,' Ben went on, 'what did you do in the end?'

'About what?' she muttered, drifting towards the kitchen and the new modern cooker they'd managed to squeeze into a gap to the left of the range.

'About lunch. Did you eat the stuff you'd bought, or did you save it?'

Daisy was poking about in the casserole dish with a wooden spoon. 'I ate most of it,' she mumbled. 'The bagels would have been stale by tomorrow.'

'Oh, well . . . Never mind. Another time.' The smell of the food mingled with her perfume was curiously irresistible. Standing behind her, Ben wrapped his arms round her waist and buried his face in her neck, avoiding the straggling end of the towel balanced like a turban on her head. It was so good to come home to her like this, knowing that she'd gone to all this effort because she cared. He hadn't felt cared for in a long time . . .

'Roses were my mother's favourite, you know,' he stated flatly, although he hadn't meant to say it aloud.

'Were they?' Daisy sounded distracted. 'I like them, of course. They're really romantic, but my absolute favourite has to be—'

'Of course,' Ben smiled. 'Daisies.'

'No . . . tulips, actually. That's why I love this time of year.'

Ben groaned and shook his head.

'What's wrong?' frowned Daisy.

'Nothing. It's just . . . at times like this, I realise how little we really know about each other.'

'What do you mean?'

'Sometimes I feel as if I've known you all my life, then something like this happens, and I realise that it's actually only a tiny part of my life, and yours. Yet everything's changed, everything's so much better.'

A smile crept on to her face and they clumsily ended up in each other's arms again, indulging in a languorous kiss until they both came up for air.

'I hope nothing ever changes,' murmured Ben, as the towel slithered off her head. Running his fingers through her damp hair, he added, his voice soft and resonating with emotion, 'I hope everything stays as close to perfect as it is now.'

'But things do change,' she sighed. 'That's life. I suppose we just have to learn to adapt.' Gently, she extracted herself and retrieved the towel from the floor. Her smile looked oddly wistful. 'I'd better put the flowers in water,' she added. 'Before they die on me.'

'So, my dear,' began Vivienne, her voice dulcet and charming – although to Daisy it seemed to carry undertones of

Cruella De Vil – 'do tell us about your family, I'd love to know more . . .'

It was the moment Daisy had been dreading since she'd arrived in Nettlesford; the interrogation she was surprised no one had mounted during her first night at Greenacres. But then, perhaps Ben had warned his family not to mention it, and his presence at the dinner table that evening had been enough to deter them. Although he was in sight now, he wasn't within earshot. He was over by the hotel bar with his father.

Smiling nervously, Daisy settled into an armchair. It seemed to give way beneath her. She sank into it, her feet almost lifting from the plush carpet. It was only then that she noticed that Geri and Vivienne had perched demurely on the edge of the sofa opposite. They were obviously accustomed to the pitfalls of swanky country hotels. Wriggling forwards, Daisy braced herself to reply. She'd rehearsed the basic formula often enough, so why should she be worried? The trick was to keep it simple.

'I'm an only child, and my mother's dead,' she said, staring at the ornate glass coffee table in front of her. 'My dad travels a lot, and I haven't seen him in ages.'

'When did your mother pass away?' asked Vivienne, at the same time as Geri said, 'So what does your father do?'

Hating to be sidetracked, Daisy frowned and continued where she'd left off. 'I was brought up by my aunt in Norwich, until I left home at seventeen.'

'Oh, did you go to college or—'

'I just went to London, and I was lucky that I managed to find a job fairly easily.'

'So you really don't have much family at all?' said Vivienne, tilting her head and toying with a pearl earring.

Was that supposed to make her look more sympathetic, as if she were hosting a daytime chat show?

Daisy glanced in her husband's direction, willing him to hurry up. Ever since he'd told her that they had been invited here tonight, Daisy had been dreading it. 'Dad and Vivienne's wedding anniversary,' Ben had explained, sounding slightly nettled. 'I don't know about the last couple of years, obviously, but they've never seemed able to keep it to a romantic meal for two at an intimate little bistro. They always want to turn it into a "family occasion" at some posh restaurant or hotel. The only bonus point is that Robert's considered too young to go.'

Whether Ben's half-brother was going to be there or not, it had equalled three days of torture for Daisy. Three days of working out what she was going to wear and what she was going to say and how she was going to evade the very subject they were on now.

'No, I haven't got much family,' she stated dully. 'And I can't say we're particularly close. So don't expect a visit from them any time soon.'

'I didn't mean that,' said Vivienne, suddenly sounding less like Cruella De Vil, which paradoxically increased Daisy's distrust. 'But Ben's said so little . . .'

That 'little' was all anyone need know. What was the point in dredging up the past? Perhaps it would win Daisy the sympathy vote, but she had never used it to her advantage. The ordeal of remembering would easily outweigh any gain.

'I could have sworn Ben mentioned your father's line of work.' Geri looked as if she was racking her brains to remember. 'I'm sorry, I feel terrible for forgetting.'

Daisy flapped her hand in a dismissive gesture. 'He's

in the leisure industry, which is why he travels so much. But don't ask me exactly what he does. As I said, we're not close.'

'Was he always travelling about, even when you were little?' Geri seemed to empathise. 'My father was the same – still is – except that he imports wine. Constantly dropping into some exotic vineyard or other to sample the produce. He drags my mother round with him, though. As a kid, when I wasn't away at school, I was always being shunted on to relatives, however distant.'

'Geraldine Parr!' Howard had returned from the bar with Ben. His tone was surly and headmasterish. 'I won't have you talking about your parents like that.'

'Sorry. But I thought you disapproved of Dad, anyway.' Geri winked furtively at Daisy.

Howard waggled a finger at her. 'He doesn't know his arse from his elbow, but that's not the point.'

'Darling,' hissed his wife mildly.

'It's OK, Vivienne. I quite agree.' Geri leaned towards Howard and pinched his cheek. Daisy winced as she waited for the gruff reprimand. But it didn't come. It was only as the banter continued that she realised her father-in-law was enjoying the verbal sparring match. It struck her that Geraldine might be the closest he'd ever come to having a daughter. According to Ben, she'd spent a fair chunk of her childhood at Greenacres.

'So what have you ladies been nattering about?' Ben smiled and squeezed Daisy's knee as he sat down.

'We were just . . . chatting,' she said off-handedly, not wanting to bring up the subject of her past again. The present and the future were all she needed to concentrate on now that she had Ben. 'Geri was telling me about her parents.'

'Oh?' He grinned. 'She was always moaning about them to me, too. Used to drive me round the bend.'

'Oi, you!' Geri pretended to slap his thigh. 'I had a terrible childhood, as you well know.'

Daisy didn't consider gallivanting round Greenacres with a cohort like Ben a terrible childhood. Her stepmother-in-law seemed to agree.

'From what I understand, Geraldine, you were always well looked after,' Vivienne pointed out. 'And when your parents were home, they spent as much time as possible with you. I don't think you have too much cause for complaint.'

There was silence for a moment. The criticism seemed to have come as a surprise to everyone, not just Daisy.

Geri looked uncomfortable. Patting her hair, she mumbled, 'It was only a joke. I know my life could have been much worse. I won't argue that I've been lucky.'

Ben coughed, and stared at the floor.

Howard glanced at his watch and muttered diplomatically, 'Where the devil is he? Our table will be ready soon.'

Vivienne frowned. 'You know what Jerome's like. Time-keeping isn't his forte.'

The hairs on Daisy's neck rose instantly. 'Jerome?'

'Jerome Wallace,' said Ben. 'Did I forget to mention he was coming? You know he's a partner in the firm—'

'Well, seeing as Declan's still away,' Geri interrupted, 'Vivienne asked Jerome along as my . . . what do you call it these days? My escort?'

Vivienne tutted. 'That makes it sound seedy.'

'I thought it made him sound like a car.' But Ben's joke fell flat.

Daisy was frantically trying to work out what she was going to do.

'An odd number at dinner isn't the done thing,' Howard was murmuring.

'Boy, girl, boy, girl . . .' Ben pretended to lay an imaginary dinner table. Geri, who appeared to have recovered from Vivienne's remark, giggled.

Daisy felt herself break out in a cold sweat. *Why* had she been so stupid and short-sighted? *Why* hadn't she just come out and told Ben about meeting Jerome in the pub and having lunch with him in the park? To begin with, she'd half-expected Ben to bring up the subject anyway. Perhaps Jerome would have casually mentioned it to him, or that receptionist or secretary – Michelle, was it? – might have commented on it. But as the days had gone by, Daisy had felt more of a coward, and the more often Ben mentioned Jerome in passing when talking about work, the harder it had become to say anything.

But anything would have been better than the here and now. She knew Ben would be annoyed about being kept in the dark, but finding out among the present company would be even worse.

'Talk of the devil . . .' Geri nodded towards the entrance.

Daisy gripped her small beaded handbag. Her nails – still short, but at least all the same length now – dug in so hard they were probably turning white. Out of the corner of her eye she saw a flash of khaki bounding towards them.

'Bloody man,' she heard Howard murmuring. 'Never wears a tie out of the office. No wonder his wife left him.'

'Don't worry,' Geri whispered archly, 'there hasn't been an official dress code here since the 1930s.'

Daisy was compelled to look up, her pulse leaping into a gallop. Jerome Wallace might not be wearing a tie, but that only made him more attractive. The look wouldn't have suited Ben, yet it was perfect for Jerome. His suit, including another matching waistcoat, was tailored from olive-brown linen, and his white shirt was open at the neck just enough to look dashing and urbane but not tacky. He seemed to fit into the understated elegance of the hotel bar more comfortably than any other man in the room.

Ben, whose subtle grey tie was endearingly crooked, stood up to shake Jerome's hand. It was the first time Daisy had seen them together, and she couldn't help drawing comparisons. Ben was taller, but Jerome seemed more self-assured. His handshake looked firm and confident, whereas Ben's, although far from limp, wasn't quite as enthusiastic.

'I'd like to introduce you to Daisy.' Ben's voice filled with pride as he added, 'My wife.'

For the first time since his arrival, Jerome turned to look at her. 'I know,' he said, after a moment's hesitation. His gaze scoured her face. She looked away, desperate for the armchair to swallow her up like a television commercial she'd seen once. 'I've already had the pleasure of meeting her,' Jerome went on, his tone slightly droll. 'Although, if she hasn't bothered to mention it, then it's obvious the pleasure wasn't mutual.'

9

On the one hand, thought Ben, he would be relieved if the silence went on indefinitely. The moment someone spoke he would be forced to speak himself, and he didn't have a clue what he was going to say. On the other hand, the sooner the silence ended, the less embarrassing the situation would seem.

In reality, it was only a few seconds between Jerome speaking and Geri piping up, 'If I were Daisy, I wouldn't want to remember you either.' She stuck out her tongue at him. 'And I'm only going to flirt with you because Declan's not here. Don't take it as the start of something deep and meaningful.'

For the rest of his life – or that evening, at least – Ben would be indebted to his ex-girlfriend for defusing the melodrama. There was no valid reason to overreact. Daisy and Jerome had already met, but what of it? No doubt Jerome was right in implying that Daisy hadn't found him particularly memorable. It had probably slipped her mind to mention it.

Probably.

Ben tried to laugh, but it came out as a weak splutter, like a knackered car engine. 'So when . . . ?'

'In the Headless Horseman,' said Daisy, at the same time as Jerome said, 'At the office.'

Ben glanced from one to the other. Jerome looked

unperturbed and cocksure, much as he always did. Daisy, however – fidgeting with the shiny black beads round her neck – looked blotchy and clammy.

'So which was it?' pressed Ben. 'In the pub, or at the office?'

'Both,' said Jerome. 'The pub was the first time we met, but it was only for a few minutes. She was at the bar, and I didn't let on who I actually was.'

'But she let on who *she* was?'

Jerome sat back in a free armchair, and chuckled in a self-deprecating manner. 'I'd had one pint too many, and you know how these things go. A pretty girl pops up out of nowhere, and before you spot her wedding ring you make a complete idiot of yourself.'

This sounded plausible enough. Ben looked at Daisy. She was blushing, but then she normally did when someone paid her a compliment.

'So what happened next?' asked Howard. 'You met again at the office?' He turned to his wife to explain. 'Daisy dropped by earlier in the week, looking to have lunch with Benjamin. It was his first day, when I took him to the Headless Horseman. We already had plans, it wasn't my fault she was trying to surprise him.'

Vivienne smiled thinly, patting her husband's arm. 'Yes, I see. So you bumped into each other a second time.' She offered Daisy a supportive look. 'I'm sure you were a little surprised to see Jerome at Kavanagh & Co., of all places?'

'Er . . .'

Her black choker was in danger of snapping, thought Ben. Little plastic beads would scatter everywhere, and she would look even more agitated.

'Of course she was surprised,' Jerome interjected. 'And

caught off guard, especially when I spotted a half-decent lunch going to waste. You know what I'm like when it comes to food, Howard. And I never could resist smoked salmon, so I commandeered the picnic basket. Fortunately or unfortunately, whichever way you want to look at it, Daisy was attached.'

'You had lunch together?' Ben frowned.

'I don't think Daisy minded too much.' Jerome turned to her enquiringly.

Ben looked at her, too. Although she was still flushed, her eyes were glittering mutinously. 'No,' she said. 'No, I didn't mind. It was nice to have some company, considering I was disappointed that Ben couldn't join me. Anyway, Jerome knew who I was by then and had stopped trying to chat me up. We got on relatively well considering he's an arrogant know-it-all.'

Geri sniggered into her gin and tonic. Vivienne tittered politely.

'There,' said Jerome, grinning broadly. 'No harm done. We had lunch in the park, in full view of the general public.'

Ben knew he was making a spectacle of himself by continuing to exude suspicion. Yet the fact that Daisy could make jokes at Jerome's expense, without Jerome minding, meant that their acquaintance had already gone beyond a certain point. It made Ben feel insecure, as if a shadow was suddenly being cast over his marriage. OK, so he was probably blowing this out of proportion, but he couldn't seem to help it. This was unfamiliar territory. He'd never been the jealous type when he'd been dating Geri.

'Speaking of food,' said Vivienne, 'now that we're all present and correct, we should probably think about going in to dinner. The table was reserved from eight.'

'Quite right.' Howard heaved himself to his feet and took his wife's arm.

Geri rose, too, and grabbed Jerome's hand. 'Come on, Wallace. If you're chatting up anyone tonight, it'll have to be me. Leave the newlyweds to fawn over each other. They'll catch up in their own time.'

Ben felt far from newlywed. Disconcertingly, Daisy was making no move to stand up. Ben cleared his throat and said lightly, 'Just think of this as the part in *Titanic* where Leonardo DiCaprio escorts Kate Winslet into the first-class dining salon.'

Daisy gazed at him, frowning. 'Ben, I feel terrible . . .'

Just stand up, he willed her. Stand up, take my hand and carry on as if everything's fine.

If she just sat there, looking mortified, he would have no choice but to give in to his fears that she had something to feel mortified about.

Slowly, she rose to her feet, clutching her little handbag and tugging at the iridescent shawl draped loosely over her shoulders. The shoestring straps of her mauve dress were made of gold braid; they glittered in the soft, ambient hotel lighting as Ben threaded his fingers through hers.

'Listen,' he said, 'we can talk later.'

'But that's just it,' she muttered. 'I should have mentioned it before – the fact that I'd already met Jerome. It's straightforward enough, but somehow I've made it complicated. And now you're angry with me—'

'I'm not angry. Well, OK . . . maybe I am a bit. I feel like a prat for finding out this way, and I don't know why you just didn't tell me.'

Her voice rose plaintively. 'It wasn't intentional. I suppose – I sensed that you didn't like him. From what you were saying about him—'

'But that was after you'd already met him at the pub and had lunch with him in the park. Remember, you knew him before I did.' Ben couldn't help it, he couldn't stop himself sounding accusing and bitter.

Daisy looked stung. She stalked off after the others, without glancing round to check if he was following. Feeling lousy, Ben hurried to catch up with her, fumbling for her hand again and squeezing it with what he hoped she would interpret as the prelude to an apology.

The group was in the process of making a toast to Vivienne and Howard when Vivienne's mobile phone began to purr. The skin between her delicately arched eyebrows furrowed as she took the phone out of her bag, glancing at the screen before answering the call.

'It's home,' she mouthed at her husband. 'Yes, hello. Henries?' With a finger pressed against her free ear, she listened with fixed concentration. Her brow grew more creased by the second. 'It's Robert,' she sighed heavily, ending the call. 'He's had an accident. Nothing major, just a fall off the unicycle. He's banged his head, though, and he's got a nasty gash. Henries isn't sure if he'll need stitches.'

'Bloody contraption,' Howard cursed under his breath.

'A shame Dora was going out . . .' Vivienne looked pale and thoughtful as she rubbed her brow with a long, tapering finger. 'She knows a fair bit of first aid, for a cook. I'm sure she could have handled it.'

Daisy, deducing that Dora was Mrs White, stared down at the breast of duck in Grand Marnier and felt a mixture of disappointment and relief at the interruption. The meal was mouthwatering, but the atmosphere still felt charged, in spite of Geri's valiant efforts to entertain and divert. At any moment Daisy had expected her to appropriate the grand piano in the corner and try to lead them all in a singsong. Chas N Dave rather than Chopin.

'Howard,' said Vivienne, deftly folding up her napkin with one hand, 'I think we ought to go home. We might have to take Robert to A&E.'

'Nonsense,' he snapped.

Vivienne blanched further.

'Of course we ought to go home,' Howard added. 'But I'll get Doctor Keithley to come out and see him. I'm not having Robert shunted round some hospital department with a bunch of inebriates.'

'But Doctor Keithley retired last year.'

'John Keithley has been coming up to Greenacres for the last thirty-five years. He brought Benjamin into the world, and he would have brought Robert in too if you'd—'

'Yes, fine,' Vivienne intercepted the remark, which was probably going to be rather personal, guessed Daisy. 'But Doctor Keithley isn't working at Nettlesford Surgery any more. If you ring—'

'I'm not phoning the surgery. I'm phoning him at home.' Howard sighed impatiently. 'Now come along, Vivienne, don't dawdle.' He leaned towards Ben and said quietly, 'Don't worry about the bill. Just put it on your card at the end of the evening and we'll sort it out later.'

Ben had already folded up his napkin too. 'But aren't we all leaving?'

'There's no need for you to come.' Vivienne was rummaging distractedly through her bag. She took out her car keys. 'Jerome can give you a lift back, can't you, Jerome?'

He rose gallantly to his feet and nodded. 'But this is supposed to be *your* evening . . .'

'Yes, well.' She waved her hand. 'It can't be helped. Just promise you'll all stay and enjoy yourselves. Don't worry about us – or Robert. He'll be fine. Really.'

'I don't mind going back now,' Daisy heard herself say.

'Neither do I,' agreed Ben.

But Jerome seemed determined to see the meal through. 'What good would it do? You heard what Vivienne said. You'll only make her and Howard feel bad.'

'He's right,' Vivienne nodded. 'Please stay.'

When her in-laws had gone, Daisy frowned down at the duck again. So far, she'd done her best to avoid meeting Jerome's gaze. Concentrating on the food in front of her helped.

'Well, this is turning into an eventful evening,' remarked Geri, who was working her way through an exotic salad comprising virtually every colour of the rainbow. 'I hope Robert isn't scarred for life.'

'I hope he is.' Jerome had sat back down and was demolishing his fillet steak.

'Sorry?' scowled Ben, displaying brotherly support for the first time since Daisy had met him.

Jerome waved his fork about. 'You know what boys are like. He'd love it if he had a scar. It'd make him look hard at school.'

'I don't really think that looking hard is an issue.'

''Course it is! How old is he again? Nine? Ten? Peer pressure's going to start meaning everything to him, if it doesn't already.'

'St Stephen's isn't like that. It's not some gang-orientated, inner city comprehensive.'

'Oh, the illustrious St Stephen's, brainwashing inno-cent little boys from the age of about three. I forgot he went there. Vivienne engineered it, didn't she? From all accounts your father was quite happy, although he grumbled a bit about the fees. You'd have probably gone there yourself, wouldn't you, Ben? But from what I've heard your mother was anti-Establishment.'

'There's no need to bring my mother into this.'

'Into what?' asked Jerome ingenuously. 'You make it sound as if we're arguing.'

'Come on, you two.' Geri voiced Daisy's own thoughts. 'You might consider yourself rivals at work – which is silly considering you're both on the same team – but we don't want any bickering at the dinner table. No,' she cut in, as Jerome opened his mouth to protest, 'no backhanded comments, thank you. Daisy and I didn't get all dressed up just so we could sit here and listen to you two behaving like children yourselves. Now, we all hope Robert's fine, perhaps with a thin scar *à la* Harry Potter. We've done our duty and toasted Howard and Vivienne. May there be many more anniversaries, although hopefully less traumatic for them than this one. So, now that we've got all that out of the way, we can get on with the business at hand.'

Jerome twitched an eyebrow. 'Which is?'

'Ordering more champagne, naturally!' She rapped his knuckles, and added threateningly, 'But not for you, Wallace. You're driving.'

After dessert, the depleted group retreated to the hotel bar again. Daisy tottered out of the Ladies' for the third or fourth time, wishing she hadn't felt the need to join Geri (who had made it plain that she was missing Declan) in drowning a few sorrows. The champagne was swirling round her system like a mini tidal wave, churning up what she'd eaten to the point where she'd been convinced she was going to be sick. But she'd managed to keep it down, although she was having to pop to the loo every ten minutes or so to pee. A combination of stress and too much alcohol.

This time round, though, in the corridor leading back to the bar, someone collided with her outside the door to the Gents'. She glimpsed a blur of khaki and felt herself stumble to one side, her funny bone jabbing into the wall. 'Ouch!'

'Sorry,' said a concerned voice, 'are you all right?'

She glared up. Jerome was hovering over her; so close, she could see her distorted reflection in his eyes.

'Did you hurt your arm?' he went on.

She rubbed at it indignantly. 'You should look where you're going!'

'I was. I was looking out for you. It's not my fault you lost your balance.'

'If you hadn't crashed into me . . .'

'I'm the sober one, remember. And why are you scowling at me like that? I thought we were friends.'

'Friends don't cause trouble.'

'How am I causing trouble? It's not my fault your husband took an instant dislike to me when we met for the first time, and it's not my fault he thinks I'm out to shaft him job-wise. I was never hired to replace him as a son, so I don't know what he's worrying about. Howard will always put him first.'

Daisy suddenly felt dishevelled. A lock of hair seemed intent on brushing against her nose, when a moment ago she could have sworn it was all still neatly pinned up on her head. 'Shouldn't you be telling Ben this, rather than me?' She swept the hair aside and exhaled heavily.

'Over a beer, you mean?'

'Over anything,' Daisy shrugged, impatient to get back to her husband before he noticed she was taking longer than usual.

'You're very defensive about your marriage, aren't you?'

'Why shouldn't I be?' Daisy felt her spine stiffen and her chin stick out. 'It's the best thing in my life.'

'Right now, it seems to be the only thing in your life.'

She hesitated. 'What do you mean?'

'You haven't got kids, or a career.'

'I've got the Gatehouse . . . and my gardening.'

'Gardening?'

Pulling out a few weeds was the extent of her experience, but it was a start. 'I like being a housewife. One day I hope to have children, but I'm not in any hurry.'

'So you're not pregnant then?'

Daisy scratched her head, dislodging a hairpin. Another tendril of hair corkscrewed down, this time over her left ear. 'Pregnant? Where d'you get that idea from?'

Jerome was nodding pensively. 'I didn't think you were, considering the way you've been drinking like a fish this evening. But it's just a rumour going round. You know how these things spread.'

'But who started it? Who did you hear it from?'

'Stella Paighton. She's an old friend of Ben's.'

'Yes, I know. I've met her.'

'Of course you have. Well I saw her in the Headless Horseman the other night, and she was convinced you had to be expecting.'

'But . . . why?'

'She said it was the only logical reason why Ben would have got married as quickly as he did.'

'Oh . . .' Daisy's head seemed to spin. Her three-inch heels suddenly felt more like six.

Jerome reached out to steady her. 'I tried to assure Stella that it was all for love. After all, it was – wasn't it?'

Daisy frowned again.

How did you distinguish the supposed 'real thing' from the dozen emotions that had spurred her on to become Ben's wife? Where did love end and her need to belong to someone and something begin? Getting married had been an escape route. A ticket out of the life she'd been existing in. But she wouldn't have done it if she hadn't cared deeply about Ben. She could never have kept up such a pretence.

'Yes,' she said simply, because the issue was too complicated to expand upon, least of all here and now.

'Good. Next time someone tries to tell me otherwise, I'll put them straight.'

Daisy glanced pointedly at her watch, then realised she wasn't wearing it.

'Would you mind clarifying something else for me?' said Jerome. 'Why didn't you tell Ben that we'd met? It's as if you had something to hide.'

'Well, why didn't *you* tell him?' Daisy sniffed.

'I thought it was your prerogative, as his wife.'

'Why—' she stammered. 'Why are we turning this into something it isn't? I didn't tell him, but I should have. I'm sorry, it was awkward. As you said yourself, he sees you as some sort of rival at work.'

'Perhaps you could have a word with him about that. He'd probably listen to you. I'd rather be his friend, if it's possible, than rub him up the wrong way for no reason.'

Daisy thought about it. 'Maybe I will.'

'Then you could both come round to dinner one night

or something. I'm a dab hand at chilli. In fact, it's the only thing I'm a dab hand at.'

Daisy was about to reply that kidney beans gave her indigestion, when her husband's voice resonated down the corridor. She realised that Jerome was still holding her arm.

'Ben!' Her own voice seemed to have shot up an octave. 'Darling . . .'

'I was wondering where you'd both got to . . .'

'We just bumped into each other,' explained Jerome.

'You seem to keep doing that.'

Jerome raised his hands sarcastically, as if he was being held at gunpoint. 'Look, Ben, your wife's a lovely girl, but I've lived through one wrecked marriage, I'm not about to be party to another. And I'm not trying to drum up more business for myself, if that's what you're thinking. Now, I'm well aware that spirits are running high tonight, in more ways than one—'

'Are you implying that I've had too much to drink?'

'No,' said Jerome smoothly, 'your wife has.'

As if to ram this home, Daisy swayed precariously. Both Ben and Jerome reached out to steady her. She was reminded of a pole propping up a washing line in the middle. In some curious, obscure way, she felt as if she was supporting them rather than the other way round.

Jerome pulled a face. 'I think that we ought to put aside our imaginary differences, and concentrate on getting Daisy and Geri back to Nettlesford.'

'Fine. You go and sort out Geri then. I'll take care of my wife.'

After a moment's hesitation, Jerome acquiesced and strode off down the corridor.

Daisy slumped into Ben's arms. 'I'm shattered,' she

sighed, as he tucked a strand of hair behind her ear in a safe, familiar gesture. She smiled up at him dozily. 'I love you, Ben Kavanagh. I hope we have twelve anniversaries, like your dad and Vivienne. I hope we have *twelve* times twelve.'

His own smile was worryingly grim. 'Well, if scientists can put together a formula for longevity and somehow reverse the soaring divorce rate, you never know . . . with a bit of luck, we just might.'

IO

May burst on the scene like a military invasion. It was virtually a destructive force as it swept aside any April showers with day after day of unbroken sunshine. A few trees and shrubs, which until now had stubbornly resisted the arrival of spring, were forced to concede, and suddenly, overnight, they burgeoned with shoots and buds and vibrant, glossy leaves.

The garden was starting to resemble a rain forest. It was Geri who said this, quite good-naturedly, as she arrived to have coffee with Daisy one morning while Ben was at work. Daisy, who had never had a garden before, had reacted defensively, but even she had finally realised that before long she wouldn't even be able to sit outside on the lawn, it would be too overgrown. Pulling up weeds wasn't a good enough attempt at keeping things in check.

So Ben gave in to another area of domesticity and bought a small Flymo and some lethal secateurs, and in the long light of a particularly gorgeous Friday evening, mowed and pruned and tamed the garden into a semblance of order while Daisy cooked supper.

'There! I can't believe I've just done all that.' He sighed and collapsed into an armchair, only to have Daisy nag him out of it.

'Get up! You're all sweaty. You'll make the chair smell.'

So he slouched upstairs to take a bath, while Daisy added the finishing touches to the salad accompanying the lasagne and set about opening a bottle of wine.

The phone rang. She answered it distractedly, tucking it under her chin while she grappled with the corkscrew.

'Daisy? It's Jerome.'

The shattering of the wine bottle on the quarry tiles brought Ben charging down the stairs, wrapped in a towel but still dripping wet. 'What's wrong? Are you OK?'

Daisy stood over the shards of glass and felt the wine trickling coldly down her bare legs. 'I'm fine . . .'

'Don't move,' Ben commanded, his blonde hair so wet it looked almost black. 'You'll cut yourself. Let me deal with it.'

Daisy became aware of a muffled noise, like a distant voice calling her to attention. She put the phone back up to her ear and muttered, 'Hello?'

'What's going on?' demanded Jerome. 'Are you OK?'

'Er – I was just trying to do too many things at once.'

'I thought women were good at that.'

'Usually. I was being over-ambitious.' Her voice sounded tired and strained.

'Who is it?' mouthed Ben, lifting his eyebrows enquiringly.

Daisy flapped her hand, as if to say, 'Wait a sec.' Fobbing him off while she tried to find out why Jerome was calling. 'What do you want?' she asked.

'Have you had a word with Ben yet, on my behalf. I know it's only been a week . . .'

'No . . . No, I haven't.'

Jerome sighed. 'I didn't think so. Are things still bad between you?'

Daisy frowned. She wanted to state that things were

not the least bit bad. In fact, all it had taken was a wildly spontaneous bout of lovemaking the day after the anniversary meal, and the tension had dissipated, like a storm clearing the air. They hadn't mentioned Jerome again since then, and when Ben spoke about work, he would skirt around the issue.

Now, though, in spite of feeling miffed at Jerome's question, hearing his voice again – distinct and pleasant and slightly husky – made Daisy realise that ignoring him didn't mean the matter had gone away. In fact, speaking with him made her conscious that she was missing something. Like a child convinced of having lost out on a treat, she felt robbed. Pretending Jerome was a problem that didn't exist was an irrational way to go about it. All it was achieving was storing up trouble for later. She had to deal with it tonight, and so did Ben.

'Everything's fine,' Daisy replied, after a long pause. 'We've just been busy. Besides—'

'Argh!' Ben was clutching his hand.

'Shit,' frowned Daisy. 'Listen, I'll have to go. Ben's cut himself.'

'Oh dear,' said Jerome, with a hint of insincerity. 'You'd better do your Florence Nightingale bit then. But when he's sufficiently recovered, can you ask him to phone me back. That's why I was calling. I wasn't actually after you, in case that's what you thought.'

'Er . . .' Daisy was thrown. 'Fine, I'll tell him.' And she hung up.

Heedless of her own safety, she ran in her bare feet to the kitchen to fetch a clean cloth. By some miracle, she managed not to cut herself. Ben was perched on the arm of the sofa, bleeding over his bath towel. Daisy wrapped the cloth tightly round his hand.

'It looks awful.' To her untrained eye it seemed as if he'd already lost a pint of blood; there was so much of it on the floor and over the towel. She felt terrible for causing the accident in the first place. 'That might need stitches. Do you have that Doctor What's-His-Name's number?'

Ben grunted. 'He didn't come out to Greenacres for Robert, so why would he come out for me?'

'Oh . . . I forgot. You did tell me. Your Dad was livid.'

'Well no one likes being put in their place. And I don't much fancy four hours at A&E, either, so I'll chance my luck.'

'Maybe Mrs White can have a look at it?' Daisy suggested. 'Vivienne said she was good at first aid.'

Ben shrugged. 'I've got the glass out. It's just a case of stopping the bleeding. Do we have any plasters?'

Daisy regarded him dubiously. 'A plaster isn't going to stop that.'

'These things always look worse than they really are. I'm just sorry it was the Chardonnay you broke. We've only got the Merlot left, and I didn't really fancy red tonight.'

Typical of Ben, making jokes when he was obviously in discomfort. But he was right about the bleeding, though. One dab of Savlon and an Elastoplast later, and the cut was satisfactorily patched up. With trainers and rubber gloves on, Daisy cleared up the rest of the mess while Ben went off to get dressed. He came back downstairs five minutes later, looking agreeably rumpled in a checked shirt and faded blue jeans. Daisy felt a tugging sensation in the region of her heart, almost painful in its intensity. It propelled her to hurry out of the kitchen and fling her arms round him, squeezing him tight as he hugged her back.

'Hey,' he smiled, 'what was that for?'

'I don't know,' she murmured, burying her face in his shirt and drinking in the citrus scent of his bath gel. The compulsion had been almost out of her control. Hot on its heels, a flood of happiness rushed through her, as if she was the luckiest woman on the face of the earth. Her arms tightened round Ben, the root of all this abundance of emotion. 'You smell so good I could eat you,' she added, as if that was the only explanation she needed. Exhaling deeply, she peeled herself away. 'But before I forget, you'd better phone Jerome back. It sounded important.'

She was so blasé about it, throwing it in so casually, that Ben clearly didn't absorb the information first time round. 'Sorry?'

'On the phone. It was Jerome Wallace just now. He wanted you to call him back – about work, I suppose.'

'Oh. I'd assumed it was Geri,' said Ben, a frown crinkling his brow. 'She's the only one who seems to ring you. I just thought . . .'

'Look,' sighed Daisy, 'we can't avoid the subject indefinitely. It's ridiculous. You've got to work out why you don't like Jerome and do something about it. As if – as if you have to learn to face spiders when you're terrified of them. What's it called? Conditioning?' She scratched her head meditatively. 'No, that's not it.'

Ben was well and truly frowning now. 'You don't like my father or Vivienne, but I put up with it.'

Daisy waggled a finger at him, catching him out. 'But just because *you* don't like Jerome, you think I shouldn't like him either. That's not fair. I don't openly dislike your dad or your stepmum. I'm nice enough to them, and I don't bitch about them behind their backs. And that's another thing, everyone knows there's no love lost between you and Vivienne, so don't get on your high horse with me.

In your opinion, she's practically the wicked stepmother out of *Cinderella*.'

'Well, Robert's definitely an ugly brother. Oh, damn,' Ben groaned, 'I shouldn't have said that. He's just a kid. I wasn't much better at his age. Not that I'm saying I'm great to look at now, but . . .' He groaned again. 'What are you trying to get at, Daisy? That I ought to go out for a drink with Jerome after work or something? Act like his best buddy, just because he's a partner in the firm?'

'No.' Daisy took a deep breath. 'Not just because of that, but because . . . because he's my friend.'

She stood staring at Ben, hands on her hips in the most defiant stance she could strike, dimly thinking that her great-great-grandparents would be horrified to see her so flagrantly opposing her husband. It was hardly the ladylike or biblical thing to do. But wasn't there another passage in the Bible about husbands respecting their wives, or something along those lines? Daisy wasn't sure.

Ben was chewing his thumb. After a few moments he stopped and asked softly, 'Why are you acting as if you've known him all your life?'

Daisy let her hands drop from her hips. 'I appreciate that you've known Adam and Kieran and the rest of your mates for a really long time,' she said earnestly. 'But I've never had anything like that.'

'What about Ellie?'

'Who?'

'Ellie Fingus or Findus, your old friend from Norwich.'

'Oh.' Daisy swallowed hard. 'Well, apart from her. But that's different, she's miles away. You're back here living among the people you grew up with. You belong here.'

'So do you.'

'Only as your wife. I'm still trying to work out how I

fit in as a person in my own right. I know that sounds a bit New Age, like needing "space". But it's how I feel.'

Ben sat down on the arm of the sofa. Daisy didn't pester him to sit on the chair properly. 'Is there any way I can help?' he said.

'You can let me have my own friends, for one thing. You don't need to vet them first.'

'But what about *my* friends? You won't give them a chance.'

'OK.' Daisy admitted that this was true. 'They're so cliquey, though. I get on better with Geri. In a way, she's on the outside, too. She didn't go to your school, so she wasn't really an "official" group member, just a hanger-on like me.'

'I think you're blowing it out of proportion. We're not that bad.'

'Not in *your* eyes.' In exasperation Daisy let out a puff of air, blowing her long fringe off her face. Typically, she wondered if she ought to have it cut into a short, blunt line across her forehead again – a familiar pattern since her teenage years, as if she couldn't decide what she preferred. She quickly dismissed it, though, remembering how much she had hated it last time round. 'I just want to be able to have my own friends, without it mattering who they are,' she added.

'Fine.' Ben held up a hand. 'I'll make a deal with you.'

Daisy wrinkled her nose in suspicion. 'What kind of deal?'

'The kind that involves compromise, because I always thought that was an essential part of marriage; of any successful relationship, really. If you'll try to be civil to Stella and Adam and the others, I'll do the same with whoever you decide to be friends with.'

'Including Jerome?'

She noticed Ben hesitate, but this was his deal, not hers. 'I'll even try and be civil to him, even though I don't understand—'

'There's nothing to understand,' said Daisy huffily. 'Nothing that isn't straightforward, anyway. We met, we chatted, he's interesting, and he seems like a loner of sorts; but then I've always got on better with people like that because I know where they're coming from.'

Ben nodded and reached out, drawing her towards him. 'I'm sorry . . . Really. I wasn't the jealous type, not till I met you.'

Daisy hung her head briefly. 'And I should have told you sooner – about Jerome. But you made your feelings about him plain, it was an awkward situation.' She was vaguely aware that she'd said something along those lines before. Was it going to be her standard reply? And why shouldn't it be – if it was the truth?

With a sigh, she wriggled out of his embrace, and drifted towards the kitchen. The lasagne definitely smelled ready.

'The phone,' she said, as Ben looked as if he was about to offer a helping hand.

He stopped in his tracks. 'I can't hear anything.'

'You're supposed to be ringing Jerome back,' Daisy reminded him.

'If it's about work, it can probably wait until Monday.'

'If that was the case, then he probably would have waited until Monday to bring it up with you.'

'I hate female logic,' Ben grumbled. 'It's so . . .'

'Logical?' Daisy gave him a half-smile. 'Come on, get it over with while I dish up the grub.'

Ben hummed and hawed, but finally gave in. He dialled

1471, then 3, while Daisy looked on as if she didn't trust him to go through with it.

'You, young lady, concentrate on the lasagne,' Ben scolded. A second later he was muttering, 'Hello, Jerome? It's Ben.' He listened carefully for a few moments, then said, 'Can I think about it over the weekend and let you know next week? No, no, I won't put it off . . . I understand . . . If I can't do it, then you need to find someone else. Yes, I see . . . OK . . . Bye.' He hung up.

'He hasn't invited us to dinner, has he?' Daisy asked, although it didn't sound as if he had. She'd just felt the need to say something to fill the gap.

'What? Oh . . . No, but it's unexpected all the same.'

'How come?'

'He's captain of a five-a-side footy team. Quite relaxed and informal, but they're in a small league with some other villages, just local. I guess he's not as much of a loner as you thought.'

'Hmm,' shrugged Daisy. 'Maybe he just does it to keep fit.'

'Maybe. Anyway, they've just become a man down – an ankle injury or something – and Jerome wanted to know if I fancied playing.'

'Oh. Don't they have an understudy or a reserve, or whatever it's called?'

'Apparently he's working down south at the moment.'

'I see. So – do you want to play?'

'I wouldn't mind, and you did more or less say that you wanted me to socialise with Jerome, didn't you? This is the ideal opportunity.'

'Well then, you ought to play. You need to keep fit, too.'

'It's on Friday nights, though, after work. And they go for a drink afterwards.'

This time, Daisy hesitated with her encouragement. She looked forward to Friday nights with Ben. It was one of life's simple pleasures to snuggle up with him on the sofa, watching TV and knowing that she had two full days of his company before the working week started all over again.

Trying to look industrious rather than upset, she lifted off the plate covering the salad and carried the wooden bowl to the table, along with the matching serving spoons.

'If you want to play,' she said at last, 'then it's up to you. I'll find something to do.'

'You could always come and watch.'

She had a vision of herself in the village colours, whatever they were, waving a scarf above her head and cheering, 'Come on, you Nettles!' But in the vision, she was also the only supporter there, like a lonely, pathetic cheerleader without her pompoms.

'Er . . . I'd rather not. Thanks all the same, but you know football isn't my thing.'

'Well, maybe you could go out for a drink yourself, with Geri or whoever. We could meet up later somewhere.'

'Maybe. We'll see, all right? I'm a big girl, I can amuse myself.'

'If you're sure . . .'

Daisy gestured for him to sit down, and took a seat herself, smiling stoically as he poured the Merlot. If this was going to be her last Friday evening alone with him for a while, then she ought to make the most of what was left of it.

I I

The bicycle wobbled beneath her as she crossed the narrow verge to the gate. Daisy jumped off, managing to retain her balance before she ended up impaled on a fence post. She had never owned a bike until two days ago, and she couldn't remember having ridden one either, not even as a child. *Especially* not as a child. Her mum and aunt had thought them a waste of money. 'Daft girl, who needs one of those when you live six storeys up?'

'The same sort of people who need cars,' Daisy had always wanted to retort, but she hadn't had the balls back then. And no real friends whose bikes she could have borrowed.

After a painfully fraught driving lesson with Ben, Daisy – who had spotted the second-hand bicycle for sale on the Co-op's customer notice board – had rung up Mr Jones of Bryn-y-Baal, which was somewhere north-west of Nettlesford, and told him she wanted to view the bike. Apparently his daughter worked at the Co-op and had put up the advertisement for him following a garage clear out. Promising to pay cash if the bike was suitable, Daisy had managed to knock him down another fiver, and Geri had driven her round there first thing Monday morning. It had turned out to be a bright pillar-box red and looked quite old, but it was still a bargain. They'd just about managed to fit it into Geri's car with the back seats folded down.

'What kind of bike is it?' Geri had asked, as they'd driven home. 'I don't know all the different types, do you?'

'I don't care as long as it's the kind that gets me out and about without having to resort to any more driving lessons. Put it this way, it's got a basket for my shopping and it doesn't look as if I could win the Tour de France on it, which is just fine.'

'Well, the wheels are rather small. And there's a fitting for stabilisers. I only noticed as we put it in the boot.'

When Ben had come home from work, the first comment he had made was that it would stand out in traffic; the second had been that it was a child's bike. 'An older child's bike,' he had added hastily at the look on Daisy's face. 'An adult could ride it. Not a large adult, mind, but someone like you . . .'

'Well *I* like it, and that's all that matters,' Daisy had snapped. 'I'm not too high off the ground, which is perfect considering I'm a beginner. And I don't look that stupid on it . . . do I?'

'Of course not. You look incredibly sexy. Very *Darling Buds of May*, especially in that blouse. It's just . . .' He had frowned. 'I joked about traffic before, but it isn't what it used to be, and you've never ridden a bike before. I could give you a hand with the basics.'

'Thanks, but no thanks,' Daisy had been quick to reply. 'It's your teaching skills – or lack of them – that drove me to this anyway.'

Neither Daisy nor Ben had the right temperaments to be pupil and teacher; at least, not with each other. Daisy had slammed Ben's car door once too often, scrambling out in the middle of nowhere after a heated argument. The last time, Ben had actually driven off, leaving her standing stroppily beneath an oak tree on a deserted country lane, wondering how she was going to get home. Two minutes later, he'd driven back up again, unable to sustain his anger as long as Daisy could, which was just as well.

'If you want, you can have *proper* driving lessons. I'll pay for them. You don't need to do this.' Ben had frowned as she'd wobbled up and down the track outside the Gatehouse on the quaint little bike.

But Daisy wasn't in a hurry to get back behind a steering wheel. Handlebars, complete with rusty bell and basic gear switch, were just about manageable. 'A break from driving might do me good,' she'd said. 'Maybe I'll have another go in a month or two.'

So Ben had grudgingly given in, although the following night he'd come home with a bicycle helmet (also bright red), a security chain and a road safety leaflet which had a list of bike riding courses in the local area, if she was interested.

Now, feeling smug after her first trip to the village and back, Daisy pushed the bike up to the front door of the Gatehouse and chained it to one of the posts propping up the wooden porch. There had been a particularly large spider in the shed this morning when she'd taken the bike out, so when Ben got home she would ask him to lock it away for her, just in case the eight-legged squatter was still around. Hearing a sound behind her, she looked over her shoulder. To her surprise, she saw Robert Kavanagh. He was also on a bike, although this one looked brand new and expensive. He jumped off and leaned it against the fence, staring at her as she unlocked the door.

'Hi,' he said.

Daisy was immediately suspicious. Since the incident with Mrs White on Daisy's first morning at Greenacres, she'd hardly spoken to the boy. Not through choice, but because she seldom saw him. Not that she trusted him anyway. Ben's attitude towards his half-brother was so . . . unbrotherly, she realised now that some of it must have rubbed off on her.

Daisy didn't consider herself the naturally maternal type, but she assumed that was because she hadn't had much experience of children apart from when she'd been a child herself. At twenty-four, her biological clock was still ticking away at a safe, regular rate. She didn't coo over every dimpled baby or cute child she saw, but at the same time she wasn't put off by the seemingly incessant dribble and runny noses.

Something about her half-brother-in-law as he gazed over the picket fence intrigued her. It was almost as if he didn't know his way home. He wasn't a baby, and with his long, thin face and watery blue eyes he couldn't be considered cute, but something inside her reacted spontaneously to the lost look about him. She couldn't help thinking that she must have worn that look herself at times.

She turned and walked back down the path. 'Hello,' she said, affably enough to sound nice, but not patronising, 'is that a new bike?'

Sometimes small talk just consisted of stating the obvious.

The boy nodded. 'Dad got it for me. He reckons two wheels must be safer than one.'

'But you don't agree?'

Robert shrugged. 'It's OK.'

'How's your head, by the way? Have you had the stitches out? I suppose you must have by now.'

He lifted his fringe to show off a short, jagged scar, still quite angry and red. 'I'll live.'

On a genuine impulse, Daisy smiled. 'Good. I haven't seen you come this way before, though. How long have you had the bike?'

'About a week. And I'm only really allowed to ride it in the grounds at the moment.' He didn't appear to be in any hurry to get away.

Daisy hesitated. 'Would you like to come in for some tea or lemonade or something? I've just cycled back from the village. I could do with a drink, I'm parched.' It struck her that she hadn't exactly made her invitation sound very appealing to a boy of ten.

Robert hesitated, too, but then he clicked open the gate and wheeled his bicycle through. 'Can I leave this round the side? I haven't got a chain with me.'

Daisy decided to humour him. After all, it was obviously far more valuable than hers. 'Go on round, and I'll open the kitchen door for you.'

The boy disappeared round the side of the house. Daisy went in, wiped her shoes on the doormat and went across to unlock the door.

'Have you got a Coke?' asked Robert as he entered the Gatehouse, gazing round curiously. Daisy guessed he had never been here before.

'I think there's one left in the fridge.' She bobbed down to have a look. 'Yes, here you go. It's Ben who drinks it, not me, but I don't think he'll mind.'

Robert's finger hovered over the ring-pull. 'You sure?'

Pouring herself a lemonade, Daisy nodded. 'I wish I'd had a brother like him when I was your age.' She wasn't sure why she'd said this, except that suddenly she felt as if she was some sort of mediator.

She heard the hiss of gas escaping the Coke can, but the boy didn't reply. Daisy gazed outside at the wisteria bobbing heavily in the breeze, framing the kitchen window like a pale purple canopy. She hadn't known it was wisteria, of course, until Alan Titchmarsh had enlightened her on the subject of climbers. Daisy watched every gardening programme on TV. And every home improvement show, daytime or otherwise. And every cookery programme. Anything that would inspire her to become a better home-maker; or, at the very least, encourage her to enjoy her new role.

The wisteria made the Gatehouse feel cottagey, Daisy realised. As a young girl, six storeys up and surrounded by concrete, she had imagined herself living in a cottage in the middle of a rose garden, like something from a storybook. It had usually been by the sea, though. There had always been a glimpse of blue between the rose bushes, and the sound of gulls echoing overhead. But maybe that was because there had been so few trips to the seaside as a child, the details had implanted them-selves firmly in her head. The smells and the sounds and the candyfloss on the promenade. She could taste that candyfloss now – feathery sweet, dissolving on her tongue.

'Are you all right?' Robert's voice dragged Daisy back to reality.

With a wistful pang, she turned round and smiled. 'I'm fine,' she said. 'How's the Coke?'

'Er, OK. Do you have any biscuits?'

'We've got KitKats, will that do?'

Robert nodded eagerly as she reached for the chocolate tin, then seemed to realise that this might be deemed uncool, and drawled nonchalantly, 'S'pose so.'

'Do you want to sit in the garden?' Daisy asked, although perhaps slouching might be more appropriate.

Why couldn't kids stand up straight these days? 'It's another nice day.'

'This weather won't last,' said Robert. 'The radio said so this morning.'

'Great.' Daisy opened the door again. 'Better take advantage of it while we can then . . .' And she drifted outside, leaving the boy to follow her.

Ben put down the phone, a dart of satisfaction running through him at a job well done. He'd managed it, against the odds. The problem with the boundaries had been the worst part. It had made things a little hairy, although when the middle link in the chain had threatened to pull out . . . Ben shuddered at the recollection. But now, all was as well as it could be. Every party involved had just exchanged, and the date for completion had been set for the second Friday in June. The most pressing matter now was to phone the couple who had employed the firm's services almost nine weeks ago, before Ben had even returned to work there, and put their minds at rest. They were first-time buyers from Wrexham in their early twenties, their hearts set on an old cottage on the outskirts of Nettlesford. They were getting married in September and were keen to do up the cottage before they moved in. Well, thought Ben, casting a cursory glance at the calendar on his desk, they would have almost three months.

He was about to pick up the phone again when there was a loud knock on the door.

'Hard at it?' It was Jerome, grinning in his usual irritating manner. He didn't wait for Ben to answer. 'Couple of things,' he breezed on. 'Firstly, Michelle wanted me to let you know that it looks as if the searches have come back for number eight, Hawthorn Close, and secondly – do you fancy doing lunch?'

Ben frowned. 'Michelle wants to do lunch with me?'

'Actually, I think *I'm* the one she fancies.' Jerome chuckled. 'No, seriously, I thought you and I could go for a pint and a ploughman's.' He swaggered in, still grinning. He wasn't wearing his jacket, it was too warm for that, but he hadn't forsaken his waistcoat yet. Why did the man dress as if he were living fifty years ago? Did women find it appealing? Ben smoothed down the wrinkles in his own toffee-coloured shirt, and noticed he had a smudge of jam on his tie from his mid-morning doughnut. Damn.

Jerome was at the window now, peering out through the blinds. 'Another scorcher,' he said lazily. 'The weathermen got it wrong, yet again.'

'Mmm,' said Ben. 'Listen, I've got to make a call. And about lunch – Daisy packed some sandwiches.'

'You can still manage a pint, surely?' Jerome perched on the low windowsill, folding his arms over his chest. 'I want to go over some new tactics. Pennyfford thrashed us last week, I don't want it happening again.'

Ben rolled his eyes. 'No, Ferguson, sir! We're not bloody Man United, you know. It's just meant to be a friendly five-a-side—'

'Ewloe were hardly friendly the week before, were they? They're out to win the league, you can see it in their eyes, they're hungry for it.'

'I know that 7–2 to them was a little galling for us, but why do you want to discuss tactics with me, anyway? I'm new to the team.'

'But you're a better player than any of the others. You don't hog the ball, and you know when to pass. We work together, too, which is convenient for lunchtime discussions like this. I only wish we were doing it down the pub. Besides, I have another motive for being sociable.'

'Oh?'

'I promised your wife I would be.' As he said this, Jerome straightened up and reached for the photograph of Daisy which stood in a pewter frame on Ben's desk. 'This is a nice picture. Heavy, too.'

Ben swallowed his defensiveness and said casually, 'Yes, it is. A good picture.'

It was a close-up of Daisy as she stood on the registry office steps: eyes shining, smile playful over the top of her simple bouquet. Her dark red dress and matching coat reflected the flush in her cheeks. It was Ben's favourite photograph, capturing Daisy at her gorgeous, radiant best. Not a good idea for Jerome Wallace to be pawing it.

'She tells me she's getting quite close to Geri,' Jerome remarked, as he finally replaced the picture on the cluttered desk.

'Why shouldn't she be?' asked Ben, stopping himself asking *when* exactly Daisy had told him this. Over another lunch in the park when Ben had had to work through? On the phone? Or at the Headless Horseman, while Ben had been hanging out with his own friends? 'Geri's popular in her own way, but she doesn't follow the herd.'

'You mean, she's not keen on cliques? Which is, I suppose, why she and Daisy are getting on so well. And I'm not keen on gangs, either, so that makes three of us. We could form our own clique without even realising it.' He sighed and added theatrically, 'The irony and the hypocrisy.'

'Yes,' frowned Ben, thinking that Jerome had a mad streak which only became apparent on rare occasions but was unsettling all the same. 'Daisy just gets on better with Geri than with Stella or Alice. There's nothing wrong with that. It's good for her to have a friend—'

'Who happens to be a girl?' Jerome interjected. 'Unlike me? Well, I suppose you've got a point there. You won't catch me going shopping with her or indulging in similar girly pursuits. That's strictly for another female – or a husband. Sorry, Ben, you lose out there I'm afraid.'

'I don't mind shopping!' said Ben, who hated it.

'That's fortunate. But the thing that gets me about Daisy and Geri is . . . well, don't you think it's a bit weird? After all, you were engaged to Geri once.'

'If they don't find it strange, why should I? Geri's been great about it. It wasn't a one-way thing when we split up, you know. Geri wasn't happy with the relationship, either. And if she still had any doubts about the break-up, now that she's with Declan she knows it was for the best.'

'Yes, but – you've slept with both of them, haven't you? Don't you ever worry that they'll start discussing your, er, sexual prowess or something like that?'

Ben ran a finger around the inside of his collar. Sod it, it was stuffy in here. He really would have to raise the question of air-conditioning with his father, or if that wasn't feasible then maybe they should look at ceiling fans. If all else failed, he thought flippantly, he would go and work in his car. It was better equipped than these Dickensian offices.

'I – um – don't think it's likely they'll be discussing anything like that over caffe lattes or cappuccinos,' Ben replied stiffly. 'Daisy isn't like that.'

'I'll take your word for it.'

Miraculously, for once, Jerome wasn't inferring that he knew Daisy better than Ben did. 'Actually, you might not be aware of this, but Geri's asked Daisy to be her matron-of-honour,' Ben went on, as if it were a breaking story on Sky News. 'Which just goes to show how highly she thinks of her, and how much she wants her to feel welcome here. She's already got a couple of bridesmaids lined up – old school-friends – but she wanted to include Daisy, too.'

Jerome raised his eyebrows. 'Really? How did Daisy react to that, considering her feelings about large, extravagant weddings?'

'Er . . .' Ben pursed his lips. He knew that it didn't matter to Daisy about the simple way they'd gone about getting hitched themselves. She'd told him she disliked big weddings, but why would something like that come up in conversation with Jerome? 'Daisy's fine about it,' he said. 'Each to their own. She's not going to pass judgement on Geri and Declan.'

'Of course not. But still, she couldn't have been over the moon about being asked.'

'I think she was honoured,' Ben said. 'She didn't complain, at any rate.'

'Does she complain? About anything, I mean? She doesn't seem the type.'

Ben didn't like the way the conversation was going, not that he'd been keen from the outset. Discussing his wife with Jerome was unnerving. It stirred all the negative emotions he'd been grappling to suppress. It made him feel vulnerable, exposed and somehow at the other man's mercy.

'I don't know what you're worried about,' said Jerome suddenly.

'Sorry?' Ben found himself doing the finger around the collar thing again.

'You've got her. She's yours. You succeeded where a dozen men or more must have failed. Doesn't that count?'

'Er . . .' Ben struggled for a reply, and then the basic, honest truth hit him. 'When you have something,' he said quietly, 'it's yours to lose. It makes you an easier target.'

Jerome regarded him thoughtfully. 'I see. Well, I might not have a pretty young wife to lose, but I've got my self-respect and a vague peace of mind, which I've only just got back after the divorce.' He folded his arms over his chest again. 'Look, Ben, I'm sorry if I wind you up the wrong way. I'm sorry you don't like me and your wife does. But I'm not out to get you back for anything, so you can save your paranoia for someone else, OK?' He headed grouchily for the door, muttering something about Guinness.

'Wait!' Ben heard himself call out. 'On second thoughts, I could do with a pint myself.' He sprang to his feet and was about to follow Jerome when he remembered something. 'I just have to make a quick call, tell this couple I've exchanged on their house. They're probably nervous wrecks by now. I won't be long. Make mine a lager, though.'

'I can amuse myself at the pub on my own, you know,' sulked Jerome. 'I'm used to it. Don't feel under any obligation to join me.'

'I don't. I want to. And, besides, if you're buying . . .'

12

In the rare instances in the past that Daisy had imagined herself married, her brother-in-law – in the even rarer instances she'd also imagined having one of those – hadn't been a kid like Robert. He had been a grown man, with a wife who held regular coffee mornings and did all her own baking; two cherubic, well-behaved children, usually a boy and a girl, and a gleaming MPV parked in the drive of a four-bed detached house in the suburbs. She didn't know why she'd imagined him like this; it was just one of those things.

He definitely hadn't ridden a unicycle or a skateboard. Robert had recently been given one of the latter by his father, the flawed argument this time being that, 'It's even safer, lad! It must be. You're nearer the ground.'

Neither had this imaginary brother-in-law harboured a penchant for KitKats and Coca-Cola. Daisy was finding that she had to stock up with those items more regularly now.

This was the fourth time in a fortnight that Robert Kavanagh had graced the Gatehouse with his presence after school. He was slouching in the garden, guzzling another Coke and watching Daisy as she gardened. She hoped he wasn't developing a crush on her. Ben had teased her about it, but she hadn't felt much like laughing.

'Why are you wearing wellies with that dress?' Robert asked abruptly.

Daisy rested on her haunches and glanced down at herself. The thin cotton dress was comfortable. It allowed the air to circulate. She hated feeling constricted by trousers in the summer, and she didn't think ordinary T-shirts suited her; they made her look like a teenager. Now she realised that this flimsy, flowery attire might not be the best choice of clothing if Robert *was* infatuated with her. 'Well, I prefer to wear it with sandals, but the ground's still damp from the storm we had last night, so wellies are more practical.'

Robert, who was wearing the latest in designer trainers, nodded. 'S'pose you're right.' He carried on watching her while she planted the rest of the pansies she'd bought with Ben at the weekend. 'What kind of music is this?' he asked eventually, screwing up his face as he listened to the song drifting out through the open kitchen door.

'Country and Western. It's a compilation disc.'

'So who's this singing?'

'Dolly Parton.'

'Oh, yeah. She's the one with the big—'

'Voice, yes,' said Daisy hastily.

'Does Ben listen to this crap?'

Daisy was about to rebuke him when she remembered that she'd heard someone say 'crap' on TV before the nine o'clock watershed, so maybe it was allowed these days. Then she also realised that it was an encouraging sign for the boy to refer to his half-brother in conversation like this. It implied that he was interested.

'I reckon Ben's tastes are more your cup of tea, even if they are eclectic. Red Hot Chilli Peppers, U2, Kylie—'

Robert's eyes lit up. 'Whoa, Kylie. Nice one!'

At least the brothers had something in common there, sighed Daisy to herself.

'You're strange, you know that?' said Robert, staring at her as she patted the soil round the last of the pansies. 'But a good strange.'

She clambered to her feet, dusting down her knees. 'That's the best compliment anyone's paid me in the last hour.'

The boy thought about this, then frowned. 'It's just . . . you're different. But I like you that way.'

'So I've passed muster then.'

'Huh?'

'Never mind. What about Ben . . . do you like him?'

The boy shrugged. 'I don't know him like I know you. He never paid much attention to me before he went away, and he doesn't much now.' He puffed out his chest a fraction. 'If I had a kid brother, I don't suppose I'd like him either. He'd sort of get in the way, wouldn't he?'

'What makes you think Ben doesn't like you?'

'Well . . . he hardly talks to me.'

'He must have been at university when you were born. That's a big age gap. Practically a generation apart. I know that Ben found it difficult when his mother died, and he wasn't happy about his father remarrying. Then you came along, and things changed even more. You've got the same dad, though, so that must count for something.'

'Are you an only child?'

Daisy hesitated. For some reason, as if the truth was becoming too large to fit neatly behind her curtain of white lies, Daisy felt an urge to blurt out the whole story to anyone who would listen.

'Yes,' she said at last, accepting that she had no real option but to stick to the version she'd told Ben. 'I'm an only child.'

'You took long enough to answer.'

'My mind was on something else, that's all.'

As she stored away her tools and gloves in the shed, an idea suddenly struck her, and she wheeled round to face the boy.

'Actually – what I was wondering was would you fancy a trip to the seaside?'

'What?'

'That sounds a bit old-fashioned, doesn't it? But you know what I mean. Aren't there supposed to be some nice beaches on the North Wales coast?'

'I guess so. But Mum and Dad never go. They like the South of France. I went on a school trip to Bangor once, though.'

'Well, if Ben and I can organise something, would you like to come along? It would be a Saturday or Sunday, of course.' She was aware of sounding gleeful, and toned down her enthusiasm. It seemed childish to be thrilled at the prospect of a day by the sea, yet nowadays even a trip into Chester, which was only a few miles away, was something to get excited about. 'It shouldn't be a long drive, should it?'

'I don't think so.' Robert looked pensive. 'I like arcades.'

Daisy preferred walking barefoot in the sand and paddling at the water's edge, but she could do that while Ben and Robert bonded over a pinball machine.

His face clouded over suddenly. 'I don't know if Mum and Dad will let me go, though.'

'Why shouldn't they? Ben and I are family.'

The boy blinked up at her. He appeared to like the

sound of that, as if he hadn't fully appreciated the fact before. 'OK . . . I'll ask them tonight.'

'And I'll speak to Ben.'

Suddenly, Daisy was no longer so convinced of the wisdom of her idea. Ben would resist it to begin with, but if she employed her feminine wiles, hopefully she could talk him round. In spite of what he thought, his half-brother was far from being a clone of their father. If Ben could only see that for himself, it might make all the difference.

'It'll be fun,' said Daisy enthusiastically. 'You'll see.'

'Talking of fun' – the boy pulled a face – 'I was nearly forgetting. I'm supposed to be asking you over for dinner on Friday.'

'Dinner? On Friday? We can't,' said Daisy, attempting to look crestfallen. 'Ben plays football—'

'Yes, I know. That's why Mum's asking *you* over. Dad's off playing golf in Scotland for the weekend, and Mum's on her own, too.'

'Oh . . .' Daisy frantically tried to think of an excuse to get out of it, but her mind was blank. For once, her imagination had failed her.

'I'll tell her it's fine then,' said Robert, glancing at the bulky sports watch strapped to his wrist like a gadget from a spy thriller. 'I'd better go. Mum worries if I'm late getting back. Dad says she's paranoid, but he's just as bad. The other day *Ransom* was on TV. They only watched a bit of it – Dad called it a load of old tosh – but afterwards I thought neither of them would let me out of their sight for a week.'

'Is that the one with Harrison Ford?' Daisy hovered by the garden gate, still desperately trying to think of a reason why she couldn't go to dinner at Greenacres on Friday night, apart from having nothing new to wear.

'Mel Gibson.' Robert grinned at her as if she was the child and he was the grown-up. 'Oh, and Mum said not to bother to dress up or anything. It's just going to be the three of us.'

'Right.' Daisy smiled back thinly. Maybe she could catch something in the meantime. A common cold would do. It needn't be anything serious.

'I'll see you Friday then,' said Robert. 'You can have a go on my PlayStation.'

'Sounds fun.' Daisy was useless at computer games.

'Mum said to come round about six.'

'Six? Good. Fine.' Damn.

Frowning, Daisy closed the gate after him.

'I can't help thinking there's more to it than Vivienne feeling lonely . . .'

'It's just a simple dinner,' sighed Geri, steering Daisy out of the changing room towards the larger room beyond, where subtly lit mirrors took up three of the four walls. 'So – what do you think?'

'I think it's suspicious. She's never gone out of her way to be nice to me before. I just don't—'

'*No.*' Geri rolled her eyes impatiently. 'I was talking about the dress.'

'Oh . . .' Daisy diverted her attention to the matter at hand. She'd been lost in thought as Geri and a sales assistant had helped her into the bridesmaid gown. This wasn't her idea of fun, having to strip down to her undies and then clamber into something that was gold and voluminous and . . . breathtaking, actually. Daisy blinked in surprise. She could see herself from a number of angles, and it wasn't what she'd been expecting.

'If we pile up your hair like this . . .' The sales assistant frowned a moment over her glasses, whipped out some pins from her suit pocket, then deftly coiled up Daisy's hair, sliding in the pins to secure it in place. 'We can tuck the tiara in the middle here . . . like so . . . and there you have it. Of course, we haven't got the small bouquet you'll be carrying, but you get the general idea.' She smiled at Daisy in a sharp, professional manner and then turned to Geri, waiting for the vital seal of approval from the bride.

'Wow . . .' Geri nodded vigorously. 'Daisy, you look stunning. Ben'll want to marry you all over again.'

The whole thing was like something conjured up by a fairy godmother, thought Daisy, who hadn't believed such a transformation could be possible. She would never have picked out this gown for herself in a million years. When she had first seen it, dangling on the hanger from discreet gold loops that were currently tucked away on the inside, it had struck her as a gilded meringue. Now that it was on, it was a completely different dress.

Even the diamanté tiara had taken on a new life. Daisy had thought it too flamboyant, but now that it was crowning her head, it seemed to make the natural dull brown of her hair look warm and interesting; she actually seemed to have highlights shooting through it. The colour of the gown even set off her skin tone to perfection, accentuating her light honey-gold tan.

Amazed and perplexed, she turned to Geri. 'I know I haven't seen your dress, but doesn't it have a hard time competing with this? I didn't think the bridesmaids were supposed to look as glamorous as the bride.'

'You're in for a shock then,' winked Geri. 'My other two bridesmaids haven't seen my dress either. It's shrouded in secrecy. But let me assure you that it's still every bit my wedding, and no one – not even you, Daisy Kavanagh – is going to outshine me on my big day.' She grinned impishly, happily, utterly content with her lot.

Daisy sighed, and gazed at herself in the mirrors again. Had she felt like that on her wedding day, or during the short run-up to it? It was less than three months ago, but it seemed longer. So much had happened since then. There was no doubt that she had *looked* radiant on her big day, there was a small photo album back at the Gatehouse to prove it, and a few favourites dotted about in frames, but why couldn't she recapture her feelings as she'd repeated her vows? Why did it already seem such a distant memory? She was sure it had nothing to do with the nature of her wedding. Even if she'd had fifty guests – or five hundred – it wouldn't have made it any more memorable; she was convinced of that. No, it was something to do with her current mood, a feeling of displacement. It was almost as if she was trying to fit into a mould that had never been meant for her.

'If there's a nip in the air,' the sales assistant was now saying, 'which I doubt there will be in August – but you can't be sure these days – there's a gold satin wrap which goes with the dress.'

Daisy nodded, still captivated by her reflection. She wished she could take the outfit home with her right now. 'What, er, happens to the dress after the wedding?'

'It's yours to keep,' smiled Geri. 'My way of saying thank you. You never know when you might want to wear it again.'

In spite of her mounting apprehension about dinner that evening, Daisy's heart did a little jig. This dress was effectively hers! After the wedding she would be able to put it on whenever she wanted, like a child dressing up as Cinderella. And hadn't Ben mentioned that Vivienne and Howard held an annual New Year's Eve Ball at Greenacres? The prospect didn't seem so daunting now, not with Ben looking like James Bond in a dinner jacket at her side, and especially not if she was wearing this dress.

'Of course, you'll need shoes,' the sales assistant reminded her, dragging her out of her reverie.

'I'd prefer to have the girls looking more or less the same height,' explained Geri, 'so it won't be too odd for the photos. One of the bridesmaids is wearing high heels, like me, and another will be in flat shoes.'

'So we're probably looking at something fairly low again in this case.' The assistant scrutinised Daisy. 'You're a size five, yes?'

The assistant waited for Daisy to nod before swanning off to the far end of the shop, expertly dodging fresh flower displays mounted on ornate, Grecian-style pillars. The whole atmosphere reminded Daisy of a florist's just before Valentine's Day. It was one of those intimidating boutiques she had avoided when she'd been scouring London for her own wedding outfit. Surely if you worked here, day in, day out, the perpetual state of romance would start to pall? After all, how many of the brides-to-be that had passed through those baroque doors were still with the same man they'd walked down the aisle with? The notion was too cynical and sobering for her own good. By the time the assistant returned with a pair of strappy cream sandals, Daisy's spirits were ebbing again.

'If these are suitable,' said the older woman, 'we can dye them gold to match the dress.'

They fitted perfectly, which might have conjured back a sense of Cinderella, if only they hadn't served to remind Daisy of a pair she had owned when she'd been seventeen.

'Are you OK?' frowned Geri. 'They're not too tight, are they?'

'No.' Daisy shook her head. The tiara wobbled slightly. 'They're fine.'

The sales assistant was now behind her, fiddling with the safety pins she'd used to secure the strapless bodice round Daisy's bust. 'We'll order a size twelve then,' she murmured. 'And considering that this is rather a last-minute arrangement . . .'

'I don't mind if it's going to cost more to have it made on the quick,' said Geri assertively. 'There's no need to worry about the financial side of things. Obviously, I want Daisy to have as much time as she needs for her fittings. There mustn't be a mad panic.'

'Of course not.' The assistant nodded, then smiled briskly at Daisy in the mirror. 'I'll help you take it off now, shall I?'

Daisy's rapture was all but extinguished. She should have known it would be too good to last. Even this particular dress wouldn't be hers. She would just have a replica. She slunk after the assistant into the changing room again, drawing the brocade curtain behind them. As the dress rustled to the floor, Daisy unravelled her bra straps, which she'd tucked under her armpits, and slid them back over her shoulders.

The sales assistant frowned in an authoritative manner over her silver-rimmed glasses. 'I think it would be a good idea to buy yourself a good-quality strapless bra, and bring it along to your first fitting. With a dress like this, it's essential that it sits correctly over your bust.'

Daisy was about to retort in schoolgirl fashion, 'Yes, ma'am.' But just in time thought better of it.

*   *   *

'My parents are paying for the bulk of the wedding, including the bridesmaids' outfits,' confided Geri, as they finally left the shop. 'It's an obvious guilt trip, you know, for neglecting me as a child.'

Daisy hesitated, then asked cautiously, 'But don't fathers-of-the-bride pay anyway? Isn't it traditional?'

'Not necessarily. Not nowadays. They don't hand out dowries either. Did your dad pay?'

'Er . . . no.' It would have been about as feasible as drawing blood from a stone.

'Well then.' Geri looked distractedly in every shop window they passed. 'Although, thinking about it, you and Ben had a small wedding, so there couldn't have been much to pay for.' There was no malice in her voice. She just genuinely lacked diplomacy sometimes. 'Your father wasn't even there, was he?'

'It was just Ben and me,' said Daisy. 'The way we wanted it.'

'And your witnesses were complete strangers, weren't they? You must have made their day. Ooooh, look at that bag!' Geri tugged Daisy into Browns of Chester.

'Do you honestly feel that your parents neglected you?' Daisy asked, a while later, as she fiddled absentmindedly with the price tag of a stylish tote bag.

'Honestly?' Geri was still examining the glossy black handbag she'd spotted in the window. 'No . . . They were just busy people. Still are. But they used to phone me every day when I wasn't off at school, and they weren't away *that* much. I could have been left with a nanny, but Mum felt I ought to have family around. Staying at Greenacres was my favourite. Growing up with Ben and having a playmate of my own age was brilliant.' Geri smiled at the recollection. 'He should have felt like a brother to me, but I was always a hopeless romantic. The thought of having a childhood sweetheart was far too tempting, although I know he didn't see me in a similar light until he was older. But men are slow to catch on, aren't they? I suppose Stella was too much of a distraction, but then blondes usually are.'

'Stella?' Daisy stopped fidgeting with the price tag.

'You know Ben went out with her . . . Oh.' Geri bit her lip. 'You didn't. We were only about fourteen or fifteen, but I was jealous as hell. She got to snog him before I did.'

'What, um, happened . . . ? Why did they break up?'

'*Because* they were fourteen or fifteen.' Geri looked anxiously at Daisy. 'Don't get all jealous about it now. It was so long ago. They were just kids, which is probably why Ben hasn't bothered to mention it.' Geri hesitated, studying Daisy. 'You're not jealous of *me*, are you?'

Daisy considered it, then shook her head. 'I was, when we first met. But I'm not any more.'

'Why not?'

'Because you've got Declan, and you're obviously head over heels in love with him. And because I like you.'

'So you're saying that you're jealous of Stella because she's single?'

Daisy shrugged. 'Maybe . . .'

'And because you don't like her?'

'Does that sound awful?'

Geri led the way to the counter, hunting for her credit card. 'Personally, I'd say you were just human. And if I let you into a secret, you've got to promise not to blab.' When Daisy nodded, Geri continued, 'I'm not keen on Stella either. She rubs me up the wrong way. Always has. But I'll tell you one thing, you don't have to worry about her when it comes to Ben. Kieran's after her; has been for ages, and I think she's finally realising he's not such a bad catch. Besides,' Geri broke into an assuaging grin, 'anyone can see Ben's crazy about you.'

As they left Browns, the first spots of rain began to fall. Like an omen, the clear blue sky was now blurring to a sombre grey. The raindrops were cold. They felt sharp on Daisy's bare arms, like needles bouncing off her skin.

'Bloody hell,' groaned Geri. 'Where did this come from?'

'I don't know. I didn't listen to the forecast this morning.' Not that she usually did, anyway. Daisy ducked her head, trying to shield herself with her hair, which had come tumbling down in a riotous mass when the sales assistant in the bridal boutique had brusquely reclaimed the hairpins. 'Maybe we ought to think about getting back to the car,' she added.

'There was somewhere else I wanted to take you.'

Oh hell. Not another shop. Daisy's feet were aching; each toe felt three times larger than nature had intended. 'Another time perhaps . . .'

'But this is important, and it's not far. Come on, let's make a dash for it. Follow me!'

Daisy sighed. In her unsuitable summery attire, including flamingo-pink, wedged mules, she trailed after the trouser-suited Geri in the direction of the canal.

13

They had only been walking for five minutes, but Daisy felt as if they'd covered miles. The instant Geri had announced she was going to buy an umbrella, the rain had eased. Daisy felt damp and uncomfortable now, though. Her hair was sticking to her neck and giving off that distinctive, unpleasant smell of wet hair. It wasn't the same as after a bath or shower. The scent of the shampoo had worn off.

'It's just up here,' said Geri, veering under a grey stone arch.

'What is?' moaned Daisy.

'You'll see.'

They were now in a picturesque cobbled courtyard. There was a café on the left, with a few small tables outside, sun umbrellas dripping on to wrought-iron chairs. Straight ahead was a restaurant, closed until evening. Geri headed right, where there was a small shop, the understated frontage consisting of a half-glazed door and bay window. There were five paintings on display behind the small square panes of glass. Attractive cityscapes of Chester. A couple were formal and traditional, while the other three were more relaxed and seemed to be by the same artist. Geri pushed the door and a bell tinkled. They went inside, where it was so warm and cosy, Daisy felt as if her damp clothes would start giving off steam.

A startlingly handsome man appeared through an inner door and rounded a small, possibly antique desk that evidently doubled as the counter. The stuff of romantic heroes – tall, dark, rugged, with strong eyebrows and a charismatic grin, his eyes seemed to melt with adoration at the sight of them. Or rather, Daisy was reminded, at the sight of Geri, who without hesitation flung herself into his arms. Daisy stared hastily at her feet. The suede of her mules had never looked this bedraggled. So much for flamingo-pink, more a case of splashed-about-in-dirty-puddles-pink now.

Eventually, the amorous couple seemed to remember that she was there and peeled themselves away from each other.

Declan Swannell stepped forwards, and almost pounced on Daisy's hand. His grip was firm. For the second time in a fortnight, she warmed to his smile, which rippled upwards into his eyes with an easy, enviable charm.

'Great to see you again,' he said, still grinning. 'Recovered from that dinner yet? Geri said you were troubled by the oysters. An allergic reaction?' His tongue was firmly in his cheek.

'I think it was the wine I was troubled by,' Daisy replied pertly. 'And it was the quantity rather than the quality.'

It had been the first time either she or Ben had met Geri's fiancé, over an elegant, yet intoxicating dinner on the Wirral, in a popular restaurant boasting scenic views of the River Dee.

'I thought your gallery was in Liverpool, though.' Slightly bewildered, Daisy gestured round her, while Declan and Geri chuckled in unison.

'It is,' he explained. 'This is new. A sideline. And it's a shop rather than a gallery.'

'Strictly speaking, it's not even yours,' added Geri.

'True, true. But for the moment, I feel as if I'm the only one doing any work round here.'

'Setting it up, you mean. Don't you realise I'm going to come in here first thing Monday morning and rearrange everything?'

Daisy looked from one to the other, then focused on Geri. 'Is this place yours?'

'Uh-huh.' She nodded exultantly. 'My wedding present from Declan. I'm fed up with being a lady of leisure and a financial drain on my parents, not to mention my future husband.'

Daisy was speechless. Declan Swannell, tall, dark, handsome, and now generous with it, truly *was* the stuff of romantic heroes. Mr Darcy, in chinos.

'I'm only going to be selling original pieces,' Geri was explaining. 'Mainly by local artists. It's an extension of the gallery, really. And off the beaten track for a good reason. Clients will come here because it's been recommended to them. They'll be serious about buying, not just dropping in for a quick browse.'

'Besides, I'll be advertising it at the gallery,' said Declan.

Daisy studied the painting closest to her. *Watercolour of the Dee.* Then she spotted the price tag, and realised that, much as she'd like to, she wouldn't be buying a picture in here herself to hang over the marital bed back at the Gatehouse. She would have to make do with the print she'd seen the other day with Ben in Tesco's.

Something was still nagging her, though. 'Why here – in Chester? Why not Liverpool? You aren't still going to be staying at Greenacres now and again once you're married?' She looked at Geri as if the idea was repugnant.

'No, of course not. Howard and Vivienne have been

great for putting up with me, but Declan and I want to find a house of our own. Nothing huge, but somewhere to put down roots. Maybe raise a couple of kids.'

Daisy waited for the mention of chickens, but instead Declan said, 'I'm still going to keep the flat. It's too much of a commodity, and I need a base near the gallery. But it would be great to know I had somewhere with a bit of land round me.'

'We might buy somewhere old and renovate,' added Geri. 'I'd prefer to do that than build from scratch. There are some lovely old farmhouses around.'

'And you're going to be looking near Chester?'

Declan nodded. 'Cheshire, Flintshire . . . somewhere round these parts.'

'I may have been born in London,' said Geri, 'but I've always felt more at home up here than anywhere else, and so has Declan. That's what it's all about, isn't it?'

Daisy tilted her head to one side. 'What's what all about?'

'Life,' said Geri. 'Love. Marriage. The whole shebang . . . *You* know.'

Daisy stared at her. Her friend against all the odds, Geri Parr, soon to be Geri Swannell – madly in love and obscenely content. And suddenly Daisy realised that she didn't know. She didn't know what Geri meant.

It was as if a bucket of cold water had been thrown in her face. Marriage was a state of mind, a state of being, but by itself, with everything else seeming so fragile around it, it couldn't provide what she lacked, what she craved. Not just someone to belong to, but somewhere. She had thought Ben could give her that. He had brought her to the place where he'd been born and bred, and she'd naively believed that this would be enough. Through marriage, everything that was his would become hers. But with each passing day, Daisy was finding herself more isolated. That feeling Geri spoke of . . . that sense of homecoming . . . it couldn't be forced. It had to happen as naturally as breathing.

'Where are my manners?' Declan was saying. 'I haven't offered you ladies a drink. Well, a coffee, to be precise. That's all I've got at the moment, apart from milk. But you look as if you could do with something hot and caffeinated anyway.'

'We got wet,' said Daisy dimly, patting her hair, which felt horribly matted.

Geri, whose own hair had re-fluffed itself into a chic bob without her having to lift a finger to it, seemed to be making a liar out of Daisy. Her suit already looked bone dry, and her make-up was obviously waterproof.

'Come into the back.' Declan ushered them through. 'I'll make a pot of coffee, so there's plenty to go round.'

'Not too much,' warned Geri, 'and not too strong. I don't want Daisy jumping about like a nervous mare. Vivienne will wonder what we've done to her.'

Daisy had been trying so hard to forget about dinner at Greenacres that evening, she had actually succeeded. As the apprehension coursed back into her veins, she collapsed into a chair, wilting fast.

'I can't face it,' she said, shaking her head and looking beseechingly at Geri. 'You're going to have to come with me.'

'Tonight?' Declan lifted an eyebrow at Geri. 'But we've got a table at Antonio's.'

'Yes, I know, darling.' Ruefully, Geri turned to Daisy. 'I'm sorry, I would have already offered otherwise. But Declan's had this table booked for ages.'

'Antonio's,' echoed Daisy, abandoning all hope of salvation. 'I haven't heard of it.'

'It's only been open a few months. It's tiny, you'd hardly notice it from the street, but it was in some good grub guide or something. Declan's been dying to try it out, especially as it's so hard to make a reservation. That usually only makes him more determined.' Geri squeezed Daisy's hand. 'Come on, don't look so glum. You'll be fine without me. I'm sure it's only a simple meal. Nothing fancy.'

'On the other hand,' piped up Declan, 'you look a little peaky. Couldn't you cancel?'

It was no good catching a cold *now*, thought Daisy despairingly. It was far too late. Vivienne would get suspicious.

'I've got to go,' she sighed. 'At least for Robert's sake. He's probably looking forward to it.' Daisy's head drooped as she took solace in her coffee. She only looked up again when Geri asked Declan where he'd put her dress.

'You said to hang it up, my sweet, so I did.'

'I asked Declan to bring me my favourite black dress – from the flat,' explained Geri. 'I thought I might wear it tonight. That's the problem with living in two places. Keeping track of what clothes you've got where is a real pain.'

Daisy glanced at a clock hanging over the sink. It was already ten past five. Where on earth had the time gone . . . ? That was easy, she realised. Where it usually went when she forgot to wear a watch.

She turned to Geri in confusion. 'So are you planning on taking the dress back to Greenacres and getting changed there?'

'Now that time's pressing on, it probably isn't worth it,' said Geri. 'I can change here. After all, it's – ooops. You've got to get home somehow, haven't you?' She frowned at the clock. 'I should have time to get to Greenacres and back—'

'No need.' Declan rose gallantly to his feet. 'I'll call Daisy a cab.'

Daisy didn't know if she had enough change in her purse for a bus, let alone a taxi. 'Oh, no. It's OK. I'll—'

'I insist,' said Declan. 'This is Geri's fault, so I'll put it right. Theoretically I should make her cough up herself, but I'm too big-hearted for my own good.'

'I'm sorry! I need my head examining,' Geri apologised profusely, looking abashed. 'I just didn't think it through. I'm so, so sorry, Daisy. I should have kept a closer eye on the time, and I ought to have mentioned about tonight sooner. You know what I'm like, though. Declan's set on getting me a personal assistant, but she'd end up running this place. I need to do something on my own to knock me into shape.'

'It's fine,' said Daisy. 'I've still got loads of time. And a cabby will know all the short cuts.'

As it turned out, there weren't that many short cuts to take, and rush hour traffic was heavy. The driver had used the new road, and Daisy found herself at the wrong end of the Greenacres estate. It was already gone six. There wasn't time to go to the Gatehouse and get freshened up and changed, even if she asked the taxi to wait for her.

Cursing under her breath, she climbed out of the cab into another downpour, even heavier than the one earlier. Crunching gravel underfoot and trying not to slip, Daisy dashed towards the entrance of the huge house, running up the stairs to the portico and yanking on the bell before she had a chance to back out.

It wasn't Henries who answered the door, but Vivienne.

'Hideous weather, isn't it?' She hustled Daisy inside. 'I tried calling you at the Gatehouse, to tell you I'd come and pick you up. I didn't want you cycling over here on a night like this.'

'Geri and I were in Chester,' gasped Daisy. 'We got caught in a shower, but then we went and met Declan, and when it turned out that Geri wasn't planning on driving back here, Declan called me a cab. Which was generous of him, I thought.' She remembered to take a breath.

'This isn't just a shower now,' said Vivienne, leading Daisy into the cavernous depths of the house. 'There's a storm coming. I suppose that's the price we have to pay for all the gorgeous weather we've been having. Come into the kitchen. I've just put the soup into the blender.'

'Oh . . . Where's Mrs White?'

'Visiting friends for the evening. Besides, I prefer to cook myself when Howard's away. He doesn't enjoy the majority of my culinary efforts, you see, so I don't often bother. Too bland for his taste. Says they remind him of school dinners.'

Daisy stared round the vast expanse of kitchen. With the illumination from the subtle strip lighting under the cupboards, it didn't look quite so cold and clinical. The work surface by the sink and round the hob was cluttered with dirty utensils and soiled pots and pans. Vivienne noticed her staring, and pulled a face.

'I'm a disaster area in the kitchen when it comes to clearing up. Thank God for dishwashers. Even when I cook something simple like scrambled eggs, I seem to use five spoons, two bowls and goodness knows what else. Would you like a cardigan or a jumper, Daisy?'

'Er . . .' The risk of getting food over one of Vivienne's expensive sweaters didn't bear thinking about. Daisy shook her head. 'I'm OK,' she murmured, even though she wasn't. 'Maybe I'll just pop to the loo – I mean, the cloakroom – and try to do something about my hair.'

'The toilet's two doors down on the left. If there's anything you need, just shout.'

Alone again, and faced with a huge mirror with a carved wood surround, Daisy tried not to feel too much of a drowned rat disguised as a panda. She patted her hair dry with a towel exotically labelled as Egyptian cotton, then took a wide-toothed comb out of her bag, and carefully – with a few winces thrown in – ran it through as much of her hair as possible. Next, using a wet tissue, she dabbed at the fuzzy grey streaks of mascara under her eyes. Ironically, that was the only make-up she was wearing today apart from some loose powder round her nose, which had a tendency to shine. That had all come off, too. Her nose was red, and looked as if she'd polished it. With a clean, dry tissue, she patted it gently until most of the shine was gone. There wasn't a great deal she could do about the redness.

When she returned to the kitchen, Vivienne smiled at her enquiringly. 'Better now?'

Daisy nodded. 'A lot, thanks.'

'Good. Now you can get some home-made chicken soup down you. That'll warm you from the inside out, as my grandmother used to say. This is her recipe, in fact.'

Daisy took a seat at the glass-topped table to the right of the door. It was only laid for two. She frowned. 'What about Robert? Isn't he eating with us?'

'He's staying over at a friend's from school. It was a last-minute invite, but I encouraged him to accept. It doesn't happen very often, but I try to egg him on when it does. I wish he had more friends of his own age from the village, but not going to the local school, he finds it hard mixing with them. He's too shy for his own good at times.'

'Why does he go to St Stephen's when it's such a distance away?' asked Daisy, somewhat daringly.

'It's not that far. I drive him there and back, and I never spend more than an hour a day in the car. He could board during the week if he wanted, but he prefers to be at home. Anyway, as you were coming over tonight, I reassured him I'd have company. But I think it was the fact that you were coming that was making him dither.'

Daisy felt her cheeks sting as a blush crept over them. 'I'm sorry,' she said sheepishly.

'What for?'

'Because . . . I think he might have a crush on me.'

Vivienne swept back a wisp of her light blonde hair, tucking it into the ponytail at the nape of her neck. A smile played round her mouth as she brought two generous bowls of soup over to the table.

'My son's only ten,' she reminded Daisy, as she settled opposite her. 'He likes to hang out with you because you're cool – which is his way of phrasing it, not mine.'

'Why would a ten-year-old boy find me cool?'

'Because girls his own age petrify him? Because he can't stand Barbie dolls, or whatever not-so-little girls play with these days?' Vivienne shrugged. 'Or because, through you, he's somehow closer to Ben.'

The soup was surprisingly good, but Daisy paused with the second spoonful halfway to her lips. 'Do you think Robert would like to be closer to Ben? Does he need a brother, considering the age gap?'

Vivienne avoided her gaze. 'Wouldn't any boy? Ben's

a fairly competent role model, apart from that running-away-to-find-himself episode. But I suppose most people need to do something reckless at least once in their life. As long as no one gets hurt . . .' She tailed off, smiling grimly. 'Of course, I'm not saying what he did didn't upset his father . . . just that . . . looking back now, I actually think it's done their relationship good.'

Daisy was finding herself wondering why she'd ever felt intimidated by Vivienne, or so apprehensive about this evening. Looking across the table, her stepmother-in-law didn't seem much older than herself, although Daisy knew she was thirty-seven. But that wasn't old either, was it? Did Vivienne grow younger the further away she was from Howard?

'I don't suppose marrying me could be considered good role-model behaviour,' said Daisy lightly.

'That was reckless of him, too, you're right. But only the way in which he went about it, not his choice of bride. I think he was quite sensible on that score.'

Daisy felt herself blush again. 'I thought . . .' But she couldn't finish what she'd been about to say; it would make her sound neurotic.

'I have to confess, though,' Vivienne continued, 'that the way I saw it initially, Ben was too immature to settle down. And you, Daisy – you were also too young to get married. I suppose I was angry with you both for coming to Greenacres the way you did, so . . . so *suddenly* and disruptively. I was worried about Howard and how he'd deal with it. When Ben first told us what he'd done, I was livid. It was as if he was trying to spite us. As if he couldn't just come home and apologise for leaving the way he did – not without having one final dig by marrying a virtual stranger.'

'It wasn't like that.' Daisy found herself on the defensive again, but her earlier cowardice was forgotten.

'I realise that now. But it seemed that way at the time. And you've got to admit, you hadn't been together long.'

'Sometimes you don't need to be. Sometimes you just *know*.'

'I understand. Really I do,' sighed Vivienne. 'But sometimes . . .' She hesitated. 'Sometimes even knowing isn't enough.'

Half an hour later, they were well into the second course. Daisy had managed to turn the conversation on to Vivienne, and was now being regaled with anecdotes of life as a struggling actress.

'That's how I met Howard, you see,' said Vivienne, concluding a particularly colourful tale. 'I was playing Ophelia at the Gateway in Chester. He was there on opening night, and he claims he fell for me instantly. After that, he'd see to it that I got a fresh bouquet of flowers after every performance.'

'Expensive,' pointed out Daisy, stabbing her fork in the remains of her fisherman's pie. She could scarcely believe it either; it didn't sound like her father-in-law. How could someone so crotchety and disagreeable be so wildly romantic?

'Expensive, yes. But it wore me down, and finally I agreed to have dinner with him. He sent a car to pick me up, and it brought me back here, like something from an old Hollywood movie. I took one look at Greenacres—'

'And you just knew,' said Daisy pithily, then instantly regretted it.

Vivienne's aquamarine eyes blazed, but within seconds the fire was out. 'You're right,' she sighed. 'I took one look

at Greenacres and Howard Kavanagh – a gruff, lonely, yet
fairly attractive widower – and in spite of the difference in
our ages I was suddenly playing a new leading role. I was
never going to make it big in London or Stratford. I knew
deep down that I wasn't good enough. So I took on another
part here, to my agent's chagrin.' Her voice was dry, with a
hint of bitterness. 'And I play it well, don't you think?'

Daisy wished that Vivienne wasn't coming clean like
this. She'd never asked her to, and somehow she preferred
the mystery that had shrouded her before. It had made
Daisy's own zealous attempt at privacy justifiable. Now
she felt as if she'd been led along a path that would
bring her out at the edge of a cliff. She would find
herself exposed and forced into jumping, simply because
Vivienne had jumped first.

'Do you think I'm terrible for what I did, Daisy?'

'Terrible . . . ?' Daisy struggled with the last mouthful
of fisherman's pie. It was delicious, but she pushed away
her plate with relief. 'No. I don't think that.'

'Tell me, when you first set eyes on Ben, what did
you see?'

Daisy blinked down at a smear on the glass table, which
could either be mashed potato or mornay sauce. 'He was
ordinary,' she said at last. 'In a good way. A down-to-earth,
ordinary guy.'

'And how did you meet exactly? I know you worked in
a – in a restaurant. But what were the first words he said
to you?'

Daisy thought back to the service station on the M1. It
was hardly a glamorous location like Greenacres. Off the
top of her head, she couldn't think of any films set in one,
unless you counted those American roadhouse movies.

'"I'd like a Whopper please,"' she said tonelessly. 'And

for our first date, after one of my shifts, we sat looking out over the car park, drinking coffee from paper cups.'

She didn't quite know what she expected Vivienne to do next, but nodding with empathy was not it.

'When I first met Howard, I saw an emotional safety net, with perks. I saw myself somewhere safe, with someone safe, for the rest of my life.'

Daisy chewed her lip, unable to reply because her stepmother-in-law had hit the nail too accurately on the head.

'So,' said Vivienne, 'I suppose we both wanted rescuing. In our own ways.'

'Did you make a pudding?' asked Daisy, anxious to change the subject.

Vivienne shook her head. 'I'm useless at desserts. But there's Häagen-Dazs in the freezer.'

Daisy nodded, and drummed her fingers on the table as Vivienne cleared away the dishes. She felt as if she'd swallowed a cactus, her throat was so prickly.

'Did he make you feel as if you couldn't breathe, though?' said Vivienne suddenly, turning to face her with curiosity in her eyes and a stylish, stainless steel, ice cream scoop in her right hand.

'Sorry?' muttered Daisy.

'Ben – when you first met him. Did he make you feel as if your stomach was dissolving and your blood was on fire?'

Oh help. The woman was mad. Daisy felt panic knotting her insides again.

'Don't worry,' smiled Vivienne. 'I'm a trained actress, remember? I used to get paid for it. In some ways, I still do. Please humour me if I sometimes get a little . . . dramatic.'

Daisy nodded and gulped, but didn't reply.

The rain against the window made an incessant rattling sound. There was a noise from the other direction, like a banging door. Daisy raised her eyebrows. 'That's not thunder, is it?'

Vivienne frowned. 'I don't think so . . . Oh! Hello.' She looked surprised but perfectly composed. 'You're just in time for ice cream.'

Daisy looked round. Her heart started thumping, as if she'd had a sudden rush of adrenalin.

'I'll skip the ice cream, if that's OK with you,' grinned Jerome. 'But I wouldn't say no to one of your lethal black coffees.'

14

Jerome's dark hair was so wet, he looked as if he'd been caught in an oil slick. 'You wouldn't believe how it's pelting down out there . . .'

Ben stepped out of his shadow, and leaned down to give Daisy a kiss. Water dripped off his hair on to her arm as he straightened up again. 'A coffee would be great.' He nodded at his stepmother.

'What – what are you doing here?' stammered Daisy. 'Did football finish early?'

'Had to,' said Jerome. 'The pitch was waterlogged.' He gestured to a chair. 'Do you mind, Vivienne, or do you want me to dry off first?'

Ben cringed, looking down at his football gear. 'Sorry, Vivienne, we've been dripping everywhere. We did remember to take off our boots, though. Hope you don't mind me using my key . . .'

Jerome snorted derisively. 'This git's had me traipsing round the house looking for you both. We went to the dining room first. The devil knows what rooms the other ones were.'

Vivienne shrugged. 'Ben's free to use his key whenever he likes. This is his house as much as it's mine. More so, in fact. But you should probably dry yourselves off a little, for the sake of your health as well as the furniture.'

While the men were gone, Daisy helped Vivienne

make the coffee. All of a sudden, she needed to keep occupied.

'Do you still want ice cream?' Vivienne asked. 'It's cookies and cream.'

'Er, just a couple of scoops, thanks.'

Daisy was just putting the sugar bowl out on the table when Jerome and Ben reappeared.

'I know we're still nowhere near respectable enough,' said Ben, addressing his stepmother, 'but we promise not to go near your best three-piece suite.'

'You didn't quite answer Daisy's question,' Vivienne reminded him. 'She asked you what you were doing here.'

'Oh,' said Ben. 'We're on a rescue mission.'

'My idea, actually,' said Jerome.

'Yes, well, when football finished early,' Ben continued, 'instead of going to the pub with everyone else, we thought we ought to come and pick up Daisy. We couldn't have her walking home in this weather.'

'I would have given her a lift,' said Vivienne.

'But this saves you a trip.'

She looked sceptical. 'It took two of you, did it? To perform this very daring rescue mission?'

'I would have been fine on my own,' mumbled Daisy, but it fell on deaf ears.

'I was the one with the car.' Jerome looked smug. 'Ben walked to work and came straight to Mynydd Isa with me for the footy afterwards. It wasn't too far out of my way to come and pick up Daisy and give her a lift home as well.'

'Very gallant.' Vivienne picked at a tiny loose thread on her blouse and deposited it in the bin.

'Where's Robert?' asked Ben, mercifully changing the subject.

'He's staying at a friend's,' said Daisy. As Ben's hand came to rest on her shoulder, she clasped it with her own and hung on tight. Suddenly, all she wanted was the sanctuary of their bedroom and the solace of his arms around her.

'We've had quite an interesting evening, haven't we?' Vivienne's voice lost its wry edge as she smiled down at Daisy.

If opening a can of worms could be called interesting. It had made Daisy squeamish, at any rate. She smiled back wanly, then gestured to the kitchen clock. 'Just look at the time . . .'

'It's not late.'

Daisy glared at Jerome, knowing that he'd pointed this out on purpose. He had a warped sense of humour and seemed to enjoy baiting her. But then he did it to everyone else, so why, as well as riling her, should it make her feel special?

'You haven't finished your ice cream,' Vivienne protested.

'I can't manage any more. You know what it's like trying to eat something sweet when you're already full. It starts to get sickly.'

Vivienne was having no trouble getting through her own two scoops. She shrugged. 'I suppose I'm defunct now for tonight, as far as your having company goes. I'm sure it's impossible to feel lonely with these two strapping lads around.'

Lonely, no, thought Daisy, trying to avoid Jerome's eye. Hot and bothered, yes.

'I really could do with a bath,' said Ben, rallying to Daisy's support.

'And I need a shower.' Jerome drained his coffee and

put the mug down by the sink, alongside the other dirty crockery.

'Well then, it looks like I'm spending the rest of the evening on my own in front of the TV.' Vivienne glanced round the kitchen. 'On second thoughts, I should probably make a start on clearing up in here. Dora will have kittens if she comes in later and finds all this.'

Daisy offered to help, but her stepmother-in-law shook her head adamantly and shooed them out.

'I feel bad for not staying longer,' Daisy admitted to Ben a few moments later, as he grappled to open his umbrella. 'She goes to the trouble of cooking and trying to be nice, and then I rush off at the first opportunity without even helping her clear up.'

'You did offer,' said Jerome, then made a run for his car, ducking his head as he braved the elements.

'Sod the umbrella,' scowled Ben. 'It was bloody useless anyway. Come on.' He grabbed Daisy's hand and together they negotiated the slippery steps and made their way hastily to the revving Volkswagen Passat.

A few minutes later, Jerome pulled up in front of the Gatehouse. Ben thanked him briskly and climbed out, clutching his suit, which had been hanging inside the car, and his large Nike sports bag. Daisy waited for him to hurry up the path and open the front door, then turned to Jerome to say goodbye. He twitched his eyebrows in an exaggerated fashion.

'So,' he said, 'I'm not invited in for coffee then? Or whatever else is on offer . . . ?'

'If that's an attempt at charm, it's no wonder you're still single.'

'I wasn't always. There's a difference.'

Daisy bit her lip. 'I'm sorry. I forgot . . .'

'I wish I could.' He smoothed a hand over the steering wheel, so lightly, it was almost a caress. A shiver ran down Daisy's spine.

'You shouldn't be so hard on yourself.' She glanced nervously towards the front door as Ben appeared like a silhouette, waiting for her.

'And you shouldn't be so pretty.'

As Jerome was facing forwards, and rivulets of water were streaming down the windscreen and battering the roof, Daisy wondered if she'd misheard him. The problem was, she hoped she hadn't. The only male compliments she received these days came from her husband. It wasn't that she didn't appreciate Ben's sentiments, simply that by coming to expect them they had lost some of their thrill and potency.

'I'd better go. Ben's waiting.'

'Aren't we all?'

Daisy hesitated. What – if anything – did he mean by that? She jumped out, and was about to slam the door when Jerome called, 'Aren't you going to thank me?'

'For what?'

'For picking you up and bringing you home. I saved you from getting soaked.'

'No, you didn't. Vivienne would have brought me back. And I'm getting soaked right now thanks to you, so what's the point?' She closed the door huffily, the sound of his chuckling echoing in her ears as she scurried up the path into the house. 'I hate that man sometimes,' she snapped, locking and bolting the front door, as if she was physically trying to shut him out.

It was the rest of the time that worried Ben.

He pulled his football shirt over his head, rolled it into a ball and shoved it into the washing machine. 'We should probably put a load on now,' he said matter-of-factly. 'All the wet stuff at least, or it'll start stinking out the laundry basket.'

'Oh . . . OK. Leave it to me, I'll sort it out. You go and have a bath. Just throw down the rest of your stuff when you're ready.'

He headed for the stairs, feeling Daisy's gaze on him as he climbed them, two at a time.

'I saw Declan again today,' he heard her call out, as he ran the bath.

'Oh, yes?'

Ben stripped off and climbed in. The ache in his limbs seemed to instantly melt away in the heat of the water. He submerged his head, then surfaced again, rubbing his face and smoothing his hair back.

'So,' said Daisy, 'aren't you going to ask me *where* I saw Declan?'

Ben jumped, and opened his eyes to see his wife sitting on the wooden toilet-seat lid. She was leaning towards him with her legs crossed and her chin resting in her hands. He frowned. 'What are you doing in here?'

'You're not being coy, are you? It isn't anything I haven't seen before. I just thought you were in a funny mood, that's all. I thought we ought to talk about it. Besides, you didn't throw me down your shorts and socks.'

'I'm not in a funny mood, and there's nothing to talk about.'

'Right. My mistake. We can just discuss Geri and Declan then. Did you know that he's got her a shop in Chester?'

'Sorry?' Ben reached for his bath and hair gel and started working up a lather.

Daisy recounted the whole story, then said, 'Maybe I

should ask her if she needs a sales assistant; someone she can boss about . . . On second thoughts,' a shadow crossed her brow, 'it's probably a bad idea. It might test our friendship too far.'

Ben immersed himself in the water again, then came back up and grabbed a towel to dry his face. 'Are you saying that you'd like to get a job?'

'It's just . . . I feel like I need to do something other than just tinker around here.'

'Are you really that bored?'

She hauled herself to her feet. Sighing evasively, she peered into the mirrored cabinet over the basin. 'Oh, bugger, my hair's a real mess . . .'

Ben thought back over the last few weeks. The house had never been cleaner, the garden never tidier, their meals never more adventurous. Daisy had been behaving like a workaholic bee, but that didn't mean that she'd been thriving on it.

'I suppose I'd better put the washing machine on,' she was saying now, scooping up the remainder of his dirty laundry.

'Why – um – don't you relax and have a bath first?' he suggested. 'You look as if you need it.'

'I can't have one till you've finished, so I might as well sort out all this stuff.'

'There's room for two . . .' His heart pounded in anticipation as she hesitated in the doorway. 'Besides, you'll probably want to put what you're wearing in the wash, won't you? You got caught in the rain a couple of times, you said, and I think that's a smudge of ice cream on your top. But you can't put it in the washing machine unless you take it off first . . .'

She was already undoing her buttons. The blouse and

skirt dropped to the floor, joining the small bundle of laundry she'd already discarded. Ben stood up, alert with excitement. It had been days since they'd last made love. Sunday morning, in fact. Since then, they'd been too tired to bother, snuggling up in bed with a book each, or a newspaper, until it was time to say goodnight, switch off the light and go to sleep.

As Daisy's lips met his, he reached round her back and unhooked her bra, sliding it off her shoulders and tossing it over the towel rail. She removed her knickers and climbed into the bath. They sank down, Daisy ensconcing herself in the space between his legs. He massaged her feet, kissing each toe and taking mischievous delight in watching her squirm. Then, as the mood shifted from playful to tender, he picked up the bath gel and a sponge and gently, slowly, massaged her body, her breath cold and erotic against his wet skin.

'Here, let me do that,' he said, when she eventually climbed out and reached for her towel.

They stood drying each other, the most sensual foreplay Ben had indulged in. His excitement was at fever pitch by the time he took her into the bedroom and lay with her on the bed. As he entered her, she moaned. With each thrust, her breathing grew shallower. When he climaxed, crying out with pleasure and release, she cried out beneath him, her fingers digging into him as if it would be painful and terrible to let go.

A while later, her head against his chest, his own head on a pillow, Ben closed his eyes and stroked her damp, dishevelled hair. No one could pretend to make love like that, he realised with an all-pervading sense of relief. Daisy had to have meant every moment. She was his wife and nothing could change that, even though the world would try. She was the miracle that had entered his life when he'd least expected it, when he hadn't been looking, when he'd reached a dead-end in the path he had stumbled down and was facing the depressing prospect of retracing his steps.

'I love you,' he murmured, a lump in his throat. 'I love you so much I—'

She pressed a finger to his lips. 'I love you, too,' she whispered back, her voice soft, raw, trembling in the semi-darkness. 'Don't you ever imagine that I don't.'

15

Ben fell asleep almost immediately, but Daisy was too restless. The air felt charged, the rumbles of thunder were drawing closer and the wind was circling the house, rattling the windows like an obstinate ghost.

With a shudder, Daisy slipped into Ben's towelling robe, much cosier and fluffier than her tatty old thing, and went downstairs to make herself a mug of cocoa. While she was at it, she put on the washing machine with a full load.

Curling up in front of the television, she wondered how other housewives coped. It was a job in itself, as worthy as any other, but personally she wished she could do something else besides; something that would mean a change of scene and the camaraderie of customers or colleagues. Perhaps her inability to adjust was down to the fact that, since she'd dropped out of college at seventeen, she had nearly always drifted from one job to another, scrimping and saving and surviving, by herself. Yet how many of the girls she had worked alongside over the years would kill to be in her shoes now?

It was also a fact that she'd never lived anywhere as remote as the Gatehouse before, she realised, wondering if that was adding to her present woes. She had always had neighbours a few yards away, some friendlier than others, but still human contact. And Nettlesford was a village;

she'd never experienced one of those either, not for any length of time. They were a different ball-game from the anonymity of towns and cities. All things considered, what she had once regarded as a bid for freedom, a providential chance for a new start, had gradually turned into another cage in itself.

She squeezed her eyes shut, as if to block it all out, then opened them again and stared mistily at the news with the sound turned down so low she could barely hear it; although it was illogical to fret that the TV would wake her comatose husband when the weather hadn't.

Of course, there were instances when her life didn't seem devoid of meaning. When Ben was with her, when he held her, touched her, made love to her, simple bliss streamed back in, as if he'd opened a window to drive out the mustiness and gloom. But it didn't last. It couldn't. He wasn't around twenty-four hours a day. And even if he were, how could that level of happiness be sustained?

She jerked her head up. Beyond the whistling of the wind, the drumming of the rain and the low growls of thunder, there seemed to come the incongruous sound of tapping on the front door. Was she hearing things? But after a pause, it grew louder and more insistent.

It was unlikely to be a visitor at this time of night, and if it was someone she knew with a problem or an emergency, wouldn't they have phoned? Perhaps it was a motorist who had broken down on the Old Nettlesford Road and had been drawn to the lamp in the Gatehouse window.

Daisy peered through the letterbox, too wary to open the door and too conscientious to ignore it. She doubted even her screams would wake Ben if it turned out to be an axe murderer. The first thing she spotted was a belt and someone's flies and then a nose and eyes thrust themselves toward hers.

'Hello,' came the accompanying voice, as she sprang back in alarm. 'Daisy, it's OK, it's me. Let me in.'

Oh, damn. She fumbled with the bolts and the key, and drew back the door as a blast of cold wind and rain followed Jerome into the Gatehouse. He closed the door behind him and turned to face her. His hair was dripping wet again, his jeans and jumper as saturated as his football gear had been earlier.

'Don't know why I bothered having a bloody shower,' he grumbled.

It was then that she noticed he was carrying her cream and purple rucksack. 'Oh . . . Did I leave it in your car?'

'You hadn't realised it was missing? I'm amazed, considering you seem to carry most of your life around in here.'

Daisy had been too preoccupied to notice that she didn't have it, but she wasn't about to go into detail. Something struck her, sparking annoyance rather than gratitude. 'You looked inside?'

Jerome circled the lounge, staring round curiously. 'I just checked to make sure it was yours.'

'Who else's would it have been? I thought you hadn't been seeing any women lately, and this is obviously a woman's bag.' She pulled back the flap and peered inside.

'I may be nosy, Daisy, but I'm not a thief. Everything's still there.'

'So you came all the way back here to return it?' She frowned, acutely aware that she was naked beneath the towelling robe, and worried that it might be gaping indecently. It felt slithery and sluttish all of a sudden, almost hanging off one shoulder, the belt slackening in spite of her efforts to knot it tight. Minutes ago it had smelled comfortingly of Ben, now it just seemed to reek of sex. But this wasn't bothering her half as much as her body's wanton desire for an encore. It appeared to have a life quite detached from her mind and her emotions. Her loins, or whatever term she was supposed to use without being lewd, were throbbing and aching for more.

'You could have waited until tomorrow,' she said raspily, dumping the bag on the sofa.

'I could have, but I thought you might need it.'

Daisy's brow creased further as she glanced at the kitchen clock. 'Why did it take you so long? You must have got back to your house ages ago.'

'I, er, didn't go straight back. I went to the pub first. Just for a quick one. It wasn't till I got home and grabbed my stuff from the back seat that I noticed the bag. To be truthful, I was going to wait until tomorrow to bring it to you. I even had a shower, ready for bed. Then I made the mistake of looking inside and thought you might be worried.'

'I would have phoned you if I was. I had it with me when I left Greenacres, so it would have had to have been in your car.'

'Not being psychic, I couldn't know what your train of thought might have been. Anyway, it's not as if it's midnight. I thought you'd still be up.'

'We are,' said Daisy. 'Well – I am. Ben's flat out. You could have just called first, you know.'

'You've got tablets in the bag.' He coughed, and scuffed the toe of his shoe along the floor. 'I thought they might be the pill. I know what can happen if you – um – miss one.'

Daisy fished in the rucksack and pulled out a half-used

strip of tiny white tablets. 'These things? They're antihistamines. Ben gets hayfever. Sometimes it's really bad, so I
tend to carry them round with me, in case he forgets his,
or runs out.'

'Oh . . .' To her surprise, Jerome coloured.

She'd always envisioned him as worldly. Had she been
under a huge misapprehension, or was he just pulling her
leg? Knowing Jerome, the latter would have been more
likely. But then he went on to explain his ignorance.

'I've always relied on Durex,' he muttered, scratching
his head. 'And then when my wife and I were trying for a
baby . . .' He pulled a stern face. '*Ex*-wife.'

'Not a lot of call for antihistamines, I know.' Daisy
looked at him in what she hoped was a mollifying manner
rather than an inquisitive one. 'It's OK. I appreciate the
gesture.'

'It all seems pointless now, considering I was probably
shooting blanks.'

She blinked, caught off guard.

Jerome dropped sullenly into an armchair. 'Although
I suppose safe sex is still an issue,' he went on, clearly
absorbed in thought. After a short, awkward silence, he
glanced up at her. 'Sorry. I'm making you uncomfortable
talking like this, aren't I? It's just . . .' he ploughed on, 'I
think that's one of the reasons I'm so crap with women . . .
I can't help thinking they're going to run a mile when they
find out I can't give them children. Sometimes I think I
should be honest from the start.'

Daisy perched on the armchair opposite, tugging a
flap of towelling robe over her bare knees and tucking it
beneath her. 'Aren't you being a bit presumptuous about
it? I mean, have you had proper tests?'

'I'm just going on evidence, although not clinical as

such. My wife and I tried for ages to have a baby. We were on the verge of seeing our GP about it, when practically the first time she sleeps with someone else – hey presto, she's up the duff! Now what does that say to you?'

It did seem pretty conclusive, but it wouldn't stand up in court. 'I think,' she began tentatively, 'that you ought to see a doctor and find out for certain. It might be that you and your wife were trying too hard. I've read that can have an adverse effect. It could just be, in a moment of madness, she looked to someone else to help her ignore her problems. Maybe she forgot about trying to make a baby, and simply got on with making love instead.'

Oh, bloody hell. Had she really just said that? Daisy looked at the floor, avoiding Jerome's gaze.

'You're amazing,' he murmured. 'Do you know that? You make me want to laugh and howl in agony at the same time. You make me want to—'

'Would you like a cocoa?' Daisy leapt to her feet and scurried into the kitchen. Jerome hesitated, then followed her.

'Thanks all the same, but no.'

'A coffee?'

He grabbed her arm. 'Listen, this is the last thing I want.'

'What is?' She looked away, frowning in panic at the washing machine. The drum was doing that funny gyrating thing, even though it wasn't technically on the spin cycle yet. She wished it would just shut up. It would be ironic if Ben were to wake up now that the storm sounded as if it was passing.

'I don't want you to be afraid of me, Daisy.' Jerome was still holding her arm, his fingers squeezing gently through the sleeve of the robe. 'Since you came to Nettlesford, things have been . . . Well, let's just say I don't plan to jeopardise our friendship. I've lost track of the times I've reassured Ben that he's got nothing to worry about. I'm not out to ruin your marriage, at least that part's true.'

Daisy slowly lifted her gaze. 'That part?'

'I don't want to trash your life. Yours or Ben's. I don't want to do what that man did to me . . . the bastard who took my wife. I could never live with myself, do you understand?' As his tone became surly, almost fierce, his grip on her arm tightened. His eyes seemed to be trying to impart information that his tongue couldn't spell out.

Daisy felt dizzy. His breath was hot, stirring her hair, brushing against her brow. Her mouth was dry. She could already feel his lips on her skin, his hands inching beneath the robe, even though he hadn't moved a muscle. Her imagination had never worked so deliriously.

He let go of her arm, then took a step back. 'You know how I feel . . . don't you?'

She couldn't bring herself to answer.

'I didn't mean for this to happen when I came here tonight. I didn't mean to tell you about . . .' He coloured again, and rubbed a hand over the faint shadow of stubble on his jaw. 'Anyway, I assumed Ben would be around. I thought . . .' He shook his head. 'Who the hell am I trying to fool? Any excuse to set eyes on you will do.'

She stared after him as he strode towards the door. His shoulders, usually so straight and arrogant, hung forward. She was rooted to the spot. Words formed in her mouth . . . *Stop! Don't go. Don't leave it like this.* But she couldn't have called out, even if Ben hadn't been asleep upstairs. Her throat was too choked up. The ability to move crept back into her limbs. Still, she waited. Finally, she crossed to the window by the front door and drew back the curtain just as lightning sliced the sky in two.

Jerome had gone. But his words, the final look he had given her, still lingered.

Daisy yanked a hand through her hair, fighting the tangles in agitation.

Maybe it had been the drink talking. He had probably had more than one pint. She'd also heard that during storms people could act out of character. Like werewolves and full moons. They could turn into someone else, *something* else.

She let the curtain fall back into place. An ocean of guilt crashed down on her as she sank on to the sofa in front of the TV again. A documentary about the nation's drug culture flashed images of white pills in clear plastic bags and teenagers dancing frenziedly beneath strobe lights. Daisy had danced like that once, but she hadn't used drugs. She knew the damage they could do.

But what about the heart . . . why did people never learn about the havoc that could cause? And why had she been so naive as to believe that just because someone might make a statement of intent, the body would immediately step into line and comply?

She grabbed her rucksack and tipped the contents on to the sofa. With relief, she spotted the familiar red and white capsules. She still had a couple left. Daisy fetched a glass of water and downed the paracetamol, then collapsed on to the sofa again, her fingers pressed hard against her throbbing temples.

'Daisy . . . ? Is something wrong?'

She jumped. A bleary-eyed Ben was staring at her over the banisters. She felt herself pale. 'Nothing. I couldn't sleep. It was too early, and the storm was so bad . . .'

'It seems to be passing now.' He yawned, slurring his words. 'I'm sorry, sweetheart, I must have dozed off.'

'I know. Don't worry, go back to bed.'

He hovered on the second-to-bottom step. 'I thought I heard voices.'

She hesitated. Somehow she knew Jerome wouldn't mention that he'd been here tonight. 'Just the TV . . . Sorry if it disturbed you.'

'Are you sure you're OK?'

'I'm fine.' She tried smiling, but it was more of a grimace. 'Honestly. I won't be long . . .'

A spontaneous rush of tenderness overtook her as she watched him trudge quietly back up the stairs. He reminded her of a child, minus the teddy bear and Bob the Builder pyjamas. She would give anything to protect him; her life if she had to. But she'd never once imagined the worst thing she would have to shield him from was herself.

16

Ben knew that Daisy wasn't pleased. He could tell by the set of her mouth and the fact that she hadn't spoken to him for the last hour. It had all begun when the minibus – driven by Stella, with Alice, Kieran and Adam as passengers – had pulled up in front of their garden gate that morning at half past nine.

'What's going on?' Daisy had demanded.

'We're going to Llandudno for the day,' Ben had pointed out cheerfully.

'I know *we* are,' Daisy had frowned. 'But what's it got to do with that lot?'

'Well . . . you know I didn't really fancy a party for my thirtieth birthday—'

'Apart from that small "soirée" up at Greenacres.'

'That was Dad and Vivienne's idea; nothing to do with me. I've got no input towards it. They could have a string quartet and fireworks planned, for all I know. Anyway, when you first brought up the idea of this day trip, I wasn't too keen, but then I got to thinking: wouldn't it be a laugh if my mates could come along as well. At any rate, it'd make a change from getting mullered at the Headless Horseman.'

From the look on Daisy's face, Ben had thought she would dig her heels in and refuse to go. 'You didn't think of discussing it with me?' she'd asked, her voice glacial.

'I thought it would be a surprise.'

'No, you didn't. You just knew I wouldn't like it, so you planned all this behind my back.'

'Don't get dramatic.'

'Me?' she'd harrumphed. 'As if!' And she'd turned away, rubbing her eye as if there was something in it. 'I was really looking forward to today . . .'

'It'll still be good. And it's not as if it was ever just a romantic picnic on the beach. Not with Robert tagging along.'

'Robert,' Daisy had lectured crabbily, 'was the whole reason for today. It wasn't about your birthday, or your friends, or anything else apart from taking your younger brother on a fun day out.'

'I thought we could kill two birds with one stone.'

'Don't give me that.' She'd regarded him with disappointment and a hint of disgust. 'You're just scared. Scared that if you had to spend longer than five minutes with Robert, you'd realise he's not like your father. You'd actually find yourself liking him, which would go against everything you've thought and felt for the last ten years. No, don't look at me like that. I won't shush, and especially not because you're worried your friends will overhear. I don't care if they hear or not. This has nothing to do with them anyway.'

And before he could reply, she'd stormed into the house, gathered together her things and flounced back out to the minibus, leaving him to lock up. He had been relieved that she hadn't said she was staying behind, but in some ways the brooding silence was going to be worse. Would she have calmed down by the time they reached the A55, or would it last all the way to Llandudno, Ben had wondered.

'The minibus belongs to my parents,' Stella had explained

to Daisy, as they'd driven to the main house to pick up Robert. 'As you know, they run the local stables, and they also have a riding school for disabled children. We do a lot of ferrying backwards and forwards, but it wasn't needed today, so Dad said I could borrow it.'

Surely Daisy wouldn't be offhand after the mention of disabled children, Ben had hoped.

In fact, the whole of today was based on hope, to one degree or another. On Daisy's part, Ben knew that she was trying to get him to spend more time with his half-brother. At first, on a rebellious note, Ben had engineered a twist to the plan. It was only as it had developed that he'd realised it was the ideal opportunity for Daisy and his friends to get to know one another better. Away from the noisy, smoky confines of the Headless Horseman, she might start to see them in a different light.

'You OK, Robbie?' he asked his half-brother, as everyone clambered down from the minibus.

'Yeah, I guess.' The boy looked round. 'But don't call me that.'

'Oh . . . Right. I thought you wouldn't have minded, because of Robbie Williams and um . . .'

'I don't like it. Call me Rob or Robert, but not Robbie.'

'Er – OK, Rob it is then.'

Ben turned his attention to helping Daisy down, but she shunned his outstretched hand. It probably wasn't a wise move, but he took her arm anyway and squeezed it, leaning towards her to murmur, 'Come on, it'll be fun if you give it a chance. At least look as if you're enjoying yourself – for Rob's sake.'

She gave him a withering look, then stalked across the road to the sloping stretch of pavement overlooking the sea. As the group fussed around getting their gear organised and Stella grumbled at a temperamental ticket machine, Ben went across to join his wife. Everyone was probably aware that they were having a domestic, but Ben was determined to act as cool as possible. It wouldn't further his cause if his friends finally grasped the extent of Daisy's hostility towards them.

'You're such a hypocrite,' she glowered, as he reached her side, 'telling me I should take Robert into account when it's pretty obvious that you don't.'

'I do! It's just . . . I thought that if you got to know Stella and the others better, you might realise they're not such a bad bunch.'

She sighed hotly. 'I never said they were bad, they're just not my cup of tea. Of course, now that I know about you and Stella, I can see why you're so keen to stay friendly with *her*, at least.'

'What are you talking about?'

'Geri told me that you used to go out with her.'

Daisy had probably been privy to this information for a while, Ben guessed, but she hadn't thought it worth mentioning until now. It was crazy how things could get blown out of proportion during an argument.

Unable to restrain his sarcasm, Ben said, 'Yes, I went out with her. About fifteen years ago. Why – are you jealous?'

'No.' She pursed her lips and stared down at the water lapping and crashing against the rocks below. They were at the western end of Llandudno Bay. To the east was the pier and the wide curve of the North Shore, the tide far out enough to reveal a strip of sand between the water's edge and the shingle. 'But if I was, I'd be justified.'

'Why?' asked Ben. 'Because of a few clumsy, teen-age fumbles? We weren't quite as sophisticated as kids nowadays. Unless you're trying to tell me it was already different in your day.'

'I know of a couple of girls who got pregnant at fourteen and fifteen, and I know who the boys were who helped them.'

'Well it wasn't like that for Stella and me. We went to the cinema or bowling, and most of the time her dad used to drop us off and pick us up. It ended because we both got bored and were nagged by our respective families into studying for our end-of-year exams.'

'I think she still fancies you.'

Ben shook his head, exasperated. 'She may have done – before I left Nettlesford. But she doesn't now. If you ask me, she's got a soft spot for Kieran.'

'Geri said there might be something going on between them, but I haven't seen much evidence.'

'That's because you don't see that much of them,' Ben reminded her.

'Talking of Geri,' said Daisy after a pause, 'why didn't you invite her along today?'

'I did, as a matter of fact. She and Declan already had plans.'

'But you didn't invite Jerome?'

Ben hesitated. He hadn't seen much of him lately apart from at work. Jerome had apparently pulled a muscle somewhere in his back, and hadn't played football for the past two weeks. Not since the night of the storm. He didn't appear to be hobbling in any way, though, and the other day Ben had spotted him bending down to pick up some files that had fallen off his desk. But playing sport was different, wasn't it? Jerome was probably worried he might aggravate the condition.

'No, I didn't ask him along,' Ben admitted at last.

'Because it's still one rule for you and another for me,' Daisy challenged. 'You don't like him so—'

'I've bloody well made an effort, though! Unlike some people.'

Ben had had enough. With gritted teeth, he crossed the road again. Perhaps he was feeling jealous himself. He had been, not so long ago, but he'd assumed he was over it. Maybe he was wrong. Maybe he hadn't felt the need to be jealous lately because Daisy hadn't mentioned Jerome, and they hadn't bumped into him at the Headless Horseman. Usually Daisy would natter to him for ages while Ben drifted off to join Stella and the others.

'Too busy,' Jerome had said, when Ben had remarked on his uncharacteristic absence from the local pub. 'Sorry, mate, but I'm finally getting a life.'

It was possible that Jerome might have a girlfriend, Ben speculated. And if it was still early days, it would explain his reluctance to broadcast the fact. Ben couldn't deny that he'd be relieved if Jerome was involved with someone. It was only because Daisy had mentioned his name just now that Ben's patience had worn thin.

'Come on,' he said, instilling vigour into his tone as he looked round the group by the minibus. By his friends' slightly embarrassed countenances, it was obvious that they sensed the tension between him and Daisy and were possibly linking it to their own presence there. 'Who's for the beach then?'

'Fish and chips first,' said Adam, who was governed by his stomach. 'Just for elevenses.'

'You're the only person I know who has cod, chips and mushy peas for a mid-morning snack,' scoffed Kieran. 'But just this once, I think I'll join you.'

'I'll pass,' said Stella, turning up her nose. 'Alice, do

you fancy doing some exploring? I've heard there's a really nice shopping centre here. And we can always grab a coffee somewhere.'

Typical, frowned Ben.

As the women sauntered off without asking Daisy if she wanted to join them, Robert started heading down the slope, too.

'Where do you think you're going?' Ben called.

'The pier.'

'On your own? No way. I promised your mother I'd keep an eye on you.'

'But I'm ten.'

'Exactly.'

Ben glanced back at Daisy. She was staring out to sea, her hair billowing behind her, streaked with gold in the sun. Angelic yet implacable, she looked lost in thought. Ben called out to her, not just once but twice. She didn't seem to hear. Meanwhile, Robert was walking faster. Doing the brotherly thing, Ben hurried after him.

High clouds scudded across the bright blue sky, throwing shifting, dappled shadows over the sand as Daisy flopped on to her towel and started drying her feet. She had paddled herself silly, and seemed to be the only person on the beach on their own. Rucksack hooked over her shoulders like the weight of the world, she'd attracted curious glances from the groups, families and couples there. Or was she just imagining it? She felt as if she had 'Outcast' stamped on her forehead.

The other members of her party had disappeared. One minute they had been hanging around the minibus; the next, they hadn't. Not even Robert or Ben. She knew she'd been deep in thought, but hadn't realised quite how much. Still, she would have expected someone to have made sure she was tagging along to wherever it was they'd gone. So she had made her way to the beach to see if they were there, but enticed to the water's edge, she had found herself distracted again as she'd paddled up and down.

Now, tucking her knees under her chin and wrapping her arms round her legs, she sighed and contemplated if she would ever know peace of mind again. It was as if she were possessed by a recalcitrant spirit. Every time she had an immoral thought, her conscience launched a backlash. And even when the thought wasn't immoral; even when it was just a comparison to Ben, such as, 'Jerome wouldn't have been so immature. Jerome wouldn't have huffed at me. Jerome wouldn't have turned such and such into a joke,' she still found herself assailed by guilt.

As if she didn't have enough to demoralise her. She hadn't gone looking for this sort of trouble, and didn't know why it had come looking for *her*. When she'd first met Ben, she knew there had been more chemistry on his side than on hers; but that had soon changed, and now she would argue with anyone who claimed physical attraction had to be instant. Ben had grown on her, and relatively quickly. There was passion between them. Heart-racing moments when he looked at her and she knew exactly what was on his mind.

She was aware that the thrill couldn't last forever, though. She might have expected temptation to rear its head – and to be resisted – a few years down the line when complacency set in, but why had no one warned her that it could well happen sooner?

Her reverie was disturbed by a green and red ball, which rolled under her legs. She looked up as a toddler in a frilly pink sundress staggered across the sand to retrieve it.

'Ball!' said the little girl, beaming toothily as Daisy handed it back to her. There was a tugging in Daisy's stomach, a longing she recognised. It didn't happen often as yet, but this time it was accompanied with the knowledge that Ben would probably be able to give her a baby one day. The chances were that Jerome couldn't.

Oh, help. She shook her head in a vain attempt to banish these thoughts. Ben was her husband. He would be the father of any children she might have. She was a terrible person for visualising Jerome in that role, but she hadn't been able to help it. She was glad that he had been frank with her about his problem. It implied that he respected her too much to lie by omission. Inconveniently, though, this honesty had only made him more attractive.

With a ragged, frustrated sigh, she looked around her. A short way along the beach, Stella, Alice, Kieran and Adam were spreading out towels on the sand. Daisy found herself in another quandary. Should she pretend she hadn't seen them, or should she join them? They might already have spotted her, but were feigning ignorance themselves. On the other hand, they might know where Ben and Robert had got to.

With another sigh, this time of surrender, Daisy clambered to her feet, rolled up her towel and ambled over to join them.

'She let me down,' said Robert, blurting it out over the clamour of voices and the electronic arcade music. It sounded as if he'd been wanting to say it for ages, but hadn't had the bottle.

Ben glanced up from the fruit machine. 'Who did?'

Robert hesitated. 'Daisy.'

'Daisy let you down? How?' Ben frowned as he hit the wrong button. 'Bugger.'

'They weren't supposed to be coming today.'

'You mean, my friends?'

'Yeah . . .' Robert looked down at his trainers. 'She didn't tell me they were coming.'

Ben gave up trying to win the jackpot, and leaned against the machine instead. 'That's because Daisy didn't know. It was my fault. I surprised her with it this morning. She wasn't very pleased herself.'

'Oh.' The skin between the boy's pale eyebrows furrowed. It reminded Ben of Vivienne.

'I'm sorry, Rob. You know it's my thirtieth birthday this week, well I thought it would be a laugh to have a day out with my friends. I didn't want a proper party.'

'Mum and Dad are throwing you one on Friday.'

'More of a family dinner. Stella and the others won't be there.'

'But your friends aren't here now, so it isn't much of a laugh, is it?'

Ben looked at his watch. 'No. By now they're probably on the beach, so maybe we should think about joining them and finding Daisy.'

'But I want to try out the Rally game.'

'You already had a go on the Grand Prix, Rob.'

'Yeah, but you beat me. I want to have a go at the Rally one on my own.'

Ben sighed. 'Fine. Have you got enough change?' When Robert nodded, he went on, 'I just need to pop to the Gents'. I'll meet you in a minute, OK?'

The boy nodded and headed off. Ben hurried to the toilet. When he returned, he went straight to the Rally machine. There was a queue, but Robert wasn't in it. Ben muttered under his breath, and went to the Grand Prix ride instead. His half-brother wasn't there, either. Damn. Ben milled through the arcade, scanning it for a blond head above a navy T-shirt and baggy stonewashed shorts; but he had no luck. He even checked in the Gents', in case Robert had gone there to look for him and they'd missed each other.

Eventually, Ben went outside, blinking in the sunlight. The pier stretched off into the sea to his left; to his right was the promenade with its sweeping row of pastel townhouses, most of them probably hotels and B&Bs. Ben looked in vain round the crowd. There was no sign of Robert. Anxiety starting to gnaw in the pit of his stomach, he made his way down to the beach.

'I can't believe you're hungry again.' Stella rapped Kieran's hand as it edged towards the vegetable samosas, which were crammed into a Tupperware container on the picnic blanket. 'Is Ben the same, Daisy? A walking rubbish bin?'

Trying to smile and not retort, 'Well, you should know,' Daisy shrugged and said, 'Sometimes.'

This was so hard. She couldn't keep up the convivial front much longer, not while she somehow felt that they were laughing at her behind her back.

'I don't mind being a rubbish bin,' said Kieran, 'as long as it's Brabantia.'

'One of those really expensive ones where you just press on the lid and it pops right up,' said Adam. 'Cool.'

Daisy wondered why pressing on the lid was so much cooler than pressing on a pedal. She and Ben only had a yellow plastic swing bin; cheap and cheerful, it did its job fairly well, except for when it came to tea bags. Why there always seemed to be streaks of tea on the lid, when she was usually so careful, was a mystery to her.

Rummaging in her rucksack, she pulled out a packet of crisps. She was starving, and couldn't wait any longer for Ben and Robert to turn up. There were provisions in the bag for three people, and Daisy felt hungry enough to devour the whole lot.

'Would you like some pitta bread and taramasalata?' Alice asked her. 'Just help yourself if you do.'

Daisy was tempted, but it seemed easier to shake her head. What if she stretched across the picnic blanket and knocked something over?

'Would you like some salt and vinegar crisps?' she found herself asking, out of politeness, which would mean stretching over anyway to share them out.

Alice declined.

'Thanks, just a couple,' said Kieran, scooping as many as he could.

After eating the remaining three crisps, Daisy was about to open another packet when she saw Ben hurrying across the sand towards them.

'You haven't seen Robert, have you?' he called.

'Should we?' said Stella.

'I've been with him in the arcade all this time,' Ben explained. 'But I went to the loo, and when I came out he was gone.'

Alice's eyes grew wide. 'And you don't know where he went?'

'If he knew,' snapped Daisy, 'he wouldn't be here talking to us.'

'I don't know what to do . . .' Ben raked a hand through his hair. A few shaggy curls stood to attention. 'Do you think I should call my dad and Vivienne?'

'And worry them unnecessarily?' Daisy scrambled to her feet. 'They're an hour's drive away, at least, so there's not much they could do. If I were you, I shouldn't panic. There's probably a simple explanation.' She gently touched Ben's arm, as if to reassure him, her earlier annoyance with him forgotten. Seeing him stride across the beach had made her heart soar with relief, only for it to sink again rapidly at the announcement that Robert had done a disappearing act.

Ben glanced round the group. 'Maybe we should all split up and look for him. When it comes down to it, he's only ten, and he doesn't know his way round Llandudno.'

'Unfortunately, neither do we,' said Stella, packing away the picnic things.

'Shouldn't someone wait here?' suggested Kieran, halting Stella in her tracks. 'I volunteer.'

'What for?' frowned Adam. 'To keep an eye out for Robert, or eat what's left of the food?' He shook his head. 'Listen, Ben, do you want me to go to the arcade and hang around there, in case he goes back to look for you?'

'Good idea. Alice, maybe you could go with him but then carry on up the pier. There are all sorts of kiosks and things up there. Do you mind?'

''Course not. But, Ben, you don't think he would have gone off with someone, do you? I mean a stranger, *you* know.'

'He wouldn't be that stupid.' Ben paused, and thought harder about it. 'He might have got talking to some other kids, though, and decided to hang out with them. But I don't know why he'd have gone off without telling me first.'

Daisy didn't believe that Robert would have made friends quite that easily. Vivienne had been right; her son had a shy streak. In Daisy's view, something must have happened to upset him. Perhaps Ben had provoked him without realising. But Daisy didn't get a chance to talk to her husband privately.

'You'd better come with me.' Ben was gesturing to Stella. 'You're the only one insured to drive the minibus. We can cover more ground if we try to spot him from the road.'

'Er – what should I do?' Daisy frowned. 'Is there anywhere you think I should try looking?'

Ben glanced back at her. 'There's no point coming with Stella and me, two of us are enough. Just wander round, or use your initiative. Out of everyone here, you probably know Rob best.'

He sounded almost resentful, as if he was blaming her. OK, so this day trip had been her idea, but if Ben had been irresponsible enough to let Robert out of his sight – not to mention abandoning her at the first instance, just because she was cranky with him – then this was his fault. He was so bloody bull-headed at times, she wanted to scream.

Jerome wouldn't have been so petty, she found herself thinking, as she struggled with the zip of her rucksack. Jerome would have been a man about it. Jerome would have . . .

Daisy straightened up, narrowing her eyes after Ben and Stella.

Jerome would have wanted her by his side come what may, she thought gloomily.

17

What appeared to be Llandudno's high street struck Daisy as very Victorian. Not being an expert on architecture, though, it was an assumption rather than a fact. With its ornate buildings and canopied shop fronts, she wished she was at her leisure to soak up the nostalgic atmosphere rather than dash about glancing through windows in search of Robert. It was almost forty minutes since she'd left the others, and for all she knew the boy might have turned up by now. Then again, her mobile was switched on; she was sure Ben would have rung to let her know.

Just as she was passing a bookshop, she glimpsed the back of a familiar blond head poking up above a shelf. Daisy went in, rounded the shelf and saw to her immense relief that it was her half-brother-in-law. His nose was buried in Shakespeare's *A Midsummer Night's Dream*. Or rather, a revision guide instead of the straightforward text. He looked up at her, blinking for a moment in surprise. But then the corners of his mouth curled downwards, and his gaze dropped to the floor.

'How did you know where to find me?' he asked.

'I didn't! Just call me lucky.' Daisy's relief turned to anger. 'What do you think you're playing at? You've got everybody searching for you! Ben's been frantic—'

'Where is he?'

'Driving round with Stella, trying to spot you from the road.'

'He, er—' the boy swallowed, 'he hasn't called the police, has he? Or Mum and Dad?'

'Not as far as I know . . . but Robert,' Daisy sighed despairingly, 'why did you just wander off on your own without telling anyone?'

'I didn't think he'd care . . .'

'Who . . . ? Ben?' The boy nodded, and Daisy frowned. 'I know you haven't had the best of starts, but of course he cares about you! He isn't a block of wood. You could do a lot worse than have a brother like him . . .' She stopped. If that was true – and it was – then why was she so lacking in appreciation of his good points herself? Because she was unhappy? Or was there another reason?

She had once believed that love would sustain her through anything. As a girl, she had escaped into enough romances to know that women (and occasionally men) would go to the ends of the earth for their loved one, their soul mate, their other half.

Leaving London and its environs for the North West had hardly been the ends of the earth, but it had seemed far enough. She couldn't say that she missed anyone there, either. She hadn't been particularly sorry to leave, and nothing was pulling her back . . . And yet, she felt as if there was a gulf between her and Ben, between his life in Nettlesford and hers. For the most part, he seemed content in his job – when he wasn't sparring with either Jerome or his father.

Daisy longed for something like that for herself. She would settle for quiet contentment rather than exhilarating, short-lived rushes of happiness, yet in many ways it was harder to attain.

Had she been wrong to have put all her faith in love a second time? Or – even worse – was it possible to have got love muddled up with something else, such as gratitude?

'But Ben asked his friends along today,' Robert was saying. 'He didn't want to have to spend time alone with me.'

Summoning her attention back to the here and now, Daisy regarded the boy with what she hoped was a look of incredulity. 'Who told you that?'

'Ben.'

'He said that he didn't want to spend time with you?'

'No . . . he didn't say that as such. But he didn't have to. He wouldn't have asked the others to come otherwise.'

Daisy sighed, and took the book from Robert's hand, staring distractedly at the design on the front cover. 'Grown-ups don't always get things right.'

'You don't have to tell me that. I already know.'

'I was hard on Ben earlier,' Daisy continued. 'I told him he was scared of getting to know you. I think he feels guilty for leaving Nettlesford the way he did. You were only a little boy then, and he didn't know how to relate to you. He still doesn't, but that's not really his fault. He'll learn – if you give him a chance.'

By putting it like that, it might make Robert feel as if he had the upper hand; as if it was up to him to be magnanimous.

He didn't reply, just stared blankly at the book in her hand.

'Are you doing *A Midsummer Night's Dream* at school?' she asked, turning it over and reading the blurb on the back.

'Nah.'

'I bet you hate Shakespeare at the moment. Nothing makes sense probably.'

Robert shook his head. 'It's not so bad, once you know what's supposed to be going on. I've seen a few films on DVD. Mum wishes I hated it, though.'

'Oh? I thought she'd be pleased, considering her background.'

'That's why she isn't. She doesn't want me to be like her, not that way. Dad thinks acting's not good enough for me, and Mum agrees with him.'

'So you've spoken to them about it then?'

'I've tried, but they don't want to know. I'm only saying I *like* acting; it doesn't mean I'll want to do it when I'm older.'

'Have they stopped you doing stuff? School plays or—'

'I've only been helping backstage, but I want to do more. There's this drama workshop in Chester over the holidays. I put my name down, but now I have to tell Mum and Dad. I need one of them to sign for me, and to pay the fee. It's not much, not compared to what they pay for me to go to St Stephen's.'

'And you're worried they'll get upset?'

He nodded glumly, just as Daisy's mobile began to trill 'Greensleeves'.

'Damn,' she hissed. 'It's Ben.'

'Daisy,' said her husband firmly, before she could even say, 'Hello.' 'I'm calling Vivienne, and then I'm going to the police—'

'There's no need.' She cut him off. 'I'm with Robert now.'

'What?' There was a moment of stunned silence. '*Where?* When did you find him?'

'We're in a bookshop in the high street. I only found him a few minutes ago. I was going to call you . . .'

'I'll try to round up the others,' he said grittily, then proceeded to give Stella all the relevant information in a muttered aside before he addressed Daisy again. 'I'll meet you back at the beach, OK?'

She ended the call. 'We'd better get back,' she told Robert. Ben had sounded relieved but annoyed. 'Are you going to buy this book?'

The boy shook his head, and watched as she slid it back on to the shelf. 'There's no point thinking about it, is there? The workshop, that is. Mum and Dad aren't going to let me go.'

'Is this workshop doing *A Midsummer Night's Dream*?'

He nodded. 'They do old stuff as well as modern, and they try to relate Shakespeare to things that are going on today, to make it easier to understand. That's the idea behind it, anyway. I've got a leaflet on it, see?' And he pulled it out of his pocket: the most dog-eared, cherished scrap of paper Daisy had ever laid eyes on.

Without too much vacillation, she pulled the book back out and headed for the counter.

'What are you doing?' asked Robert, hot on her heels.

'Signing my own death warrant.'

'Huh?'

She handed a ten-pound note to the shop assistant. 'This is a gift,' she told her half-brother-in-law. 'From Ben and me.'

'The book?' said Robert, looking confused.

'For starters.' Daisy took the change and receipt and put them away in her purse. 'But Ben can be very persuasive.'

'I don't get it.'

'You will,' smiled Daisy confidently, and passed him the small bag the shop assistant had given her.

Daisy didn't feel quite so confident when she told Ben her plan later that day.

'Sorry?' he spluttered, coughing.

He was sitting up in bed reading a newspaper, but he crumpled it to one side and stared at her as if she'd grown two heads.

'I think you should ask your dad and Vivienne about this drama workshop on Robert's behalf,' Daisy repeated.

'But that's madness! They'd see it as interfering.'

'You're his half-brother, Ben. You've got a right to put forward your opinion. You've always said that one of the things that made you want to get out of this place was that you couldn't bear to watch Robert being "moulded" by Howard and Vivienne. But he's too much of his own person for that, and this is your chance to really help him.'

Ben groaned, and rubbed a hand over his face. 'You have such a knack, my darling.'

'Knack?'

'Of making me feel bad.'

With a stubby fingernail, Daisy followed a ripple of embroidery in the duvet cover. She was sure that he didn't know the meaning of guilt. Not compared to her. 'Oh?' she said nonchalantly. 'How else have I done that?'

'Today. This morning.'

'Because you'd invited your friends to Llandudno with us?' She shrugged. 'I *wish* I could like them, Ben. But I don't hate them. That's saying something, isn't it?'

'If you don't actually like my friends, then you *dis*like them, which isn't strictly hate, I know. It still puts me in a spot, though. What I want most is for you all to get along. I can't understand why you don't.'

'I know, I'm sorry.' She stared out through a gap in the curtains. Darkness hadn't fallen completely, there was still a touch of blue in the sky. 'It's just . . . how many times do I have to explain? They're so—'

'Cliquey? And I still think you're exaggerating. We're nothing like . . . like *Friends*.'

Daisy wanted to dispute that by drawing a few parallels, but she felt as if she'd come up against the same brick wall as usual. 'Why do you act differently when you're around them?' she asked instead. 'Do they regard you as the clown of the group?'

'Sorry?'

'You always seem to try so hard to be funny around them, hopping from one joke to the next. You don't relax.'

'That's a bit over the top.'

'Maybe. But you never seem to talk seriously when you're with them, as if they're expecting you to be the comedian. As if there isn't more to you than that. It gets my goat, I'm sorry. I find myself becoming all defensive, because I know the other side of you better than they ever will. The way I see it, if you can't be yourself with your friends, especially the ones you've known for years, then what's the point?'

'Spoken like a true expert,' retorted Ben, sounding aggrieved. 'Oh no, I forgot. You don't have any old friends, apart from Ellie What's-Her-Name.'

Daisy bit her lip. What *was* her name? She'd forgotten. It began with F, didn't it? Oh help, fabrications on this scale were no good if your memory started failing you.

'And who knows when you last spoke to her?' Ben went on. 'Not recently, anyway.'

'You can't know that for certain!'

'Well, have you?'

'No . . . But that's not the issue. We're not talking about my friends, or lack of them. Maybe I resent you for having Stella and Kieran and the others, as well as the fact that they share so much history with you. I've never had the good fortune, or however you see it, of being in a "gang". I've never had the particular gift of making friends in large numbers. I always seemed to attract bullies rather than . . .' she tailed off, having said more than she'd intended.

Ben turned to her, his entire manner softening. 'Were you bullied at school? You never told me that.'

'Not bullied, exactly. More . . . picked on. Silly things, nothing major. I just wasn't one of the popular girls, one of the in-crowd. I always used to wonder – sometimes I still do – who decides who's popular and who isn't? You go to school on your first day, with a load of other kids who don't necessarily know one another, but suddenly you all get invisibly divided up into cool and uncool. Who does that? How does it happen? It isn't necessarily based on looks.'

'I can't say I've thought of it like that. But I see your point,' he added hastily.

'You were one of the popular ones, though.'

Ben shifted uncomfortably. 'I never lacked friends, no, but I used to wonder if people were nice to me because I lived up at the big house and my mother was a Greenwood by birth. I did ask myself if things would have been different if Mum had been plain Mrs Jane Bloggs.'

'The realist in me says that they would.'

'The realist in me tends to agree.'

'So,' sighed Daisy, aware that she'd been sidetracked, and determined not to switch off the light and go to sleep without securing a positive response. 'Are you going to ask your dad and Vivienne about this drama workshop then? It's the least you can do for Robert.'

'Because I ruined his big day out? Well, he didn't exactly make it a barrel of laughs for me either. Running off like that – a typical case of attention seeking.'

'You sound just like your dad,' scowled Daisy. 'And there's a history of running away in your family,' she reminded him pointedly. 'Don't throw stones in glass houses.'

'Yes, well,' grumbled Ben, 'I get your drift.' He paused, rubbing his eyes. 'Listen, my love, I'll think about it, OK? I'd need to go about it tactfully, and at the right moment. I can't just wade into Greenacres and say, "Look here, you two, the boy deserves some consideration and a chance to prove himself."'

'Why not?'

He snorted in derision. 'You really take the biscuit, you know that. If you're so keen for Robert to do this drama workshop, why don't you speak to Dad and Vivienne yourself?'

'Fine,' said Daisy, sensing an opportunity to get her own way. 'I will, considering that you're too much of a coward. I'll tell them that it's just a bit of fun, and that he's young enough to grow out of this acting phase just as he's old enough to know he wants to give it a go right now. What else is he supposed to do over the summer holidays?'

'Normally, the three of them would go off to France for a couple of weeks, but I know they're not doing anything like that this year. Geri's wedding's too big a deal; there's still loads to organise as far as I can make out. And the idea of a huge marquee on the lawn is starting to make Dad wet his pants.'

'Well, then! With all this wedding stuff going on, Robert's going to be bored stiff, as well as getting in everyone's way. It'd be much better if he had something of his own to concentrate on.'

Ben snorted again, this time in admiration. 'You never give up, do you?'

'Not when I'm passionate about something.'

'Are you passionate about me?'

Daisy shrugged coquettishly. She was tired, it had been a long day, but if a kiss and a cuddle might clinch the deal, she was ready and able to oblige.

18

Ben folded his arms behind his head, and swivelled his chair to stare out of the open office window. The pavement below shimmered in the midday heat. He was all too aware of the sweat patches forming on his shirt, but hopefully from down there on the street no one would notice. The new ceiling fan – which took up less room in an already cluttered office than a free-standing one – wasn't cooling him down as efficiently as he'd anticipated. In fact, in spite of its clean, modern lines, the main purpose it seemed to serve was as a poignant reminder of that last family holiday before his mother died – an unparalleled, month-long tour of the Far East, starting and ending in Singapore. Ben sighed heavily. The bloody fan hadn't been quite so evocative when he'd seen it in a catalogue and pointed it out to his father.

There was a knock on the door, and a second later Michelle came in.

'Remind me never to build a conservatory,' said Ben. 'At least, not without state-of-the-art-air-conditioning.'

Her brow wrinkled. 'Sorry?' She handed him the letters she'd typed that morning.

'Nothing.' He wet his lips. 'Don't worry.' Skimming over the mundane correspondence, he picked up his pen from the desk. 'They seem fine. Thank you. I'll sign them now, shall I, so you can get them sent off?'

When she'd left, he twirled the classic black-and-gold pen through his fingers. It was a Mont Blanc. A birthday present from Geri and Declan. Ben had to admit that it was one of his favourite gifts. His father had had a brass door plaque engraved for him – which made Ben feel as if he were working in a doctor's surgery – and his stepmother had opted for a Dolce & Gabbana sweater, which was tasteful enough, if not quite his thing. But he wouldn't be wearing it until Christmas, the way the temperature kept soaring.

Daisy had bought him a leather-bound photo album, for all those photos he kept loose in his bedside-table drawer, a DVD of the latest *Star Wars* instalment and a loud Hawaiian print shirt (as a joke really, from the charity shop, she'd explained). He didn't quite know how to tell her that he liked it. Stella and the others had grouped together to buy him a stash of CDs he'd been after for ages and a 'Coping with your Thirties' survival kit, which included hair dye, 'disguise your beer belly' underpants and a large tub of anti-wrinkle cream for men, allegedly loaded with pheromones in case you were still single and searching.

'They couldn't give you something that would actually come in useful,' Daisy had complained, in a voice barbed with sarcasm.

Ben had flapped the shirt at her. 'You don't expect me to wear this, but you gave it to me anyway.'

Daisy hadn't replied to that, just held up the huge elasticated underpants, and said worriedly, 'These are as tight as a girdle. They could seriously diminish your sperm count, you know.'

Ben had almost spat out his coffee. Part of him had hoped she wasn't starting to get broody just yet, the other part, which consisted primarily of his sense of humour, had found her remark hilarious.

She'd turned to him sternly. 'Infertility isn't a laughing matter.'

'I know, I know. It was just the way you said it. I'm sorry, and I promise not to wear the pants. In fact, I don't think any sane man would be seen dead in them.'

Of course, sanity often went out of the window the instant vanity swooped in. Slouched in his office chair now, Ben patted his belly, which was only marginally bigger than it had been ten years ago, thank God, and not as flabby as it could have been if he didn't do a few sit-ups practically every day. He was one of the lucky ones, unlike poor Adam, whose paunch seemed to expand weekly and head south at the same time. On the other hand, there were men like Jerome and Declan who seemed inherently fit without having to do anything. Somehow, Ben couldn't visualise them slogging away on their bedroom floor or in a gym. Jerome's back, for one, was still bothering him, and Declan seemed too busy in between all those nights out with Geri and running his increasingly successful art gallery.

Which reminded Ben about the show or exhibition, or whatever that sort of thing was called, which he and Daisy had been invited to the following week. He wasn't particularly looking forward to it. Still, life couldn't be roast beef and Yorkshire puddings all the time, as Aunt Eleanor used to say.

Thinking about the past, about his mother and aunt and the way they had suddenly and tragically become absent from his life, made Ben soberly consider the future. There was a history of repression and control in the Greenwood family that the Kavanaghs had done nothing to alter. Ben knew that his father had been glad when he'd followed in his footsteps, and in spite of a temporary lapse, as Howard had referred to those years Ben had been gone, everything was more or less running to plan. He'd said all this in his speech at the family dinner last Friday – in honour of Ben turning thirty – pompously toasting his elder son and the future of Kavanagh and Co., and implying that Robert would also opt for a career in law. 'A barrister in the family would cap things off nicely,' he'd concluded, half-jokingly.

Ben knew that Daisy had almost picked an argument, but by some miracle she'd managed not to. Maybe because it was his birthday, or because she was aware that it wouldn't further Robert's cause. Either way, Ben had been thankful to get through the evening without a scene. But had he missed his opportunity to talk to Vivienne and his father about the drama workshop? Daisy had nudged him a few times, but he'd let the moment pass, each time with a rational, whispered excuse which hadn't exactly placated her, but at least she hadn't pressured him further at that point.

It was odd leaving the first flush of youth behind, he reflected now, staring down at a pensioner in the street below. He was the first of his close friends to do so, to join the ranks of professional, thriving thirty-somethings like Declan and Jerome. He ought to feel . . . different somehow. Perhaps more confident. But he didn't. He felt as if he was the same teenager who had watched his mother die of cancer, and, less than a month later, learned that his aunt had died in a car crash on the M6, her Citroën 2CV crushed between a coach and a Land-Rover. He still felt as insecure, and as much of an innocent, and as terrified of such a loss again.

Ben suddenly remembered Kipling's poem 'If' about being a man, but he couldn't reconcile it to his own life. Leaving Nettlesford had made him feel stronger; yet it was just that – a feeling. It hadn't lasted. And, mulling it over now, he realised he'd come *back* rather than coming home. He still wasn't sure if he knew what the latter really meant.

Marrying Daisy was the only thing he felt he had done right. He knew the speed with which it had happened didn't make sense to a lot of people, yet it did to him. It always had. He prayed it made sense to her, too, but lately she'd seemed so disheartened and beyond him that he wasn't sure what to think. Nothing he did or said appeared to help. All his efforts seemed futile. On the other hand, perhaps there was something he could do . . .

Not for his half-brother, or for the sake of his own conscience, but for Daisy – he could speak to his father, today, right now. He could take the opportunity that was staring him in the face.

He could start being a man.

'I don't usually go round quoting song lyrics,' said the voice from behind, 'so forgive me in advance, but I just can't get you out of my head.'

Daisy jumped in shock, and almost rolled off the new sunlounger Ben had surprised her with last week. She looked round, her heart thudding.

'What the hell . . . ?' She put a hand to her chest, as if that would calm the palpitations. Instead, it made things worse. There was too much bare flesh to be felt when she would have preferred to have been buttoned up to her chin. There was nowhere to hide in this old turquoise bikini, however, and there were definitely no buttons. Just a few knots and bows which, sod's law, were probably going to choose this moment to slither undone.

'You scared me!' she hissed, peering at Jerome over her sunglasses. 'And stop hovering above me like that.'

'I'm sorry, but there isn't a chair, otherwise I'd sit down. I take it you weren't expecting guests?'

'Do I look as if I am?'

'That would depend on who they were and whether they were bringing their own seats.'

'You're awful,' she groaned, grudgingly adding, 'there are some folding chairs in the shed, help yourself.'

'So you don't actually mind me dropping by like this, then? Only I saw Ben heading off to the pub with Howard, and thought you might appreciate some company.'

Daisy tried swatting a pesky fly, but missed. 'I wasn't expecting him home for lunch today, anyway.'

'Good.' Jerome had found a chair, and was positioning it beside the sunlounger. 'We need to talk.'

It was just a cliché, thought Daisy. Probably not as important as it sounded. It still felt as if the sun had got hotter and its rays more intense, though. She wished there was some sort of sunscreen she could slap on that would shield her from more than just UV radiation.

'You know, you shouldn't be sunbathing at this time of day,' Jerome scolded.

'I've got factor twenty-five on.'

'Doesn't matter. And you're not wearing a hat.'

She flicked indignantly at one of the low bunches she was sporting. As opposed to a ponytail or bun, they allowed her to lie flat on the lounger without digging into her neck. Her parted hair hung halfway down her back, clinging to her damp skin.

'I don't have a hat,' she said.

'Doesn't Ben own a cap?'

'It's lying around somewhere.'

'Maybe you should find it. Or, on second thoughts, perhaps we ought to go inside.' His face was beginning to look shiny. He loosened his tie. 'I thought the office was bad enough . . .'

'We could always sit in your car. You can switch on the air-conditioning,' quipped Daisy, who didn't want to go indoors with him dressed like this. Outside was bad enough, but in the airless gloom of the house she would feel even more exposed; as if she was only wearing her bra and knickers, rather than a bikini.

'Let's compromise.' He rose, picked up the chair and moved it into the shade of the apple tree. Then he gestured for her to get up, and moved the sunlounger over as well. 'There. Could I have a drink now? I'm parched. One of those beers you're drinking there will do, if you've got any more in the fridge. It's only a small bottle, I don't think it'll affect my concentration.'

'I've got one left. Wait here.' Daisy went into the kitchen, took off her sunglasses in order to see, and then fished out the beer from behind the fruit juice cartons in the fridge. As she flipped off the lid, she spotted her denim shorts lying over a stool. Quickly, she tugged them on. They were a little on the snug side, and she only tended to wear them round the house, but they were better than just those itsy-bitsy bikini bottoms. She padded back outside, trying to appear insouciant and hoping Jerome wouldn't mention the additional item of clothing that had materialised on her body.

He didn't. He launched straight in with the heavy emotional stuff instead.

'I've missed you, Daisy.' He took a long swig of beer.

'I won't ask you why you've been drinking on your own, seeing as I've been doing the same.'

'One beer!' she defended herself. 'That hardly makes me an alcoholic.'

'One beer, two beers . . . I'm on the tequila, myself.'

'Tequila on your own doesn't sound much fun.'

He looked at her squarely. 'It isn't meant to be.'

She wriggled on the sunlounger, and, having left her sunglasses in the kitchen, squinted in the brightness at a ladybird that had landed on the checked upholstery. It was easier than looking at Jerome. 'I thought we were supposed to be avoiding each other.'

'Was that the unspoken rule? I think we've done pretty well. Fleeting glimpses, brief hellos and goodbyes. We last spoke properly a month ago, the night I brought your bag back.'

As if she wasn't acutely aware of the fact. 'It's for the best. I – I don't know why you're here now.'

'Like I said, I've missed you. It's the stupid little things that you notice most, isn't it? Those cupcake things you used to send into work with Ben sometimes. Did you know that he used to share them out during our coffee breaks?'

'I haven't done any baking lately,' she said dismissively. 'And that's hardly missing me directly.'

'Well, what about the fact that I've lost a friend, just because I was reckless enough to fall in love with her.' Jerome sighed. 'Actually, that's not a stupid thing. Or little,' he added. 'Wrong categorisation, sorry.'

Wide-eyed, Daisy stared at him through a gap in her straggly, sweeping fringe. It was one thing for him to imply how he felt, quite another to actually come out and state it like that. She felt as if she were standing in the middle of a level-crossing with the barriers lowering on either side of her.

'Jerome . . .' She rebuked him, but so quietly it was almost a whisper.

'I shouldn't have said that.' He held up his hand in a gesture of concession. 'But I had to . . . I need to know – I need to find out exactly how you feel.'

'I'm married to Ben.'

'That doesn't answer my question.'

She shook her head. 'I miss you, too, but I can't tell you what you want to hear . . . Oh hell, that sounds so corny.'

He reached out and took her hand, gazing at her studiously. Then he looked down, turning her wedding ring round her third finger, as if examining it for flaws. 'Why can't you tell me?'

'Because I don't *know*,' she sighed roughly, extracting her hand from his. 'I don't know exactly how I feel about you . . . I just know that I can't hurt Ben.'

'What about hurting me?'

'I'm not your wife. I met Ben first, I married him because I wanted to. No one twisted my arm. You were the one who said you couldn't live with yourself if you messed up another marriage. And you were the one who said you weren't prepared to jeopardise our friendship.'

'Screw our friendship.'

She was too shocked to reply.

'Don't look at me like that,' scowled Jerome. 'I can't win either way. Apparently it's for the best if we don't make contact, so I've lost out on that score. And as for not being able to live with myself . . . I'm having trouble living with myself now, so what's the point? I don't think either of us are happy – are we?'

'No,' she admitted at last. 'I'm not. But that isn't because of Ben. Not exactly. It's this place . . . Greenacres . . . Nettlesford . . . I'm not welcome around here.'

Jerome's dark eyes were hooded as he regarded her warily. 'What do you mean?'

'Nettlesford's pretty, but . . .' She shrugged. 'I don't know. "Pretty" doesn't seem enough when practically everything else seems wrong. Maybe it's because of Greenacres and all that family history. It sounds so sad. I like hearing about Ben's mum and his aunt, but there's something about that house . . .'

'I thought most girls would kill to be in your position – married to the heir of a large country estate.' Jerome was mildly sardonic.

'At face value, maybe. But it's not really like that. Ben's not loaded, and any Greenwood money that's left is tied up in running the estate and maintaining the house.'

'Yes, I know. The Greenwood name has died out, and the Kavanaghs aren't wealthy, landed gentry types, even though that's always been Howard's ambition. In my opinion – but please don't repeat this to anyone – he's failed. For all the conservatism and show. Don't you think the house and land will have to be sold off one day?'

'I – I don't get involved, so I don't know what's going on. Ben hasn't said anything.'

Jerome brushed a finger against her knee, tracing the shape of the bone with his fingernail. Daisy froze, her throat constricting. Then she shook her head, and swung her legs out of range. 'Don't,' she mumbled.

'Don't what?'

There was something in her voice that reminded her of sandpaper as she muttered, 'Jerome, I think it's time you left.'

'So you don't feel anything? Not the slightest—'

'I'm not bloody well made of stone! Of course I feel something. You can call it lust if you want, but how . . . how mixed up it is with anything else, I don't know.'

'What are you saying?'

She turned to face him again, hostility the safest form of resistance. 'Maybe I care about you,' she frowned. 'Maybe it's more than just platonic, and it might be more than just a physical thing. But I promised myself when I got married that however I felt in the future, I wasn't, *wasn't* going to turn into some sort of . . . of adulteress.'

'That's an old-fashioned way of putting it . . .'

She blinked at him incredulously. 'But that's the point – it *isn't*. It happened to you, remember? And you can call it whatever you want in our case, you can delude yourself or try to pull the wool over my eyes, but it would still be adultery. Society might call it an affair, make it sound as if we couldn't help ourselves or something, but I couldn't glamorise it like that. We *can* help ourselves, Jerome. We can choose not to devastate Ben just for the sake of a quick shag. We can—'

He took her hand again, clasping it so tightly it hurt. She knew it wasn't deliberate. He was just afraid; his eyes said it all. 'An affair wouldn't be enough, Daisy.'

There was a catch in her voice as she asked, 'So what do you suggest? We run off and leave Ben a note? That bodes well for a long and happy life together – starting out as if we were fugitives.'

'I thought you weren't going to glamorise this?'

'I'm not.' That honestly hadn't been her intention. 'I just haven't got any reason to be optimistic.'

With a sudden groan, he heaved himself to his feet and dragged both hands through his hair, pausing as he reached the back of his neck. He stood over her, looking as if he'd just woken up and had frozen in mid-stretch. She waited for him to say something, to move again. Eventually he did, directing his gaze to his watch and staring long and hard as if it took more than just a second to work out what time it was. 'I – I'd better get back.'

She swallowed with difficulty, managing a nod.

'I'm sorry I bothered you.' He turned to go. As if it was that simple.

'Jerome, wait . . .'

He looked back at her. A flicker of hope passed across his countenance.

Daisy took a deep breath. 'If we don't mention this again . . . we can pretend that today . . . that it never happened.' But that wasn't what he wanted to hear. The words had just come out of her mouth, as if she was reading from an Autocue.

He shook his head. 'I'm tired of pretending, Daisy. It's a crap way to live.'

And looking as helpless and dispirited as she felt, he crossed the lawn towards the front of the house, tightening his tie as he went.

19

'I'm home!' called Ben.

Daisy inhaled deeply, then clattered down the stairs. 'Hello, darling.'

Easing off his shoes, he looked at her in surprise. 'Have you just had a bath? Your hair's all wet.'

'Just a quick one. I'd been sunbathing, and I'd gone for a ride on the bike—'

'In this heat?'

'Just a short one. Not up hills, of course. It was the only way I could think of to cool down' – she made the motion of air whizzing past her face – 'apart from sitting in a cold bath, or spraying myself with a hose. Anyway, when I came back, I was all sticky from the sweat and the suntan lotion, so I, um . . .'

'Had a bath anyway?'

'But not a cold one.'

'No.' Smiling, he bent down to kiss her. She noticed he had a pleased air about him, as if work had gone well today.

Tugging at her sundress, which had a tendency to ride up, she wondered when would be the best moment to say what she had to say. Ben's chirpy mood indicated that Jerome hadn't told him he'd been here, but that wasn't any reason for keeping quiet about it herself.

'I've some good news,' began Ben, slinging his tie over the back of a chair.

'Jerome dropped by today,' Daisy interrupted, taking the plunge. If she'd waited, she might never have told him, and it seemed easier to slip it in like this, as if it wasn't of any real consequence.

'Sorry?' said Ben.

'Jerome – during his lunch-hour – he dropped by for a chat.'

'Oh . . . He didn't mention it. Then again, I only saw him briefly this afternoon.'

'Yes, um, he had a beer and told me what he'd been up to lately.'

'Really?' Ben was rooting round in the fridge. 'What has he been up to? Did he tell you he has a girlfriend?'

Daisy dropped one of Ben's shoes, which she'd been tidying away. She picked it up again without fumbling too much and peeked to see if he'd noticed. Mercifully, he hadn't. 'Sorry, what did you say?'

'Jerome,' said Ben, straightening up with a can of Coke in his hand, 'did he tell you he's got a girlfriend?'

'Er, no. Has he?' There was a quaver in her voice that she couldn't disguise.

'I'm guessing that he has. You've got to admit, he's been hard to pin down lately. As if he's been busier elsewhere.'

The light dawned. 'I see,' said Daisy.

'I thought that maybe he was reluctant to talk about her, in case it went wrong.' Ben's forehead creased slightly. 'He didn't confide in you, though?'

'No . . . No, he didn't mention anything like that. About girlfriends. You know.' Daisy frowned back. Bugger, she was talking rubbish. 'Just normal stuff, about work, his car.'

'His car?'

Oh hell, she felt as if all her brain cells had died off in the space of a few minutes. What had started off as an honourable desire to tell the truth – albeit an edited, toned-down version – had ended up as nonsense. She had no idea what she was supposed to say next.

'The air-conditioning's brilliant,' she mumbled. 'Apparently.'

'Right.' Ben looked perplexed. 'I'm glad. Especially in this weather. Not exactly what I wanted to hear, though.'

'Oh?' Daisy drifted into the kitchen and opened the fridge herself, collecting ingredients for a salad.

'I just . . . It would have been good if he was seeing someone – for his own sake. Maybe he was, but it hasn't worked out. Perhaps he came to see you today to cry on your shoulder or something, but decided not to. You're a woman, after all, you would have been more sympathetic than a bloke. Not that he's got many male friends that he's close to. Well, not as far as I can make out, but then I can't know for sure, can I?'

He was waffling. Daisy sensed his anxiety, just as she'd sensed Jerome's, although the latter had been more overt. She'd gone out on her bike that afternoon to calm her own mounting fears, hounded by the possibility that Jerome might have returned to the office and said something rash to Ben.

'I'm sorry I mentioned it,' she muttered, making room for a chopping board on the worktop near the sink. 'I thought that if I didn't, and you heard about it later, you might get the hump with me.'

'Why should I?'

'Because you always have in the past. Do you want spring onions in the salad? I've washed them now, so . . .'

'Er – OK. I'm going up to get changed.' But Ben hesitated, and turned back at the foot of the stairs. 'By the way, before you brought up Jerome, I was about to tell you I went to lunch with my dad today.'

'Yes, I know.' She paused from chopping and stared down at the knife in her hand. If she wasn't careful, she'd take off her finger. 'Jerome told me. Did you go to the pub?'

Ben nodded. 'I spoke to him about Robert's workshop.'

'Oh!' Daisy looked up expectantly. 'What did he say?'

'I can see his point of view. Acting's a tough profession.'

'But Robert's only ten, in a few years he might not even—'

'I know, I know. That's what I told Dad. He said he'd think about it, and speak to Vivienne, of course.'

Daisy nodded. This was a breakthrough on more than one level. She was glad that Robert might get to go to the workshop during the holidays, and pleased that Ben had finally plucked up the courage to confront his father. 'So he didn't accuse you of interfering, then?'

'No,' said Ben, wetting his lips, 'he accused *you*. But I told him that's what daughters-in-law are for. In my opinion, and please don't take this the wrong way, my love, I think he's finally warming to you.'

With a false smile, Daisy tossed the salad, wishing she could add, 'And vice versa.' Instead she said, perhaps too gaily, 'Tea won't be long. You'd better hurry up and change, darling.'

'So is that all we have to do?' asked Robert. 'Shove the sacks through people's letterboxes?'

Daisy jumped off her bicycle, and propped it against a low wall beside Robert's. The bikes weren't going to be out of their sight, so it was safe enough to leave them here for a few minutes. '*You* don't have to do anything,' said Daisy. 'This is my job. You just said you wanted to tag along.'

'It's not a proper job, though. You're not getting paid for it.'

'No, I'm a volunteer. But the definition of work doesn't just mean paid employment. This is something to keep me busy, and it's for a good cause, so everybody wins.'

'But isn't it . . . boring?'

Daisy sighed. 'Are you going to help me, or just stand around debating the merits of my new endeavour?'

'Huh?' Robert looked blank.

'Here.' Daisy handed him a wad of sacks. In their present condition, each individual sack was flat and rectangular and sealed inside a plastic envelope bearing the logo of Nettlesford's charity shop. Hopefully, by Monday morning when a van went round the village collecting them up again, most of them would be full of surplus-to-requirements clothes, toys and bric-à-brac, for the charity shop to sell.

'You do the right-hand side of the street,' Daisy suggested, 'and I'll do the left.'

She watched him walk off, and asked herself if she was doing the right thing letting him help. It was nice to have the company, but the job would be done faster with two pairs of hands and feet. This meant that she'd be home earlier, defeating the issue.

When Daisy had spotted the advert for part-time volunteers at the charity shop, she'd jumped at the chance. Apart from keeping her occupied, she'd also hoped it would help her feel part of the local community. The fact that it was all for charity was a bonus.

On this, her first day, she hadn't bargained on Robert presenting himself at the front door at nine a.m.

'Why aren't you at school?' she'd interrogated him suspiciously. 'I thought you didn't break up till next week.'

'Gas leak,' Robert had grinned. 'Didn't you hear about it on the radio? They're trying to work out where it's coming from. But in the meantime, they've had to shut the school. Just bad luck it didn't happen when we were all there. It would have been brilliant to be evacuated. We might have been on TV!'

There obviously wasn't much news to report today, Daisy had thought wryly, but had kept it to herself, not wanting to miff Robert. It had soon become apparent, though, that the boy's excitement wasn't just due to an unforeseen day off from St Stephen's.

Daisy eyed his progress as he wove up and down the front paths of Chesterfield Close. He reminded her of a lamb gambolling in a meadow, his step had such a spring to it.

'It's all because of you, you know,' Robert had gabbled, when he'd blurted out his even more personal piece of news, far more interesting than a mere gas leak.

'It's hardly got anything to do with me.' Daisy had tried to make light of her role. 'It was Ben who spoke to your dad about it.'

'But if you hadn't persuaded him to speak to Dad—'

'He didn't need much persuading,' Daisy had fibbed. 'He thought the workshop was a good idea, too. Keep you out of trouble during the holidays,' she'd teased.

And so, that was that, one problem out of the way. If only the rest of her life could be sorted out with the same relative ease. The business of having 'something to do', for instance. Ben had been supportive about her volunteer work for the charity shop, but he'd urged her to broaden her horizons, too.

'You can get a proper job, if you want,' he'd encouraged her gently. 'You don't have to sit at home all day. I mean, I know you don't sit. You work bloody hard, but if it's getting you down and you find this volunteer work isn't enough for you . . .'

At the beginning of the year, when Ben had whisked her away from her last job, he'd told her he was happy to support her for as long as she wanted, although at first he'd been concerned she'd find his attitude old-fashioned. He wasn't expecting her to start an instant production line of children, and he would be just as happy if she decided she did want to work, whether full or part-time. The idea of being a lady of leisure, though, had appealed to her after years of struggling to get by. But now she often found herself wondering if that struggle to survive was too deeply entrenched in her system to be overridden.

'I'll start with the charity work,' Daisy had decided, 'and see how things go from there.'

So far, she wasn't exactly on cloud nine, even though she was out and about away from the Gatehouse and Greenacres. Robert's good news had naturally raised a smile, yet it had also thrown the complexity of her life into sharp relief. Oh, to be ten again! Except not the ten-year-old girl she'd once been, but someone else. Another ten-year-old, belonging to another family, with a different future ahead of her.

No Greenacres, no Nettlesford, no Stella and the gang, no Jerome . . . no Ben.

Daisy frowned, thinking harder along those lines. Instead

of wondering more and more about the validity of her feelings for her husband, perhaps it would make sense to ask how she would feel if he *wasn't* around? If he didn't exist. If he had never appeared in her life and turned it completely upside down. If she were still plain Daisy Miller – not Mrs D. Kavanagh.

But she had to admit that even that was complicated, because it was impossible to remember if she had been marginally 'happier' back then than she was now.

20

'Declan's been looking at me strangely since we got here,' Daisy whispered to Ben. 'Then again, so has Geri. Do I look OK? I haven't got my skirt tucked into my knickers or anything?'

'You look stunning. Maybe that's why they're both staring. They're wondering how a great bumbling oaf like me ended up with such a gorgeous young wife.'

'Oh, you!' She gave him a gentle prod.

'I'll tell you one thing, my love, I'm feeling like a complete philistine. I just can't make out why people call this kind of thing art.' He tilted his head to one side, as if trying to work out some sort of pattern or structure from what seemed nothing more than a few random splodges of primary colours.

'It's *modern* art,' Daisy reminded him, in hushed tones, as another group of onlookers drifted by, evidently mesmerised. 'And I don't understand it, either,' she sighed.

Ben scratched his head. 'I'll probably get strung up for saying this in a place like this—'

'Say it quietly,' Daisy advised.

'Well, all this contemporary stuff seems a cop-out compared to the old masters.' He gestured to the painting in front of them. 'When you're three or four years old and you do this kind of "abstract" thing, Mum proudly puts it up on the kitchen wall or the fridge door. Do it when you're twenty-something, and it ends up in Swannell's, or the Tate Modern.'

Daisy pinched Ben's arm. 'You're terrible.' She giggled, and stretched up to kiss him. But before either of them had a chance to savour the moment, Geri butted in.

'Now, now, you two! Snogging's strictly forbidden here.'

'Didn't you read the small print on the invitation?' added Declan with a smirk.

Ben and Daisy regarded the other couple in embarrassment.

'Can't you save it till later?' Geri tutted. 'When you get to the hotel room.'

'I don't know if I can,' said Ben, looking worried. 'I think it's some sort of addiction. Do you think it's treatable?'

Declan stroked his chin thoughtfully. 'I've heard of a few alternative therapies.'

'None of them repeatable in public,' Geri swiftly intervened. Then she turned to Daisy, and looking as if she was about to do an impression of Mount Vesuvius, asked, 'Why didn't you tell me you'd done some modelling?'

Daisy couldn't speak; her mouth suddenly felt bone dry.

Ben frowned. 'Modelling?'

'If those pictures were of me,' gushed Geri, 'I'd have them plastered on my living-room wall.'

Daisy could feel Ben's gaze on her. 'It was so long ago,' she managed to mumble.

'Why didn't you tell me?' He looked puzzled. 'What kind of modelling was it?'

'I was only seventeen,' said Daisy, as if that would clarify everything.

'It's nothing she might feel ashamed of,' added Geri

hastily. 'Hardly page three, or top shelf at the news-agent's stuff.'

Declan was looking a touch more sober than he had five minutes ago, as if he'd realised what he and Geri had unleashed. 'Why don't we go to my office. I'll explain how I found out about it . . .'

Ben hesitated, then followed Declan. The girls lagged behind.

'I'm so sorry about blurting it out like that,' murmured Geri. 'I assumed Ben knew—'

'It's fine,' said Daisy mechanically. 'It's just . . . I haven't thought about it in ages.'

Now, whether she liked it or not, she would have to extricate the memory.

'The thing is,' began Declan, closing his office door behind them, 'I'm trying to lure this hot new photographer to have a show here in the autumn. Justin G. Maybury.' He paused, as if waiting for a response.

'I used to call him Greg,' said Daisy dully. 'His middle name. He hated Justin back then.'

'If you were seventeen' – Declan was trying to work out the maths – 'then Justin would have been—'

'Twenty-one. We met at a college near Norwich. I was doing my A levels. He was just finishing an advanced photography course.'

Ben's brow grew more crumpled. 'I didn't know you'd done A levels.'

'I never finished. I dropped out to go to London.'

'So you and Justin Maybury were friends then?' said Geri.

'Of a sort.' Daisy shrugged. 'I only modelled for him once, and it was inadvertently. I don't know why it's such a big deal . . .'

'They're amazing pictures,' said Declan. 'You've seen them, obviously?'

'I had copies, but I threw them away.'

'Well *I'd* like to see what all the fuss is about,' said Ben, moving to stand beside Declan, who was sitting at his PC, clicking on the mouse.

'How –?' stammered Daisy, rubbing her forehead. 'Why –?'

'They're on the Internet,' said Geri. 'On Justin's website. Well, a few of them are. I don't know if there were more.'

'But they're so . . . so *dated*,' frowned Daisy.

'They're among his earlier work,' said Declan. 'He's been striving for recognition for years, and now he's finally getting what he deserves.'

Daisy wanted to snap accusingly that Greg Maybury deserved nothing more than to be fried in hot fat, but the only person she needed to explain herself to was Ben.

'Websites like this are only designed to be a taster,' Declan was saying, 'but it's a good place to publicise your talent.' He clicked the mouse one last time, then sat back in his leather chair. 'There you go!'

From where she was standing, Daisy couldn't see the monitor; but there was no need to, anyway. The images were being projected in her head, as if they were part of an old slide show which had been stored away for years in someone's attic. She watched her husband's face. His expression wavered eloquently between confusion and admiration. Eventually, he looked up at her.

'I don't understand why you didn't tell me about this. Like Geri said, you've got nothing to be ashamed of . . .'

It wasn't the photographs she was ashamed of. Greg had never asked her to pose naked, not for the benefit of his camera lens, at least. And the pictures had been taken on the spur of the moment, totally unstaged. It had been late July; a balmy day, warm and sunwashed. They'd been for a drive, and had ended up at the coast. Perched on a rock in a plain white summer dress, the crinkly fabric furling round her thighs, Daisy had stared out into the hazy blue-grey of the North Sea. At first, she'd been unaware that Greg was taking pictures, and then, when she had realised, she'd thought they were just snapshots. Nothing serious. Nothing that would end up as huge, half-metre-by-one-metre images in simple black and white, hanging on the wall of Greg's studio. 'The Siren Collection', he'd called them, after the mythological creatures who draped themselves on rocks and sang sweet songs to lure hapless sailors to their doom.

Ben offered Daisy a supportive smile, but behind it she could still see a barrage of questions. 'Well,' he said, 'it certainly looks like this Greg knew what he was doing with a camera.'

Pity he'd had no idea what to do with a young girl's heart, apart from crush it.

Daisy felt her lips harden into a thin line. 'Greg was a genius, even then,' she murmured. 'He could make any subject look interesting.'

She only half-listened as Declan launched into a lecture about lighting and contrast and the other crap Greg had been fond of going on about. Daisy just wanted to get out of there. It was Geri who unwittingly started the ball rolling.

'I wish he was doing our wedding photos,' she sighed, massaging Declan's shoulders, her nails sparkling in silver, matching the platinum of her engagement ring.

'He wouldn't lower himself,' sniffed Daisy.

'That's the problem with artists like Justin G. Maybury,' said Declan. 'They could easily make a living out of the ordinary, day-to-day stuff, but in their view, they'd be compromising themselves.'

'Our wedding's hardly going to be "ordinary"!' Geri flicked indignantly at her hair. 'Which reminds me, Daisy, I need to talk to you about the hen night . . .'

Daisy, who was reliving the afternoon she'd found Greg in bed with two of his regular models, one of them male, could easily have screamed if Ben hadn't interrupted.

'Can't you girls discuss it another time, over coffee or something? Time's getting on and—'

'You've a suite booked at The Mersey,' winked Declan.

'Not exactly a suite . . .' Ben shrugged, almost apologetically, as if somehow he'd failed a set task.

'Whatever you've got will be good enough, believe me, mate. I wouldn't have recommended it otherwise. I always put up clients there if they need somewhere to stay and I'm out to impress them.'

A shame Declan wasn't footing the bill this time round, Daisy couldn't help thinking. Especially as he'd been the one who, in a roundabout way, had tarnished the magic of the evening.

The hotel was only a few streets away from the gallery. When Ben had suggested they stay over in Liverpool and make the most of their night out, Daisy had jumped at the chance. It would probably do them good to spend time in a swish, four-star no-man's-land with en suite Jacuzzi. Not that she missed the bright lights and hubbub of life in a big city – she knew she never wanted to live in one again – but once in a while it made a change from the quiet, slow-paced microcosm of society that was Nettlesford.

The evening had started out so promisingly. The more distance they had put between them and Greenacres, the more Ben had seemed to turn into the man she'd first met. By the time they had reached Declan's gallery, Daisy was beginning to wish they could go straight to the hotel instead. They had been so at ease, so affectionate with each other. And Ben had made such an effort to update his image, with his hair slightly spiked at the front and a new, loud, striped tie contrasting with his black shirt. But try as he might, he still hadn't fitted in among the crowd that had gathered to admire Declan's 'latest sensation' – a young artist with yellow hair and countless piercings.

Now, however, he was back to being the Ben she'd grown uneasy around these past few weeks. The Ben who, somehow, she couldn't relate to, swinging from moments of introspective silence to the exhausting glee of a court jester. By the time they reached the hotel and went up to their room, he was trying so hard to act as if everything was fine that he was simply coming across as manic.

'Did you order champagne?' Daisy pointed to a bottle in an ice bucket, on the table by the window.

'I thought it would be a surprise.' He was bouncing up and down on the bed like a young boy. 'Wow! Come and feel this mattress.'

But Daisy couldn't bear it any longer. 'Ben, listen, I think I should explain a few things . . .'

He looked up at her with a smile, but it seemed as if he was wearing it like a mask. 'I thought you already had. About the pictures, that is.'

She was shaking her head. 'They're not really important, that's why I didn't mention them before. As I said, it was all unstaged. I never felt like a proper model. It wasn't a job or anything.'

'And you and this Justin – Greg – guy, or whatever he's called – you were friends at college?'

Daisy paused. 'We were more than friends, Ben. He was the reason I left Norwich and went to London.'

'Oh.' Her husband stared at her without blinking.

'I wasn't happy at home, and college wasn't working out . . . When I met Greg, he did literally sweep me off my feet, but I was so naive about the whole thing, so . . . *blinkered*. He was the first . . .' She hesitated. 'Well, you know. It all happened so fast. I ended up moving in with him, and then, when he finished the course and said he was going to London, I went, too.'

'But you told me you'd never had a serious boyfriend. From a commitment point of view, not the physical.'

'It was hardly a commitment on his part, or long term. Just a crummy couple of months in which I finally grew up and learned the only person I could rely on was myself.'

'He treated you badly?'

'It didn't seem so bad then. There were days when he was wonderful. Casanova reincarnated. But the majority of the time he treated me like some sort of slave, not a girlfriend. Before that day at the beach, he hadn't seemed to think me a good enough subject to photograph. He tried to say that he wanted to keep his professional life separate from the personal, but looking back . . . I suppose I never argued with him because I respected his talent. I wasn't good at anything in particular, and whenever I saw Greg with a camera – he was so extraordinary, so gifted. I suppose I put up with it in a kind of stoical, martyred way.'

'He didn't . . . hit you?'

Daisy shook her head. 'It wasn't physical abuse. You could call it verbal, in a way, because the things he said . . . he used to make me think I'd be completely useless without him.'

'So what happened? Why did it end?'

'I found out he'd been cheating on me with his models. The ones he paid, the ones who came into his studio and our bed when I wasn't there.'

'So you left him?'

Daisy stared at the floor. 'He dumped me. Told me to stop snivelling and whining and dragging him down. According to him, when we'd first met he'd regarded me as his muse, but then I started to "block" him rather than inspire new work.'

Ben looked aghast. 'So he made you totally reliant on him, and then he just threw you out?'

'But I coped,' said Daisy, poking her chin in the air. 'I found a job and somewhere to live, and I got by. I've always got by, wherever I've been—'

'As if you had something to prove?'

'Maybe . . .' Daisy sat down on the bed, just as Ben stood up.

'You know,' he said carefully, 'we don't have to stay here tonight if you don't want to. We can go home.'

'The bill for the room will still go through on your card, won't it? It's too late to cancel.'

She knew Ben would need time to digest everything she'd told him; she couldn't begrudge him that. The flame which had flickered so tantalisingly between them at the start of the evening wouldn't even be considered a puny little spark now. It had gone, and Daisy couldn't predict when it might return, except that it wasn't going to be tonight.

'Anyway, I'm tired,' she added. 'I don't fancy the drive back.'

Ben nodded slowly as he opened their overnight case

and extracted the washbag. He drifted towards the en suite, and she heard him unpack their toiletries and start brushing his teeth.

Daisy glanced at the champagne, guessing it would remain unopened. She slipped out of her dress, put on her nightie and flopped back on to the bed, slumping against the mound of pillows. When she spotted the remote control, she switched on the TV and started flicking through the satellite channels on offer. By the time Ben came back out, she was watching *Brief Encounter*.

'You know,' he began, wetting his lips, 'you could have told me about Greg. It wouldn't have changed anything . . . It still doesn't.'

Except that it had just wrecked their evening. Daisy frowned, and snuggled further into the pillows. 'Telling you about him . . . it would mean he was always there. I'd tried so hard to forget, it seemed pointless to rake it up again . . . until tonight, when I had no choice.'

'I won't mention it again.' Ben climbed under the covers. As if they were sitting on their sofa at home, Daisy automatically passed him the remote control. 'There's just one thing bothering me, though,' he went on, 'and I need you to tell me, then that'll be the end of it. If Greg treated you so badly – and no one could blame you if it put you off relationships for life – what was it about me, about *us*, that made you feel differently?'

'Greg was a long time ago,' Daisy answered at last, 'and you're nothing like him. I suppose I found it easy to trust you. That was the hardest part about having a boyfriend after Greg – the lack of trust. I kept expecting it to happen again.'

'But I was different?' murmured Ben, staring ahead at the TV screen.

'You made me feel good about myself. How you looked at me – it wasn't just sexual.'

Her husband was quiet, still staring ahead – one of those introspective moments that had grown to trouble her.

'I only ever wanted to make you happy,' he said finally, his voice guttural.

'I know.' Daisy patted his hand as she slid under the covers. Suddenly she felt too worn out even to use the bathroom; yet in spite of her exhaustion, her mind was so fired up that she couldn't relax, and her heart was banging away in her chest as if she'd had half a dozen cups of coffee.

It was Ben who fell asleep first, and it was Daisy who had to reach over and gingerly prise the remote control out of his hand to switch off the TV.

21

This was only the second hen night Daisy had been on. The first had been a few years ago, which she'd helped organise for one of the barmaids she'd worked with. The pattern followed then was pretty much the same as the one now. The women met up in a trendy bar, limbered up with a few drinks, whereupon the paraphernalia that seemed to accompany these occasions made their appearance.

Geri's two old school friends, Heather and Jane, had made her a sash decorated with an L-plate; a veil spangled with stars and glittery hearts; and for a tiara, they produced an Alice band with two antennae-like springs attached, fluffy pink pompoms bobbing about at the tips.

One of Daisy's earliest memories was of some girls in a playground wearing similar headgear. There had been a huge craze for them, apparently, but Daisy had been too young to have a pair. The majority of the other women now assembled in the bar sounded as if they remembered them well, which just went to prove the difference five or six years could make.

Geri's humiliation seemed tempered by the Long Island iced teas she'd already downed. 'What do I look like?' she cackled, winking at Daisy, who was feeling hungry and wishing they would get a move on and proceed to the next stop on their itinerary – the restaurant a few doors away.

'Don't worry,' laughed Heather, whipping out another pair of antennae from her carrier bag. 'The rest of us aren't going to let you suffer on your own.'

Daisy gulped down her vodka and lemonade. Oh drat. It appeared that they were all going to parade around Chester like aliens who hadn't quite mastered the guise of looking human.

Each pair of pompoms was a different colour. Daisy ended up with the red set, which at least complemented her lipstick and scarlet dress. Smugly, she observed that Stella and Alice weren't happy with their green and blue ones. Vivienne, on the other hand, was trying her best to look at ease in her silver pair, which Daisy thought quite flattered her. Next out of the carrier bag came some fluffy pink handcuffs, but auspiciously there was only one set and they were meant for the bride-to-be. She dangled them from her wrist, and threatened to try them out on Declan.

'I hope the boys are treating him kindly,' she sighed, wiping a tear of mirth from her eye.

'Don't worry. Ben will take care of him,' Stella assured her, 'he won't let things get out of hand.'

Daisy frowned. That ought to have been her line.

'I know, you're right.' Geri sighed, and flicked at her veil. 'Well, the truth is, girls, that I'm starting to feel peckish, and that always stresses me out. I suggest we go get some grub.'

Daisy seconded the motion. 'We don't want to be late. We might lose the table.'

'No chance of that,' said Heather, 'Geri's chummy with the management.'

The restaurant, which Geri had organised herself because she and Declan were acquainted with the manager, special-ised in Italian cuisine, although it was far less exclu-sive than Antonio's. The décor was rustic yet chic, the atmosphere informal. A couple of square tables had been joined together to make one large rectangular one, and as everyone scrambled to sit down, Daisy found herself sandwiched between Vivienne and Stella.

She sighed. She could happily have stayed in on her own with some popcorn and a DVD. She wondered if Vivienne would have preferred not to come either, but had made the effort for the same reason as Daisy – neither of them wanted to let Geri down.

'Howard doesn't really approve of this hen night busi-ness,' Vivienne confided in Daisy, after everyone had placed their food orders. 'He thinks I'm demeaning myself. "Married women shouldn't go out with single women," if you forgive the ambiguity. The poor man didn't know why I found that funny.' Vivienne sighed, adjusting her pompoms. 'He said that if Celeste – Geri's mother – wasn't prepared to make a spectacle of herself, why should I? I told him that Celeste was over fifty, and reminded him that I wasn't.'

'Somehow,' said Daisy, 'I don't think Geri would be letting her hair down quite as freely if she knew her mum was watching.'

Vivienne smirked, looking younger than ever. 'Mind you, I intend to let my own hair down, so I'm glad Celeste didn't make the trip up here to come out tonight, or she'd report straight back to Howard.'

Stella suddenly turned to Daisy and gave her a dazzling smile, which immediately put Daisy on the defensive. 'I hope I don't sound patronising,' she began, sounding anything but. 'And I don't suppose I'm meant to tell you this, but Ben made me promise to keep my eye on you. Sweet of him, I thought. He probably got Vivienne to promise, too, didn't he?' Stella popped an olive in her mouth. Daisy wished it was a cork.

'I wouldn't put it like that.' Vivienne frowned and sipped her wine. 'He asked me to make sure she had a good time, that's all.'

Daisy felt as if she wasn't there, sitting right between them.

'Of course. I'm sorry if I implied anything else,' Stella went on assuagingly, looking directly at Daisy again. 'Ben just meant that he wanted you to enjoy yourself, so I'm going to make sure that you do. Starting with the wine. Come on, drink up!'

'Give me a chance,' Daisy spluttered, as Stella thrust the Frascati towards her. 'It's only just been poured.'

But as the evening wore on, the wine flowed copiously round the table, and Daisy was feeling agreeably mellow by the time they headed for the club. She was still hoping that a stripper wasn't on the cards, though. Geri had confessed to her privately that she would die of shame if a man in a G-string so much as came near her, let alone asked her to massage his buttocks with baby oil. But it was no good pleading with Heather or Jane not to book one; they would simply ignore her and go ahead and do it anyway.

As the group joined the queue outside the nightclub, Stella – who seemed the worst for wear out of the lot of them and had linked arms with Alice – decided to loop her arm through Daisy's, too.

'I'm glad we're friends now,' she blurted out passionately, with a slight slur.

Daisy frowned, and glanced at Vivienne and Geri, who

were ahead of them in the line, in front of Heather and Jane. Strange how she would have preferred to stay close to her stepmother-in-law, when not so long ago, given the choice, she would have made haste in the opposite direction.

'Mmm,' she said non-committally.

'And I'm glad you married Ben,' Stella slurred again, as they moved forwards a few paces.

This surprised Daisy even more, considering that she had always believed in *in vino veritas*.

'When you first came to Nettlesford,' Stella continued, 'I've got to admit, I thought you were pregnant. I was convinced that was why Ben had married you so quickly.'

'So did I,' piped up Alice sheepishly.

This was nothing new. Daisy gritted her teeth, but tried to sound forgiving when she finally replied, 'It was an easy assumption to have made, given the circumstances.'

'Good. I mean, I'm glad you understand.' Stella nodded, her blonde hair swishing symmetrically on either side of her head.

In front of them, Geri and Vivienne were batting their eyelashes at the bouncers, the neon sign flashing like an artificial rainbow above their heads as they passed through the wide, smoked-glass doors.

'I know Ben's crazy about you and all that,' said Stella, 'but I appreciate now why you couldn't really take your time over getting married. You wouldn't have needed to rush if it hadn't been for that stupid business with the Gatehouse. It seems such a shame that you missed out on a decent wedding, just because Ben's aunt was barking.'

The words struck like a hammer-blow at the very moment Daisy was smiling and fluttering her eyelashes at the doormen herself.

'Enjoy yourself, love.' The taller of the bouncers winked at her.

Daisy glanced at him vacuously, then turned back to Stella, who had reclaimed both her arms, possibly in case the doormen thought she couldn't stand up by herself and refused her entry. 'What are you saying?'

'Paying?' Stella blinked. 'What am I paying? I think admission's free before ten thirty. What's the time now?' She fumbled up her chiffon sleeve for her watch.

Daisy could already hear music pulsating from the nether regions of the club. But surely it wasn't loud enough for Stella to have misheard? Or was she being obtuse on purpose? Perhaps she was just too drunk to remember what she was saying from one moment to the next.

The evening was warm. Neither Daisy, Stella nor Alice had a jacket to leave at the cloakroom. They negotiated the wide steps that circled downwards and found themselves in a basement room that seemed far too small for the crush of bodies already present. As if she had a homing device implanted in her brain, Stella led the way to the bar.

Daisy's mind was whirling. She wondered if Ben was somewhere similar in Manchester, pining for her among the cloying haze of booze, aftershave and perfume, not to mention stale sweat. A dull ache of longing stirred inside her, but it was rapidly chased away by curiosity and an obsessive desire to know what Stella had been referring to.

Alice was standing closest to her at the bar. Daisy spoke as loud as she dared over the music. 'Do you know what Stella was talking about?'

Alice didn't look her in the eye. 'When?'

'When she mentioned Ben's aunt, and why Ben and I had to get married in a hurry.'

'I'm – I'm not really sure. Stella wouldn't actually say how she found out.'

'Found out what?'

'I don't know how much of it's true . . . It seems ridiculous to me, but then apparently Ben's aunt wasn't all there. That doesn't make sense to me either, though, because I didn't think a will was valid if the person who wrote it was certifiable, or near enough.'

'Can't you just tell me what you *do* know?'

'Nothing . . . Well, just that Ben could only inherit the Gatehouse once he was married. It wasn't legally his until he could produce the marriage certificate.'

Daisy's blood seemed to run hot then cold.

'Look,' Alice went on, 'there's no use interrogating me. If anyone here knows the full story, it'll be Vivienne, won't it?'

Daisy scanned the crowd in search of her stepmother-in-law. She spotted Geri instead, her veil glittering under the strobe lights on the dance floor. In slow motion, Daisy forged her way over, her movements jerky, almost robotic.

She reached the bride-to-be and raised her voice in competition with the latest dance hit. 'Where's Vivienne?'

'Sorry?' Geri cupped a hand round her ear.

'*Vivienne.* Where is she?'

'Oh. The Ladies', I think. Are you OK?'

Daisy nodded vaguely, and began pushing her way back towards the main entrance and exit. The ladies' toilets were halfway up the stairs, leading off from a broad, carpeted landing. There was a queue outside the door already, but Daisy fought her way in, attracting menacing glances.

'I'm looking for someone,' she muttered, hardly caring if anyone believed her.

To the right were the basins and hand-dryers, with the toilet cubicles beyond; to the left were a couple of marble-topped counters with large mirrors at eye level and white globe lights dotted round the frames. It reminded Daisy of a backstage dressing room. Vivienne must feel right at home. Daisy spotted her retouching her make-up, her handbag open in front of her to reveal lipstick, mascara, a compact and eyeliner – all by Chanel. Noticing Daisy in the mirror, she smiled. Then something must have registered – probably the look on Daisy's face – and she turned round.

'Is it true?' Daisy asked, before Vivienne had a chance to speak. 'About Ben not inheriting the Gatehouse until he was married?'

'Sorry?' Vivienne stared at her blankly for a moment. 'Who told you that?'

'Stella. Well, she implied something, but then I couldn't get much sense out of her, so I asked Alice.'

'I . . . I didn't think Ben had confided in his friends. His father advised him not to, although I thought that was making it into more of a drama than it already was.'

'So it is true?'

'More or less. But I don't think this is the place to discuss it.'

Daisy ignored her. 'I want to know the truth, and I want to know it now.' That sounded so lame, she instantly felt worse.

Vivienne clicked her bag shut. Taking Daisy's arm, she guided her out of the Ladies', to the obvious disappointment of the women who had already tuned to listen in. She steered her to one side, as far from the queue as possible.

'Daisy, look, firstly you have to remind yourself that

Ben loves you. I seriously doubt that what I'm about to tell you clouded his judgement in any way.'

'Go on,' Daisy insisted, with a shiver. Her spine already seemed to be chiselled out of ice.

'His aunt Eleanor was a hopeless romantic, in spite of her unmarried state, or maybe because of it, I don't know. I never knew her, but from what Howard told me, she was as sharp as a pin, even if she didn't always act it. If you want to put it in legal terms, she was of sound mind, even if the will was hardly conventional. I think Howard was just relieved that she didn't want to leave all her worldly possessions to an animal shelter, even though she left a modest amount to a local hospice.'

'You're sidetracking,' frowned Daisy.

'I'm just trying to give you all the facts. Eleanor Greenwood's main asset was the Gatehouse, and, as you know, she left it to Ben. But there was a stipulation. It would be held in trust, and he couldn't live there, or do anything with it, until he was married. I suppose, if he'd found himself a wife while his aunt was still alive, the will would have been changed somehow . . . But that's just speculating. We'll never know. Ben was only young when it was written.'

In spite of Vivienne corroborating what Alice had said, Daisy looked at her incredulously. 'It's all madness . . .'

'I don't think it would have sounded strange if it were a hundred years ago. I'm sure that all Eleanor wanted was for Ben to be happy. Maybe she didn't go about it in an orthodox way, but why change the habit of a lifetime? If you ask me, it showed she had faith in him as a person. And I don't think Ben let her down. After all, he could have married Geri when he had the chance, but he didn't. He chose to wait for the right girl.'

'It's just bricks and mortar, though, isn't it?' Daisy was

trying to rationalise the revelation, to somehow make it less significant. 'Or stones and mortar, at any rate. And it's not as if it's a mansion. Some might say it's smaller than some of those little terraced houses you see. It can't be worth that much.'

'The historical value alone . . .' Vivienne seemed to stall.

'What?' Daisy masochistically pressed her to continue.

'It's a listed building, and although there isn't much land involved, it's on the edge of the Greenacres estate. It used to be part of the estate, with no defining boundaries, until Eleanor had it signed over to her by her parents. I think it was meant to be a gift from them, perhaps to smooth over the fact that she'd reached thirty without attracting a "suitor", but Howard put it all down in writing. Convenient having a solicitor in the family.'

'So basically, what you're saying is that the Gatehouse is worth more than it looks.'

'I don't think its value is the issue here. Just think about it, Daisy. If Ben was in this for mercenary reasons, don't you think he would have been trying to sell it already? He's more or less handed it over to you. He's given you a home, and if you want my honest opinion, I think that's something you've never really had before.'

Daisy stood reeling, irritated by the other woman for being that astute and for spelling it out. 'Why didn't Ben tell me, though?' She focused on the pattern in the short-pile carpet, frowning so intensely her brow ached.

Vivienne sighed. 'I know it doesn't do him any credit, but he probably kept it from you because it made the situation surrounding your marriage seem incriminating.'

'Oh, so he just told everyone else, and now they're all laughing about it behind my back!'

'I'm sure it isn't like that . . .'

Daisy clutched her small beaded bag tighter. She had to get out of here. Her mind felt as if it were stuffed with Brillo pads. Every thought struggling to make its presence felt was painful and abrasive. 'Will you tell Geri I'm sorry . . .'

'You aren't leaving?' Vivienne's face was pale and drawn. The newly applied make-up was too much of a contrast; it made her look like an anxious china doll.

'I can't stay. I just want to—' About to say 'go home', Daisy realised that returning to the Gatehouse would only add to her disoriented state.

'I'll come with you,' said Vivienne.

'No!' Daisy stepped back. 'I need to be on my own. I'll get a taxi. Just apologise to Geri for me. Tell her I've got a migraine. *Anything.*'

Vivienne seemed to waver, torn between respecting Daisy's wishes and forcibly accompanying her wherever she was going. Daisy didn't hang around. She hurried up the last flight of stairs to the foyer, ignoring the doormen's appreciative glances as she brushed past them into the street.

22

'If I could have picked you up, I would have, but I've
been drinking . . .'

Daisy shrugged in reply as she stepped over the thresh-
old. 'There was no need. I got a taxi.'

'You were lucky to get hold of me at all. Almost didn't
hear my mobile ringing above the racket at the Headless
Horseman.'

'I know. You said. It was just funny . . . I knew you lived
on this estate – I've even delivered sacks round here for the
charity shop – but I didn't know your exact address.'

'I suppose you had no reason to. I never got around to
inviting you and Ben over for dinner.'

Jerome looked jumpy as he ushered Daisy out of his
cramped little porch into the lounge. It appeared that he'd
started tidying up in a hurry and wasn't quite done. He
whipped some magazines and his briefcase off the sofa
and motioned for Daisy to sit down. She was aware of
the split in her dress as she did so. It was the first time
she'd been bothered by it all evening.

Jerome appraised her in one swift glance. 'You're looking very elegant.'

'Geri's hen night.'

'So you told me. Is that dress new?'

She pictured herself the first time she'd worn it, in a
changing room at Browns of Chester. Ben had persuaded

her to try it on, even though she'd raised her eyebrows at the price. Yet she had been won over the instant she'd zipped it up and turned to face the mirror. It was a perfect fit, the shape accentuating her figure more flatteringly than anything she could remember wearing, apart from the bridesmaid gown. Although there was something retro about the plunging V-neck and floaty cup sleeves, that only made it more fashionable.

'Ben bought it for me,' she said tonelessly. 'It was meant to be a treat.'

'Oh? Was he trying to cheer you up, or was he just being nice for no particular reason?'

'I think he was feeling guilty about agreeing to go on Declan's stag do.' As Daisy spoke, she wondered if Ben lived in a perpetual state of guilt, able to hide it adequately enough while he was with her. Her stomach knotted with bitterness. 'I've just found out my marriage is a sham,' she said, still in that same toneless voice.

Jerome, who was perched on an armchair, leaned closer. His face crumpled as if he was hard of hearing and hadn't made out what she'd said. 'Sorry?'

'I found out something tonight. Something that seemed common knowledge to most people, but not to me . . .' She explained what had happened in the nightclub, ending acerbically, 'So how does that make me look – the fact that I didn't know?'

Jerome stood up, passed under an archway into the dining room and went over to the sideboard. He took out two small glasses and a bottle of tequila, then returned to the lounge and poured a couple of shots.

'I've salt, but no lemon.' He slid one of the square, thick-bottomed glasses across the coffee table towards her.

'It doesn't matter. This'll do.' And she knocked it back, coughing as she held out the glass for a refill.

'Are you sure?'

She nodded. It would dull the pain, topping up the wine, and the vodka and lemonade, she'd drunk earlier.

'I don't think you should be so hard on yourself,' Jerome said, after he'd downed a second tequila himself. 'The fact that you weren't aware of the clause in Eleanor Greenwood's will makes you an innocent party.'

Something in his words, and the way he spoke, triggered another cold surge of suspicion. 'Jerome . . . did you know about the will?'

'I'm a partner in the firm. The Kavanaghs made me part of their lives. It was hard to conceal anything . . .'

'But you didn't tell me.' Daisy was besieged by a whole new set of questions.

'No. At first, I assumed Ben had explained it all to you. I didn't bring up the subject, but as I got to know you, I realised that you didn't have any idea about it.'

'But if you'd told me—'

'It might have changed things between us, and between you and Ben?' Jerome shrugged. 'Maybe. But whatever you think, I'm not that kind of person. You know how I feel about you, Daisy, but basically what that means is that I'd never do anything to hurt you, not deliberately. Telling you about Ben and the Gatehouse, whether it was deliberate or not—'

'I'm more furious than anything.'

'Are you? The thing is, if you didn't marry Ben because you were pregnant, or because of the Gatehouse, or for anything else you might have been accused of at the time, then you married him for the best, most simple reason of all.'

Jerome was so articulate and polished. His house didn't fit in with the image Daisy had of him. She glanced round, trying to breathe slowly and come to terms with what he was saying. She had imagined him in a bachelor-like divorcee pad, decked out in calming, contemporary classics. Not this sloppy mishmash of MDF and saggy eighties' three-piece suite. The house, possibly three-bed judging by the size of the downstairs, was on the small, relatively new estate on the northern fringe of Nettlesford. The original magnolia walls hadn't been touched. They looked powdery and matt, and the settlement cracks had been left unfilled. Venetian blinds hung from the window as a testament to the current trend, but in such a bland space the lack of curtains, cushions or rugs made the lounge cold and uninviting.

With a sigh, Jerome glanced round, too, as if seeing his home through Daisy's eyes. 'This place is a time warp, I know. When my wife and I split up, she bought replacement furniture, courtesy of her new partner. I stayed with all the old stuff. I haven't had much inclination to replace anything, even when I moved to Nettlesford.'

'Did you keep all the furniture because it reminded you of her?'

'Maybe at first, in some perverse way. Not any more, though. Like I said, I can't be bothered to do anything about it. The whole house needs a woman's touch, really.'

Daisy stared at the coffee table. For the first time, she wondered what legal right she would have to the Gatehouse if she and Ben split up. None whatsoever, probably. Would Ben even get to keep it? Maybe there was another clause stating that his ownership could be revoked if his marriage broke up within a year, or even five. Oh, God, help. She was so naive about this sort of thing. The law had always seemed so convoluted, and it was even more so now.

'Can I have another drink, please?' She slid her glass towards the bottle of tequila.

'Wouldn't you rather have a coffee?'

'Don't patronise me. And anyway, you were the one who got the alcohol out.'

'I know . . . My fault.' He poured them both another shot.

The warmth spread through her stomach. It reminded her of sunbathing on a blisteringly hot day, which had the immediate effect of transporting her mentally and emotionally to the last time she had seen Jerome.

He had said that he loved her, and that an affair wouldn't be enough. His words filtered back to her. Each one seemed to stand alone and make her pulse race. Why had she come here? Had she been looking for comfort from a friend – or something more?

As if they were on the same wavelength, Jerome asked, 'Did you come here to get back at Ben? You said that you were angry—'

'So I'm using you as some sort of revenge?'

'You're asking as if you're not sure yourself.' He smiled thinly. 'I'm not blaming you. We all say and do things we regret when we're not thinking straight. I've a feeling that you would have gone back home if Ben was going to be there. You need to thrash this out with him, and one of the reasons you're angry is because you can't.'

Daisy frowned in concentration, desperate to focus her thoughts. Seeking out Jerome had been instinctive, a knee-jerk reaction. She felt caught up in a nightmare. Apart from a few rare moments of insecurity, she had always been so certain of Ben's affection for her. She had made herself vulnerable from early on in their relationship, letting herself fall; and with what she had taken for passion and integrity, he had caught her. But now she felt as if she were falling again, for an entirely different reason. This time, it was as if he had let go of her.

'I'm sorry,' said Jerome, 'but there's something I've been dying to do since you got here . . .' He stood up and loomed over her. Daisy caught her breath, her heart hammering. The next instant, she was aware of a pulling sensation as her hair was snagged. 'Shit,' he mumbled, 'I'm sorry. It's tangled. Wait. Keep still . . .'

With a sinking feeling, Daisy remembered the scarlet pompoms. A moment later, Jerome stood examining them in his hand, shaking his head in bemusement.

'I'd forgotten I was wearing them,' mumbled Daisy. 'They're so light . . .'

'It could have been worse. The last time I was in Chester, there was a hen night where all the ladies were kitted out as French maids. I think you had a lucky escape with these.' He sat down next to her, and handed them back.

Daisy could feel her face hotting up. 'Now I know why the taxi driver was giving me weird looks. You sod, Jerome, why didn't you tell me sooner?'

'I was waiting for the right moment to break it to you gently.'

She lunged out to thump him amiably, but he intercepted her hand, catching it in his. The features of his face seemed to grow fuzzy, as if Daisy was suddenly seeing him through a soft focus lens.

'Having you here,' he said, 'in my house like this . . . I'm starting to think that any time spent with you would be better than nothing.' He tilted her face until it was level with his own. 'Daisy, I know how you feel about Ben . . .'

'How can you? I'm not sure myself right this minute.'

'If you didn't care, you wouldn't be hurting so much.'

She shrugged despairingly. 'I trusted him . . . but that isn't the same as love. I let myself depend on him, because of everything he was offering me, but what if I mistook gratitude for something else? What if I *wanted* to love him, and made myself believe I actually did?'

'Is that what you really think?'

'I told you, I don't know . . . All I do know is that I've been more and more miserable these last few weeks. Ben's happy here in Nettlesford, but I don't think I ever could be. So what sort of a future do we have? I can't ask him to leave, and I don't even know where we'd go.'

'What about this work you've been doing for the charity shop; hasn't that helped? Ben mentioned something about it in the office one day, and you said something just before about delivering sacks. Is that all you have to do?'

'That's just part of it. I help sort out the stuff that people don't want, that kind of thing. But working there hasn't helped as much as I'd hoped. I still feel as if I'm treading water, but I don't know why, or what I'm waiting for. Everything to do with Greenacres is like a giant claustrophobic shadow hanging over me.' She sniffed, and rubbed her eyes. 'I probably sound completely doolally.'

'No. You don't. The Kavanaghs aren't the easiest of people to get along with, and neither were the Greenwoods before them, as far as I can make out. It's not a crime to feel depressed.' He hesitated. 'But I swear, if I knew how to make you happy . . .' Daisy didn't flinch as his lips brushed against hers. It was a kiss, soft and warm, nothing more.

Jerome pulled away, studying her cautiously. 'I'm sorry.'

'What for?'

He swooped again, but now his lips parted and the tip of his tongue darted through, like a tiny persistent flame. Daisy felt the scarlet pompoms drop to the floor as her arms slid round him. Desire stirred, rippling in every direction until her entire body was gripped by it.

The kiss went on, growing more heated. Jerome's hand found its way to her breast, kneading gently, and his lips left her mouth and trailed down her throat. As his fingers tugged at the neckline of her bodice, his tongue followed their progress. Daisy slumped back, sinking into the sofa. A moan swelled in her throat as Jerome pushed up the folds of her dress, exposing her thighs, but when nothing more seemed to happen, she opened her eyes.

Jerome was staring at her. 'I don't want it to be like this.' He sounded different, as if his voice was coming from deeper in his throat. 'I don't want to rush it.'

Daisy gazed at him mutely as he stood up and held out his hand. She took it, and rose to her own feet, swaying in front of him.

'I've waited too long.' Jerome led her across the room. 'I want it to be exactly how I imagined it, those nights I was on my own . . .'

But at the foot of the stairs, Daisy froze. She literally couldn't go further, as if there was an invisible wall in front of her, penetrable to Jerome, but not to her. He was so beautiful tonight, in a Greek god-like way, and she believed in him, in everything he had said, but now that their impetuous foreplay had been suspended, a flash of clarity was forcing her to realise that she believed in something else more.

'I can't,' she murmured, shaking her head. 'I can't do this.'

Jerome hesitated, then stepped back down to her level. 'Why not?'

'When you imagined us together, did you ever see me acting out of vindictiveness? Was sex between us ever just pain relief on my part?' She groaned. 'I'm sorry. You don't deserve this, Jerome. For a few minutes back there, it all seemed to make sense. Maybe that was why I went along with it.'

He regarded her for a long moment. 'I was fooling myself again . . . wasn't I?' Daisy suddenly wondered if he would tell her that he didn't care what her reasons were, or what happened afterwards, but instead he asked solemnly, 'Would you still consider it adultery?'

Slowly, agonisingly, she nodded. 'I'm still married.'

'You make it sound as if it could be over.'

'Even if I were able to see into the future, I might not be able to work out what I really want. Maybe that's my biggest problem. I might never feel satisfied or . . . complete. But I can't wish away the fact that I *am* married, not even for a few minutes, not even for you.'

'So you're backing out on a technicality?'

Daisy paused, blinking beneath the white glow of the energy-saving light bulb, hanging above their heads in a chipped glass pendant. Visual details trickled into her brain again. The heavily doodled-on jotter on the telephone stand. The graduation photograph of Jerome above the television. He looked so young, proudly holding his diploma, or whatever that scroll-like thing was called, standing shoulder to shoulder with another fresh-faced graduate.

'Who's that with you?' Daisy asked, her diversionary

tactics shrewd, honed by years of practice, even though her curiosity this time was genuine.

Jerome frowned. 'My best mate at university.'

'He looks nice.'

'He was killed in a motorbike accident, a couple of years after that picture was taken.'

Daisy bit her lip. 'I'm sorry.'

Jerome shrugged. 'Like a lot of things, it's in the past. Someone's got to remember him, though. He didn't have much family.'

At a loss for what to say, Daisy drifted over to the sofa and opened her handbag, checking how much money was left in her purse. Enough for another taxi. She glanced back at Jerome. He was still by the foot of the stairs, looking wrapped in thought. There was so much about him that she didn't know and probably never would. Even the seemingly trivial things made up the tapestry of a relationship.

Right now, realised Daisy, in spite of everything that had happened, there were far more tiny, tenuous threads linking her to her husband than the man whose lounge she was standing in. However much Jerome might profess that he loved her, the fact that she would never have put him down as someone who doodled while he was on the phone – however silly and inconsequential that seemed – only served to strengthen her resolve that nothing more was going to happen between them tonight.

'You're leaving?' Jerome asked, as if coming out of a trance.

'You were right,' said Daisy, 'I was using you . . .'

'Do you feel better?'

'Calmer, I think.'

'That's a start.'

She shook her head disbelievingly. 'How can you say that when I've been a complete bitch to you?'

'I'm not about to start begging. After the proverbial cold shower, and a night's sleep, I'll be fine tomorrow. As fine as I was before you rang me tonight. "Getting by" I think they call it.' He picked up his phone. 'I know a good taxi firm. They're normally reliable.'

She frowned. 'Maybe I should walk . . .'

'It's too late and too far, and I'd be obliged to walk with you.' He punched out a number. His call was taken almost instantly. 'About ten minutes,' he told Daisy, putting the phone back on the hook.

'Right.' What was she supposed to say or do now? An uneasy atmosphere had developed.

'Time for a coffee,' said Jerome briskly, heading for the kitchen. 'Milk and sugar?'

'Er, just milk.'

'Keep a look out for the cab, in case it comes early.'

When Jerome returned, Daisy was hovering by the window, peering through a gap she'd made in the blinds. He handed her a mug.

'I put in a touch of cold water,' he said, 'to make it drinkable.'

'Thanks.' She took a welcome sip.

'The night feels cooler now. You don't have a coat, do you?'

'No, it was so warm before. Besides, you always seem to queue up forever in a club to get it back from the cloakroom.'

Jerome disappeared into the porch. He returned with his denim jacket. 'Here, borrow this. I don't think it'll swamp you too much.'

'Oh. It doesn't matter—'

'It does. You'll catch your death in that dress.'

Daisy acquiesced, feeling humbled and grateful. Jerome was magnanimous, even when dealing with rejection.

'And, Daisy, you're not a bitch,' he added matter-of-factly. 'I know better than to have got involved with another one of those.'

23

At this time of night, the drive back from Manchester would probably take less than an hour. After the call from Vivienne, Ben had drawn Declan aside and, to keep the explanation simple, told him that Daisy wasn't well.

'Too much to drink? Well, you know what these hen nights can be like.' Declan had chuckled, but in spite of the alcohol he'd already consumed himself, the look on Ben's face must have made him realise it was serious. 'So, you want to head back to Nettlesford then? Is that what you're saying?'

Ben had nodded. 'I feel bad about letting you down . . .'

'Come on, mate, some things are more important. And I've enough company to see me through the night. Now the least I can do is pay for your taxi back. Now, no arguing. I insist. I dragged you all the way over here, so I ought to be the one to see that you get home. I'll drop off your bag tomorrow, or have Geri get it back to you at some point. There's nothing in it that you need urgently?'

It was still in the boot of Declan's Audi, but Ben hadn't been desperate for it.

The stag party had met up at a pub by Piccadilly Station, having travelled to Manchester from various parts of the country. Declan had given Ben and a couple of other friends a lift into the city. His best man had organised a smart hotel in the centre, which meant that the group wouldn't have to stagger too far to reach the sanctuary of their beds after the pubs and clubs shut. Ben had been in two minds about leaving Daisy on her own all night, but she'd reminded him that she would be late home anyway.

'I'm getting a lift back with Geri and Vivienne. Don't fuss so much.' She'd tossed her head loftily. 'I'm sure I can manage without you for one weekend. After all, I'd been doing it for twenty-four years before we actually met.'

Hearing Vivienne's concerned voice crackling out from his mobile had made Ben's blood turn to ice. She'd been uncertain whether to ring him, but he was glad that she had.

'You did the right thing,' he'd assured her. 'Don't worry, I'll get home as soon as I can and sort it all out.'

But now, sitting in the back of the cab rattling down the M56, he wasn't feeling very confident. He knew he ought to have told Daisy the full story behind his aunt's will, but when would have been the right time? When they were first going out? Somehow, he had known that he would want to marry her sooner rather than later. The chances of her learning the truth about the Gatehouse and still saying yes to his proposal had been minimal. She was too principled for that, and he wouldn't have blamed her for misinterpreting his own motives. No, there was no easy way to have told her before the wedding. And afterwards . . . ?

He had put it off, agonising even more over how she would take it. She would look at him differently. How could she not, knowing that he had kept something on this scale from her?

He felt as if he had been cornered – as had his mother

and aunt and possibly generations before them – by some strange sort of Greenacres' curse. Or was there a rogue Greenwood gene which meant that anyone who inherited it would end up tormenting members of their own family, even if that was the last thing they intended?

At first, Ben had regarded the clause in his aunt's will as one of her many vagaries. Once the pain of her death, and of his mother's, had eased a fraction, he had even viewed the matter of his inheritance with faint amusement. At that stage of his life, he hadn't given it much thought, not seriously. He had doubted he'd actually want to live at the Gatehouse, anyway, although he couldn't imagine wanting to sell it either. Escaping Nettlesford had been in his mind even then. Perhaps his mother's death had triggered it.

Leaving for London two and a half years ago had made the issue fade even further into the back of his mind. It was only as he had found himself wondering if it was time to return to his roots, and then had actually begun planning his homecoming, that he'd given it the consideration it was due. Meeting Daisy had brought it all rushing to the fore. Inheriting a house this way suddenly seemed archaic and absurd. And so Ben had stored up trouble for later, convinced that he had no choice, riskily relying on the few people who knew about the will not to bring up the subject in front of his wife.

It was eleven forty-five when he arrived at the Gatehouse. The only light visible was the small Cornish pottery lamp in the front window, controlled by a timer switch. Ben watched the taxi vanish round the tall hedgerow, then unlocked the door and went inside.

There was no one downstairs. Ben stood glancing round. Perhaps Daisy was already upstairs in bed. That might explain why her mobile was going straight to voice mail and their home line was diverting to the 1571 answering service. He'd been trying to get through to her all the way back from Manchester. Of course, he hadn't been expecting her to be waiting for him with open arms, but the fact that she might already be asleep was somehow more disturbing. He didn't want to wait until morning to discuss this with her. He needed to do it now, while he was feeling reasonably brave, and while his explanations still seemed coherent and believable.

But Daisy wasn't in bed, asleep or otherwise. Frowning, Ben came slowly down the stairs again. There was no sign of her. It was as if she hadn't come back to the Gatehouse after leaving the nightclub. And if that was the case, then where had she gone? Had something happened to her?

His anxiety mounting, he rang his stepmother's mobile, but that went straight to voice mail too. Perhaps Vivienne had rung earlier from outside the club, and then been asked to switch off the phone before going back inside. Some clubs were like that. Damn.

Ben tried his father next. Eventually Howard answered. 'Yes?' he barked, his gruffness implying that he'd been asleep.

'Dad, it's me.'

'Benjamin? Do you know what the bloody time is?'

'Is Daisy there? Has she been round there tonight?'

'Daisy? What are you talking about? She's with Vivienne at that bloody hen thingy.'

'She left early, and I don't know where she's gone. She's not here at home.'

'Hang on a minute. Aren't you supposed to be in Manchester?'

'I was. Vivienne rang and—' He couldn't be bothered to

explain now. 'Never mind, she'll tell you about it herself. I've got to go. If you hear from Daisy, just let me know.' And Ben hung up, gazing bleakly round the lounge.

At twenty-five minutes past midnight, Daisy unlatched the rickety garden gate and rummaged in her bag for her keys. But before she could unlock the front door, it swung open, making her jump in fright. She felt herself blanch as she stared up at an equally pale-faced Ben.

'Wh – what are you doing here?' she demanded hoarsely.

'I was worried about you. Vivienne called me. She told me what happened.'

'How – how did you get home?'

'By taxi, the same way as you.' He gestured to the cab she'd arrived in, the tail-lights retreating down the drive. Then he stepped back, leaving Daisy room to enter.

She did so shakily, staring at him as he locked the door. He slid the bolt at the top, just as he always did at night before they went to bed.

'The way Vivienne was talking,' Ben went on, 'she made me imagine the worst.'

'Which was?'

'That you were on the warpath.'

Daisy shrugged. The denim jacket, which had been so welcome a few moments ago, now seemed to be burning her skin. 'I'm sure you've got a reasonable explanation . . .'

'Have *you*, though?'

'Have I what?'

He was regarding her oddly. His relief at seeing her seemed to have abated already. 'Have you got a reasonable explanation for why you've been missing for the last couple of hours and why you're wearing Jerome's jacket?'

Daisy stared at him, feeling sick. It struck her that he might only be bluffing about recognising the jacket. After all, it was plain denim, with no obvious distinguishing features. On the other hand, he would know it wasn't hers either.

She had already come to the decision that she would tell him the truth about going to Jerome's tonight. He was hardly catching her out. But she hadn't expected to be confessing quite so soon.

When she'd pictured herself telling him, it had been Sunday afternoon – an hour or two after Declan had dropped him back home and he'd had a chance to relax and get comfortable. Hopefully she would have managed to get some sleep the night before, and she would have had time on her own to reflect on everything that had happened. Jerome's jacket would also have been safely stowed away.

As it was, in spite of the caffeine boost, she felt emotionally raw and physically exhausted. At least the strong coffee had taken away the taste of Jerome's kisses, but she could still smell him – that hint of sandalwood he always wore. Was the residue of the scent strong enough for Ben to detect, too?

'I haven't been "missing",' she said quietly. 'If I'd known you were on your way home, I would have come home myself to have it out with you. Vivienne was right – I *was* upset. After leaving the club, I couldn't face coming back here to an empty house—'

'So you went to Jerome's.' Ben finished the sentence for her, then added, 'Have you been there before?'

'No.'

'Then how did you know where to go?'

'He's my friend, Ben.'

'So you keep saying.'

'It wouldn't be unusual for me to have a vague idea of where he lives. Anyway, I phoned him first. He was at the Headless Horseman.'

'That's a surprise. So why didn't you just arrange to meet him there?'

Daisy felt a resurgence of bitterness at Ben's inquisition. What had changed to put him back in the driving seat? Her own sense of guilt? The fact of the matter was, he had kept an important truth from her, and she was still just as anxious and afraid to hear why.

'I'd already left one crowded bar behind,' she rationalised. 'I didn't feel like walking straight into another. Not in the mood I was in.'

'So what happened when you got to Jerome's?'

Daisy slipped off the jacket and tossed it on to the sofa. 'Why don't you tell me, Ben, seeing as you already seem to have an idea.'

This clearly threw him. He stood glaring at her. 'You do know that he fancies you? You're not so naive that you haven't noticed?'

'Actually,' hissed Daisy, her acrimony fully stoked again, 'to be perfectly precise – he's in love with me.'

Ben looked as if she'd slapped him. His eyes darkened. 'In love with you?'

'That's different to just plain fancying,' Daisy hurtled on dangerously, her hands on her hips.

'How – how long have you known this?'

'For a few weeks.' Although, to be accurate, it was longer than that. 'I suppose I already suspected before then. We've been avoiding each other, or he's been avoiding me, I'm not sure. But tonight . . . I didn't have anyone else to talk to.'

'Why didn't you tell me about it? About how he felt?' Ben's voice seemed to shudder. 'When you first found out, Daisy, why didn't you just *tell* me?'

She shook her head scathingly. 'Oh, come on, Ben, you work with the man. You saw him as a rival from the minute you walked back into your dad's office. I wasn't about to make the situation worse. I just had to deal with it the best way I could.'

'And how was that then? By flaunting yourself in front of him dressed like that?' He gestured to her dress.

Daisy conjured up an image of the skimpy turquoise bikini, but quickly reassured herself that she hadn't worn that deliberately, either. Every nerve seemed to prickle with hostility as she glowered at her husband. 'I wasn't intending to go to his house tonight when I got ready to go out. The only reason I went there is because I needed someone to talk to. The fact that we're even having this argument is your fault anyway.'

'Because I didn't tell you the truth about the Gatehouse?' Ben's vehemence faltered. He collapsed into an armchair and leaned forward with his head between his hands. Something about him reminded Daisy of a condemned man in a dock. 'How did you find out exactly?' he muttered. 'Vivienne was vague on the phone, and the connection wasn't clear.'

'Stella was drunk. She let it slip . . . . I don't think she meant to.'

'Stella?' Ben screwed up his face. 'But I've never told Stella.'

'Well someone has.' Daisy paced the rug in front of the TV. 'I was bound to find out sooner or later. Why didn't you just tell me the truth when you had the chance?'

'And when was that? Think about it, Daisy, when

would have been the best time? I never asked for any of this, I never expected it. When my aunt died, I thought ownership of the Gatehouse would simply revert back to the estate. But, no, she wanted me to have it, even though I'd never hinted that I was interested. Frankly, at the time, I wasn't. I was little more than a boy. Then she also had to go and put in that clause about my being a married man, and it wasn't until I met you, until the workings of it became clear, that I realised what an impossible situation I was in.'

'So,' said Daisy, 'what it boils down to is that you didn't trust me enough to confide in me?'

Ben looked pale again. 'Is that what you think? That I didn't tell you because otherwise I'd always wonder if you'd married me for my money? It wasn't like that, though, was it? As far as you knew, the Gatehouse was already mine. And you were also aware that there *was* no money, not really. The little that's left of the Greenwood "fortune" is being poured straight back into Greenacres. I haven't a clue what Dad and Vivienne are going to do when it finally runs out. I only wish I could help, but I don't know how I can.'

'The Gatehouse is worth something. It might be small, but—'

'It isn't on the market. It's our home. And even if I considered selling it to help Dad, it wouldn't be anywhere near enough.'

Her stubborn streak more evident than ever, Daisy pursued the matter further. 'Look at it this way. By keeping me in the dark, you've made what you did seem incriminating. You've made it look as if it was your main reason for marrying me so quickly – or for marrying me at all.'

'You know that's not true!'

'But you didn't give me the chance to work that out for myself. If you'd had enough faith in me . . .'

'Daisy, it wasn't that simple.'

'Everyone knew about it except me. Your family *knew*, and I feel so stupid now, so—'

'They understand why I married you. OK, so maybe they thought it was dubious when we first turned up here, but they don't think that way any more. No one does.'

'How do you know that? You can't read their minds.'

Ben shook his head wearily. 'No, I can't. And there's not a lot more I can say to vindicate myself. I married you because I loved you, not because I wanted a roof over my head. The thought of my aunt's will somehow coming between us, changing us, was too much for my pathetic brain to handle. I'm sorry.'

Slowly, Daisy rubbed the tips of her fingers over her brow, as if she was trying to smooth out the creases. 'You can see why I was upset, though?' she asked softly, plaintively. 'Finding out like that . . .'

'Yes,' said Ben. 'What I can't see, though, is why you had to go running to Jerome about it. Why didn't you just call me?'

'I was mad with you,' spluttered Daisy, 'and I didn't expect . . . I didn't know you were going to come charging back from Manchester. I thought it would help to talk to someone who didn't have a vested interest in all this.'

'But you said it yourself,' Ben reminded her, a steely quality in his voice suddenly, which only unsettled her further, 'Jerome's in love with you. If that isn't a vested interest, I don't know what is.'

24

'Why was your mobile switched off?' Ben asked, when the silence between them seemed to have evolved into a form of torture. 'I tried calling you, but it just kept diverting to messaging.'

'I've hardly got any battery left. I switched it off to try to conserve it, in case I needed to use it again.'

'Convenient,' mumbled Ben. Not having meant to say this aloud, he quickly backtracked. 'I suppose I should have thought of phoning you at Jerome's. After all, how many shoulders were left for you to "cry" on? Not Geri's, obviously. And Rob's a bit young, although I did phone my dad to check if he'd seen you.'

Daisy scrunched up her face. 'I'd hardly go crying to your dad, would I?'

'No, but you might have demanded to know more about the will.'

'Confronting your dad would have only made things worse,' Daisy retorted thornily.

'Can they get worse?' Ben took a deep, steadying breath. 'I work with Jerome, but how am I supposed to face him now? How can I even *look* at him? All this time, he's been saying one thing, and thinking and feeling another. I just want to . . .' Ben clenched a fist, by way of demonstration. 'But that's hardly the most civilised course of action.' Stretching his fingers again and sighing, he raked a hand through his hair, which felt tousled and unsophisticated already even though he'd only had it trimmed a fortnight ago. He had never considered himself a violent man, but his antagonism towards Jerome alarmed him.

'Why do you think I carried on as normal,' said Daisy, 'or as relatively normal as possible, once I found out how he felt? You see him day in, day out. I suppose I was trying to protect—'

'Him?'

'No,' she frowned. 'Both of you. All of us. I don't know . . . Can't you see, maybe if it was someone else, I would have confided in you, but *Jerome* . . .'

'Perhaps that's because you're attracted to him yourself.'

Ben watched as Daisy opened and closed her mouth, either in outrage or because she couldn't summon up the words to deny it. At last she said, 'Yes, he's an attractive man. But I think Brad Pitt and George Clooney are attractive men. I think *you're* attractive. I'm sorry, but it's in my genetic make-up, somehow I can't help it.' Sarcasm leaked into her voice, like a self-defence mechanism.

'But Jerome's readily available. Brad Pitt and George Clooney aren't.'

'Oh, for pity's sake!' She started pacing again. 'You're doing my head in! I'm tired of going round and round in the same old circles.'

'Then maybe we should have it out, once and for all.'

She made an impatient 'grrrrr' sound deep in her throat, punctuated with a brief, cold silence. 'Anything to make you happy.' The saccharine smile she offered him was as false as they came.

'Are you prepared to swear that nothing's happened between you and Jerome?'

The smile stayed put, her jaw clenched, as if the wind had changed and she would be stuck with that expression forever. But by the time she spoke, the smile had evaporated. 'Why are you even asking me that, Ben?' A look of fatigue crept over her. With a small groan, she sank into an armchair and grabbed a cushion, holding it tightly across her stomach.

'Because I want to know. I want to believe you, but I don't seem to know how any more.'

'Did you ever?' asked his wife dully.

'Yes. Yes, I did. I believed in you totally. But I suppose it's the little things that grind faith down. And then, the way you didn't tell me about Greg, it started me thinking – what else don't I know about you? What's real, and what's a lie?'

'So what's to stop me lying now?'

'Nothing. Except—'

'Except that you'll only believe me if it's an admission of guilt, anyway.'

Ben didn't reply. Churning deliriously in his head was the consciousness that if he found Daisy more beautiful and desirable tonight than ever – captivating, stunning, haunting, in that red dress which seemed to have been made for her – then wouldn't Jerome, who claimed to love her too? And what would have stopped Jerome trying to act on his basic instincts?

'In a way, Ben, you lied, too – about the Gatehouse,' Daisy went on. 'I'm not saying that makes us even, just that people tell the truth selectively. We both had our reasons.'

'You haven't answered my question yet.'

'About Jerome and me? No, nothing had happened.'

She looked like someone taking the bull between the horns. And she'd said 'had', past tense.

'But?' gulped Ben.

'Something did almost happen tonight.'

He paused to take this in. 'Define "almost".'

'Ben, you've got to remember I'd had quite a bit to drink, and I was furious with you . . .'

'Just tell me, Daisy.'

'We didn't have sex, if that's what you're afraid of.'

Stupefied, his countenance crumpled. 'Of course that's what I'm bloody afraid of . . .'

'We stopped before it went that far,' Daisy muttered, frowning at the rug.

'Stopped what exactly?'

'I'm telling you this because—'

'—the guilt's getting too much for you?'

'Yes, I feel guilty!' Her bottom lip quivered. 'Of course I do! I should never have let Jerome kiss me. It happened so suddenly, though, and one thing could have led to another . . . But it didn't. We stopped ourselves.'

'I see.' He inhaled slowly. 'So, in other words, Jerome wasn't up for it. Remember, I'm a man, Daisy. I'm aware of how men think, how we react in particular situations. I can't see him backing off – unless he was afraid he couldn't see it through.'

'So even if I'd suddenly called a halt to the proceedings, he would have ignored me, is that what you're getting at?' She shook her head wretchedly. 'You've got a screw loose, do you know that? Would it help if I told you that I *did* call a halt to it? That I couldn't go further, but that Jerome didn't just ignore my wishes and carry on regardless? We both stopped it there, and then wondered what the hell we were supposed to say to each other. Is that what you'd prefer to hear? Probably, if only you'd believe it. I don't know what you want any more.' Her tone was acrimonious, even though her eyes were beginning to look watery. 'I just know I couldn't go to bed with Jerome and shag him senseless, even though a part of me wanted to. Even though I needed to get back at you somehow. I couldn't go through with it, no matter how attractive I found him, or how totally he'd convinced me that it wouldn't have been just a one-night stand. I'm sorry, am I too crude for you? Or simply too honest?'

Ben sat with his elbows on his knees and his hands over his ears, as if trying to shut out her voice and her words and the terrible, terrible realisation that he didn't believe her. She was right. He wasn't prepared to accept anything but the worst. The fact that it had come to this made everything seem so desperate and futile.

Meeting Daisy had reaffirmed his confidence in humanity, especially women. Since Geri, the few he had been out with had been so samey and hard to please. If he'd been himself with them, they'd got bored; if he'd tried harder, they'd accused him of suffocating them. But when those relationships had been over, he'd never felt the way he did now – as if his whole life was caving in on itself.

Daisy was the only one who had reached far enough and deep enough to make a difference, and it followed that the pain of her betrayal would be greater than anything he had known or could have imagined.

She was looking at him with her light brown eyes seemingly full of remorse. And yet, there was something else there, even now that she'd half-confessed. That flinty, tempestuous look that could so easily spark into a full-scale show of defiance. From early on in their relationship, he'd accepted that it was part of her. He couldn't change it, and to be fair everyone had their weaknesses, so why should he even try? But was this contentiousness in her nature part of something darker?

'Ben,' she said suddenly, 'I'm sorry . . . I never meant to hurt you.'

That was such a cliché. But as Ben reflected on it, he realised it was also a valid statement. Few people ever meant to hurt others to such a degree, it was just one of life's crueller ironies that they didn't think that way *before* the event.

'Ben,' she persisted, 'if I'm not telling the truth, if I'm really having an affair with Jerome, why did I even bother to come home tonight? I wasn't expecting you back, was I? I could have stayed out until tomorrow morning and you wouldn't have been any the wiser.'

'I – I don't know. It doesn't prove anything. Vivienne could have phoned you, to warn you I was coming home.'

'But that doesn't make sense. If she'd known what I was up to, why would she have phoned you in the first place? And if she was on your side, then why would she tip me off?'

Ben shrugged, dismissing this. He didn't want to think logically; his heart seemed unable to allow it. 'For all I know, you and Jerome might have had an argument. You might have left earlier than you'd planned. There could be a dozen reasons why you didn't spend the whole night with him.'

'And you'll listen to every single one, except the one that counts.' Daisy heaved herself upright, discarding the cushion and smoothing a hand over her face. 'I'm going to bed,' she said flatly. 'It's late, I'm tired and still not completely sober. Maybe we can make sense of all this in the morning. Right now, I don't think we're getting anywhere.'

'You expect me to join you?'

She faltered on her way towards the stairs, her back to him. For a moment, her shoulders trembled, then they straightened and her head lifted. 'You can do what you want,' she muttered.

Ben watched her climb the stairs. The effort she put in seemed immense. When she disappeared from view and her footsteps sounded overhead, making the floorboards creak, he gazed round their home as if nothing in it was familiar or comforting.

Rising unsteadily to his feet, he glanced towards the stairs, then turned in the opposite direction, scooping up something from the sofa as he walked past.

25

When Daisy heard the front door slam, she stopped brushing her teeth on automatic pilot and spat into the basin. Her reflection in the lightly misted mirror looked wan and lifeless. Had she really been expecting Ben to come upstairs and get ready for bed, as if nothing had happened? She was so worn out, there only seemed to be haphazard, scant communication between her thoughts and feelings.

When she heard the car engine rev, her stomach lurched and then sank. Where was Ben going? Up to the main house? If so, what would he tell his father? The truth – as he saw it? Then something else struck her. He'd been drinking too; she had smelled it on him. It didn't appear that he'd been indulging at home, but he must have been knocking back the lagers when he'd been in Manchester. After all, he had had no reason to think that he would be driving that night.

Daisy hurried out of the bathroom and down the stairs, then scanned the memory facility on the phone until she came to Vivienne's mobile number. Her stepmother-in-law would know what to do. But it went straight to messaging. Daisy rang off and put down the phone. She didn't want to risk ringing Greenacres and having to speak to her father-in-law. But just then, another notion stole over her chillingly. What if Ben had gone round to Jerome's?

In the movies, there would be a classic fight scene, with chairs splintering dramatically and men hurtling backwards over tables. In English TV murder mysteries, someone would get stabbed or shot. Outlandish scenarios played themselves in her head as she wondered if crimes of passion were actually that common. At last, she shook herself together and reached for the phone again.

Jerome's answering machine was on. As soon as Daisy heard the tone, she started to gabble wildly. 'Hello, it's me. I know you're probably there, so if you can, please pick up. I need to talk to you about Ben. He knows something happened tonight and he's stormed out. He's taken the car, and he's been drinking. Apart from that, he's all wound up, so he probably shouldn't be driving anyway—'

'Daisy, are you OK?' Jerome sounded groggy as he interrupted.

'Were you asleep?'

'Not quite. But what are you on about – "Ben knows"? How? And *what* exactly?'

'He got all suspicious because I wasn't there when he arrived home—'

'Hang on, slow down. I thought he was staying in Manchester?'

'He was. But because I was so upset when I left the nightclub, Vivienne got worried and called him. He came dashing home, and I wasn't there. I wasn't at the Gatehouse, and he wanted to know where I'd been. He recognised your jacket . . .' Daisy tailed off, glancing round. 'Oh, shit, Jerome, your jacket's gone. He must have taken it with him.'

There was a brief pause. 'Then I'd guess Ben's on his way over here right now. He can't get his hands on a gun at short notice, can he?'

'Don't joke like that!'

'I've just got visions of Howard owning a pair of antique duelling pistols or something, to go with his "country squire" image.'

Daisy felt ill. 'I – I don't know. I've never seen any. Are they still legal? Owning them, I mean.'

'Not my area of law.' There was another pause. 'I think Ben's here now, I can hear a car. Don't panic. I know he has a temper at times, but he's not psychotic.'

Daisy suddenly heard knocking coming from the other end of the line. It sounded ominously loud.

'I'd better go,' sighed Jerome, sounding as if he were heading off to face the guillotine.

'I should come over—'

'No! You stay put. There's nothing you can do here. You'd only make things worse.'

'He knows how you feel about me, Jerome. He knows that something almost happened tonight. He's just not convinced about the "almost" part.'

'Daisy, I know he's not here to pat me on the back, but I can handle it. Please don't worry. I'll call you when he's gone, OK?'

There was a click, and the line went dead.

The worst part, thought Ben, thunderously rapping on Jerome's door, was the knowledge that nothing could ever go back to the way it had been before. He hadn't deluded himself that he was the first man in Daisy's life, but it had been preferable not to know about her past sexual encounters in graphic detail.

It had disturbed him to find out about Greg, and to acknowledge this other man's significance in Daisy's life, even though it was long since over. The whole matter would have been easier to understand and dismiss from his thoughts if she'd told him about it earlier, when they'd discussed their previous relationships and he had explained candidly about Geri. Since the night at the art gallery in Liverpool, though, only a couple of weeks ago, Ben hadn't been able to shake off the feeling that she was still hiding something. Now it was glaringly obvious that this 'something' was the reality behind her so-called friendship with Jerome Wallace.

'Your jacket,' said Ben, hurling it into the porch as the front door swung open.

Jerome caught it by one of the cuffs, and with his characteristic equanimity hung it on a coat hook. 'Hello, Ben. Thanks for returning this, but there was no rush.'

With a sour taste in his mouth, Ben realised that Jerome had been expecting him. 'I suppose she called, to warn you I was coming?'

'By "she", I assume you're referring to your wife?'

That was enough for Ben to charge in and slam Jerome up against the nearest free wall. 'My *wife*,' he spat resentfully. '*Mine*. You're a sick bastard – you know that? Reassuring me over and over again that you weren't interested—'

'Actually,' rasped Jerome, winded, 'I can't recall saying I wasn't interested. I just said I wouldn't interfere. And I never meant—'

'What? You never meant *what*?'

'You're right. I'm a sick bastard, and I'm sorry.'

Jerome's coolness and self-control only antagonised Ben more. 'What am I supposed to say now? Apology accepted? Do you have any idea what you've done?'

'Yes. But I think it might be better if you let me get my breath back and we went into the lounge and discussed it in less barbaric terms.'

'"Barbaric",' growled Ben. 'You've got no idea . . .'

'Actually, I do. The tragedy of all this is that I know exactly how you're feeling. At the worst you want to kill me, or hack my balls off. At the best, you'd be prepared to draw just a drop of blood, even if it's a cut lip. I know exactly what's going through your head because it went through mine two years ago, and I still remember it as clearly as if it were last week.'

Jerome had obviously got his breath back. Ben found himself releasing him. 'You're sicker than I thought.'

'As I said, I agree. But if there can possibly be a mitigating circumstance in a situation like this, then I think I have one. It would never have been just a casual affair. It could never have been that simple.'

'As I recall, your ex-wife ended up marrying the wanker she had an affair with. I'd hardly call that casual.'

'The wanker got her pregnant. I'd say that was reason enough for her to leave me and shack up with him. In my case, I wouldn't have needed to stay with Daisy out of any sense of obligation. The way I feel about her would have been enough.'

Ben couldn't stand to hear him spell it out. 'And you knew you'd win, didn't you?' Suddenly overcome with exhaustion and despair, he leaned against the door frame for support.

Jerome shook his head and straightened his shirt collar. 'I haven't won. If you're too wrapped up in yourself to see that . . .'

Ben felt as if he was choking, but managed to utter, 'Then we've both lost.'

'Bullshit,' scowled Jerome. 'It isn't a case of winning or losing. Can't you see what this is actually about? Not you or me. Pathetic, selfish gits that we are, we don't really deserve much of anything. No, this is about a young woman who was once called Daisy Miller. I've never met anyone as confused as she is. Even my clients . . . well, most of them seem to know when a relationship's at an end. What happened here tonight was out of anger, on Daisy's part at least. And something did happen, but it wasn't half as much as I wanted, and it wasn't as unforgivable as you seem to imagine. You shouldn't make her suffer when you're as much to blame as anyone.'

'Me?' Ben frowned at him.

'For not seeing how this place is sapping her dry. For bringing her here and installing her in your world, and either deliberately ignoring how miserable she's become or being completely insensitive and blind to it. Something was going to happen, and if it wasn't what happened tonight, it would have been something else.'

'I – I don't understand.'

'Go home, Ben. Go home and talk to her. And perhaps attempt listening for a change. Try seeing her for who she is, not what you've created her to be in your mind. She's looking for something, and I wish to God I knew what it was. I wish I could be the one to give it to her. But I don't think I am, and I'm not satisfied that you are either. Something tells me that she'd like you to be . . . but maybe hoping for that, waiting for it, has only messed her up more.'

Ben took a few faltering steps out of the house. The night felt airless. The sky was devoid of stars. The hours around midnight seemed to have dragged on forever.

Jerome stood framed in the doorway. 'I don't think you ought to drive . . .'

'Fuck you,' spat Ben. 'I hope you rot in hell.'

In times of crisis, the old lines seemed to recur with a strange, reassuring banality. Ben climbed into his car and turned the key in the ignition.

26

Dawn had been and gone by the time Daisy woke up. Her joints were stiff and her limbs ached, but it was her neck that had taken the brunt of a night cramped on the sofa. She had collapsed on to it in a relieved little heap after Jerome had called her to say that Ben was almost certainly on his way home again.

Apparently there had been a heated exchange, but nothing worse. 'I've still got all my teeth in place,' Jerome had reassured her, before his voice had softened and grown less flippant and he had told her she ought to try and get some sleep. And in a way, she had. Just not upstairs in bed. She'd decided to wait up for Ben, and must have dropped off anyway.

Watery grey light was filtering through tiny slits in the curtains. Yawning, Daisy drew them back and welcomed faded colour to the ground floor of the Gatehouse. With gummy eyes, she stared round her, her gaze resting on the digital clock on the stereo. Why hadn't Ben woken her up when he'd got home? And where was he? In bed? But as this thought seeped into her mind, she turned in slow motion to look out of the lounge window. The space where Ben normally parked his car was still empty. Daisy's chest seemed to cave in.

He hadn't come home.

Oh, God. What if there'd been an accident? What if . . . ?

Daisy ran towards the stairs, and almost tripped in her agitation to climb them. She went into the bedroom and flung open the wardrobe. With the same unwavering sense of urgency, she wrenched off the ill-fated red dress and scrambled into a pair of jeans and an old misshapen sweater. Even though it was still July, there was a peculiar crispness to the morning that reminded her of autumn.

She rushed downstairs again, grabbed her set of keys, tugged on boots and opened the front door. She paused only to lock it behind her, as if someone with a moderate degree of logic had taken over her brain, then hurried round the side of the house to the shed to fetch her bike.

The bell clanged through the old house like a warning knell. Daisy waited impatiently, peering through the rippled, diamond-shaped glass panes on either side of the oversized oak door. At last, a distorted figure appeared, dressed in blue and gliding across the hall like a ghost. Daisy couldn't make out who it was until the door was heaved open. Vivienne didn't look surprised to see her. In fact, she seemed wearily resigned. Shadows clung round her eyes, her skin looked sallow and there were still traces visible of last night's make-up. Her hair was piled up in an untidy mass on her head, as if she hadn't bothered letting it down for bed. The only part of her that was as flawless as usual was her dressing-gown.

'I'm not hungover,' she sighed. 'In case that's what you're thinking.'

Daisy ignored this and launched right in. 'Ben's gone. I'm terrified he's had an accident. What should I do? Phone the hospitals or the police or—'

Vivienne was shaking her head. 'Ben's all right. That's why I haven't had much sleep. Well, practically no sleep . . . He turned up here, not long after Geri and I got in ourselves.'

'He's here?' Daisy's relief was short-lived. 'I don't understand . . .'

'You'd better come in.' Vivienne started leading her through to the back of the house. 'Dora's got a stomach bug – not very good news for a cook, is it? – so I'm afraid I'm in charge of breakfast today. What would you like, or have you already had yours?'

'No, thanks . . .' Daisy frowned. 'I just want to talk to Ben.'

Vivienne didn't say anything for a moment. 'I see Howard just about managed to rustle up a coffee,' she grumbled, examining an empty cup by the sink. 'I'm surprised he didn't bang on my door and demand I get up and grill him some bacon.'

Daisy realised her stepmother-in-law was stalling. 'I slept on the sofa last night, waiting for Ben to come home from . . .' Daisy hesitated. 'I was frantic this morning when I saw he hadn't. I thought his car might be lying in a ditch somewhere. I couldn't just sit around waiting for the phone to ring, or something to happen.'

Vivienne's brow was almost as pale as alabaster, but not quite as smooth. 'Daisy, he told me what happened yesterday. How you didn't go straight home after leaving the club . . .'

Daisy felt the colour drain from her own face. 'You know the mood I was in better than anyone. You had no right to call him. If you hadn't interfered—'

'Yes, OK.' Vivienne stopped pottering about the kitchen. 'In a way, this is my fault. I take responsibility for some of it, but not all. I called Ben because I was worried about you, and I thought he was the only one who could make a difference. If I'd known what was going to happen—'

'You'd still have done it,' said Daisy scornfully. Deluged with self-pity, she found herself too weak to ward it off. 'Neither you nor Ben's dad ever wanted me here. You're probably both secretly gloating that Ben and I have had this row.'

Vivienne seemed taken aback by this. She came over to where Daisy was still hovering skittishly by the door and ushered her into a chair. She scraped another chair closer and sat down herself, clutching Daisy's hands with a firm, intense grip, as if she wanted to impart her message with every available form of language, physical as well as verbal.

'Daisy, I don't *ever* want you to think that way again. This was never going to be an easy transition for you, and in the beginning, as I've told you before, I had my doubts. I still think you rushed into this marriage, but as to your . . . suitability, I don't see any problem with that. I honestly think you and Ben were made for each other.'

'I just want to speak to him . . .' Daisy rubbed a hand over her face. It was strange how her skin felt grey to the touch, as if she were seeing it through her fingertips. 'How does the saying go? Marry in haste, repent at leisure . . . Well, I'm not very good at the repenting part. I'd just rather get it over and done with.'

Vivienne sighed and sat back in her chair. 'Daisy, I think you should just give it a bit more time. I've never seen Ben like this, and I hate saying it, but I think he needs some space.'

'You mean he doesn't want to talk to me?' Daisy translated.

'He's so wound up right now. He might be fine in a few hours—'

'Or he might never want to see me again.'

Vivienne shook her head emphatically. 'It isn't like that. Just let him cool down. It'll work itself out, these things always do.'

Daisy stood up. 'I might as well not be here.'

'Wait.' Vivienne put out her hand. '*I'd* like to talk to you. I want to hear your side of the story, if you're OK about telling me.'

Daisy hesitated, then sat back down. Her stepmother-in-law made coffee, insisting that she have one, and Daisy heard herself recounting her own version of events, slowly and haltingly, but the absolute truth. When she'd finished, they sat in silence.

Eventually, Vivienne spoke again. 'If it's any consolation, *I* believe you. I don't think you were unfaithful, not to the extent Ben's convinced you were. And I think I know why.'

Daisy raised her eyes to meet the older woman's gaze.

'I know your feelings have been confused lately,' said Vivienne, 'but I don't think you care about Jerome in the same way you care about Ben. It's good to have principles to uphold, especially when it comes to marriage, but more often than not they go out of the window when passion comes in. Jerome's been your friend, a stalwart shoulder to lean on, but if he was the man you really wanted, you'd be with him right now. There'd be nothing to stop you.'

'I've hurt them both,' Daisy uttered, sounding desolate.

'But you didn't mean it.'

'That doesn't make me feel any better. I've lost a husband and a friend . . .'

'Daisy, they'll get over it. You haven't lost anything. You're just feeling sorry for yourself, like Ben is. And that doesn't help anyone. Look at me, don't turn away, just look at me properly. I'm a sight this morning, aren't I? Usually I try my hardest to be faultless; I won't leave my bedroom until I'm completely satisfied. As if I'm still playing some theatrical role, and my make-up needs to be just right. But I'm not deluding myself any more that this is going to last, or at least, not the way we've grown accustomed to it.'

'What's not going to last?' asked Daisy, experiencing a pang of curiosity.

'Greenacres – this stately, old-fashioned country existence, with me swanning about as the lady of the manor. And it gets harder and harder to see Howard pretending that everything's fine. That this life, as we know it, is going to stay like this until we're dead and buried. The cracks are beginning to show, and they're getting wider.'

'Are you talking financially?' said Daisy quietly.

'Mainly. But I'm almost thirty-eight years old, and what have I got to show for it, apart from living here? A ten-year-old son who's so much like the old me that it's painful to watch. He's got the fire and the drive and the talent – I know, I've seen him reading Shakespeare and Wilde aloud in the library when he thinks no one's around. And it isn't that I don't want him to succeed, just that I know how devastatingly easy it is to fail.'

Oh God, thought Daisy, why do I keep putting my foot in things? 'I'm sorry I butted in about the drama workshop,' she said, only partially penitent. 'I should have accepted that you had a good reason not to want him to go. I should have—'

'But I'm glad you butted in. I'm pleased he's going. Howard and I can't suppress Robert's dreams just because of the past, or because it's not what we'd hoped for him. I should know . . . There were people who tried to stop me from following my ambition, and I turned against them. I don't want that happening to Robert and me, or to Robert and Howard. It isn't worth it. He's my only son – I can't lose him.'

'I don't think you ever would.'

Vivienne pushed back a frond of hair that was intent on dipping itself in her coffee. 'I hope not.'

Daisy rose to her feet again. This time she was going to make it out of the door. She wanted to be alone, waiting and thinking and absorbing everything her stepmother-in-law had said.

Vivienne sighed. 'You're going?'

'Thanks for the coffee. And for listening . . . You'll tell Ben I was here . . . won't you?'

'Of course.' Vivienne nodded. 'And I'm sure, by tonight, he'll be over at the Gatehouse desperate to make things up with you . . .'

But he wasn't.

Daisy spent the evening wrapped in a travel blanket on the sofa, staring at the TV without really paying attention to what was on. Her mind was ticking over at full speed. A couple of times, her hand reached for the telephone, wondering if she should try calling Greenacres. But if Ben wasn't ready to speak to her, there was no point. And more than twice, she found herself halfway through punching out another number, gearing up to ask Jerome what the hell he'd said to her husband. He'd made her believe last night that his altercation with Ben hadn't been as bad as she'd imagined. Had he been deliberately misleading her, or just trying to make her feel better? She hadn't gone through with making that call either, though. Each time, she'd been afraid of what she'd say to him, and what would happen if he came round to see her, because the answer was *nothing*. Nothing would happen. And in all fairness, how could she keep leading him on like that?

For the second night in a row, Daisy fell asleep on the sofa. And for a second morning, she woke up to an empty house and a crick in her neck.

The taxi dropped her off at the station at ten past twelve, and she used what she'd taken out of the 'emergency cash' tin in the kitchen to pay the driver. She bought the train ticket with her credit card. Her suitcase seemed to weigh more than it ever had in the seven years that she'd owned it. She pulled out the handle and wheeled it behind her to the nearest Link machine. The most she could withdraw in one day was two hundred and fifty, which she did without qualms. That was about as much as she'd taken with her into the marriage, it was only fair that she should take it out again. She wouldn't resort to either her credit or debit card again unless she was completely strapped – assuming Ben didn't put a hold on her using them. She'd never had a joint account before, and wasn't sure if he'd have the authority or not.

Daisy sat down on a bench and stared round, her heart thumping violently against her ribcage, as it always had when she'd left one place behind and set off for somewhere new, into an unplanned future. She could try to persuade herself that this was no different from those other times, but that would be making light of what had happened. She was leaving because her last reason to stay had turned away from her. Their lives had become too disparate, and maybe what had happened the day before yesterday had made Ben realise it too.

Daisy didn't know if it was forever, or if it was just a case of needing time apart to think things through. But as the train pulled out of the station four minutes behind schedule, the wave of finality that swept over her was enough to make her lurch down the carriage to the nearest toilet.

27

Howard Kavanagh's study at Greenacres had always reminded Ben of a gentlemen's club. The kind that you saw in old technicolour movies, or TV period dramas, with dark wood panelling and green leather armchairs. He had no idea if they were still like that these days, because he'd never been in one. The few times that he had sat in his father's study had always seemed momentous, as if only matters of great importance were ever conducted there, such as the day he had heard about his aunt Eleanor's will.

Sitting here now opposite his father, Ben half-expected Howard to whip out his prized cigar box and offer him one, even though he knew his father only ever handed those out to his closest cronies. Instead, he got the offer of a whisky, which he accepted with worrying eagerness; but anything that dulled the misery inside him even marginally and muffled the conflicting voices in his head was welcome.

Ben didn't know why he was here, except that his father had extended the invitation to join him in the study after dinner, while Vivienne helped Robert in the library with his history homework. As his father prepared the drinks, Ben gazed round with nervous eyes. At last Howard returned to his chair and passed him the whisky.

'You haven't been back to the Gatehouse for a few days, have you?'

Ben stared into the amber liquid. 'Not since I picked up some things I needed, no.'

'And how long do you intend to stay with us? I mean' – Howard swiftly raised a hand in a conciliatory gesture – 'not that I believe you could outstay your welcome. For one thing, you have as much right to be here as I do. I was just wondering if you had any plans for the future – either long or short term.'

It had been just over a week since Daisy had left; since Ben had ventured to the Gatehouse and found her things gone. No note, no hint of where she might have headed to. And no one he could contact, not even that friend of hers in Norwich whom he'd never spoken to or met, the one whose surname he couldn't remember.

'I – I don't know,' he said to his father. 'I haven't made any firm plans yet.'

He hadn't made plans at all, of any description. He was even drifting in a desultory fashion from one thought to another; from believing that Daisy must have been guilty of *something* to have left so abruptly, and then wondering if he had driven her too far and that this was all his own fault.

It was as if he were existing in a bubble, with people too scared to come close to him in case they burst it and something terrible flooded out. Like Geri, who was spending most of her time with Declan in Liverpool in spite of the last-minute wedding arrangements to take care of at Greenacres. And Vivienne, who always seemed to have a small frown indenting her brow, and only spoke to Ben when it was necessary about matters that were mainly inconsequential. Finally – and in a strange way, the worst of all – there was Robert, who avoided him as if he had the lurgy, except at the dinner table, when Ben sometimes caught his half-brother peering at him from under his floppy fringe with narrowed, resentful eyes. Ben felt about as welcome at Greenacres as an infestation of dry rot, but going back to the Gatehouse before he was ready, while the pain was still so raw, would be a hundred times worse.

'It's just . . .' his father spoke haltingly now, 'with Jerome leaving—'

Ben jerked his head up. 'What do you mean?'

'It's not permanent. But he hasn't set a date, as such, for his return.' Howard sighed. 'I know I told you both to take some time off – for the good of the firm, not simply yourselves – but I can't cope on my own much longer.'

'Dad, if you needed me, you just had to ask. I'm not . . . ill. I'll be back at work tomorrow. I'll—'

'I'm not sure that your returning will solve anything,' said Howard solemnly. 'Your heart wasn't in the job *before* she left, let alone now.'

Ben frowned. 'What are you saying?'

'Don't get me wrong, Benjamin. I'm glad that you came back to Nettlesford, and I'm grateful that you've put in so much effort at Kavanagh & Co., but it wouldn't have worked out in the long run, even if she hadn't left . . . would it?'

'I – I don't understand.' Ben shook his head helplessly.

'You only ever became a solicitor because it seemed a logical progression in your life. If there'd been something else you badly wanted to do, you probably wouldn't have taken my "advice" on board. But you never grew up wanting to be a footballer, or a rock star, or even an actor.' Howard looked away for a moment, pressing his lips together, the edges curling downwards slightly. 'I don't know if people are born for a career in the law. Perhaps I only went into it myself because of my father before me, but I could tell from an early age that you were never cut out for it. I suppose I've always just turned a blind eye. Even when you came back saying you wanted to rejoin the firm. I tried to convince myself that you'd matured, that you were ready for it this time . . . but I was wrong.'

Ben didn't know what to say. His father had never voiced these doubts before, and to hear them now, of all times, filled Ben with dread. 'Dad, I . . .' But the words failed him; his throat was so tight it felt as if a snake were coiled round it.

'You're not a failure, Benjamin. I'm not implying that. You do a fine job because you're conscientious and diligent and you care about your clients, but the longer you do it, the harder it's going to get for you and the more mistakes you'll start to make. I don't want to see you slip down that route, and if you're going to leave Nettlesford again, then it would be best for everyone if you did it now.'

'Leave Nettlesford?'

Howard sighed again, and twirled the now empty, lead crystal whisky tumbler round in his fingers, as if examining it for flaws. 'You're not going to stay, Ben. Even if you don't know it yet. It might only be a temporary absence, but I'd rather you did it sooner rather than later.'

Ben opened and closed his mouth. It crossed his mind that maybe his father was asking him to leave in a subtle, round about fashion. But this didn't make sense, and the more he considered it, the more he realised that the older man wasn't having an easy time saying any of this.

'But, Dad, what about Kavanagh & Co.?'

Howard shrugged laboriously, and rose to pour them both another whisky. 'In spite of anything I might have said in the past, I have no delusions about Robert following in my footsteps. Even if he doesn't pursue this acting lark, he won't want to be a solicitor or a barrister. He wasn't . . . *designed* to sit behind a desk.'

'But if Jerome's gone, and I'm not there either, who will you get—? I mean, you do expect him to come back?' Ben frowned, because it wasn't easy to discuss the other man like this. 'I can't just leave you to sort everything out yourself. He must have left some unfinished business. You're supposed to be working towards full retirement, not increasing your workload—'

But Howard interrupted, 'Would you be disappointed if Kavanagh & Co. became Kavanagh & Campbell?'

Ben looked at his father in shock. This wasn't Howard Kavanagh talking. It was an impostor who had the same whiskery grey exterior and deep, gruff voice, but a completely contrary way of thinking. 'Are you talking about Anthony Campbell?'

'Who else? I've known him for years, but what you might not know is that he's been on at me to amalgamate the two firms for a while now. To be frank, retirement in any way, shape or form doesn't suit me. I can't stand the thought of all those brain cells dying off while I'm sitting around doing nothing. If the two firms joined together, we'd have branches in Nettlesford and Mold. Anthony also has more staff, a couple of whom would be more than happy to come to Nettlesford, at least in the short term. With our breadth of experience we could be more competitive, more on the ball—'

On the ball? 'Hang on,' said Ben, because this only confirmed that it wasn't his father speaking, 'what about keeping the "exclusivity" of Kavanagh & Co.? I've heard little else since the day I was born. It was Kavanagh & Co.

before the Second World War, and you've always said it
would be Kavanagh & Co. till the day you died.'

'That was when I imagined I might at least have a
son who would be involved in the business. Since you
left the last time ... Let's say that Jerome was a good
stand-in; a hard worker and a shrewd business brain,
but no replacement for my own flesh and blood. But
who knows, perhaps it might be Campbell, Kavanagh
& *Wallace* – there's a lot still to thrash out. The point
is, as Vivienne's so fond of telling me lately, a man has
to move with the times.'

So, it was his stepmother in his dad's body, thought
Ben, trying not to laugh maniacally from the sheer absurd-
ness of it all. And yet, it made perfect sense. It was only
ridiculous because it was the last thing he would have
expected from a man he thought he knew inside out.

'And where do I fit into all this?' he asked instead, with
a voice that sounded puny.

'That's your decision, Benjamin. As I said before, I
don't believe it's here, but I'm not asking you to leave the
firm against your will. I'm just telling you to give serious
thought to your future. It isn't a threat, it's more of a plea
– don't prolong something if it isn't destined to last.'

Ben stared at the oriental hearthrug by his feet. 'Like
my marriage, you mean.'

Howard didn't answer, just sipped slowly at his drink.

'So,' Ben broached, trying to sound blasé when in
reality the answer seemed crucial, 'did Jerome say where
he was going? Is it a holiday, or . . .'

'Or is he with Daisy? Is that what you want to know?
You're hardly asking out of polite interest.'

'I wasn't imagining for one minute—'

Howard's shaggy, grizzled eyebrows twitched darkly,

but his lips were still downturned. 'Weren't you? Then you're the only one who won't be thinking it. I'm warning you now, there'll be speculation and gossip. That's the only thing that concerned me about Jerome going away – the impact it would have on you.'

Ben felt his face set like clay. 'I'm not sorry to see the back of him, even if it's indefinitely. I won't pretend otherwise.'

'It *is* just a holiday. Or extended leave, as he put it. But then he hasn't had a proper break since he came to Nettlesford. It always seemed to be work, work, work, but after what he went through with his wife and the divorce, I couldn't blame him for trying to forget her by concentrating so obsessively on something else. I'm not saying that you'd never find him playing football, or that his habitual haunt at the weekends wasn't the Headless Horseman, just that work perhaps was the only thing that had any meaning for him, the only reason he ploughed on.'

Ben couldn't help feeling even more isolated and pushed out. 'So you're vindicating him, is that it? You're saying that the poor bloke had been through so much, no one could blame him for trying to steal another man's wife.'

Howard shook his head. 'No, Benjamin. I'm just trying to explain that in a situation like this, it isn't necessarily just the couple involved who get hurt. If Jerome honestly cared for Daisy, then you can comprehend what he's going through himself right now. You can understand better than anyone.'

Because I'm going through it all myself? Ben completed the sentence in his head, feeling that familiar urge to strike out in his own defence – but what was there actually left to uphold?

'If you must know,' Howard continued, 'Jerome has gone to Portugal. He has a relative – a cousin, I think – who owns a bar out there. Apparently he's been putting off an invitation to pay a visit, but finally decided the time was right.'

'Convenient,' muttered Ben.

'Daisy isn't with him.'

'How do you know?' He couldn't prevent the scathing note in his voice. 'Did you ask him and accept a simple "yes" as his answer?'

'I did,' nodded Howard. 'And I also know it's the truth because I can recognise a man who's gambled on love and lost for a second time in his life,' he said vehemently, with a touch of impatience. 'Something like that takes its toll on you, believe me.'

Ben stared at him. It was almost as if the older man was speaking from experience. But he'd been married twice, so how could he claim to have lost out? Both times he had done well for himself, and Vivienne was still here, with no sign that the marriage was going through a rough patch, if you discounted the separate bedrooms, an arrangement that was hardly recent.

'Dad, what are you talking about?'

'Jerome Wallace. What do you bloody well think I'm talking about?' said Howard, with an incisiveness that Ben recognised as the conversation drawing to a close. At this stage, nothing and no one would persuade Howard otherwise. 'I'm not asking you to feel sympathy for him. Just to accept that people are going to spread rumours, and they're going to point fingers, and you'll have to walk as tall as you feel you're able to. Even if you think they're laughing at you behind your back, you know the truth – wherever your wife is, it isn't in Portugal with another man.'

Ben looked down at the floor, the conflicting voices echoing in his head again, in spite of the alcohol, or maybe because of it.

If only he did know where Daisy was. If he had some sort of idea, some *clue* . . . But even if he did, could he put aside anger, pride and the lingering consciousness that she'd broken his trust? Would he even go to her, and try to mend something that seemed so damaged?

And then the other voices circling round those initial, instinctive thoughts – what trust had she really broken, and what exactly was she guilty of, when maybe it had been his lack of faith that had pushed her away in the first place?

28

Instead of Saturday night at the Headless Horseman, for once, Adam and Alice had invited everyone back to theirs.

'We'll cook,' said Alice.

'But nothing fancy,' said Adam, who knew how hopeless they were in the kitchen.

The home the twins shared had always struck Ben as cramped but cosy, in a different way from the Gatehouse, because everything seemed curiously Lilliputian. But neither Adam nor Alice was tall, and their grandfather, who had left them the terraced house just off the High Street, had only been five-foot-one. The décor might have been different if they were a couple rather than brother and sister, but as it was, Adam's taste for chrome, leather and lava lamps clashed defiantly with Alice's chintz cushions and Laura Ashley-style wallpaper.

Ben sat slumped in an old easy chair by the hi-fi, which was styled after a classic Bang & Olufsen model, watching the CD whirling round as it played, the design on the label merging into a rainbow blur like a Catherine wheel. About to start on his third bottle of lager since he'd got there, the doorbell rang and Alice hurried out from the kitchen to answer it.

Stella and Kieran shuffled in, loaded with wine and beer respectively. 'Are we late?'

Alice shook her head. 'Not really. Adam still hasn't liquidised the soup yet. He's fiddling with that cook's blowtorch you bought him for Christmas.'

'He's blowtorching soup?' Stella frowned in confusion.

'No, just the pudding,' Ben piped up, from his strategic spot in control of the music. 'Something along the lines of crème brulée.'

Stella and Kieran looked at him with half-smiles on their flushed faces, as if smiling fully would mean they were inconsiderate, and not smiling at all would be even worse. His friends had been like this since they'd found out Daisy had left him; tiptoeing round his feelings and trying their hardest not to talk about it. The curious thing was, he wasn't sure that he wanted them to act that way. Wouldn't normal behaviour have been preferable? Or if that was unrealistic right now, then couldn't they just let him have a rant and a rave at the injustice of life without him feeling that it wasn't the done thing? Because he *would* be uncomfortable discussing his true feelings in front of them; yet ironically, he had assumed he'd been doing just that since he'd ganged up with them all those years ago. Maybe, when he was younger, he had. So what had changed now?

Kieran came over and patted his shoulder. 'All right, mate? What are you listening to?'

'Nothing much. Just the usual rubbish they've got here.'

Kieran chuckled politely.

'Hello, Ben,' said Stella, as she came over to kiss his cheek. 'How are you keeping?'

He had only seen her two days ago, but she made it sound like two weeks. 'Fine,' he mumbled, as she flopped on to the sofa.

'I'll go open your wine then?' Kieran lifted his eyebrows at her as he headed for the kitchen.

She nodded. 'Please . . .'

It seemed to Ben that she'd badly wanted to tag 'darling' on the end.

'Looks like you two are getting along well,' he remarked, when they'd sat for thirty seconds without making conversation.

'Oh, you know,' Stella shrugged. 'It's early days.'

Ben would hardly have called it that considering she had known Kieran since junior school, but he didn't pursue it. She was probably just referring to the romantic aspect.

Now, she was twiddling a strand of hair round her index finger and staring into the bowl of dry roasted peanuts on the coffee table.

Since Ben had tried talking to her about his aunt's will, confronting her about how she'd found out about it, things had been strained between them, even more so than with the others. It wasn't that he didn't believe her – the fact that she hadn't meant to tell Daisy, but she'd been so drunk on Geri's hen night it had inadvertently slipped out. He couldn't imagine why she would lie, apart from saving her own skin. If she'd known the truth about his inheritance for ages, then she would have had the opportunity to have told Daisy before. Ben didn't believe for one moment that Stella would be that callous or vindictive, but he did know how much of a blabbermouth she could turn into when alcohol got the better of her.

If, as she'd said, she had overheard about the will from gossip at the Headless Horseman – in the Ladies', to be exact, from a couple of women she knew by sight if not by name – then sooner or later Daisy would probably have heard it, too. As for the person who had let it slip in the first place, there were likely candidates near enough to home. His father kept very little from his close friends and associates, although he hypocritically expected others in the family to keep Kavanagh affairs private. And as for Vivienne . . . ? Ben didn't really know if she had any close confidantes in her small social circle, but she wasn't above sharing a snippet of juicy local scandal with Mrs White. Why would she have bothered to keep her mouth shut about the will, especially during those two and a half years when he'd been out of the picture?

No, he accepted Stella's story, and had told her as much, assuring her that the break-up of his marriage hadn't been her fault. But perhaps that wasn't enough to convince her. She might be acting uneasily around him because she still felt bad about it.

'It's for the best,' he heard himself say suddenly. 'The fact that Daisy's gone. It doesn't matter how it happened, or who did what. It was doomed from the outset.'

'Ben—' said Stella.

'No, listen. Please. I don't want you blaming yourself. I should never have asked her to marry me so quickly. I ought to have known the success rate would be practically nil. I should have got to know her first, found out there was a whole side to her I wasn't aware of. But looking back, I don't know what I was thinking.'

He was vaguely aware that it wasn't just Stella listening to him now. The others were all crowded in the kitchen doorway, Alice carrying a stack of soup bowls. But he found himself speaking as if from a script, each word carefully crafted to create an effect, to move the drama forward. It wasn't what he really wanted to say, it was just what he thought the others needed to hear. To absolve them, somehow. To reassure them that they could treat him as an ordinary guy.

'Actually, I probably *do* know what I was thinking,' he continued. 'It just either makes me sound like a fool or a terrible person. You choose. Because maybe I didn't just marry her so quickly because I was in love with her . . . Maybe it was to deflect attention away from me, and the way I'd screwed up at trying to make it on my own, without my family's help.'

'Ben,' Stella leaned over and touched his knee, 'you don't have to say any more.'

'I do. That's the point. I was hardly coming home in a blaze of glory, but with a wife in tow . . . especially someone like Daisy – it would prove I hadn't messed up every aspect of my life. And maybe that mysterious thing she had about her – maybe that was to my advantage, too. People would be so busy trying to work her out, they wouldn't bother about me. I could get on with working for my dad again, without too much fuss.'

'I don't think any of that makes you sound terrible,' said Alice feebly, ending the tense silence that followed Ben's admission. 'Just . . . human. Anyone could see that you weren't just using her. You did care about her, and you tried your hardest to make her happy.'

Ben's head drooped towards his beer. 'Maybe.'

Oh, God, why was he doing this? Why couldn't he tell them the truth, not this psychobabble that might only have its basis in a tiny grain of fact? Yes, Daisy had been attractive enough to lessen his sense of failure. With a girl like her at his side, no man could possibly feel that they hadn't been successful in one way, at least. But that had only been a derivative of his reason for marrying her, not the reason itself.

He had loved her. Worshipped her as if she were more than just mortal. Had Jerome been right when he'd accused Ben of expecting too much, of regarding her as the woman he wanted her to be and not the woman she was? It killed him to even consider that that man might have been right, and that he'd seen something in Daisy which Ben had overlooked because he'd been too absorbed in himself and too neglectful of her.

But, in another way, it was just as painful not to be able to express himself to the handful of people he had thought of for so long as his true friends.

Daisy had once said that he put on an act for them, that he didn't let them see the real him. If that was the case, how long had it been going on, and why? Were the others putting on a show, or was it just his own way of handling things? Some deep-seated insecurity that prevented him from admitting that he wasn't always Fun-To-Hang-Around-With, Make-A-Joke-Out-Of-Anything Ben. As if they'd go off him if they saw how needy and pathetic he really was. Even now, when they were pussyfooting round him, he couldn't seem to bring himself to allow it. He couldn't help looking downcast – most people would expect that in his situation, anyway – but he wouldn't let them see how total his loss truly was. He couldn't let them know how his world had been shattered, and how impossible it felt to piece it back together.

29

The day of Geri and Declan's wedding dawned overcast, but by ten o'clock, the sun had broken through. It made the vast marquee on the back lawn at Greenacres sparkle with a brilliant whiteness that Ben had only seen up to now on soap powder commercials.

He had got up late, as usual, and skipped breakfast, and after a quick shave and bath was now struggling with the cravat of his morning suit. As an usher, he had been fitted out for the suit weeks ago, but he hadn't given it much thought until it had arrived at Greenacres yesterday. It consisted of a dark burgundy jacket, navy pinstripe trousers and a lavishly embroidered gold waistcoat. The cravat was gold silk, and a bugger to adjust to the right fit.

Just as he'd succeeded, there was a knock on his bedroom door. It was Vivienne, already impeccably dressed in a pale grey suit that was almost silver, depending on how the light caught it. The dress below the jacket was straight and went down to her ankles. Ben guessed she would probably tart it up later for the evening reception with one of those shiny scarf things or fancy jewellery. It seemed the fashion nowadays. Daisy had been contemplating something along those lines herself.

'Ben, good. You're almost ready,' said his stepmother with her characteristic briskness. 'I considered giving you a wake-up call, but then it slipped my mind.'

'Is there something you need me to do?' he asked dutifully.

'Not this minute. It's Geri – she wants to see you.'

'Now?'

Vivienne nodded, and glanced at her watch.

'But isn't she busy getting ready?' Ben protested. 'Hasn't she got a hairdresser and make-up artist and all sorts of people fussing round her?'

'Not at this present moment,' said his stepmother impatiently. 'But if you don't hurry up . . .'

'OK, OK, I'm coming.'

He grabbed the burgundy jacket and followed her down the corridor, aware of the hustle and bustle rising from the depths of the great house. Muffled conversations emanated from temporary guest bedrooms on either side as they made their way to Geri's room. Greenacres seemed a different world today from the cold, echoing, slightly eerie house it usually was. It had the ambience of a hotel, but an exclusive, stately home retreat, rather than some of those modern versions masquerading as old country houses and catering primarily for business people.

At the top of the staircase, Vivienne turned to Ben. 'I've got to sort out something with the caterers, but you go ahead and see Geri. She wanted to talk to you alone, anyway.' And with that, she started to make her way downstairs, deftly hitching up her dress with one hand as she held on to the banister with the other.

Ben crossed the galleried landing and walked a few yards down the east-wing corridor before knocking on Geri's door.

'Come in,' he thought he heard someone say. Cautiously, in case she was only half-dressed, he turned the brass door knob and pushed the door open.

Geri was on her own, sitting hunched in front of her huge antique dressing-table. Considering the official photographer was supposed to arrive at eleven, Ben was surprised to see Geri wasn't looking anywhere near ready. In her kimono-style dressing-gown and her dark hair in curlers, she looked like a tiny schoolgirl auditioning for an amateur production of *The Mikado*.

'Hi,' he said, tentatively moving closer. 'Vivienne said you wanted to see me . . . ?'

At that, she swivelled on the stool and confronted him with misty, anxious eyes. 'I need to talk to you, Ben. It's really important. I've been pretending it isn't, but it is, and I can't keep putting it off. Not any more.'

A cold frisson of dread sliced through him. Was she having second thoughts? She seemed more agitated than a blushing bride ought to be. What if she was going to reveal something cataclysmic, along the lines of 'I'm still in love with you'? What could he say to that? How would he react? What about Declan? He was crazy about her. And the wedding preparations? All those people involved, all those guests . . .

Ben felt physically sick.

'I did something terrible,' she gabbled on, sounding breathless, as if her lungs were being crushed. 'It seems so long ago now, and I didn't think much of it for ages, not until – until the morning after my hen night, when I found out exactly what had happened between you and Daisy . . .' As she mentioned his wife's name, her eyes looked beyond him, and slightly sideways. Ben turned to follow her gaze.

A fairytale gold dress hung from the top of the wardrobe door. It appeared to be strapless, with a tight bodice and full skirt, and it was still wrapped in clear protective plastic.

As his eyes fell on the gown hanging beside it, which was every bit as glamorous, if not more so, even though it was slightly shorter and made out of a pearlescent ivory material, Ben twigged who the gold one belonged to. It was Daisy's bridesmaid dress.

'Geri,' he said slowly, 'this is *your* day, yours and Declan's, regardless of what's gone on before. I don't want you to feel bad for me, or even give me a second thought. I can get through it OK.' He paused for a moment to swallow the lump in his throat, hoping she wouldn't notice. 'I'm still here and dressed up in this foppish suit, because I want to be. Because I care about you, and I'm not going to let you down.'

Geri's eyes seemed glazed. 'I had the dress delivered because I was still hoping, still praying that she might turn up today. But she isn't going to . . . is she?'

Ben shook his head. 'No. I don't know where she is, and this isn't a Julia Roberts movie. The happy ending isn't just round the corner. Daisy isn't going to suddenly burst in and make everything all right again.'

'Do you want her to?' asked Geri quietly.

Ben shrugged. 'I don't know. I don't know much any more . . . Just that you've got to stop crying or your mascara's going to go everywhere in a minute.'

Geri grabbed a tissue and blew her nose. 'Sod my make-up, I can have it redone. The photographer will just have to wait. I've got to tell you this now, or it'll be too late. I won't get another chance, and I'll go off on honeymoon and after that you'll never know. I'll never get round to saying it. And I'll always feel awful, because you'll still treat me as if everything's OK. I'd rather have you hating me than have it on my conscience any longer.'

This sounded ominous. The same cold sense of dread cut through him as Ben stood staring at her, waiting.

'I was the one who told Stella about your aunt's will,' said Geri. 'Or rather, about the clause that stated you had to be married before you could inherit it.'

Ben couldn't seem to register this properly. 'But Stella heard about that from a rumour at the pub,' he contested.

Geri was shaking her head. 'She did hear it at the Headless Horseman, but it wasn't just a rumour . . . I was the one who opened my big mouth.'

'But . . .' Ben shook his head back at her. 'Why would you do that?'

'The only person I'd told up until then had been Declan. It wasn't long after I came back from Cuba that I told Stella. I didn't really know Daisy that well yet, and I wasn't out to imply that you'd married her because you wanted the Gatehouse, or that you didn't love her. Stella was just going on and on about her suspicion that Daisy was pregnant, and trying to get out of me if I knew. I was arguing that you really did love her when I found myself adding that maybe you wouldn't have *rushed* to get married if it hadn't been for your aunt's will. I only meant that you might have taken your time otherwise. But as soon as I'd said it, I panicked. I made Stella promise not to tell anyone, not even Kieran, but she obviously didn't keep her word.'

Geri stopped to blow her nose again, the sound echoing round the room as Ben stood regarding her in shock. He would never have believed it if he hadn't heard it from her own mouth. Even if it had been Stella who had told him, he wouldn't have been able to go along with it. And yet, had Geri been nursing a grudge without him realising? Had she really been pleased to see him return to Nettlesford as part of a couple?

'I know that when you and I broke up, it might have looked to other people that it was all my doing,' he said tersely, as she sat there snivelling into her tissue. 'You didn't resist the break-up, but it can't have been fun for you being the one left behind to face everybody.'

'You're saying I did this on purpose?'

'I'm saying no one could blame you if you felt some degree of resentment when I came back with Daisy.'

She sighed wretchedly. '"Resentment"'s too strong a way of putting it. "Miffed" might be better. But I *am* happy with Declan, and anything bitchy I might have felt wore off really quickly once I got to know Daisy.'

Ben scuffed a shoe along the carpet, staring down at it. He'd forgotten to polish the leather; it looked dull and slightly grimy, but he hadn't paid attention up until now, not even when he'd put the shoes on.

'I suppose I felt a bit miffed myself,' he said.

Geri looked up, her eyes ringed with smudges of make-up. 'How?'

'Because you'd obviously done better for yourself without me. In two and a half years, you'd completely transformed yourself. As if you hadn't missed me at all.'

'Of course I'd missed you! But just the friendship side of things, the fact that we'd been so close for so long. When I met Declan, I realised what love really meant. And if you're honest with yourself, Ben, that's the way you feel about Daisy.'

She started rummaging around distractedly on her dressing-table. Ben took a step closer, compelled to say something that would put her mind at rest. This was her wedding day. Nothing else ought to matter. Even if he didn't completely mean what he said, even if he was still upset and shocked by her confession, he had to pretend that he wasn't. He cared about her now as if she were his sister, not just a friend and distant cousin, and it wouldn't make him feel any better if he let her leave this room believing she was instrumental in ruining his marriage.

He found himself repeating what he'd told Stella and the others. *Something would have given sooner or later . . . It was ill-fated from the outset . . . Best that it happened now and not further down the line.*

All the while, Geri sat looking up at him with an envelope in her hand. At last, she said, 'You don't really think Daisy and Jerome are together, do you?'

Ben didn't reply.

'Daisy wouldn't do that to you,' said Geri adamantly.

'She did everything else.' But he hadn't meant to say that. It was just hard to get the image of Jerome and Daisy out of his head.

'She might have made a few mistakes, and I know I never got the chance to speak to her about what happened on my hen night, but I believe what she told Vivienne. I don't think she did go the whole way with Jerome.'

'So she's fooled you, too.'

Geri frowned and tossed her head, the curlers quivering indignantly. 'I think the only person deluding himself is you. But I don't want to get into an argument with you today. It's been bad enough, without ending it like this. Here,' she said firmly, 'before you say anything else, I think you should see something.' And she passed him the envelope. It felt like a card, and was addressed to Geri at Greenacres.

Ben recognised the handwriting instantly. A hot flush ran through him. His hand shook.

Geri tilted her head to one side in a defiant pose. 'That's not a Portuguese stamp, as far as I can tell . . .'

Ben only glanced at it quickly. 'Can I . . . ?'

She nodded, and he drew back the flap to find a wedding card, plain but elegant. The message inside was equally simple. Daisy apologised for her absence and for leaving Geri without a matron-of-honour. She wished the happy couple well for the future, signing off 'Love Daisy', in her swirly, girlish, familiar hand. There was nothing that hinted at what had happened; nothing that would strike anyone as strange.

And no return address.

Ben felt the void inside him opening up further. Geri was looking at him expectantly, an eyebrow cocked, as if she were Sherlock Holmes to his Doctor Watson. And then he realised, in his haste to read the card, he'd neglected a vital element. Flipping over the envelope again, he peered at the faint, fuzzy postmark. He could just about make it out, and his heart seemed to stop and then start beating again at an accelerated speed.

'Now that's hardly in Portugal – is it?' said Geri.

The make-up artist had achieved the remarkable feat of making the bride look naturally radiant and composed, considering it was a touch-up job.

Ben drifted through the day as if he'd taken a strong painkiller, the kind that left you feeling woozy and as if you were taking part in a dream rather than reality. He couldn't stop wondering when the photographer and journalists from *OK!* or *Hello!* were going to turn up. By the number of spectators who had milled round outside the archetypal, grey-stone church, anyone might have assumed that Geri and Declan were local celebrities.

Ben glanced round the marquee as the speeches finally came to an end. He felt as if he'd had enough wine and champagne to last until New Year, but that wasn't going to stop him starting on the lager as soon as the evening reception was underway. Which wouldn't be long now, he acknowledged, consulting his watch. The string quartet were already packing up to make way for the live band, who Ben had never heard of even though they had apparently been the support act in a Rod Stewart tour.

Or was it Elton John?

Ben heaved a sigh, tired of the stilted, polite conversation he'd had to make at the table with his father and Vivienne and other family members who were closer to Geri's side than to his and whom he'd never even met before. Throughout the meal, he had been unable to resist imagining how Daisy would have been captivated by the whole setting, even though it was a wedding. With its glittering chandeliers, opulent velvet chairs, pristine white tablecloths and dazzling crystal, it was more than redolent of *Titanic*.

As he stared into the lavish flower display in the centre of the table, Ben was disquietingly aware of the envelope folded up in his breast pocket, even though he couldn't physically feel it against his chest through his jacket, shirt and waistcoat. He just knew it was there, waiting for him to act on it or not, and his mind reeled with the possibilities.

The guests at his table were beginning to move away, making courteous little noises about going upstairs to freshen up. Ben wondered dimly why women didn't say that they were off to powder their noses any more. It struck him as a genteel, ladylike euphemism for nipping to the loo. His mother had always used it, even when the family had just been sitting in front of the television of an evening.

Ben sighed heavily again, contemplating how keenly his mother would have revelled in a day like today and how much her sister Eleanor would have loathed it. They had been so different and yet so devoted to each other. But he still missed each of them for the same reason, the one characteristic they had unwaveringly had in common: their affection for him, and their ability to make him feel cared for and protected.

Blinking hard, Ben scraped back his chair and muttered something about needing to freshen up himself. As he headed quickly out of the marquee, he caught sight of Stella and Kieran at another table. She was draped all over him, giggling, and Kieran's own knowing smile stretched from ear to ear. Ben couldn't help feeling a jolt of resentment. To make matters worse, he collided with Geri and Declan as they were re-entering the marquee arm in arm. Both of them asked how he was getting on, but they couldn't stop grinning and glowing even though they were probably trying their hardest not to, and when Geri offered Ben a look of sly complicity, he felt as if the cravat round his throat had shrunk two sizes.

It was obvious that she was expecting him to jump in his car at the earliest opportunity and race off to find Daisy, now that her whereabouts had been significantly narrowed down. Geri seemed to think it would be easy, and perhaps finding his wife once he got there would be. It was the deciding whether to go that was the hard part.

Minutes later, Ben sought solace on his own in the conservatory. The daylight was already creeping across the lawn like a retreating tide. The partially hexagonal-shaped room had barely changed since his mother's day.

It was seldom used now, and had a dated look about it, as if trapped in a time that was neither historical nor contemporary. There was a faded photograph on the windowsill. Ben picked it up, the slightly tarnished frame heavier than he remembered. He stared at his father in the posed, black-and-white studio shot. Taken over thirty years ago – as a birthday present for Ben's grandmother – Howard Kavanagh, with a hint of an enigmatic smile, looked more like a Hollywood movie star than a lawyer. All that was missing was an autograph to a devoted fan scrawled across the bottom. Ben could recall always having found this amusing, but he didn't feel much like laughing now.

'You could almost believe he was happy, couldn't you?' came a voice from behind, making Ben start.

He swung round to find Vivienne, who had discarded the tailored jacket in favour of a swathe of silvery chiffon. In her long, pale grey dress, she looked like a ghost.

'I saw you going in the opposite direction to everyone else,' she went on.

'And decided to follow me?' Ben concluded, in annoyance. 'I'm all right, you know. I don't need mothering.'

'Don't you?' Vivienne arched an eyebrow. 'I may be only eight years older than you, but I should have thought a little mothering was exactly what you needed.'

30

B en couldn't reply. The words didn't seem to exist. After a pause, Vivienne came to stand beside him.

She gently prised the photograph from his hands. 'Your father can hide his feelings so well, you wouldn't really guess that when this picture was taken your mother was in love with another man.'

Ben stared at his stepmother as if she'd just told him she had irrefutable proof that the earth was flat. 'What – what are you talking about?' he stammered.

Vivienne returned the photograph to its original position on the windowsill, then sighed, as if embarking on something arduous yet unavoidable. 'I'm trying to tell you that it's time you stopped comparing Daisy to an impossible ideal. As far as I can tell, your mother was just one in a line of Greenwood women who were weak enough to fall for the wrong men. From the little research I've done, the history of this house seems littered with false hopes and broken promises. Women having affairs during both world wars while their husbands were off doing battle seems mild compared to some other things.'

There was a pause, and then Vivienne's voice grew sterner as she continued, 'I'm not saying the men didn't have their faults, just that the women's seem more well known. And it wasn't just the Greenwoods who were guilty of being fickle, the Kavanaghs didn't exactly alter

the pattern. In a way, I've probably been the worst of
the lot. But your wife . . .' Vivienne sighed and shook her
head. 'She was the one who could have broken the trend –
if only you'd let her. Because the fundamental difference
between her and the rest of us was that she honestly and
truly loved the man she married.'

'But Jerome . . .' mumbled Ben, breaking the silence
that followed Vivienne's speech.

'Was just there for her when she needed someone, and
that's all you can accuse them of. He couldn't help the way
he felt about her. You pushed them together with your
suspicions and your jealousy, and I'm not saying that your
feelings were unfounded, just that you made the situation
so much worse than it would have been.'

Ben glanced over his shoulder, checking there was a
chair behind him before sinking into it as if he was
carrying more weight than he could hold. Vivienne's
words felt like a barrage of criticism directed solely at
him, but as he tried to make sense of what she was
saying, he realised that she was holding herself in equal
contempt. And not merely herself, but other wives who
had passed through Greenacres before her – including his
mother.

'What you said about my parents . . .' he muttered,
going back to how his stepmother had started the conversation. 'They loved each other. You can't tell me
otherwise, you weren't even there. It was obvious—'

'—that they got on well? That's probably true. She had
the money and the advantage of her social position, and
your father had the ambition and the brains. Unfortunately, he hasn't got much common sense, so the brains
didn't come in as useful as your grandfather had probably
hoped.'

'My grandfather?' Ben frowned, perplexed. 'What's he got to do with it?'

'He was the reason your parents were together in the first place. You see' – Vivienne wrapped the shawl tighter round her shoulders and dropped into the chair beside Ben's – 'as far as he was concerned, your mother was developing an infatuation for an unsuitable young man, and as you know, your granddad was somewhat old-guard. The thought of a car mechanic in the family—'

'A car mechanic?' echoed Ben. 'What's wrong with that? It wasn't the *186*0s.' Not that motor cars as they knew them had existed back then, he thought vacuously.

'Time seems to move slower around here,' Vivienne went on. 'And it wasn't just his profession that was beneath the Greenwoods, he also had a reputation for being a bit of a lad, if you know what I mean. He was dangerously good-looking, from what I can gather, and it wasn't just your mother who was developing a fondness for him.'

'He had a few women on the go?'

'That's what I've heard. And although your mother was plucked out of his clutches in the nick of time, I'm afraid your aunt Eleanor wasn't quite as innocent as she might have seemed. Not after this young man was through with her.'

Ben's eyes felt as if they were on stalks. 'They *both* fancied him? But they were sisters. They were so close . . . You mean Aunt Eleanor actually—'

'As far as I'm aware. But she never told your mother, and she managed to keep it a secret from your grandparents.'

Ben stared round him for a moment or two, blinking in stupefaction as he absorbed what he was hearing. Finally, he looked up at Vivienne again with a puckered brow. 'How come *you* know all this? I don't understand.'

Picking fluff off her dress, she said carefully, 'Your father told me. Eleanor confided in him after your mother died . . . Listen, Ben, something you've got to understand about all this is that the Kavanagh and Greenwood families have known each other for years. They had a business relationship going long before your parents married. When your grandfather was trying to lure your mother away from this unsavoury young village lad, he hit upon using a late friend's son as bait.'

'My dad?' said Ben shakily.

'A respectable young lawyer was a far more attractive alternative, in the family's eyes. Your mother wasn't too hard to persuade, especially when she caught the man she claimed to love in a clinch with another local girl. Besides, your father can be quite charming when he wants to be.' Vivienne pursed her lips. 'As I can testify myself.'

Ben felt queasy as he murmured, 'But you're saying that Mum never really loved him . . .'

'Not to begin with,' Vivienne went on hastily. 'Not in the way you're implying. But after a few years . . . after they'd had you, and were bringing you up together . . . she probably did come to care for him. It's a different sort of love, but it shouldn't be undervalued.'

Ben rubbed a hand over his forehead. He could feel the beads of sweat smearing under his fingers. He felt hotter than ever in his morning suit as he gazed across at his stepmother and remembered something else she'd said. 'So where do you fit into all this?' he asked. 'Is that how you feel about Dad? You said something about being the worst of the lot . . .'

Vivienne stared outside, a faraway, glazed look settling on her countenance. 'I was hoping you'd forgotten that.'

'Were you in love with someone else, too?' Ben pressed, almost sadistically, before realising that punishing her for what she had told him so far was tantamount to shooting the messenger.

She hesitated. 'Not at first . . . That is, when I married your dad, there wasn't another man on the scene; I wasn't on the rebound. It might not have been love on my part – not the usual kind – but I'd had an unsettled life up until then . . . I think that's why I saw so much of myself in Daisy when she came here. I suppose, at first, I was worried about her motives. Anyway, my acting career was hardly offering me the security I was looking for, so when I met your father . . . To put it simply, I was carried away by it all, the whole Greenacres thing. I saw a new dream, and I followed it.'

'So what went wrong?' prompted Ben, unwittingly beginning to look upon his stepmother as a complex human being – with a childhood and an adolescence – and not just as a stereotype.

'It was while you were at university . . . I met up with an old friend I knew from drama school. He wasn't quite the gawky boy I remembered. He was handsome, athletic. He'd always had a leaning towards acrobatics, but not the muscles to go with it, not when he was sixteen. My first memory of him was in a play set in a circus . . . He was riding a unicycle round the stage as if he'd been doing it all his life.'

Ben knew he'd been slow about a lot of things today, but not this time. It all fell into place in his head with a resounding clunk.

'Shit,' he hissed. 'Rob's his son . . .'

Vivienne was still staring out of the window. 'Although we hadn't been married all that long, your father and I weren't at our closest around that time.' She seemed to be choosing her words judiciously.

Ben noticed her hands trembling in her lap. He felt the same inside.

It was almost inconceivable! That boy back in the marquee, awkward and bashful in an identical, albeit smaller version of the morning suit Ben was wearing . . . that boy wasn't his half-brother. He wasn't a blood relative at all. He was just Vivienne's son, which effectively made him a *step*brother, nothing more.

'So why didn't you just go off with this old "friend" when you found out you were carrying his child?' Ben asked, willing Vivienne to face him.

'I would have. That's the really awful thing. I *would* have gone – if he'd said he'd look after the baby and me. But he didn't want the hassle, the responsibility. Basically, it was the whole "it was fun while it lasted" scenario.'

'And Dad hadn't found out about the affair?'

Vivienne shook her head.

'So you just carried on as if everything was normal,' Ben conjectured. 'You pretended the baby was his and—'

She swivelled in the chair to confront him, her familiar blue eyes glinting recklessly. 'Is that what you imagine happened?'

'What else am I supposed to think? If Dad had known the truth—'

'He'd have thrown me out?' she challenged. 'And not just me, but Robert, too?'

Ben faltered. Knowing how bigoted and uncompromising his father could be, he couldn't imagine another option.

'I didn't lie to him, Ben. Not once I knew I was pregnant. I told him about the affair, and about the baby, and I went upstairs to pack my bags. But I never got as far as the front door. Howard asked me to stay.'

'My father . . . forgave you?'

Vivienne stared at Ben now with an odd look, as if she pitied him somehow. 'Eventually he did. It wasn't easy to begin with. But I learned so many new lessons about relationships, it was worth every second. Your father hadn't just seen me as some young trophy wife to parade in front of his friends. He'd always loved me, from the very beginning, the way a woman dreams of being loved; or *should* dream, at least,' she added bitingly, 'when she isn't hankering after Mr Wrong. And now, all these years down the line, no matter what happens to us or to Greenacres, I'm with him till the final curtain. Not out of any sense of duty, but because I want to be.'

The cynic in Ben had already started to argue that his father had only been trying to save face. Putting up with what Vivienne had done was better than the humiliation and ignominy of her leaving. That theory only seemed to work up to a certain point, though. It couldn't explain away everything, because there was still a child in the world who had been christened Robert John *Kavanagh*. And the man whom this child called Dad had still waited with him back in May for four hours at A&E, knowing he was the result of an extramarital affair, knowing it was all just a lie.

Vivienne was rising unsteadily to her feet. There was an element of panic about her, as if her insurgence had subsided and all she was left with was the worry that Ben would tell someone. Anyone. Or more precisely – Robert.

Ben stretched out a hand to stop her leaving, his

fingertips brushing the edge of her shawl. 'Listen . . . Don't let on to Dad that you told me all this . . . It's best that he doesn't know.'

In the fading light, her face was ashen and ethereal.

'I think I know why you felt you had to say it,' Ben ploughed on. 'And I'm sorry.'

'What for?' she muttered, sounding as if she'd just come down with a sore throat.

'For being a lousy stepson.'

She shrugged, seeming more like her old stiff self as she refuted, 'It's how you measure up as a husband that I'm concerned about at the moment. And on that particular count, I'm not the person you should be apologising to . . .'

31

The trail that had started with Daisy's wedding card to Geri had led Ben here, to this small harbour-front restaurant in the fishing village of Mevagissey. During the drive south, starting off early so that he'd caught the morning rush hour but not the evening one, Ben had felt at his most pessimistic, in spite of his favourite music blasting from the CD player. Packing his bags and heading to Cornwall had seemed a long shot. Daisy might only have been passing through for a few days. And even if she was still in the area where they'd spent their honeymoon, where would he begin to look?

But, as it turned out, that had been the easy part. He had decided to go first to the B&B where he and Daisy had stayed back in early April. It was now the last week of the summer holidays, and the 'No Vacancies' sign hung wonkily in a front window between lace net curtains. The landlady had explained that she hadn't had any vacancies either when Daisy had turned up at the beginning of August. She'd recommended another B&B, though, and the Tourist Information Centre, if Daisy had no luck there.

So Ben had gone to the second B&B – larger and more centrally located than the first, quite basic and not as fussily decorated, but by the state of the reception, clean and tidy with a friendly enough landlady. Ben's spirits had rocketed when she'd told him that Daisy was still boarding there.

'But then I get a lot of retired folk who stay here for the winter months,' she'd added, leaning her elbows on the counter, 'so you could sort of say that I specialise in long-term boarders.'

Ben had questioned the landlady further, like a private detective, unable to resist the thrill of it.

Was Daisy there now, right at that moment?

No. She'd found herself a part-time job. Or maybe she was just out. The landlady wasn't sure what time her shifts were.

Where did Daisy work? What was she doing exactly?

It was just a straightforward waitressing job. The landlady kept various business cards behind the counter, and had handed one to Ben. She often recommended this particular restaurant to her guests. It wasn't fancy, but the meals were all home-made and the fish was always fresh.

Ben knew the place well. It had been his and Daisy's favourite haunt of an evening.

As he sat in a corner booth now, waiting for her to start her shift (twenty minutes to go; she arrived just before six, according to one of the other waitresses), he mulled over how she'd managed to wangle a position here. He would have thought there would have been local girls needing the work. But then again, Daisy had a non-sickly charm about her. It might have been enough to secure her a job if there was one going, especially at this time of year when the restaurant would be busier than usual.

Ben had only ordered a snack, but was having trouble forcing it down. As the minutes ticked by, he ate less and less until at last he gave up and put down his knife and fork. Immediately a waitress swooped, asking if he'd like a dessert. But suddenly, Ben could only stare beyond her to the door as a young woman entered in a long dark skirt and black and white gingham blouse – the standard uniform, except that she was carrying her rucksack. Her hair was tied back and she was sporting large hoop earrings, like a gypsy from a storybook. She looked thinner and in spite of her light tan her cheeks had lost their bloom. Ben was virtually holding his breath as she vanished into the back, but then a few moments later she reappeared, no rucksack this time and tying a white apron round her waist.

'Excuse me, sir,' the waitress at his side was tutting impatiently, 'would you like anything else or can I get you the bill?'

It was at that moment that Daisy glanced in his direction, over the heads of the other diners. The moment when time seemed to freeze. Ben would remember it for the rest of his days. His fear peaked and his more recent nightmares seemed to be coming true – because he couldn't tell if she was glad to see him or not. Her face registered shock, and then became as blank as untrodden snow.

As if he was already too late.

On the steep sides of the valley cradling the heart and soul of Mevagissey, houses perched precariously as if clinging on for dear life. Daisy sat beside her husband on a bench by the inner harbour. Overhead, seagulls wheeled noisily in search of food, while a few yards away, small fishing boats bobbed and creaked. Beyond the boats was a row of waterfront buildings, including the bistro where Daisy worked. It was a far cry from Nettlesford, evoking vivid images of pirates and smugglers and a history steeped in the sea.

Her father had been Cornish. Maybe he still was,

because theoretically there was as much chance of him being alive as dead. That was all Daisy knew about him, though; his name wasn't on her birth certificate and her mother had never told her what it was. The only thing Beverly Miller had let slip was the Cornish connection. Apparently it was why she'd singled him out in the bar in Norwich on the night of Daisy's conception. He'd had a warm, broad accent that she hadn't been able to place. The perfect way to initiate a conversation, according to Daisy's aunt, who had been oozing sarcasm as if it were about to be made illegal and she needed to get it out of her system. Maybe, Daisy had speculated, her mother hadn't been able to remember his name. She might have been too drunk to let it sink in, or perhaps, after their frantic fumble in the back of someone's car, it had just slipped from her mind.

Strange, thought Daisy, the things that attract you to a person and alter the course of your life. With Ben it had been his eyes, faithful and devoted. Puppy dog eyes, they were known as. The same eyes that were staring at her now. *Trust me*, they seemed to say, *I won't let you down*. But she'd trusted them once before, and it had only led to this juncture. To this general awkwardness and inability to talk as freely and animatedly as they once had. To this sitting here, side by side, without touching, as if they might burn their fingers if they tried. Could it be any different a second time?

'Good of your boss to let you have the night off,' Ben muttered. 'Especially at short notice. Well, *no* notice, considering you were already there.'

Daisy shrugged. 'She actually insisted. It's not every day your husband turns up after you haven't seen him for almost a month. I think she thought I wouldn't be able to concentrate on work anyway.'

'Had you told her about . . . us?'

'She knew a bit. The job's only short term. Till the end of September. Unless other people leave, I probably won't be able to stay on. They don't need as many staff over the winter.'

Ben nodded. 'So, after this, where would you have gone? Would you have tried to get another job round here?'

She shrugged again. 'Maybe. I don't know. I've just been taking each day as it comes . . .'

She had already told him that she'd taken a train to London first, but it hadn't been long before she'd had the compulsion to come here. It had only been coincidence that there'd been a job going in that particular restaurant, but she'd blagged her way into it. She hadn't mentioned to Ben about her Cornish ancestry, but she knew the slightly embellished tale she'd spun her employer had helped secure her the position.

'The "compulsion", to come here,' Ben was saying, 'was that because of our honeymoon?'

She sensed it had taken him a while to build up the courage to ask. It crossed her mind to say that that hadn't been the reason, but any other excuse wouldn't make as much sense.

'I'd felt safe here with you,' she said eventually, staring straight ahead. 'I thought maybe . . . maybe I'd feel that way again.'

'And have you?'

She faltered. 'It's not the same.'

'That card you sent Geri and Declan – did you plan for her to show me? The postmark was faint, but I could still read it. You can't always make them out, though. If you were pinning your hopes on that . . .'

'Maybe I was leaving it up to fate. If I'd put my address down and . . .'

'And what?'

She took a deep breath. 'And you didn't come here, or try to contact me . . .' It was too much to contemplate. 'But this way . . . if nothing happened, I could always tell myself it was because the postmark wasn't obvious. Maybe then I would have tried again, in a couple of weeks. Written to Vivienne or something. The thing is, I didn't know if you'd want to hear from me. It seemed easier to put the ball in your court.'

'Since you left, I haven't been the easiest of people to get along with.' He sighed. 'I probably made everyone's life a misery, but to be fair to them, there were those who didn't let me get away with it. I don't blame you for going . . . not considering the way I was acting. I just didn't expect it. It blew me away. Knocked me off course for a while.'

There was so much Daisy wanted to ask, but the questions were causing a pile-up on her tongue, and she wasn't sure if it was the right time, anyway. The atmosphere was stilted, in spite of the content of their conversation, as if there was still a barrier between them. Perhaps, thought Daisy, she was putting it up herself, for her own sake, to prevent further pain. She knew how she felt about Ben now. The time apart had made it clear. Life without him was worse than anything she could have imagined.

If her feelings for him had been based on gratitude alone, the hurt would never have been so acute. But the separation had hit her as if it were an actual physical loss, as intense as any bereavement. And the fact that it wasn't permanent, that somehow, someday, she would probably see him again, hadn't helped console her. Now that he was here, and it was sinking in that he was real and not an illusion, perhaps she was masking her more fragile feelings in case he turned around and said that he had only come to end things properly, amicably, without recrimination. To tie up this last loose end before he could move on.

And there was another reason to hold back, she acknowledged. It had nothing to do with waiting for an apology, but everything to do with her logical, unemotional self. Ben had family, a job and a home back in Nettlesford – there was no denying the fact. She would never ask him to give all that up, and she could never return there herself, at least not to live. So where did that leave them? Where did love enter into it, if something as important as this was going to keep them apart?

'How – how is everyone?' she asked abruptly. 'How was the wedding?'

'Everyone's fine. They send their best. Especially Rob.'

'Really?' Daisy felt the stirrings of a warm glow inside. 'How's his workshop thing going?'

'Too well. I don't think it's putting him off acting. More the other way around, which I suppose is the whole point of it. Anyway, he'd been stroppy with me since you left. It was only when Vivienne told him I was coming to find you that he actually deigned to talk to me. As for the wedding, Geri looked stunning, of course, and Declan surprised her with fireworks to round off the evening reception, as if whisking her away to the Cayman Islands wasn't enough. Vivienne did such a good job organising everything, though, she's now got this hare-brained scheme – my dad's choice of words, not mine – of actually trying to capitalise on it.'

Daisy knew he was prattling because he was nervous, but at least he was coherent.

Ben had paused, as if for impact. 'My stepmother,' he continued, 'has decided to turn Greenacres into a business success story, as opposed to a drain on resources, which is what it is currently.'

'Oh? What sort of business?'

'A wedding venue,' he announced.

'You mean . . . somewhere to hold receptions and stuff?'

He nodded. 'But not just that, she wants to look into applying for a licence to hold civil ceremonies there.'

Daisy's eyes goggled. 'Your father must be—'

'Cacking himself?' Ben snorted. 'Vivienne claims she's been thinking about it for ages, ever since she started putting the details together for Geri's wedding; but she didn't want to say anything until after it was over, in case something went wrong. To her credit, it went amazingly well. I can see the potential, even if Dad can't. It would mean disrupting his well-oiled routine, but I think Greenacres is large enough to double up as a home and a business, with a few modifications. Anyway, he's shaking up his own professional life, so maybe it's not just Vivienne who's ripe for a change.'

'How's that?'

Ben explained about his father's plans to amalgamate with another firm. He didn't mention Jerome, and Daisy thought it wise not to either. Not just yet.

'Where does that leave you, though?' She frowned. 'Are you OK about it? The name change and everything?'

'I said I'd go along with whatever Dad wanted. And the thing is, I don't see that it has that much to do with me any more.'

Daisy was aware of her pulse beating faster through her body. 'What do you mean?'

'I handed in my letter of resignation yesterday. Well, it wasn't actually a letter, but that makes it sound more official, doesn't it? It was just a man-to-man at the Headless Horseman, but I knew Dad wouldn't be surprised. He'd already seen it coming, even before I did.'

'But . . .' Daisy felt as if she were a mechanical doll, rhythmically opening and closing her mouth and shaking her head from side to side '. . . why did you do that? I thought you were happy there.'

'Until Dad pointed out that I wasn't, I'd thought I was reasonably content there, too. In retrospect, though, and being honest with myself, I had to agree with him. Maybe I'd just been too scared to admit I'd let him down again.'

'But if you're not working at Kavanagh & Co., or whatever it's going to be known as, where are you moving to instead? Have you been headhunted by another firm?'

He made a noise like a laugh, but it didn't quite come out of his mouth. 'I was never that good. The low-down is, I'm not going to be a solicitor any more. And I'm not going to sell vacuum cleaners either, before you ask.'

'Then . . . what *are* you going to do?'

'You remind me of a school careers advisor. And to be brutally frank, I have absolutely no idea.' He seemed to find this funny, too, making that odd laughing sound again, almost as if he was choking. 'Why?' he added flippantly. 'Got any suggestions?'

Daisy couldn't believe this. Ben had seemed so satisfied, so confident in his work.

'I suppose we're alike in that way,' he went on. 'You and I. We're not career-driven. I'm not afraid of hard work, and I know you're not either, but *what* we do isn't as important as it is to other people. Maybe that's where I went wrong before. I thought I had to make a go of something, and if

I failed, it felt like a disaster. But I was too hard on myself. There's a whole world of possibilities out there, and if one job isn't working out, there's nothing to stop me trying out something else. Perhaps I'm just not a conventional person.'

Daisy jumped to her feet, too fidgety now to sit still. If she were alone with Ben – away from the people milling about taking photographs, enjoying the unspoilt sights, relaxing in the balmy twilight – she wondered what she would do. Fling herself into his arms? Recoil? Submit? Strangle him? There was so much going through her head, she could barely contain it. And she still wasn't sure what he wanted or why he was here. He wasn't spelling it out clearly.

'Ben, look.' She turned to face him, her defences crumbling because it was suddenly imperative just to *know*, to put herself out of her misery. 'You've come all this way, and I still don't know why, and I—'

'Why?' His face tilted upwards, and those eyes fixed themselves on her until she felt as if she were a rabbit mesmerised by approaching headlamps. 'Because I don't want to be in Nettlesford any more. Least of all if you're not there. I'm not here to drag you back kicking and screaming, if that's what you were afraid of.'

There was a short silence, punctuated by a child crying a short distance away, and from somewhere further off, a dog barking.

'What I was afraid of,' said Daisy, almost breathlessly, 'was that you were here to tell me it was over. That you wanted us to part permanently as friends, instead of having a huge dark cloud hanging over us.'

Ben tilted his face even further, staring up at the sky. 'I'd say it was going to be a clear night,' he murmured.

'No sign of any clouds. But unless I find somewhere to stay, I'll be sleeping under the stars . . .'

Daisy hesitated. If it hadn't already been nabbed, she knew a single room had become available at the B&B. The recently widowed old lady from Carlisle whom she'd befriended had gone back home after a month of endeavouring to come to terms with her grief. She'd been married for forty-nine years. Over full English breakfasts, which both of them had usually just picked at, Daisy's problems had always shrunk by comparison, if only for a short while.

'Let me make a quick call,' she said slowly, nodding at her husband. 'I can probably sort something out.' She moved away a few paces to a quieter spot to ring from her mobile. Less than a minute later, she walked back towards Ben, tucking the phone in her bag. 'No luck,' she sighed. 'The room's already been taken.'

'Oh,' said Ben, swallowing hard. 'That's too bad.'

32

B ack at the B&B, Daisy and Ben passed swiftly through the empty reception and climbed the stairs to the second-floor bedroom. Without a word, Daisy unlocked the door and led Ben inside. He put down his bag, having chosen the one with toothbrush, deodorant and clean underpants in it from several in the boot of his car. Then he took a moment to look around.

The smell of lavender hung in the air. Ben noticed the little oil burner on the dressing-table. Daisy's predilection for candles had always worried him, in case she left one unattended, or dozed off with her oil burner still going. If she was having trouble sleeping, she would usually infuse the air with lavender in the evening, or dab some on her pillow. Just as well that he'd grown up with the scent and didn't mind it. It had been one of his mother's favourites.

The full-length curtains at the window were a few inches too long. Daisy drew them across and seemed to spend ages neatening the folds at the bottom. At last she straightened up, and gave him a brief, watery smile before glancing round herself, as if seeing the room through his eyes. Ben followed her gaze, which came to rest on the bed. It was one of those strange in-between sizes. Too narrow to be called a double, yet wider than a standard single. Ben would have bundled Daisy into his arms then and there, raining kisses in her hair before turning his attention to her mouth, her neck, her . . . He shook himself mentally. Orchestrating time alone with her in private didn't mean that they were ready to pounce on each other.

As Ben stood in the centre of the room, Daisy by the window pulling out the tight scrunchie from her hair, he noticed some photographs on the bedside table beside her jewellery box. Automatically, without thinking, he drifted over and picked them up. Daisy was beside him in a few quick strides. She whipped them out of his hand. From what he'd seen, they were old Polaroids. The colour didn't seem quite natural enough; or maybe it had just faded over the years. The top picture had been of Daisy's mother – so like Daisy it was jarring – but the little girl holding her hand had jet-black hair and dark eyes, and the features were too angular to be Daisy's. Besides, Ben had seen a few pictures of his wife as a child, and this definitely wasn't her.

He blinked, puzzled, as she clutched the photographs defensively against her chest.

'What's wrong?' he said. 'Why can't I see them?'

She shrugged. 'It's silly . . .'

'What is?'

'I hardly ever get them out. It's just lately . . . I've been looking at them more.' She brushed past him to the bedside table, and lifted out the inner tray of the jewellery box, revealing what was virtually a secret compartment underneath. 'I usually keep them here,' she muttered.

'One of the pictures was of your mother, wasn't it?'

She nodded. 'Most of them are.'

'I'm sorry I just grabbed them,' said Ben. 'I should have asked you first.'

She sighed. Her shoulders themselves seemed to rise and fall with the effort. 'It's OK . . . You can see them if you want.' And without meeting his eyes, she passed them to him.

Ben studied each one carefully. They seemed to have been taken on separate occasions, but the underlying feature was that Daisy's mother looked happy, whether she was with the black-haired girl or a tall dark man with a wide grin. In the few other pictures Ben had seen, Beverly Miller hadn't been this young or quite this at ease in her own skin.

He turned to Daisy. 'You're the spitting image of your mother when she was about your age. But who's the bloke? And the little girl? Relatives of yours?'

Daisy hesitated. 'Those photos were taken in the early seventies, when my mother was known as Beverly Carmichael.'

'I thought her name was Miller?' Ben frowned.

'It was. Miller was her maiden name. While she was married, she didn't live in a poky flat with her sister but a four-bed detached house in the best area of Norwich. She had a husband called Martin and a daughter called Sophie. And it was the happiest time of her life.'

Ben's eyes widened. 'You've got a half-sister?'

Daisy shook her head. 'No . . . No, technically, I haven't. She died when she was eleven. Five years before I was born. And I was never enough to keep my mother happy. I wasn't a good enough replacement. I was just me – just Daisy. And what Mum wanted most was Sophie . . .'

Switching on the small kettle that stood on a shelf by the dressing-table, Daisy glanced at their reflections in the full-length wall mirror. Ben was sitting on the edge of the bed, still studying the photographs. He didn't notice her looking at him. When the water eventually boiled, Daisy made tea in plain white cups and carried one over to him, rattling it in the saucer. 'Here.'

He finally put the pictures to one side. She brought over another cup for herself and sat down next to him. For a while, neither of them spoke.

At last, he said, 'I knew you didn't have a great childhood. I guessed that was why you didn't talk about it much, but I wish you'd told me what it was really like.'

'There was this old lady staying here, too, until yesterday,' began Daisy. 'I got to know her a little. She was married for almost fifty years, but she said to me that there were things she'd never told her husband, and she was sure there were things he'd never told her. That didn't mean their marriage hadn't been up to scratch, just that a husband and wife are still individuals. Sometimes it isn't necessary to bare your soul completely, however close you are to someone.'

Ben nodded pensively. After a moment or two, he spoke again. 'But I don't understand why you told me that story about your father working abroad. You've just admitted that you don't even know who he is. It isn't just that you're not close, or that he walked out on your mother when you were a baby.'

'No,' said Daisy. 'No, it isn't just that we're not close. It's worse than that, and that's why I've never told anyone. Or no one who didn't know me when I was a child, at least. I didn't want people pitying me. I wasn't just another social worker's case, clogging up a filing cabinet. So I made up a few things over the years, and I didn't hurt anyone, did I? It was easier to keep the story simple than to complicate it with the truth or too many lies. I never said I'd had a happy, normal childhood, but why go into detail by saying how bad it really was?'

Ben clearly didn't know how to answer that.

'In a way,' Daisy continued, 'it wasn't Mum's fault. Life had been plain sailing up to a certain point. She'd found her Prince Charming and she was living the happily ever after. Except . . . after Sophie was hit by that van . . . Prince Charming turned into someone else and so, apparently, did my mum. They couldn't share their grief, and it tore them apart. She had an affair, he threw her out of the house and she went to live with her older sister – my Aunt Fran – who'd always begrudged Mum doing well for herself while she was stuck in a crummy flat without a man to take care of her. She made Mum's life as difficult as she could and there was no one else to turn to. My grandparents were dead. There was no other family.'

Daisy put down her tea on the bedside table and picked up one of the photographs, her mouth a grim line as she stared at the smiling faces of a girl and man she'd never met, but who had known her mother as well as she had if not better. 'From what I could gather, people had always regarded Mum as the prettier sister. She had no trouble picking up men. It just took a one-night stand, and she was pregnant with me.'

'But she decided to keep you.'

'I think she thought I could make up for losing Sophie. I was suddenly a good idea. But when I arrived and I looked nothing like her first little girl . . . The harder I tried to please her, the worse Mum seemed to get. I remember when I was about six or seven, I was playing the lead in one of those end-of-term school plays. I had to sing a whole song by myself, and I was nervous, but so excited, too. It was as if – as if I could finally impress Mum enough for her to really care.'

Daisy hung her head, and her hair cascaded down on either side of her face, shielding her from Ben's view. 'She walked out. In the middle of the song, she just stood up and walked out of the hall. I was inconsolable, and it was only that night that I found out that Sophie had been able to sing, too. You see, it didn't matter that we had this in common. I think it was only then that Mum realised, however closely I might have resembled Sophie, I was never going to fill the hole in her life. And after that . . . she just got worse.'

'In what way exactly?'

'Drinking. Going out and not coming home for a couple of days. That sort of thing. Until she just overdid it and her liver packed up. I was twelve when she died, but you already knew that. I think I was too afraid of what people thought to make any proper friends, even once she'd gone. I was always on the outside, looking in, or dreaming of getting away from my aunt. I suppose that was why I leapt at the chance Greg gave me to leave. And, in spite of the fact that he was a complete sod, he never judged or pitied me. It always seems to be the good men who do that . . .'

There were tiny lines over Ben's nose, between his strong, dark blond brows. He didn't pursue her last point, but asked instead, 'Your friend Ellie, though . . . ?'

'Was another embellishment,' said Daisy, before remembering why she'd made her up in the first place.

'But you got a card from her . . .'

Daisy gulped. 'It was from Jerome,' she muttered, knowing she'd be a fool to make up another story. She felt Ben flinch. 'You remember the first night I went with you to the Headless Horseman, and someone put my name down for the karaoke? It wasn't Kieran or any of the others.

I'd just met Jerome at the bar, and he thought he'd do it for a laugh, just to tease me. He never expected me to go through with it. He sent the card to apologise.'

'And you made up a whole new best friend, just to explain it away?'

'It was the first thing that came into my head. Suddenly I had to think of something fast. I had no idea how you'd react to this strange bloke writing to me, even though it was a few silly lines saying he was sorry, nothing worse than that. And I didn't know who Jerome really was then, either.'

Ben stood up, his back to her, his shoulders straight. She felt her heart start to contract. 'So,' he said, 'where's this card now?'

'In a landfill, probably. I threw the bloody thing away ages ago.'

Ben was making strange noises again. His shoulders were trembling. 'But Ellie Findus,' he blurted out, rather squeakily. '*Findus*, for pity's sake. That was her name, wasn't it? From those Crispy Pancakes you used to like . . .'

'I never stopped liking them,' mumbled Daisy, afraid to even look at him now. 'There just wasn't much room for them in our freezer compartment.'

'I never made the connection,' he continued, still in that slightly high-pitched voice. 'In fact, I'd actually forgotten what her name was. It's only just come back to me.'

'I'd forgotten, too,' admitted Daisy weakly. 'My own best friend, and I'd forgotten her name.'

Ben spun round. Daisy felt herself hauled to her feet, but still couldn't bring herself to look at him. His hands parted the curtain of her hair and swept it back over her shoulders before his fingers crept back to gently cup her face, the pads of his thumbs stroking her cheeks. It was only then that she realised they were wet.

'You're crying,' he murmured. There was a trace of awe in his voice now, no longer squeaky, but lower and huskier.

She raised her eyes to his at last. 'I'm sorry . . .' she quavered.

'Why? What the hell are you sorry for? Crying? It's nothing to be ashamed of. *I'm* the one who's sorry, for putting you through hell when you'd already been there enough times already. And I've wanted you to cry like this since I've known you. I know that makes me seem like a bastard, but what I mean is, it doesn't achieve anything to keep it all in. I'm only wondering what's set you off now . . .'

'Because it's always going to come between us, isn't it? Jerome, and what happened. He's always going to make you turn away from me—'

Ben interrupted, hushing her softly. 'That's all over. I don't care about the card. I'm not angry. Or, at least, I'm not as wound up about it as I would have been six weeks ago. All that's important right now is that you're the funniest, sweetest, most miraculous thing that's ever happened to me. However clichéd that sounds. And thinking of how unhappy I made you—'

'But you didn't!'

'I did. All those weeks, I could see you were miserable, but I didn't try hard enough to find out why.'

'It was my fault, too. I tried to hide it because *you* were happy, or seemed to be. If I'd told you how I really felt . . . Well, just see it from my point of view. How could I admit to you that I wanted to leave Nettlesford? It was your home.'

'My home was always going to be with you.'

'Then why shouldn't it be the same in reverse?' she asked obstinately.

'Because it doesn't need to be. I don't think I belong in Nettlesford, either. I had to go back when I did, there was too much unresolved business, but it's not necessarily the place where I want to end up for good. I'd like to visit, of course, because I've got family there, but that's as far as it'll probably go.'

'And a house,' said Daisy. 'You've got a house there, don't forget.'

'It's the TV and DVD player I'm more concerned about.'

She wanted to thump him, but she was too busy clasping his waist. 'Can't you be serious?'

'Deadly,' he said, holding her face in his hands again. 'You never know, if this scheme of Vivienne's takes off, I might ask for a stake in it. Over and above the one she already felt obliged to offer, seeing as I've got more right to decide what Greenacres ought to be used for than she has.'

'What sort of stake?' said Daisy dubiously.

'Well, with a makeover, wouldn't you say the Gatehouse could make an idyllic wedding-night retreat? Or even somewhere for the bride and bridesmaids to get ready before a Daimler, or a horse-drawn carriage, transports them in fairytale fashion to the main house?'

'For someone who hates all the palaver surrounding weddings, you've got a hypocritical way of dealing with it.'

Ben grinned rakishly. 'But I bet we could save up a tidy nest egg.'

'I suppose extra income wouldn't exactly go amiss.

You'd have to replace the bed, though. Any couple on their wedding night would be well within their rights to claim compensation after a few hours on that thing.'

'Point taken.' And with that, his lips met hers for the first time in what seemed a century. The most knee-buckling experience she could have fantasised – she wished she could bottle it, or preserve it in some other way. Their relief at being together again was almost a physical thing.

As they drew back from the kiss, still wrapped in each other's arms, Daisy was grudgingly aware that there were a great many things they still had to thrash out. The nitty-gritty details. The questions that needed answering. The plans to be made. They'd never really talked enough about the important things, either before their wedding or after it. They had rushed into marriage when they should have been as wary as crossing a road, looking both ways, rather than simply straight ahead.

But now wasn't the time for that rest-of-our-lives stuff. They could save that for the morning, over breakfast. Daisy wondered if the landlady would do room service.

'I've a confession to make,' said Ben sheepishly, smoothing back her hair again. 'That vacancy here before . . . I was the one who took it. I asked if there was a room going when I came here looking for you. I wasn't sure if I'd be needing it or not. I was praying the landlady wouldn't be around when we came back. Although, thinking about it,' he frowned, 'something doesn't add up. If you asked her for a room for me, then why didn't she tell you I'd already got one?'

Daisy bit her lip. 'I've a confession to make, myself. I never actually rang here before. I just pretended to. I was praying the landlady wouldn't be around when we came back, either . . . But if I'd known it was you who'd taken the room, I'd have—'

'What?' he goaded, pulling her closer. 'You'd have made me sleep alone?'

'Don't push your luck,' she snapped archly. 'I might still change my mind . . .'

VALERIE-ANNE BAGLIETTO

THE WRONG MR RIGHT

Kate Finlay is coping – just. She wouldn't trade her precocious daughter Emmi for a million pounds, but as a single mum, holding down a job and paying the bills is hard work. If only her glamorous, fun-loving nanny Paloma were better at housework – if only she had a few more hours in the day.

When her boss Dick Anthony – tall, lithe, lean and loaded – starts showing an interest in her, Kate's tempted to reciprocate. But then she meets reckless jack-of-all-trades Tom Llewellyn, who attracts her despite her best intentions. So when Emmi's father Harry Barrett comes back into her life – a changed man – Kate's more than just a little bit confused.

Is love finally in the air, or is she going to make the same mistake again? The one that made her a single mother in the first place . . .

HODDER AND STOUGHTON PAPERBACKS